CONTENTS

PART I

THE PROTECTING ANCESTORS

CONTENTS

PART II

THE GREAT SKY LANTERN

PART III

THE BRINGER OF GOOD NEWS

PENGUIN BOOKS

108

KAI LUNG UNROLLS HIS MAT

BY ERNEST BRAMAH

Leonard H. C. Tait

KAI LUNG
UNROLLS HIS MAT

BY

ERNEST BRAMAH

*

PENGUIN BOOKS

MELBOURNE · LONDON · BALTIMORE

First published 1928
First issued in Travellers' Library 1935
Published in Penguin Books September 1937
Reprinted October 1937, 1949, 1954

Made and printed in Great Britain
for Penguin Books Ltd,
Harmondsworth, Middlesex
by Hazell, Watson & Viney Ltd,
Aylesbury and London

PART I

THE PROTECTING ANCESTORS

*

CHAPTER I

The Malignity of the Depraved Ming-shu rears its Offensive Head

As Kai Lung turned off the dusty earth-road and took the woodland path that led to his small but seemly cottage on the higher slope, his exultant heart rose up in song. His quest, indeed, had not been prolific of success, and he was returning with a sleeve as destitute of silver taels as when he had first set out, but the peach tree about his gate would greet him with a thousand perfumed messages of welcome, and standing expectant at the door he would perchance presently espy the gracefully outlined form of Hwa-mei, once called the Golden Mouse.

'As I climb the precipitous hill-side,' he chanted,
'My thoughts persistently dwell on the one who awaits my coming;
Though her image has never been wholly absent from my mind.
For our affections are as the two ends of a stretching cable – united by what divides them;
And harmony prevails.

Each sunrise renews the pearly splendour of her delicate being;
And floating weed recalls her abundant hair.
In the slender willows of the Yang-tze valley I see her silken eyelashes,
And the faint tint of the waving moon-flower tells of her jade-rivalled cheek.
Where is the exactitude of her matchless perfection – '

'There is a time to speak in hyperbole and a time to frame words to the limit of a narrow edge,' interposed a contentious voice, and Shen Hing, an elderly neighbour, appeared in the way. 'What manner of man are you, Kai Lung, or does some alien Force possess you, that you should reveal this instability of mind on the very threshold of misfortune?'

'Greetings, estimable wood-cutter,' replied Kai Lung, who knew the other's morose habit; 'yet wherefore should despond-ency arise? It is true that the outcome of my venture has been concave in the extreme but, whatever befall, the produce of a single field will serve our winter need; while now the air is filled with gladness and the song of insects, and, shortly, Hwa-mei will discern me on the homeward track and come hurriedly to meet me with a cup of water in her hand. How, then, can heaviness prevail?'

At this, Shen Hing turned half aside, under the pretext that he required to spit, but he coughed twice before he could re-compose his voice.

'Whence are you, amiable Kai Lung?' he asked with unac-customed mildness; 'and have you of late had speech with none?'

'I am, last of all, from Shun, which lies among the Seven Water-heads,' was the reply. 'Thinking to shorten the path of my return I chose the pass known as the Locusts' Leap and from this cause I have encountered few. Haply you have some gratifying tidings that you would impart – yet should not these await another's telling, when seated around our own domestic hearth?'

'Haply,' replied Shen Hing, with the same evasive bearing, 'but there is a fall no less than a rise to every tide, and is it not further said that of three words that reach our ears two will be evil?'

'Does famine then menace the province?' demanded Kai Lung uneasily.

'There is every assurance of an abundant harvest and already the sound of many blades being whetted is not unknown to us.'

'It can scarcely be that the wells are failing our community again? Fill in the essential detail of your shadowy warning, O dubious Shen Hing, for I am eager to resume my homeward way, whatever privation threatens.'

'It is better to come empty-handed than to be the bearer of ill news,' answered the sombre woodman, 'but since you lay the burden on my head it is necessary that you should turn your impatient feet aside to ascend yonder slight incline,' and he pointed to a rocky crag that rose above the trees. 'From this height, minstrel, now bend your discriminating gaze a few li to the west and then declare what there attracts your notice.'

'That is the direction in which my meagre hut is placed,' admitted Kai Lung, after he had searched the distance long and anxiously, 'but although the landmarks are familiar, that which I most look for eludes my mediocre eyes. It must be that the setting sun – '

'Even a magician cannot see the thing that is not there,' replied Shen Hing meaningly. 'Doubtless your nimble-witted mind will now be suitably arranged for what is to follow.'

'Say on,' adjured Kai Lung, taking a firmer hold upon the inner fibre of his self-control. 'If it should be more than an ordinary person can reasonably bear I call upon the shades of all my virtuous ancestors to rally to my aid.'

'Had but one of them put in an appearance a week ago it might have served you better, for, as it is truly written, "A single humble friend with rice when you are hungry is better than fifteen influential kinsmen coming to a feast",' retorted Shen Hing. 'Hear my lamentable word, however. It has for some time been rumoured that the banners of insurrection were being trimmed and the spears of revolt made ready.'

'There was a whisper trickling through the land when I set forth,' murmured Kai Lung. 'But in this sequestered region, surely – '

'The trickle meanwhile grew into a swiftly moving stream although the torrent seemed as though it would spare our peaceful valley. Like a faint echo from some far-off contest we heard that the standard of the Avenging Knife had been definitely raised and all men were being pressed into this scale or that of the contending causes. ... High among the rebel council stood one who had, it is said, suffered an indignity at your requiting hand in the days gone by – Ming-shu his forbidding name.'

'Ming-shu!' exclaimed Kai Lung, falling back a step before the ill-omened menace of that malignant shadow. 'Can it be that the enmity of the inscriber of the mandarin's spoken word has pursued me to this retreat?'

'It is, then, even as men told?' declared Shen Hing, with no attempt to forgo an overhanging bitterness, 'and you, Kai Lung, whom we received in friendship, have brought this disaster to our doors. Could demons have done more?'

'Speak freely,' invoked Kai Lung, averting his face, 'and do not speak to spare this one's excessive self-reproach. What next occurred?'

'We of our settlement are a peaceful race, neither vainglorious nor trained to the use of arms, and the opposing camps of warriors had so far passed us by, going either on the Eastern or the Western route, and none turning aside. But in a misbegotten moment Ming-shu fell under a deep depression while in his tent at no great space away, and one newly of his band, thinking to disclose a fount of gladness, spoke of your admitted capacity as a narrator of imagined tales, with a special reference to the serviceable way in which the aptitude had extricated you from a variety of unpleasant transactions in the past.'

'That would undoubtedly refresh the wells of Ming-shu's memory,' remarked Kai Lung. 'How did he testify the fullness of his joy?'

'It is related that when those who stood outside heard the grinding of his ill-assorted teeth, the rumour spread that the river banks were giving way. At a later period the clay-souled outlaw was seen to rub his offensive hands pleasurably together and heard to remark that there is undoubtedly a celestial influence that moulds our ultimate destinies even though we ourselves may appear to trim the edges somewhat. He then directed a chosen company of his repulsive guard to surprise and surround our dwellings and to bring you a bound captive to his feet.'

'Alas,' exclaimed Kai Lung. 'It would have been more in keeping with the classical tradition that they should have taken me, rather than that others must suffer in my stead.'

'There can be no two opinions on that score,' replied the scrupulous Shen Hing, 'but a literary aphorism makes a poor defence against a suddenly propelled battle-axe, and before mutual politeness was restored a score of our tribe had succumbed to the force of the opposing argument. Then on the plea that a sincere reconciliation demanded the interchange of gifts they took whatever we possessed, beat us heavily about the head and body with clubs in return and departed, after cutting down your orchard and setting fire to your very inflammably constructed hut, in order, as their leader courteously expressed it, "to lighten the path of your return".'

'But she – Hwa-mei,' urged Kai Lung thickly. 'Speak to a point now that the moment must be faced – the cord is at my heart.'

'In that you are well matched, for another was about her neck when she went forth,' replied Shen Hing concisely. 'Thus Ming-shu may be said to possess a double hold upon your destiny.'

'And thereafter? She – '

'Why, as to that, the outlook is obscure. But a brigand with whom I conversed – albeit onesidedly, he standing upon this person's prostrate form meanwhile – boasted of the exploit. Hwa-mei would seem to be a lure by which it is hoped to attract some high official's shifting allegiance to the rebel cause, she having held a certain sway upon him in the past.'

'The Mandarin Shan Tien – now a provincial governor!' exclaimed Kai Lung. 'Thus our ancient strife asserts itself again, though the angles ever change. But she lives – at least that is assured.'

'She lives,' agreed Shen Hing dispassionately, 'but so likewise does Ming-shu. If he was your avowed enemy, minstrel, you did wrong to spare him in the past, for, "If you leave the stricken bull his horns he will yet contrive to gore you".'

'It is no less written, "The malice of the unworthy is more to be prized than an illuminated vellum",' replied Kai Lung. 'Furthermore, the ultimate account has not yet been cast. In which direction did Ming-shu's force proceed, and how long are they gone?'

'One who overlooked their camp spoke of them as marching

to the west, and for three days now have we been free of their corroding presence. That being so, the more valiant among us are venturing down from about the tree-tops and to-morrow life will begin afresh, doubtless as before. Have no fear therefore, story-teller; Ming-shu will not return.'

'It is on that very issue that I am troubled,' was Kai Lung's doubtful answer. 'Ming-shu may still return.'

'Then at least do not show it, for we are all in the same plight,' urged the woodman. 'To-morrow we assemble to repair the broken walls and fences, so that in the association of our numbers you may gain assurance.'

'The spirit you display is admittedly contagious,' agreed Kail Lung. 'In the meanwhile I will seek my devastated ruin to see if haply anything remains. There was a trivial store of some few bars of silver hidden about the roof. Should that hope fail I am no worse off than he who possesses nothing.'

'I will accompany and sustain you, neighbour,' declared Shen Hing more cheerfully. 'In sudden fortune, whether good or bad, men become as brothers.'

'Do so if you feel that you must,' replied Kai Lung, 'though I would rather be alone. But in any case I will do the actual searching – it would be the reverse of hospitable to set you to a task.'

When they reached the ruin of his once befitting home Kai Lung could not forbear an emotion of despair, but he indicated to Shen Hing how that one should stand a reasonable distance away while he himself sought among the ashes.

'A steady five cash a day is better than the prospect of a fortune.' Shen Hing busied himself looking for earth-nuts, but in spite of the apt proverb his sombre look returned.

'Even this slender chance has faded,' reported Kai Lung at length, approaching Shen Hing again. 'Nothing remains, and I must now adventure forth on an untried way with necessity alone to be my guide. Farewell, compassionate Shen Hing.'

'But what new vagary is here?' exclaimed Shen Hing, desisting from his search. 'Is it not your purpose to join in the toil of restoring our settlement, when we, in turn, will support you in the speedy raising of your fallen roof?'

'There is a greater need that calls me, and every day Hwa-mei turns her expectant eyes towards the path of rescue,' replied Kai Lung.

'Hwa-mei! But she is surrounded by a rebel guard in Ming-shu's camp, a hundred li or more away by now. Consider well, story-teller. It is very easy on an unknown road to put your foot into a trap or your head into a noose, but by patient industry one can safely earn enough to replace a wife with a few successful harvests.'

'When this one lay captive in Ming-shu's power, she whom you would so readily forsake did not weigh the hazards of snare or rope with an apprising eye but came hastening forward offering life itself in two outstretched hands. Would a dog do less than follow now?'

'That is as it may be and I have certainly heard some account of the affair at various times,' replied Shen Hing craftily, for he well knew that Kai Lung's reciting voice would lighten the task of each succeeding day. 'But even a beggar will not cross a shaking bridge by night, and how are you, who have neither gold wherewith to purchase justice nor force by which to compel it, to outdo the truculent Ming-shu, armed at every point?'

'I have sandals for my feet, a well-tried staff between my hands, a story on my lips, and the divine assurance that integrity will in the end prevail,' was Kai Lung's modest boast. 'What therefore can I lack?'

' "In the end"?' repeated Shen Hing darkly. 'Admittedly. But an ordinary person inclines to something less ambitious provided it can be relied upon more towards the middle. You are one who is prone to resort to analogies and signs, Kai Lung, to guide you in the emergencies of life. How can you then justify a journey entered upon so suddenly and without reference to the omens?'

'He who moves towards the light has no need of the glow of joss-sticks,' replied Kai Lung, indicating the brightness that still lingered in the sky. 'The portent will not fail.'

'It is certainly a point to be noted,' confessed Shen Hing, 'and I cannot altogether expect to dissuade you in the circumstances. But do not overlook the fact that the sun has already set and nothing but dark and forbidding clouds now fill the heavens.'

'We can only see the clouds, but the clouds can see the sun,' was the confident reply. 'Success is a matter of luck, but every man obeys his destiny.'

With this inspired pronouncement Kai Lung turned his back upon the ruin of his unassuming home and set out again, alone and destitute, upon an unknown path. Shen Hing pressed into his sleeve the few inferior nuts that he had laboriously collected, but he did not offer to accompany the story-teller on his way. Indeed, as soon as he was reasonably sure that he was free from interruption the discriminating wood-cutter began to search the ashes on his own account, to see if haply there was not something of value that Kai Lung had perchance overlooked.

CHAPTER II

The Difficult Progression of the Virtuous Kai Lung assumes a Concrete Form

IT was Kai Lung's habit, as he approached any spot where it seemed as though his mat might be profitably unrolled, to beat upon a small wooden drum and even to discharge an occasional firework, so that the leisurely and indulgent should have no excuse for avoiding his entertainment. As darkness was fast approaching when he reached the village of Ching it would have been prudent first of all to obtain shelter for the night and a little rice to restore his failing powers, for three days had passed since the parting from Shen Hing and with scarcely a pause Kai Lung had pressed relentlessly on toward the west, journeying through a barren upland waste where nothing to sustain life offered beyond the roots of herbs and a scanty toll of honey. But the rocky path that he had followed was scarcely less harsh and forbidding than the faces of those to whom the story-teller now spoke of food and shelter with an assured payment at some future time, and however ill-fitted he felt his attributes to be he had no alternative but to retrace his faltering steps to the deserted open space and there to spread his mat and lift up his voice in the hope of enticing together one or two who would contribute even a few brass pieces to his bowl.

When Kai Lung had beat upon his drum for as long as it was prudent and had expended the last fire-cracker of his slender store, he looked around so that he might estimate what profit the enterprise held out and judge therefrom what variety of story would be adequate. To his gratified surprise he now perceived that so far from attracting only a meagre sprinkling of the idle and necessitous, about him stood a considerable throng and persons of even so dignified a position as an official chair-bearer, and an assistant tax-collector had not scrupled to draw near. At least two full strings of negotiable cash might be looked for, and Kai Lung brushed aside his hunger and fatigue as he resolved to justify so auspicious an occasion.

'It is well said,' he remarked with becoming humility, 'that the more insignificant the flower the handsomer the bees that are attracted to it, and the truth of the observation is borne out by this distinguished gathering of influential noblemen all condescending to listen to the second-rate elocution of so ill-endowed a person as the one who is now speaking. Nevertheless, in order to start the matter on a satisfactory basis, attention is now drawn to this very inadequate collecting bowl. When even its lower depth is hidden beneath the impending shower of high-class currency, these deficient lips will be stimulated to recite the story of Ling Tso and the Golden Casket of the Lady Wu.'

For a few beats of time there was an impressive pause, which Kai Lung ascribed to a pleased anticipation of what was to follow, but no shower of coins ensued. Then a venerable person stood forth and raised a forbidding hand.

'Refrain from this ineptitude and tell us the thing that we have come to hear,' he remarked in an unappreciative voice. 'Is it to be thought that persons of such importance as an official chair-bearer and an assistant tax-collector' – here he indicated the two, who assumed expressions of appropriate severity – 'would bend their weighty ears to the painted insincerity of a fictitious tale?'

'Yet wherein can offence be taken at the history of Ling Tso and the virtuous Lady Wu?' asked Kai Lung in pained surprise.

'None the less, it is reasonably said that he who hires the carriage picks the road, and should another tale be indicated this one will cheerfully endeavour to comply with the demand.'

'Alas,' exclaimed the one who had constituted himself the leader of their voices, 'can obliquity go further? Why should we who are assembled to hear what relief Ang-Liang can send us in our straits be withheld in this extraneous manner? Deliver your message competently, O townsman of Ang-Liang, so that we may quickly know.'

At this reversal of his hopes and all that it foreshadowed, Kai Lung suddenly felt the cords of his restraint give way, and for a discreditable moment he covered his face with his hands, lest his anguish should appear there.

'It is very evident that an unfortunate misconception has arisen,' he said, when he had recovered his inner possession. 'The one before you has journeyed from the east, nor has he any part with the township of Ang-Liang, neither does he bear with him a message.'

'Then how arises it,' demanded the foremost of the throng acrimoniously, 'that you have come to this very spot, beating upon a wooden drum and bearing other signs of him whom we expect?'

'I had sought this open space thinking to earn a narrow sufficiency of the means whereby to secure food and shelter before the darkness closes in,' replied Kai Lung freely. 'My discreditable calling is that of a minstrel and a relater of imagined tales, my abject name being Lung, and Kai that of my offensive father's ill-conditioned Line. Being three days' journey from my bankrupt home I have nothing but my own distressing voice and the charitable indulgence of your unsullied hearts to interpose between myself and various unpleasant ways of Passing Upwards. To that end I admittedly beat upon this hollow drum and discharged an occasional cracker, as my harmless custom is.'

'Were it not possible to take a lenient view of the offence by reason of your being a stranger, it is difficult to say what crime you may not have committed,' declared the spokesman with obtuse persistence. 'As it is, it would be well that you should return to your own place without delay and avoid the boundaries of Ching in future. Justice may not close an eye twice in the same direction.'

'Nothing could be more agreeably expressed and this one will not fail to profit by your broad-minded toleration,' meekly replied Kai Lung. 'Yet inexperienced wayfarers have been known to wander in a circle after nightfall and so to return to the point of their departure. To avoid this humiliating transgression the one who is now striving to get away at the earliest possible moment will restrain his ardour until daybreak. In the meanwhile, to satisfy your natural demand that he should justify the claim to be as he asserts, he will now relate the story of Wan and the Remarkable Shrub – a narrative which, while useful to ordinary persons as indicative of what may be reasonably expected in a variety of circumstances, does not impose so severe a strain upon the imagination as does the history of Ling Tso and the Golden Casket.'

'Any strain upon the imagination is capable of sympathetic adjustment,' put forward one of the circle, evidently desirous of sharing in some form of entertainment. 'As regards the claim of the collecting bowl to which reference has been made – '

'Cease, witling,' interposed the leader in a tone of no-encouragement. 'Having been despoiled by Ming-shu's insatiable horde are we now to be beguiled into contributing to a strolling musician's scarcely less voracious bowl? Understand, mountebank, that by flood, fire, and famine, culminating in this last iniquity at the hands of a rebel band, our village is not only cashless but is already destitute of food and fuel for itself, so that we have even sent imploring messages to less deficient neighbours.'

'In that case the historical legend of Wan and the Remarkable Shrub is exceptionally appropriate, conveying as it does the inspiring maxim that misfortune may be turned to final gain, and indicating – on broad lines – how this desirable result may be attained.'

'A recital of that nature cannot be deemed to be merely light and indulgent,' contended the one who had favoured the amusement, 'and, indeed, may be regarded as a definite commercial asset. It is true that among us we have not the wherewithal to line even the bottom of the accommodating Kai

Lung's unassuming bowl, but if a mat upon my misshapen sleeping bench should be judged an equivalent share – '

'In the matter of your evening rice this person chances to have a superfluous portion of meat upon a skewer,' remarked the official chair-bearer. 'Lean and unappetising as it will doubtless prove, it is freely offered as a proportionate bestowal.'

'Meat of itself requires the savour of mixed herbs,' interposed the assistant tax-collector, not desirous of being outdone by others, 'and in that respect this one will not prove lacking.'

'When the tide turns it carries all before it,' grumbled the headman of the community, with a supine glance at the many who were pressing forward. 'As regards tea to any reasonable amount the name of Thang stands to that detail.'

'An onion to refresh your supple throat,' came from another. 'A little snuff to bring out the flavour of each dish'; 'Look to Wei Ho for mien paste to form a staple'; 'A small dried fish, well steeped in oil'; 'The gratuitous shaving of your noble footsore limbs ' – these and a variety of inspiring cries were raised on every side.

'It is necessary to test silver upon a block, but hospitality proclaims itself,' replied Kai Lung agreeably. 'This brings in the legendary tale of Wan and what befell him.'

THE STORY OF WAN AND THE REMARKABLE SHRUB

I

The story of Wan and the Remarkable Shrub is commendable in that it shows how, under a beneficent scheme of government, such as that of our unapproachably enlightened Empire admittedly is, impartial justice will sooner or later be accomplished. When a contrary state of things seems to prevail and the objectionable appear to triumph while the worthy are reduced to undignified expedients, it will generally be found that powerful demoniacal influences are at work, or else that the retributive forces have been counterbalanced by an unfortunate conjunction of omens acting on the lives of those concerned. If neither of these causes is responsible it may be that a usurpatory and unauthorised dynasty has secured the sacred dragon throne (a not unusual occurrence in our distinguished history) and virtue is thereby for a time superseded from its function; or, possibly, a closer scrutiny will reveal that those whom we had hitherto regarded as tending towards one extreme were not in reality such as we deemed them to be, and that the destinies meted out to them were therefore both adequate and just. Thus whatever happens it is always more prudent to assume that the integrities have been suitably maintained all round, and that the inspired system initiated by the Sages ten thousand years ago continues even to-day to enshrine the highest wisdom of mankind, and is yet administered by the most scrupulous body of officials in what is still the best possible among the nations of the earth.

For this reason the story of Wan and his associates, badly told and commonplace as it must inevitably sound when narrated by this incompetent person, is appropriate for the mental nourishment of the young and impressionable, while even the ill-intentioned and austere may be discreetly influenced along a desired path by its opportune recital at convenient intervals.

At a period so remote that it would be impious to doubt whatever happened then, a venerable and prosperous philosopher, Ah-shoo by name, dwelt at the foot of a mountain in a distant province. His outward life was simple but reserved, and although he spent large sums of money on fireworks and other forms of charity he often professed his indifference to wealth and position. Yet it must not be supposed that Ah-shoo was unmindful of the essentials, for upon it being courteously pointed out to him, by a well-disposed neighbour who had many daughters of his own, that in failing to provide a reliable posterity he was incurring a grave risk of starvation in the Upper World, he expressed a seemly regret for the oversight and at once arranged to marry an elderly person who chanced at the time to be returning his purified wearing apparel. It was to this incident that the one with whom this related story is chiefly concerned owed his existence, and when the philosopher's attention was diverted to the occurrence he bestowed on him the name of Wan, thereby indicating that he was born towards the evening of his begetter's life, and also conveying the implication that the achievement was one that could

scarcely be expected to be repeated. On this point he was undoubtedly inspired.

When Wan reached the age of manhood the philosopher
abruptly Passed Above without any interval of preparation. It
had been his custom to engage Wan in philosophical discussion
at the close of each day, and on this occasion he was contrast-
ing the system of Ka-ping, who maintained that the world was
suspended from a powerful fibrous rope, with that of Tai-u,
who contended that it was supported upon a substantial bamboo pole. With the clear insight of an original and discerning
mind, Ah-shoo had already detected the fundamental weakness
of both theories.

'If the earth was indeed dependent on the flexible retention
of an unstable cord, it is inevitable that during the season of
Much Wind it must from time to time have been blown into a
reversed position, with the distressing result that what was the
East when we composed ourselves to sleep would be the West
when we awoke from our slumber, to the confusion of all
ordinary process of observation and the well-grounded annoyance of those who, being engaged upon a journey, found themselves compelled to return and set out again in the opposite
direction. As there exists no tradition of this having ever happened it is certain that the ingenious Ka-ping did not walk in
step with the verities.'

'Then the system of the profound Tai-u is the one to be
regarded?' inquired Wan respectfully.

' "Because Hi is in the wrong it does not automatically follow that Ho is necessarily right",' quoted Ah-shoo, referring
to the example of two celebrated astrologers who were equally
involved in error. 'The ill-conceived delusion of the obsolete
Tai-u is no less open to logical disapproval than the grotesque
fallacy of the badly informed Ka-ping. If a rigid and unyielding staff of wood upheld the world it is obvious that when the
ground became dry and crumbling, the upper end of the pole
would enlarge the socket in which it was embedded, and the
earth, thus deprived of a firm and stable basis, would oscillate
with every considerable movement upon its upper side. Even
more disturbing would be the outcome of a season of continuous flood, such as our agreeable land frequently enjoys, for

then, owing to the soft and pliant nature of the soil, and the ever-increasing weight of the impending structure, the pole would continue to sink deeper and deeper into the mass, until at length it would protrude upon the upper side, when the earth, deprived of all support, would slide down the pole until it plunged into the impenetrable gloom of the Beneath Parts.'

'Yet,' suggested Wan with becoming deference, 'if the point of the staff concerned should have been resourcefully embedded in a formidable block of stone – '

'The system of the self-opinionated Tai-u contains no reference to any such block of stone,' replied Ah-shoo coldly, for it was not wholly agreeable to his sense of the harmonies that the one who was his son should seek to supply Tai-u's deficiency. 'Furthermore, the difficulty of hewing out the necessary incision for the head of the pole to fit into, in view of the hardness of the rock and the inverted position in which the workers must necessarily toil, would be insuperable. Consider well another time, O Wan, before you intervene. "None but a nightingale should part his lips merely to emit sound".'

'Your indulgent censure will henceforth stimulate my powers of silence,' declared the dutiful Wan in a straightforward voice. 'Otherwise it would have been my inopportune purpose to learn of your undoubted omniscience what actually does support the earth.'

'The inquiry is a natural one,' replied Ah-shoo more genially, for it was a desire to set forth his own opinion on the subject that had led him to approach the problem, 'and your instinct in referring it to me is judicious. The world is kept in its strict and inflexible position by – '

Who having found a jewel lifts his voice to proclaim the fact, thereby inviting one and all to claim a share? Rather does he put an unassuming foot upon the spot and direct attention to the auspicious movements of a distant flock of birds or the like until he can prudently stoop to secure what he has seen. Certainly the analogy may not be exact at all its angles, but in any case Ah-shoo would have been well advised to speak with lowered voice. It is to be inferred that the philosopher did not make a paper boast when he spoke of possessing the fundamental secret of the earth's stability but that the High Powers were unwilling, at that early stage of our civilisation, for the device to become generally understood. Ah-shoo was therefore fated to suffer for his indiscretion, and this took the form of a general stagnation of the attributes, so that although he lingered for a further period before he Passed Above he was unable to express himself in a coherent form. Being deprived of the power of speech he remembered, when too late, that he had neglected to initiate Wan into any way of applying his philosophical system to a remunerative end, while it so happened that his store of wealth was unusually low owing to an imprudently generous contribution to a scheme for permanently driving evil beings out of the neighbourhood by a series of continuous explosions.

It is no longer necessary to conceal the fact that throughout his life Ah-shoo had in reality played a somewhat two-faced part. In addition to being a profound philosopher and a polite observer of the forms he was, in secret, an experienced magician, and in that capacity he was able to transmute base matter into gold. For this purpose he kept a variety of coloured fluids in a shuttered recess of the wall, under a strict injunction. Having now a natural craving to assure Wan's future comfort he endeavoured by a gesture to indicate this source of affluence, confident that the one in question would not fail to grasp the significance of anything brought to his notice at so precise a moment, and thus be led to test the properties of the liquids and in the end to discover their potency. Unfortunately, Ah-shoo's vigour was by this time unequal to the required strain and his inefficient hand could not raise itself higher than to point towards an inscribed tablet suspended at a lower level upon the wall. This chancing to be a delineation of The Virtues, warning the young against the pursuit of wealth, against trafficking with doubtful Forces, and so forth, Wan readily accepted the gesture as a final encouragement towards integrity on the part of an affectionate and pure-minded father, and dutifully prostrating himself he specifically undertook to avoid the enticements described. It was in vain that the distracted Ah-shoo endeavoured to remove this impression and to indicate his meaning more exactly. His feeble limb was incapable of a more highly sustained effort, and the more des-

perately he strove to point the more persistently Wan kow-
towed acquiescently and bound himself by an ever-increasing
array of oaths and penalties to shun the snare of riches and to
avoid all connection with the forbidden. Finally, this inability
to make himself understood engendered a fatal acridity within
the magician's throat, so that, with an expression of scarcely
veiled contempt on his usually benevolent features, he rolled
from side to side several times in despair and then passed out
into the Upper Region.

It was not long before Wan began to experience an uncom-
fortable deficiency of taels. The more ordinary places of concealment were already familiar to his investigating thumb, but
even the most detailed search failed to disclose Ah-shoo's expected hoard. When at length very little of the structural
portion of the house remained intact, Wan was reluctantly
compelled to admit that no such store existed.

'It is certainly somewhat inconsiderate of the one to whom
my very presence here is due, to have inculcated in me a contempt for riches and a fixed regard for The Virtues, and then
to have Passed Away without making any adequate provision
for maintaining the position,' remarked Wan to the sharer of
his inner chamber, as he abandoned his search as hopeless.
'Tastes such as these are by no means easy to support.'

'Perchance,' suggested Lan-yen, the one referred to, helpfully, 'it was part of an ordered scheme, thereby to inspire a
confidence in your own exertions.'

'The confidence inspired by the possession of a well-filled
vault of silver will last an ordinary person a lifetime,' replied
Wan, with an entire absence of enthusiasm. 'Further, the
philosophical outfit, which so capably enables one to despise
riches in the midst of affluence, seems to have overlooked any
system of procuring them when destitution threatens.'

'Yet are there not other methods of enrichment?' persisted
the well-meaning but not altogether gracefully animated one in
question.

'Undoubtedly,' replied Wan, with a self-descriptive smile,
'the processes are many and diffuse. There are, to example
them, those who remove uncongenial teeth for the afflicted;
others who advance the opposing claims of the litigiously in-

clined; and forecasters of the future. But in order to succeed in these various enterprises, it is desirable to be able to extract an indicated fang, to entice the confidence of the disputatious, or to be able to make what has been predicted bear some recognisable semblance to what has come to pass. Then there are merchants in gems and precious stones, builders of palaces, and robbers in the Ways, but here again it is first advantageous to possess the costly traffic of a merchant's stall, to have some experience in erecting palaces, or to be able to divest wayfarers of their store in the face of their sustained resistance. Still endeavouring to extract the priceless honey from the garden of your inspired suggestion, there are those who collect the refuse of the public streets, but in order to be received into the band it is necessary to have been born one of the Hereditary Confederacy of Superfluity Removers and Abandoned Oddment Gatherers. ... Aspire to wisdom, O peerless one, but in the meanwhile emulate the pattern of the ruminative ox. This person will now proceed to frequent the society of those best acquainted with the less guarded moments of the revered ascended, and endeavour to learn perchance something more of his inner business methods.'

With this resolve Wan sought out a body of successful merchants and the like whose custom it was to meet together beneath the Sign of Harmonious Ease, where they chiefly spoke in two breaths alternatively of their wealth and their poverty, and there strove to attach himself to the more leisurely inclined. In this he experienced no difficulty, it being for the most part their continual despair that none would give heed to their well-displayed views on things in general, but when he spoke of the one for whom he dressed in white, and endeavoured to ascertain by what means he had earned his facile wealth, even the most sympathetic held out no encouraging hope.

'The same problem has occasioned this person many sleepless nights,' admitted the one on whose testimony Wan had placed the most reliance. 'In a spirit of disinterested friendship he strove by every possible expedient that a fertile and necessity-driven imagination could devise to inveigle your venerated sire into a disclosure of the facts, but to the end he maintained a deluded and narrow-minded silence. The opinion of some here was that he secretly controlled a band of river pirates; others held that he associated with ghouls who despoiled the hidden treasure of the earth. My own opinion was that he had stumbled upon some discreditable fact connected with the past life of one now high in power. Properly developed, any of these three lines of suggestion should lead you to an honourable competence, but if the one whose foresight we are discussing has neglected to provide you with the essential clue before he Journeyed Hence the line you incautiously chose might leave you suspended in quite another position. Your obvious policy would therefore tend towards neglecting to sacrifice for him the commodities of which he must now stand most in need. Under this humane pressure his distinguished preoccupation may perhaps be brought to an enlightened end, and in the form of a dream or through the medium of an opportune vision he may find a means to remedy his omission.'

'It is easy to close a door that none is holding open,' replied Wan freely, for the period had already come when it was difficult for him to provide for the maintenance of his own requirements, 'and the course that you suggest is like Ho Chow's selection in the analogy that bears his name.'

'It is always a privilege to be able to counsel the young and inexperienced,' observed the other, rising and shaking hands with himself benevolently as the beating of a gong announced that the evening rice was laid out near at hand. 'Do not hesitate to bend your inquiring footsteps in the direction of my receptive ear whenever you stand in need of intellectual sustenance. In the meanwhile, may your capacious waistcloth always be distended to repletion.'

'May the pearls of wisdom continue to germinate in the nutritious soil of your well-watered brain,' replied Wan no less appropriately as he set out on a homeward path.

II

There can be little doubt that the Mandarin Hin Ching was an official of the most offensive type: rich, powerful, and in every way successful at this period of his career. Nevertheless, it is truly written, 'Destroy the root and the branches wither of their own accord,' and it will go hard with this obscure person's power of relating history, if, towards the close, Hin Ching shall not be brought to a plight that will be both sharp and ignominious.

Among the other degraded attributes of the concave Hin Ching was a disposition to direct his acquisitive glances towards objects with which he could have no legitimate concern, and in this way it had become a custom for him to loiter, on a variety of unworthy pretexts, in the region of Wan's not specially attractive home at such hours as those when Lan-yen might reasonably be encountered there alone. For her part, the one in question dutifully endeavoured to create the impression that she was unaware of his repulsively expressed admiration, and even of his presence, but owing to his obtuse persistence there were occasions when to have done this consistently would have become inept. Thus and thus Wan had more than once discovered him, but with his usual ill-conditioned guile Hin Ching had never yet failed to have his feet arranged in an appropriate position when they encountered.

On his return from the Abode of Harmonious Ease where the outcome of his quest has already been so incipiently described, Wan presently became aware that the chair of a person of some consequence lurked in the shadow of his decrepit door, the bearers, after the manner of their supine tribe, having composed themselves to sleep. Wan was thereby given the opportunity to enter unperceived, which he did in an attitude of introspective reverie, this enabling him to linger abstractedly for an appreciable moment at the curtain of the ceremonial hall before he disclosed his presence. In this speculative poise he was able to listen, without any loss of internal face, to the exact terms of the deplorable Hin Ching's obscene allurement, and, slightly later, to Lan-yen's virtuous and dignified rejoinder. Rightly assuming that there would be no further arisement likely to outweigh the disadvantages of being detected there, Wan then stepped forth.

'O perverse and double-dealing mandarin!' he exclaimed reproachfully; 'is this the way that justice is displayed about the limits of the Ia-ling mountains? Or how shall the shepherd that assails the flock by night control his voice to sentence those who ravage it by day?'

'It is well to be reminded of my exalted office,' replied Hin Ching, recovering his composure and arrogantly displaying the insignia of his rank. 'Knees such as yours were made to bend, presumptuous Wan, and the rebellious head that has grown too tall to do obeisance can be shortened,' and he indicated by a gesture that the other should prostrate himself.

'When the profound Ng-tai made the remark, "Beneath an integritous roof all men are equal," he was entertaining an imitator of official seals, three sorcerers, and a celebrated viceroy. Why then should this person depart from the high principle in favour of one merely of the crystal button?'

'Four powerful reasons may be brought to bear upon the argument,' replied Hin Ching, and he moved towards the door to summon his attendants.

'They do not apply to the case as I present it,' retorted Wan, drawing his self-reliant sword and intervening its persuasive edge between the other and his purpose. 'Let us confine the issue to essential points, O crafty mandarin.'

At this determined mien Hin Ching lost the usual appearance of his face somewhat, though he made a misbegotten attempt to gather reassurance by grinding his ill-arranged teeth aggressively. As Wan still persisted in an unshaken front, however, the half-stomached person facing him very soon began to retire behind himself and to raise a barrier of evasive subterfuge – first by the claim that as the undoubted thickness of his body afforded a double target he should be permitted to return two blows for each one aimed against him, and later with a demand that he should be allowed to stand upon a dais during the encounter by virtue of his high position. Whatever might have been the issue of his strategy the conflict was definitely averted by a melodious wail of anguish from Lan-yen as she suddenly composed herself into a gracefully displayed rigidity at the impending scene of bloodshed. In the ensuement the detestable Hin Ching imperceptibly faded out, the last indication of his contaminating presence being the apophthegm that there were more ways of killing a dragon than that of holding its head under water.

As the time went on the deeper meaning of the contemptible Hin Ching's sinister remark gradually came up to the surface. Those who in the past had not scrupled to associate with Wan now began to alienate themselves from his society, and, when closely pressed, spoke from behind well-guarded lips of circumspection and the submission to authority that the necessities of an increased posterity entailed. Others raised a lukewarm finger as he passed, where before there had been two insistent outstretched hands, and everywhere there was a disposition to remember neglected tasks on his approach.

In other and more sombre shapes the inauspicious shadow of this corrupt official darkened Wan's blameless path. Merchants with whom he had been wont to traffic on the general understanding that he would requite them in a more propitious hour now disclosed a concentration of adverse circumstances that obliged them to withold their store, so that gradually the bare necessities of the least elaborate life ceased to be within his reach. From time to time heavy rocks, moved by no apparent cause, precipitated themselves around his footsteps, hitherto reliant bridges burst asunder at the exact moment when he might be expected to be crossing them, and the immutable laws governing the recurrence of a stated hazard seemed for a time to be suspended from their function. 'The egregious Hin Ching certainly does not intend to eat his words,' remarked Wan impassively as a triumphal arch which lay beyond his gate crumbled for the fourth time as he passed through.

III

Who has not proved the justice of the saying, 'She who breaks the lid by noon will crack the dish ere nightfall?' Wan was already suffering from the inadequacy of a misguided father, the depravity of an unscrupulous official and the flaccidity of a weak-kneed band of neighbours. To these must now be added a cessation of the ordinary source of nature and the intervention of the correcting gods. Under their avenging rule a prolonged drought assailed the land, so that where fruitfulness and verdure had hitherto prevailed there was soon nothing to be found but barrenness and dust. Wan and Lan-yen began to look into each other's eyes with a benumbing dread, and each in turn secretly replaced among their common store something from the allotted portion and strove unseen to dull the natural pangs of hunger by countless unstable wiles. The meagre strip of cultivated land they held, perforce their sole support, was ill-equipped against the universal famine, and it was with halting feet and downcast face that Wan returned each day to display his slender gain. 'A few parched fruit I bring,' it might be, or, 'This cup of earth-nuts must suffice,' perchance. Soon, 'Naught remains now but bitter-tasting herbs,' he was compelled to say, and Lan-yen waited for the time when there would come the presage of their fate, 'There now is nothing more.'

In the most distant corner of the garden there stood two shrubs of a kind then unfamiliar to the land, not tall but very sturdy in their growth. Once when they walked together in that part Lan-yen had drawn Wan aside, and being of a thrifty and sententious mind, had pointed to them, saying:

'Here are two shrubs which neither bear fruit nor serve a useful purpose in some other way. Put out your hand, proficient one, and hew them down so that their wood may feed our scanty hearth and a more profitable herbage occupy their place.'

At this request Wan changed countenance, and although he cleared his throat repeatedly, it was some time before he could frame a suitable reply.

'There is a tradition connected with this spot,' he said at length, 'which would make it extremely ill-advised to do as you suggest.'

'How then does it chance that the story has never yet reached my all-embracing ears?' inquired Lan-yen in some confusion. 'What mystery is here?'

'That,' replied Wan tactfully, 'is because your conversation is mainly with the ephemeral and slight. The legend was received from the lips of the most venerable dweller in this community, who had in turn acquired it from the mental storehouse of his predecessor.'

'The words of a patriarch, though generally diffuse and sometimes incoherent, are worthy of regard,' admitted

Lan-yen gracefully. 'Proceed to unfold your reminiscent mood.'

'Upon this spot in bygone years there lived a pious anchorite who sought to attain perfection by repeating the names of the Pure Ones an increasing number of times each day. Devoting himself wholly to this sacred undertaking, and being by nature generously equipped towards the task, he at length formed the meritorious project of continuing without intermission either by night or day, and, in this tenacious way outstripping all rival and competing anchorites, of being received finally into a higher state of total obliteration in the Ultimate Beyond than any recluse had hitherto attained. Every part of his being responded to the exalted call made on it, save only one, but in each case, just as the permanent achievement lay within his grasp, his rebellious eyelids fell from the high standard of perfection and betrayed him into sleep. All ordinary methods of correction having failed, the conscientious solitary took a knife of distinguished sharpness and resolutely slicing off the effete members of his house he cast them from him out into the night. The watchful Powers approved, and to mark the sacrifice a tree sprang up where each lid fell and by the contour of its leaf proclaimed the symbol of its origin.'

This incident occurred to Lan-yen's mind when their extremity had passed all normal bounds and every kind of cultivated food had ceased. The time had now come when Wan returned an empty bowl into her waiting hands, and with mute gestures and uncertain steps had sought to go, rather than speak the message of despair. It was then that Lan-yen detained him by her gentle voice to urge a last resort.

'There still remain the two mysterious trees, whose rich and glossy leaves suggest a certain juicy nourishment. Should they happen to prove deadly in effect, then our end will only be more sharply ruled than would otherwise be the case; if, on the contrary, they are of innocuous growth they may sustain us until some other form of succour intervenes.'

'If you are willing to embark on so doubtful an adventure it would cover me with secret humiliation to refrain,' replied Wan acquiescently. 'Give me the bowl again.'

When she heard his returning step Lan-yen went out to meet

him, and seeing his downcast look she hailed him from a distance.

'Do not despond,' she cried. 'The sting of a whip indicates its end and your menial one is inspired to prophesy a very illustrious close to all our trials. Further, she has procured the flavour of an orange and a sprinkling of snuff wherewith to spice the dish.'

'In that case,' replied Wan, displaying what he had brought, 'the savouring will truly be the essence of our feast. The produce of the shrubs has at length shared the common fate,' and he made to throw away the dry and withered leaves that the bowl contained.

'Forbear!' exclaimed Lan-yen, restraining him. ' "It is no further on than back again when the halfway house is reached." Who knows what hidden virtues may diffuse from so miraculous a root?'

In this agreeable spirit the accommodating person took up the task and with such patient skill as if a banquet of ceremonial swallows had been involved she prepared a dish of the withered leaves from the unknown shrubs. When all was ready she set the alien fare before Wan and took her place beside the chair to serve his hand.

'Eat,' she exhorted, 'and may the Compassionate Ones protect you.'

'I lean against their sympathetic understanding,' responded Wan devoutly as he looked beneath the cover. 'Nevertheless,' he added graciously, 'on so momentous an occasion priority shall be yours.'

'By no means,' replied Lan-yen hastily, at the same time pressing him back into the seat he would vacate. 'Not until you have slaked your noble appetite shall my second-rate lips partake.'

'It is proverbial that from a hungry tiger and an affectionate woman there is no escape,' murmured Wan, and taking up a portion of the food he swallowed it.

'Your usually expressive eye has assumed a sudden glassy lustre,' exclaimed Lan-yen, who had not ceased to regard him anxiously. 'What is the outstanding flavour of the dish?'

'It has no discoverable flavour of any kind,' declared Wan,

speaking with considerable emotion, 'but the general effect it produces is indistinguishable from suffocation. A cup of water, adored, before it is too late!'

'Alas,' admitted Lan-yen, looking round in a high-minded access of refined disdain, 'none now remains! There is nothing here but the dark and austere liquor in which the herb has boiled.'

'So long as it is liquid it suffices,' replied Wan in an extremity, and seizing the proffered vessel from her misgiving hand he took a well-sustained grasp of its contents.

'The remedy would appear to be a protracted one,' remarked Lan-yen in some surprise, as Wan maintained the steady rhythm of his action. 'Surely the obstruction is by now dispersed?'

'Phœnix-eyed one,' replied Wan, pausing with some reluctance; 'not only is that obstruction now removed, but every other impediment to felicity is likewise brushed away. Observe this person's sudden rise of vigour, his unexpected store of energy, the almost alarming air of general proficiency radiating from his system. It becomes plain now that from the beginning of our oppression everything has been working in an ordered scheme to lead us to an end. This is no earthly liquid, such as you might brew, but a special nectar sent down by the gods to sustain mankind in every sort of trial. From this moment our future prosperity is assured.'

As he finished speaking there was a sudden outcry from the Way beyond, a blending of heavy steps and upraised voices; the door was thrust widely open, and with a deplorable absence of seemly ostentation the sublime Emperor of the land, accompanied by a retinue of agitated nobles, pressed into the room.

IV

Let it be freely admitted that a really capable narrator of events would have led up to this badly arranged crisis more judiciously and in a manner less likely to distress the harmonious balance of his hearers' feelings. Yet there is a certain fitness in the stress, however ineptly reached, for the august sovereign now involved was so rapidly outlined in all his movements that between his conception of a course and the moment when he embarked upon it there was very little opportunity for those chiefly concerned to engage in preparation. Thus steps into the record Ming Wang, last of his royal line.

When the famine had cankered the land for seven full moons there appeared before the Palace gate a stranger clad in fur. Without deigning to reply to any man of those confronting him with words of this or that, he loftily took down the brazen trident from among the instruments that hung there and struck on it a loud compelling note with the fingers of his open hand. At this defiant challenge, in compliance with the Ancient Usage, he was led into the presence of Ming Wang at once.

'Speak without fear,' said the sympathetic ruler affably, 'for the iron law of Yu protects you.'

At the mention of this heroic name the stranger's expression varied in its tenor and he drew up the covering of his face a little although the day was warm.

'In the north and the south, on the east and the west, there is a famine in the land, for the resentful gods withhold their natural moisture,' he proclaimed; and it was afterwards agreed that the sound of his voice was like the whetting of a sickle on a marble hone. 'For seven moons and seven more days has this affliction been, and you who stand regently between the Upper and the Lower Worlds have suffered it to be.'

'What you say is very surprising,' replied Ming Wang, 'and the more so as no appreciable scarcity has been apparent at our royal table for the time you name. Be assured that due inquiry shall be made however.'

'Let it be made forthwith and justice measured out,' said the intruder sternly, and he turned away and stood so that none might see the working of his complicated thoughts.

'When two minds are agreed what matter which tongue speaks?' remarked the liberally endowed monarch to the scandalised officials hovering round, and with truly imperial large-handedness he ordered the immediate presence of the four chancellors of the regions named, despite the fact that they were then residing in their several distant capitals. No stronger proof of the efficiency of Ming Wang's vigorous rule need be sought, for no sooner was the command issued than four chancellors immediately appeared.

'It is obligingly reported by an unnamed well-wisher that a scarcity exists in all the corners of our boundless realm,' remarked the Illimitable, in so encouraging a voice that the four chancellors began to beat their heads upon the granite floor in an access of misgiving. 'Doubtless each has a wholly adequate reply?'

'Omnipotence,' pleaded the first, 'there has been a slight temporary derangement of transport in the Province of the North, with the unfortunate arisement that here and there a luxury is scarce.'

'All-seeing,' replied the next, 'certain grain in a restricted area of the Province of the South has been consumed by subterranean Beings. Yet what are southern men that they should not turn from rice to millet with a cheerful face?'

'In the Province of the East, Benevolence,' declared the third, 'a fiery omen shot across the sky, corroding the earth to barrenness that lay within its sphere. To judgments such as this the faithful can but bend an acquiescent neck.'

'Father of all mercies,' stammered the last, who being slow-witted had no palliation ready to his tongue, 'that same blazing menace then passed onward to the Province of the West where it wrought a like disaster.'

'Nothing could be more convincing,' agreed the Mouthpiece of Wisdom heartily. 'We were sure that something of the sort would be at once forthcoming. It will certainly be a fountain of consolation to your sorrowing friends, even in the most poignant moments of their grief, that your crime – despite its regrettable consequences – was purely of a technical description.'

'High Majesty?' besought the four in harmony.

'It would appear,' explained the Supreme indulgently, 'that by withholding all mention of this distressing state of things (doubtless to spare our too warm-hearted ears) you have each inadvertently come within the Code of Yaou and Shun, under the Section: Conduct in an official whereby disaffection of the Outer Lands may be engendered. In that imperishable Statute every phase of misdoing is crystallised with unfailing legal skill into this shining principle of universal justice: one crime, one responsible official. That firmly grasped, the administration of an otherwise complex judicial system becomes purely a matter of elementary mathematics. In this case, as there are clearly four crimes to be atoned, four responsible officials suffer the usual fatal expiation.'

'Enough,' exclaimed the stranger, emerging from his reverie and confronting Ming Wang again. 'In that respect, no doubt, a fit example will be made. But what of the greater need besetting you, or who will persuade the seasons to resume their normal courses?'

'As to that,' replied the Emperor agreeably, 'we are waiting to tread in your illuminating footsteps in whatever direction you may indicate.'

'He who brings the word is not thereby required to go the way,' replied the one who thus described himself. 'You, Younger Brother, hold the Line of the Immortal Eight. See to it that you do not fail their now expectant eyes.'

'It is one thing to hold the line: it is quite another to obtain a message from the farther end,' murmured the Sublime rebelliously, but when he would have again applied for more explicit guidance it was discovered that the stranger had withdrawn, though none had marked the moment of his going.

'All-knowing,' urged a faithful slave who bore the Emperor's cup, 'if you seek enlightenment wherefore are The Books?'

'It is well said,' exclaimed the Monarch, casting off his gloom. 'What more in keeping with the theme than that a vassal youth should recall what the trusted keepers of our Inner Council have forgot!'

'Revered,' returned the spokesman of the Elder Branch, by no means disposed to have their prescience questioned thus, 'if we who guard the dark secrets of The Books forbore, it was not that our minds were tardy in your need, but rather because our passionate devotion shrank from the thought of finding what we may.'

The Divine made a gesture of reconciliation.

'Your loyalty is clear and deep, Tso Paik, nor has its source yet been reached,' he admitted freely. 'But what does the somewhat heavily scored music of your genial voice forecast?'

'That is as will presently appear,' replied the other sombrely, 'for since the day of your great progenitor Shan-ti (who chose self-ending in consequence of what he learned) the restraining cords have not been cut nor the wisdom of The Books displayed.'

'Certainly there are strong arguments against doing anything of the sort in an idle spirit,' admitted Ming Wang hastily, at the same time spilling the larger portion of his wine upon the kneeling cup-bearer. 'Perhaps after all – '

'The requirement has gone forth; the issue must be met,' pronounced the custodian firmly, 'Even the lower-class demons have their feelings in such matters.' Then raising his voice, as his especial office permitted him to do, he called for the attendance of all his satellites and for the bringing of The Books. At this unusual cry general business of every sort was immediately suspended within the limits of the Palace walls, and an interminable stream of augurs, sorcerers, diviners, astrologers, forecasters, necromancers, haruspices, magicians, incantators, soothsayers, charm-workers, illusionists, singers and dancers, thought readers, contortionists and the like, rallied to his side, bringing with them birds, serpents, fruit, ashes, flat and rounded sticks, cords, fire, entrails, perfumed wax, salt, coloured earth, dung of the sacred apes, crystal spheres and the other necessary utensils of their enlightened arts. So great was the press that very few ordinary persons gained admittance and of these only the outspoken and robust. When order was restored the splendid ceremony of Bringing in The Books was formally observed, the casket opened, and the cords released.

'Ming Wang,' pronounced the one who had made himself conspicuous throughout, 'this is the Wisdom of The Books and thus stands the passage on the bamboo slip to which my necessarily inspired finger has been led: "Drought, excessive, to assuage. Should a pestilential drought continue unappeased, a palatable extract may be made of the fermented grain of rice – " '

'Tso Paik,' muttered another of the Inner Council, from about his sleeve, 'what Evil Dragon has assailed your mental balance?'

'Imperishable,' pleaded Tso Paik in servile confusion,

'dazzled by the brilliance of your shining condescension, this illiterate person misread the initial sign and diverged to an inappropriate line. Yet his arresting finger was not deceived, for the jewelled passage that relates appears on the next slip.'

'Continue, discriminating Tso Paik,' said the Emperor pleasantly. 'Nor suffer your finger yet to lose that self-same place.'

'Sublimity, the guidance sought is that entitled: "Drought, caused by Good or Bad Spirits, to disperse," ' resumed Tso Paik in a less compelling voice. 'Thus and thus the message is pronounced: "He who stands between the Upper and the Lower Planes alone can intervene when the Immortals have so far declared their wrath" – there follows much of a circumlocutory nature connected with the Inherent Principle of Equipoise, and so forth.'

'That can fittingly be reserved for our leisurely delectation at some future date,' put in the Highest. 'Insert your chopstick in the solid meat, Tso Paik. What have we got to *do*?'

'Putting aside these gems of philosophical profundity, Benign, the nature of your submission is neither palatable nor light.' At these foreboding words a thrill of apprehension swayed the vast concourse, but it was widely noticed that the crude Tso Paik's lamentable voice took upon itself a pleasurable shade. 'Decked to the likeness of a sacrificial ox, shorn both of hair and rank-denoting nails, and riding in a farm-yard cart, it is your unpleasant lot to be taken to the highest point of the sacred Ia-ling range and there confess your sins to heaven and undertake reform. When this human sacrifice has been achieved (providing no untoward omen intervenes meanwhile), the healing rain will fall.'

At the full understanding of this direful penance an awe-struck silence fell upon the throng. The first to break it was the captain of the Emperor's chosen guard, and although he was incapable of producing more than an attenuated whisper, his words expressed the thoughts of every loyal subject there.

'Sins! Who speaks of sins?' he murmured in amaze. 'How can that which is not, be? The Ever-righteous *has* no sins!'

Never was the profundity of the All-grasping more lucidly displayed than in that exacting pause, when, whatever else happened, a popular rising, in one direction or another, seemed inevitable.

'Peace, worthy Sung,' he cried in a voice that carried to the public square outside, where it was rapturously acclaimed, although at that distance it was, of course, impossible to distinguish a word he said; 'restrain your generous zeal and whet your docile ears to an acuter edge. The obligation is to *confess* sins: not to *possess* them. Admittedly we have no sins, for, little as the censorious credit it, your Unapproachable is often denied what the meanest outcast in his realm can wallow in. Nothing that we may do is, or can be, wrong; but the welfare of the people is our chief concern, and to secure that end there is no catalogue of vice that we shall not cheerfully subscribe to.'

So unutterable was the effect produced by this truly regal magnanimity that all who heard its terms were rendered speechless. Those outside, on the contrary, hastily assuming that Ming Wang had said all that he intended, testified their satisfaction more joyfully than before, and loud cries of 'A thousand years!' filled the air.

'In the detail of promising amendment, also, there is nothing to which the most arbitrary need take exception,' continued the enlightened Monarch when his voice could once more be heard. 'What, after all, is a promise of amendment but an affirmation that the one who makes it will be more worthy of homage to-morrow than to-day? There is nothing new about that in your Immaculate's career; every day finds him better than before.'

'Your words are like a string of hanging lanterns where the way has hitherto been dark,' fervently declared an aged counsellor. 'But, Pre-eminence, your polished nails, your cultivated hair – '

'It is better to lose two spans outwards than one span inwards,' replied the practical-minded Sovereign, dropping his voice for that one's ear alone. 'Yet,' he continued, turning to Tso Paik again, 'in one respect the limit of compliance has been reached, and he who opens a hand so freely on the right may close one as tightly on the left. "The likeness of an ox" is doubtless a picturesque analogy, and the similitude is not bereft of a certain massive dignity. But if at the extremity of your prolific mind, Tso Paik, you cherish the questionable ambition of displaying your confiding Ruler to a superstitious though by no means simple-minded populace, wearing horns – '

'Mirror of Felicity!' protested Tso Paik, as one who is maligned; 'if my crude tongue offends let it cease. You wear a sword and my head has but a single neck.'

'In our romantic land there should be room both for your tongue and my sword to move without any overlapping,' reassured Ming Wang. 'Proceed, in your sublime office, therefore, to the exactitude of detail and let harmony prevail.'

v

Thus in the third year of his short but glorious reign the well-disposed Ming Wang set out to free his people from the evil that oppressed them, draped in the semblance of a sacrificial ox (the metaphor, it was found, did not demand more than a screen of rushes to enclose his lower half), shorn, and riding in a dung-cart through the land. With so liberal-minded a prince, in so ambiguous a guise, it was impossible that the journey should be devoid of incident, but this is the essential story of Wan, and he who, while gathering mast, suffers his mind to dwell on the thought of peaches, will return with an empty sack.

In due course the company reached the lower slopes of the Ia-ling mountains, and thenceforward all progress was on foot. Tso Paik, who was gross by nature and very sluggish on his feet, would willingly have remained below to offer up (he said) an invocation to the gods, but Ming Wang would not suffer this, claiming that if he did their appetites might become satiate before his own chance came. Being of a slight and strenuous cast this mode of progress was more congenial to the Emperor's taste than the restricted freedom of the dung-cart, and from time to time he inspired his train by pointing out to them that what they deemed to be the highest point was an imposition of the eye, and that yet another peak lay beyond. Finally, Tso Paik rolled bodily upon the ground and declared that, as he could go no farther, where he lay in his

official rank as Chief Custodian of The Books must constitute the limit, and this was then agreed to.

No complete record of Ming Wang's confession now exists,
all those who accompanied him having entered into a deep
compact to preserve a stubborn silence. It is admitted, however, that it was of inordinate length, very explicit in its details,
and that it implicated practically every courtier and official
of any standing. In a final access of self-reproach the Emperor
penitently admitted that he was the guilty head of a thoroughly
decayed and criminal autocracy, that he weakly surrounded
himself with greedy and incompetent officials, and that he had
thoughtlessly permitted sycophantry, bribery and peculation
to abound.

Almost before he had begun to speak, heavy clouds were
seen to drift up from the west; with the first words of definite
submission a few drops fell, and the ceremony was concluded
in a steady downpour. The conscientious Monarch did not
allow the undoubted discomfort of all concerned to stem the
flow of his inspired penitence, but when the last atrocity that
he could lay to his own and, even more pointedly, to his minis-
ters' charge had been revealed, he called upon Tso Paik.

'You, Tso Paik, as Ceremonial Director of the Enterprise,
have accomplished an end. Yet, no longer to maintain a poise,
does not the copious promptness of the response astonish even
you?'

'Omnipotence,' replied Tso Paik, looking steadily before
him, 'my faith was like an elephant tethered to a rock.'

'It is well,' agreed the Greatest, endeavouring to shake his
scanty outer garment free of moisture. 'Bring forward now our
largest state umbrella.'

At this sudden but in no way unreasonable command a very
concentrated silence engaged the company and those who had
not the opportunity to withdraw in unstudied abstraction
sought to anticipate any call upon themselves by regarding the
one involved expectantly.

'Alas,' confessed the dense Tso Paik, 'it had not occurred to
this one's bankrupt mind that there would be any likelihood – '
but at that point, understanding the snare to which he had enticed himself, he stopped abruptly.

A passing shiver disturbed the royal frame, though with high-born delicacy he endeavoured to conceal it. Only a faint elevation of the celestial eyebrows betrayed the generous emotion at the painful obligation laid upon him.

'It wrings my tenderest parts with hooks of bitterness,' he said, 'that so loyal and trustworthy a subject should have brought himself within the Code of Yaou and Shun, under the Section: Conduct in an official whereby the well-being of his Sovereign is directly or indirectly menaced. Li Tung, you are a dignitary of high justice; receive the unfortunate Tso Paik into your charge until the Palace executioner shall require him at your hands. Let us now strive to avert, so far as we can, the ill consequences of this fatal indiscretion by seeking the nearest shelter.'

VI

In this remarkable manner two of the most notable characters of any age, Wan the son of Ah-shoo, and Ming Wang (to whose memory posterity has dedicated as a title 'The Knowing'), at last encountered, for it was to the penurious home of the former person that destiny inclined the Emperor's footsteps. Recognising the languished fortunes of the one whose roof he sought, the considerate Monarch forbore to stand on ceremony, merely requiring a reclining stool before the charcoal fire.

'Beneficence,' exclaimed Wan, falling on his face to the best of his ability as he offered a steaming cup, 'admittedly the hearth will warm the muscles of your lordly body, but here is that which will invigorate the cockles of your noble heart.'

For a perceptible moment the Imperishable wavered – certainly the balance of the analogy might have been more classically maintained, or possibly he remembered the long succession of food-tasters who had fallen lifeless at his feet – but in that pause the exquisite aroma of the fragrant liquid assailed his auspicious nose. He took the cup and emptied it, returned it to Wan's hand with an appropriate gesture, and continued thus and thus until the latter person had to confess that his store was destitute. Not until then did Ming Wang devote his throat to speech.

'What is this enchanted beverage?' he demanded, 'and why has it been withheld from us until now?'

'It is the produce of a sacred tree, high Majesty, and its use but lately revealed to me by special favour of the Powers. Never before, from the legendary days of the First Man until this hour, has it been brewed on earth, and, save for the necessary tests, your own distinguished lips are the first to taste it.'

'It is certainly miraculous,' agreed Ming Wang ecstatically, and unable to contain himself he began to cross and recross the room, to the embarrassment of the assembled nobles who were thus also kept in a continual state of flux. 'It has a perfection hitherto unknown among the liquids of the world. It cheers yet without any disconcerting effect upon the speech or movements. It warms where one is cold and cools where one is hot. Already every trace of fatigue and despondency has vanished, leaving us inspired for further deeds of public usefulness, eager to accomplish other acts of justice. It stimulates, invigorates, rejuvenates, animates, lubricates – '

'Sublimest of Potentates,' pleaded the recorder of his voice, 'retard the torrent of your melodious soliloquy! How else shall this clay-fingered menial take down your priceless words which it is his design presently to set to appropriate music?'

'It will be as acceptable at the earliest gong-stroke of the yet unwakened morn, as it will become the inevitable accompaniment to the afternoon rice. Into the inner office of the commercially inclined it will be brought to smooth the progress of each bargain, and in the dim recesses of our departmental archives it will produce harmony and discreet mirth among the abstemious yet sprightly of both sexes. In the chambers of our lesser ones its name is destined to rank as a synonym of all that is confidential and inexact. The weary student, endeavouring to banish sleep; the minor priest, striving to maintain enthusiasm amid an inadequacy of taels; the harassed and ill-requited inscriber of the spoken word – '

'Proceed, O Tap-root of Eloquence, proceed!' murmured the one who plied a hurrying brush. 'To an accompaniment of drums, horns, and metallic serpents – '

'To cope the final pinnacle, it is an entirely new thing; indeed it is *the* new thing, and unless our experience of an imitative and

docile people is signally astray it will soon become "the thing".'
It is hardly necessary to insist at this late date how noticeably
the prescient Ming Wang's words have been literally fulfilled.
Known for many centuries as 'the new thing', the popular
decoction passed by a natural stage into 'the thing', and then,
in affectionate abbreviation, to 'the'. By this appropriate desig-
nation it is recognised in every land to which our flowery
civilisation carries, though doubtless on barbaric tongues the
melodious word is bent to many uncouth similitudes.

'It now only remains,' continued the even-handed law-giver,
'to reward virtue and to eradicate vice. The former is personi-
fied before us – the latter we shall doubtless very soon discover
in some form or another. What, O benefactor of mankind, is
your upright name?'

'My low-class appellation is Wan, that of my mentally defec-
tive father being Ah-shoo, we spring from the lowly house of
Lam,' replied the other suitably. 'The inconspicuous shadow
lurking in the background is Lan-yen, whose name entwines
with mine.'

'Yet how comes it that you, who are evidently under the
direct protection of the higher Forces, are in so – as it may be
expressed – ' and with commendable tact the humane Emperor
merely indicated the threadbare walls and Wan's immemorial
garb.

'Formerly, Magnificence, my state was thus and thus, lacking
nothing and having slaves to stand before my presence,' admitted Wan. 'But of late one in authority has oppressed me
for no cause, save that the proverb aptly says, "Should you
touch a rat upon the tail be assured that he will turn and bite
you", and in this latter end his malice has prevailed.'

'Ah,' commented the Enlightened, with a meaning nod at
each of his suite in turn, to which they duly responded an apt
glance of cognisance. 'What is this corrupt official's name and
the sign of his condition?' and the Justice-loving began to rub
his hands enjoyably together.

'He is of the crystal button, lord, and his forbidding name
Hin Ching. Furthermore, led on by an insatiable curiosity, he is
at this moment standing about this person's crumbling gate,
striving to peer through the prickly hedge towards us.'

'Let him be brought in at once,' was the command, and with no opportunity to prepare an evasive tale, Hin Ching was hurried forward.

'Hin Ching,' said the Emperor, who had meanwhile taken up an imposing station, 'all your duplicity is known to us and no defence will serve you. How comes it that you have so pursued this meritorious youth who has our royal favour?'

'Tolerance,' pleaded the terror-stricken culprit, seeing no other course before him, and kowtowing so passionately that his words could scarcely be heard above the steady clashing of his head upon the sonorous floor, 'be clement in your strength, for it has long been suspected that this person's heart is touched.'

'In that case,' decided the Sun of Impartiality, 'the marks should certainly be visible so that the innocent may be warned thereby.' Then turning to his retinue he continued: 'Procure a reasonable abundance of supple bamboo rods, and without disturbing the afflicted mandarin from the position which he has so conveniently assumed, remove his lower robe.'

At this awful presage of the nature of the correction shortly to be laid upon Hin Ching a shudder went up from the assembled host, and even Wan vacillated in his strict resentment.

'Brother of the peacock,' he pleaded, 'suffer justice this once to drowse. He is a man of middle years and obese beyond his age.'

'It has ever been the privilege of the wronged to condone the guilty,' replied Ming Wang, 'and to that extent your plea must hold. Yet wherein shall Hin Ching's penance lie, his case being outside the Code of Yaou and Shun? What, mandarin, is your strict equivalent?'

'Your entirely humble ranks with a district prefect, High Excellence – equal and above.'

'Henceforth you will rank equal and below, thus degrading you appreciably and at the same time enabling you to save a portion of your face. On the unbending line of pure romantic justice all your belongings should divert to Wan, but as this would probably result in your becoming a dangerous criminal the special requirements will be met by allotting to him half. To prevent any mutual delusion you will divide all you possess into two equal mounds – and Wan will make his choice.'

'May your life span ten thousand ages and your grandsons rule the world!' exclaimed Wan. 'It is enough to have seen this day,' and even Hin Ching contributed an appropriate, though a shorter, blessing from within his teeth.

'It only remains to define your duties,' continued the Ever-thoughtful, addressing himself to Wan. 'Your style will be that of "Protector of the Tree" and the scroll confirming this will follow in due season. Your chief function will, of course, be that of assuring an unfailing supply of the beverage to our royal Palaces at all times. In your spare moments you can transmit offshoots of the tree to every point of our boundless Empire, so that the seed shall never fail. The office, which will be strictly hereditary, will naturally be quite honorary, what you receive from Hin Ching being sufficient to maintain your state. It will, however, carry with it a salute of three trumpets and the emblem of a steaming cup.'

'Majesty,' reported an attending slave, entering at this pause, 'a relay of swift horses from the Capital awaits your commanding voice without.'

The All-accomplishing rose and moved towards the door with the well-satisfied smile of a person who has achieved his worthy end.

'Everything has been set right here,' he remarked pleasantly, 'and the usual edicts will follow within a moon.' Then to his suite: 'Come, let us press forward with all haste to scatter the germs of promiscuous justice elsewhere.'

CHAPTER III

The Further Continuance of Kai Lung's Quest and his Opportune Encounter with an Outcast Band, all Ignorant of the Classical Examples of the Past

THE next day, as soon as it was light, Kai Lung resumed his toilsome way, sustained by the cordial leavetakings of the villagers to whom his unassuming qualities as a relater of events had proved of interest, and no less encouraged by the tactful bestowal of such gifts as they had no further use for.

'Even a meatless bone should be tendered with both hands,' apologised one, bereft of reason, as he indicated all that he could offer – a pipe containing only ashes, and in the same harmonious spirit Kai Lung placed the stem between his lips for a few moments with the equally polite assurance, 'It is not necessary to pluck the fruit in order to admire the tree.'

At the parting of the roads a patriarchal figure was seated on the earth. As the one with whom this narration is essentially concerned approached, the inopportune person indicated that the other should retard his footsteps so that they might converse at leisure and with ease. Unwelcome as the delay would prove, Kai Lung had no alternative but to defer to the wishes of a venerable whose long white moustaches almost touched the ground. He stopped and saluted him with deference.

'What is passing through your mind is by no means so hidden as you may think,' remarked the stranger, with a penetrating glance; 'nor, considering the mission upon which you are embarked, is your reluctance to be wondered at.'

'Your insight is both clear and deep,' confessed Kai Lung. 'What you infer is all the more surprising, as no word of this has so far escaped my docile tongue.'

The ancient smiled slightly in a self-approving manner and caressed the more accessible portions of his virtuous moustache.

'It is not necessary for a philosopher to light a torch to catch glow-worms by at midday,' he replied profoundly. 'The one before you, in spite of his admittedly quite ordinary appearance, is really an experienced wizard. Last night, in return for the gratifying entertainment afforded by your story of the vicissitudinous Wan, he spent the hours of darkness in drawing up the fundamentals of your lucky system. From these it would appear that the numbers 4 and 14 are inimical to your prospects, while 7 and 41 point directly to success. The mango is a tree to be avoided, but a golden bud set on a leafless stem leads to your achievement. Finally, should you encounter two hyenas and an infirm tiger disputing for the possession of a sick cow's bones, do not hesitate.'

'It is well expressed,' replied Kai Lung gratefully. 'Yet in what precise direction should the recommended lack of indecision tend?'

The gifted necromancer raised his inspired eyebrows somewhat, as though this stress of detail did not altogether merit his approval.

'It is one thing to forecast contingencies,' was his reply; 'it is another branch of the occupation to explain what takes place thereafter. If you have led a consistent life, doubtless some benignant Influence will be told off to direct you in the crisis.'

'I can make no particular claim to anything excessive,' admitted Kai Lung with due humility. 'My usual practice has been to avoid treading on bees, ants, silkworms and industrious creatures generally, and there is a suitable hole cut in my outer door and a bowl of rice always set within so that any passing homeless ghost need not go hungry through the night. The care of ancestral spirits, of course, need not be specified.'

The aged made a gesture expressive of some doubt.

'It may be deemed sufficient in your hour of trial,' he conceded, 'but a few authentic charms, written with perfumed ink and worn at the more vulnerable angles of the body, might well be added.'

With this warning in his ears the story-teller passed forward on his way, for the pious anchorite had immediately fallen into a deep introspective haze from which it would have been unseemly to recall him. Profiting by the directions readily disclosed to him by dwellers in those parts, Kai Lung steadily followed in Ming-shu's offensive wake, not forming any very clear perception of how to act when the moment of their meeting should arrive, but content meanwhile to leave the matter to the all-directing wisdom of the forerunners of his Line.

After enduring many hardships and suffering occasional inconvenience through the really flattering but too excessively persistent attentions of brigands, outlaws, underling officials, wild beasts of various kinds, snakes and scorpions, swollen rivers, broken paths and thunder-stones, Kai Lung came on the seventh day at evening to the outskirt of a trackless morass that barred his further progress. The scanty dwellers in that sterile waste were persons of a low standard of intelligence whose sole means of livelihood consisted of the occasional wayfarer who sought their aid. These it was their custom, by immemorial use, to rob and then fatally dispose of, or to guide along the secret morass paths for an agreed reward – according to the arrangement which they found the more convenient. The appearance of Kai Lung was disconcerting to a tribe of so regular a habit.

'For here is one who has nothing in his sleeve and whose apparel is inferior to the worst among ourselves,' they said. 'Thus he is secure from our extracting thumbs, and having no complaint to carry hence against us there is no reason why we should put ourselves to the trouble of disposing of him fatally,' and they continued to look at one another askance.

'That is a matter very easily arranged,' interposed Kai Lung. 'In accordance with a certain vow it is necessary that I should cross these voracious swamps in pursuit of Ming-shu's host. By guiding me among the secret ways you will fulfil one of your essential purposes, and by supplying me with such meagre food as will enable me to justify my oath you will acquire merit of a very special kind.'

To this solution of their difficulty the better-class murderers at once agreed, but some of the more sordid-minded, who by reason of their deficient literary attainments could not follow the balance of the synthesis, began to murmur from behind their fanlike hands.

'It is all very well,' they implied, 'but Ming-shu, who began by putting us to death to exact our service, was forced in the end to succumb to our terms. Why, then, should we guide this alien wayfarer, who is plainly banded with Ming-shu, merely to gain some hypothetical distinction in a future state?'

'The reply to that is easy and concise,' was Kai Lung's ready answer. 'This being the seventh day of my pursuit it falls within my lucky zone, and thereby I cannot fail. Should you neglect to profit by my auspicious presence here, another will snatch this godsend from your grasp, for in the circumstances a powerful friend will certainly arise to foster me, even as that high official the Mandarin Wong Tsoi came to the aid of Keu Chun, the needy actor.'

'We who are men of the bogland of Yang-tze pay allegiance to the Mandarin Ho Hung alone,' the ill-contents replied. 'What is this new official with whom you threaten us?'

'The word is inexact,' maintained Kai Lung, 'nor would a throat so obsequious as mine bend to the line of menace. The Mandarin Wong Tsoi is one who had no actual existence in this world, he being but a fictitious creation of an imagined tale.'

At this the tribesmen conferred together apart and it was plain that even the boldest were shaken. Then the spokesman stood forth again.

'If the Mandarin Wong Tsoi was such as you affirm, how is it possible to say what words he used or the manner of his behaviour in any contingency of life?'

'That constitutes the story-teller's art,' replied the one before them, 'and therein lie the essentials of his craft. But is it possible,' he added, scarcely daring to voice so incredible a thought, 'that you are unacquainted with the crystalline scintillation and many-petalled efflorescence of a well-related legendary occurrence?'

'We are but the untutored brigands of this lonely waste, whose immature ideas have hitherto been bounded by the arrival of inoffensive travellers from the east and the manner of their passing out towards the west,' confessed the tribe. 'The form of entertainment to which you allude lies quite beyond our sphere.'

'Yet it would seem incredible,' lamented Kai Lung, sadly, 'that within the furthest confines of our classic-loving Empire there should be tribes so barbarous and deficient in the rudiments of a literary veneer as not to be acquainted with the "Romance of Three Kingdoms" or the more austere "Wilderness of Pearls", and to whom the graceful apophthegm-spangled masterpieces of the sublime period of T'ang are a never-opened book.'

'We certainly begin to become conscious of a hitherto unsuspected void,' agreed the leaders. 'But how can a community living so remote aspire to correct our fault?'

'As to that,' replied Kai Lung modestly, 'the one before you is himself a very third-rate relater of fabricated legends. On the understanding that you will guide him through the hidden byways of your prepossessing swamp and will supply his present need, he will, to the best of his quite unsatisfactory ability, endeavour to waste your priceless time with the narrative entitled

"The Story of Wong Tsoi and the Merchant Teen King's Thumb".'

'Is that a noteworthy example of your inimitable style?' asked the chieftain of the band politely.

'It is no better nor worse than any other threadbare makeshift of my superannuated stock,' replied Kai Lung no less reciprocally. 'It maintains, however, a certain harmonious parallelity to our existing state in that a discreditable outcast finds a beneficent protector in his hour of need, and the one who thus upheld his cause is himself rewarded for his virtuous action.'

'If that is the case we will constitute your circle,' agreed the others, 'and when you have honourably fulfilled your word you will find no disposition on our part to recede from ours.' Kai Lung accordingly unrolled his well-worn mat and indicated that his simple preparation was complete.

THE STORY OF WONG TSOI AND THE MERCHANT TEEN KING'S THUMB

It was the custom of the Mandarin Wong Tsoi to move about the streets of Hoo-yang at night unattended and by stealth. Sometimes he chanced upon an encounter of a kind that was not strictly within his province as a magistrate, at others he heard a whisper that enabled him to influence justice towards those whom he distrusted without the necessity of invoking the more elaborate forms of law, and upon one occasion – But having thus first brought to the notice of a select and proverbially open-handed band of listeners the most distinguished person of this very ordinary recital (according to the dictates of the refined models of the past), it is now permissible to begin in a more convenient manner.

When Chun, the son of Keu, returning to his father's house from a lengthy absence, made his first inquiry, after the protestations of regard and filial devotion, it was of Fragrant Petal that he spoke. Recalling little of what had gone before they told him freely, with, perchance, an added jest, that one so old and unwieldy in his bulk as Teen King, the rich produce merchant, should seek to possess a butterfly. When he knew all,

Chun reached for his hat and his staff and unlatched the door.

'I would look again upon the Ways and well-remembered quarters of the city,' he remarked evasively.

'Yet it is now dark,' they reminded him, 'and you are but just restored to us. To-morrow – '

'There is still light enough to show me what I seek,' was his reply.

As Chun turned later into a convenient byway that led down to one of the deep places of the river, he met two men running and heard a cry from the darkness of the water. The great sky lantern at that moment directing a propitious beam, he discovered one struggling vainly to regain the shore, and thrusting a long pole towards him Keu Chun succeeded at length in bringing him to safety.

'Your aid was timely,' remarked the stranger when he was somewhat recovered, 'and the measure of this one's gratitude will not be stinted. In what particular direction does your necessity lie?'

'This is in the nature of things, seeing that the origin of our meeting is your desire to avoid drowning and my determination to encounter it,' replied Keu Chun sombrely. 'Thus the foreshore of the river on which we stand becomes, as it were, a common ground to both. If you will but continue your footsteps to the north and leave me equally to press forward to the south, our various purposes will thereby be effected.'

'What you say is sufficiently surprising, and I would gladly learn something more of your condition,' exclaimed the other. 'The dilapidated hut that shelters me stands but a short li distant from this spot. Even if your mind is set on drowning, courtesy demands that I who am concerned shall at least provide you with a change of dry apparel in which to do so more agreeably. Should you still be in the same mood after this slight civility there will be nothing lost, for, as the proverb says, "Felicity slips quickly by, but affliction walks side by side along our path".'

'If you feel that the omission would leave you under an intolerable obligation I cannot reasonably deny you what you ask,' admitted Chun, with an emotion of no-enthusiasm towards any arisement. 'Therefore lead on.'

With this encouragement the stranger professed himself content, and together they sought the higher ground. Presently the more noisome district of the city where beggars, criminals, and the literary classes had their quarters was left behind, the better-reputed parts frequented by the industrious and sincere were likewise passed and soon the spacious ways and well-spread gardens of successful merchants and officials marked their further progress.

'Admittedly the path that seems long to a person when fleeing from justice appears incredibly short when he is led down it to execution,' remarked Keu Chun at length. 'Nevertheless, this small li of yours – '

'We are even now at the poverty-stricken gate,' replied the guide, stopping before the largest and most lavishly ornamented of the mansions, and with a key that he drew from his inner sleeve he unlocked a door leading to the courtyard and stood aside. 'Pass in, nobility.'

'Before one whose ancestors doubtless wore the peacock feather?' protested Chun no less agreeably. 'These rebellious knees would refuse their sustenance should I attempt so impolite an act,' and he also moved farther away.

'The circumstances are not happily arranged for a really well-kept-up display of mutual refinement,' remarked the other, speaking with some discomfort through his chattering teeth and at the same time stooping to wring an excess of moisture from his body-cloth. 'In the name of the Viceroy of Hades let us go in together.'

On this understanding they went forward side by side, though with some difficulty, the way being narrow and the one who led Chun a person of outstanding attitude.

'This is evidently an underling in the service of some noble,' thought Chun. 'His easy manner proclaims that he is not altogether without influence.' But the one concerned did not turn aside towards the living-huts. He led the way up to the great house itself and again drawing forth a key he unlocked a door.

'This is certainly a personal attendant upon a high official,' next considered Chun, 'and unless my memory is grossly at fault the yamen of the district mandarin should be hereabout.

If I have rendered this service to one who has the ear of Wong Tsoi it may turn, if not actually to my advantage, at least to the disadvantage of Teen King.'

'Let us now rearrange ourselves more in comfort,' said the stranger affably, and with the tone of authority he struck an imperious gong. 'Two changes of fine raiment here without delay,' he cried to the slave who hurried at the call. 'Later, let a repast be laid out in my inner room – a display suited to the entertainment of an honoured guest.'

'I hear and obey, high excellence,' replied the slave, retiring.

'Excellence!' repeated Keu Chun, falling back several paces from so august a presence. 'Can it be that you are – '

The broad-minded official made a gesture implying caution.

'The wise duck keeps his mouth shut when he smells frogs,' he remarked significantly. 'Be discreet, and you may rely upon the advancement of your righteous cause. But should you be so short-sighted as to maintain a special claim on this one's succour it would be his duty, as an incorruptible upholder of the law, to sentence you to a variety of unpleasant exertions for attempted blackmail.'

'So presumptuous a thought never entered this ill-nourished mind,' replied Keu Chun.

'It is well said,' agreed Wong Tsoi; 'and among virtuous friends a slight inclination of the head is as efficacious as the more painful admonition from an ironshod foot.'

With discriminating courtesy the tolerantly inclined mandarin forbore to question Keu Chun more closely until a rich and varied abundance had restored their energies. Then reclining with dignified ease among the cushions of his couch, Wong Tsoi indicated to his guest that he should seat himself upon the floor at a respectful distance away and disclose his past.

'For,' he added, 'it concerns one who is responsible for the administration of the best regulated city of our Celestial Empire to discover what flaw in an otherwise perfect judicial code prompted you to so distressing a remedy.'

'Yet, eminence,' Chun ventured to remind him, 'if your benevolent condescension is moved by so slight a matter as this obscure person's mere misfortune, with what refined anguish must you regard actual crime! The two unseemly outcasts who ventured to lay their sacrilegious hands upon your honoured person – '

'Cherish no apprehension on that score,' replied the far-seeing Wong Tsoi capably. 'In cases of absolute wrong-doing it is impossible for even the least experienced official to deviate from the iron rule of conduct. Cause and effect; effect and cause: these two facets of an integral system corollarate with absolute precision. Two persons having committed a Category One crime, two persons will automatically suffer a Category One punishment, and the Essential Equipoise of justice will thereby be painlessly maintained.'

'It is what the scrupulous would look for,' assented Chun.

'It is what they will inevitably see,' replied Wong Tsoi. 'Should your leisurely footsteps chance to turn in the direction of the public execution ground on the occasion of the next general felicity, your discriminating eyes will receive assurance that the feet of the depraved find no resting-place on the upright soil of Hoo-yang.'

'It is indeed a matter of rejoicing that your penetrating gaze recognised the degraded miscreants who will thus be brought to an appropriate end.'

A faint absence of agreement for the moment obscured the well-balanced exactness of the law-giver's expression.

'If,' he remarked profoundly, 'so sublime a principle as justice should depend upon so fallible a thread as a single human attribute, all feeling of security would be gone for ever. The two misbegotten harbingers of shame who submitted this hard-striving person to the indignity of thrusting him down into a polluted stream will sooner or later meet with a fate that will be both painful and grotesque. In the meanwhile the wholesome moral of retribution will be inculcated in the wrong by two others (doubtless quite as abandoned in their several ways), demonstrating that authority does not slumber.'

'It has been claimed that there is equally one law for the just and for the unjust,' assented Chun, 'and in a certain guise – '

'Your loyal approbation nourishes the roots of our endeavour,' interposed Wong Tsoi, rewarding the speaker with a handful of melon seeds cast in his direction. 'Now disclose your own involvement.'

'Beneficence,' replied Chun readily, 'my obscure happening may be likened to a scorpion's tail, in that it is short but sharply pointed. My lowly name is Chun, that of my father's meagre house being Keu, and having ever been of a wayward bend I earn my scanty rice as an inefficient Brother of the Peach Orchard.'

'An actor!' exclaimed Wong Tsoi, regarding his guest with a special interest.

'Alas, exalted,' confessed Chun, 'such is my offensive calling.'

The leniently inspired official made a gesture of dissent, after satisfying himself that no attendant lingered.

'That which would brand you as an outcast in the eyes of the tightly buttoned, to me contains an added flavour,' he admitted. 'In the security of this inner chamber I will confide to your specific ear that I also am of a straggling and romantic nature, though the dignity of office makes it impossible for me to go very far in any impropriety. Nevertheless, half a cycle of years ago, when I had failed for the third time to attain the degree of Budding Genius in the competitions, I had all but decided to throw up an official career and go upon the wooden platform. ... Does your refined gift lie in the portrayal of noble youths of exalted lineage who are for a time alienated from the path of happiness by the machination of an elderly vampire?'

'At one time my ambition reached in that direction, but, as the saying has it, "One learns to itch where one can scratch", and my unworthy talents are considered most effective in the delineation of club-armed guardians of the street who slip heavily backwards on overripe loquats, and similar devices of a gravity-removing nature.'

'Proceed with the recital of your story,' commanded the mandarin briefly.

'Over against my low-born father's bankrupt hovel there stands the home of Fragrant Petal, the graceful and entrancing offspring of the autumnal widow Le-she. From an early period it has been the habit of the sympathetic maiden and the calamitous earthworm now before you to meet unostentatiously in a convenient spot that was suitably screened from the windows of both houses. Here a binding arrangement was mutually exchanged, together with the pledges of appropriate gifts, that each should remain faithful to the other. Fortified with this incentive, nothing seemed too excessive, and a score of moons ago the one who is now relating his sordid experience set forth to achieve distinction and to win an agreeable superfluity of taels. To-day he returned – '

'Doubtless to entrust a few bars of gold to a discreet friend's keeping?' suggested Wong Tsoi politely, as the other paused.

'To recover a still serviceable pair of sandals that he remembered leaving in an outer shed, esteemed,' replied Keu Chun with conscious diffidence. 'Then only did he learn of the grossly unfit-to-live Le-she's perfidy. Taking advantage of this one's absence and of the obscene Teen King's infatuation she had bartered Fragrant Petal to be that glutinous-eyed produce monger's possession at the price of a hundred taels of silver.'

'In these close-handed times a hundred taels are not to be spat at,' remarked the mandarin judicially.

'Excellence!' cried Keu Chun, springing to his feet, 'it is not the equivalent of a single hair among the ten thousand glossy ones that go to crown her high perfection. When she smiles, her eyes throw out continuous beams of violet light – even sideways. At every step her classically proportioned feet leave the impress of a golden lily. The Imperial treasury within the Purple City does not contain sufficient store to buy one glance of approbation – '

'It was thus with this one also in the days of his own brightly coloured youth,' sighed Wong Tsoi reminiscently, as he removed the outer skin of a choice apricot. 'There was Che-Che who danced on pigeons' eggs at the "Melodious Resort of Virtue" in Chiang-foo, and another, whose attractive name has escaped my weed-grown memory, who was reputed to have invisible wings, for in no other way could her graceful unconcern, as she progressed upon one foot along a distended cord, be accounted for. But maidens are no longer what they were in the days before they gummed their hair. Doubtless this Fragrant Petal – '

'If your own distinguished eyes could but see – '

'Enough!' interposed Wong Tsoi decisively. 'Shall one measure the bounty of the Yang-tze-kiang by a tea-cup? But for your graceful versatility with a perverse-willed steering pole the misshapen eyes to which you so fittingly allude would at this moment be unable to regard anything beyond the ill-made bed of an offensive water-course.'

'Then, benevolence – ' begged Chun, stirred by new hope.

'The engaging qualities you display – added to the fact that the low-conditioned Teen King recently deluded this confiding person in a matter affecting the quantity of some reputed swallows' nests – establish the justice of your case. How to proceed is another matter, for the contaminating refuse-blender has both wealth and legality on his side. Speaking strictly as one loyal subject to another it may well be admitted that it is not infeasible to outstrip legal forms by means of a well-lined sleeve, nor yet to get the better of mere riches by a dexterous use of lawful methods. But to defeat both of these while possessing neither would melt the tenacity of demons.'

'Could you not,' suggested Keu Chun helpfully, 'in the exercise of your exalted office, denounce the unclean Teen King to vigilant authority as one worthy of immediate death, without disclosing too exactly the nature of his crime?'

'Undoubtedly,' agreed Wong Tsoi. 'It is by no means an unusual course, and it has the merit of ruling out a mass of evidence which is wholly irrelevant when the result has already been decided. But by a most corrupt enactment it is necessary for an official submitting a complaint to begin it with a full recital of the various times that he himself has been degraded.'

'Degraded!' exclaimed Keu Chun, incredulous of so harsh an infliction towards one so spotless. 'Surely these blameworthy ears – '

'On seven misjudged occasions – thrice charged with "ordinariness of character" and on yet four times more for "displaying originality of conduct unseemly in a high official",' replied Wong Tsoi dispassionately. 'Rearrange your composure, worthy Keu Chun; these are but formalities in the daily life of a zealous servant of the state and merely indicate that another would gladly wear his button.'

'Why then, graciousness – '

'It nevertheless bars your well-meant plan. So inauspiciously sired a plaint would be consigned by the merest official pencil-moistener to the eternal oblivion of the dove's retreat,' explained the mandarin with a meaning flicker of his wrist. 'If you hope to look forward to a hundred strong sons to venerate your name, Keu Chun, something more apt must emerge from our mutual endeavour.'

'Benevolence,' confessed Keu Chun with some dejection, 'the one before you would cheerfully face the torments to achieve his quest, but in matters involving guile he is as devoid of wisdom as a new-laid egg is destitute of feathers.'

'Certainly the enterprise will need qualities of no common order,' agreed Wong Tsoi ungrudgingly. 'To your knowledge did the maiden go unwillingly and is she still allegiant to your cause?'

Chun put a hand within his sleeve and from a hidden fold he offered to the mandarin a sheaf of polished bamboo slips tied together with a crimson thread. A score and five there would be in all, or even more.

'This missive awaited my discovering thumb within a certain hollow cypress tree which often served our need,' he said. 'Read freely, excellence, of her gracefully expressed affection and of the high-minded repugnance with which she regards her detested lot.'

'Your meritorious word suffices,' replied the mandarin hastily, as he recognised the formidable proportion of the letter. 'It is scarcely meet that another eye should rest upon the context of so privileged a message. Doubtless after this avowal you sought to approach beneath Teen King's inner window?'

'That would have served no profitable end, esteemed. For a reason not yet clear Fragrant Petal has been straightway conveyed to that corrupt spice-adulterator's summer seat, a lonely tower lying off the northern earth-road, where she is strictly held.'

'Yet Teen King himself has not passed beyond the city gates during the present moon,' observed Wong Tsoi shrewdly. 'His ardour has a strangely tardy bend, that it must loiter so.'

'Perchance the chief one of his inner chamber has raised a contentious voice – '

'There you have struck the wooden skewer on its thicker end, Keu Chun!' exclaimed the other with conviction. 'Her forbidding name is Tsoo, and hitherto she has allowed no secondary to share her place. Teen King, stricken with this corroding passion of his unsavoury old age, has acted thus and thus, hoping doubtless to sway Tsoo on one plea or another, or, perchance, failing that, to dispose of her inoffensively by some simple but well-tried method.'

'If that is indeed the case then Fragrant Petal may still – '

'May still be yours, you would say? Yet, should that come to pass, is there any secure retreat into which you and the ornamentally described one could imperceptibly fade? Assuredly in so amiable a cause some unnamed well-wisher would be forthcoming to contribute a double hand-count of taels to your virtuous success.'

'Munificence,' replied Keu Chun, 'to elude pursuit would then be easy. A propitious friend, lying at no great distance from this spot, trades a commodious junk far into the lower reaches of the river. Once there – '

'Truly. As well look for an eel in a cart-load of live adders. Forgo despair, Keu Chun. I am by no means desirous that my care-worn ghost should be under the burden of this obligation to your exacting ghost in the Hereafter. What a far from slow-witted official can do to readjust the balance now will be discreetly effected.'

'I am in your large and never-failing hand,' replied Keu Chun submissively.

Wong Tsoi waved a gesture of benevolent dismissal and closed his eyes to indicate tactfully that a concentrated reverie was necessary in which to mature his plans. So deep indeed became the profundity of his thoughts that neither Keu Chun's deferential leavetaking nor yet the various gong-strokes of the night were suffered to obtrude, and the early light of dawn found him with his eyes still closed in meditation and his body in the same pliant attitude of introspective calm

Let it be freely admitted that when Wong Tsoi stepped forth from his yamen on the following day he had not the most shadowy idea of how to bring about Keu Chun's desire and thus fulfil the obligation that the saving of his life – at the risk of incurring the malignity of the presiding demon of the river – had imposed upon him.

'Yet,' he remarked self-reliantly as he set out, 'I am pledged to the undertaking, and as the wise philosopher of Ts'i has so observantly remarked, "Where the head has already gone, the hind quarters are bound to follow".'

In pursuit of a guiding omen the scrupulous official dismissed his chair and bearers presently and bent his not entirely reluctant feet in the direction of the 'Abode of Harmony and Well-seasoned Dishes' at about the time of the evening rice. Beneath this auspicious sign might be found at that hour many of his more opulent and mentionable neighbours within Hooyang. The honour of an unceremonious visit from so high a dignitary was a conspicuous event and the gratified Comptroller of the Table, meeting Wong Tsoi at the door, preceded him backwards to his place, chanting meanwhile a happily arranged song in his honour, into which the versatile person gradually blended the names of the various delicacies available as they neared the highest seat. Wong Tsoi having made an appropriate choice, the one who had attended him retired in the same becoming order, extolling the guest's discernment in another set of verses, wherein he pronounced the selected viands in a louder key, thus to apprise the Custodian of the Grill of what was required from him. When the first dish duly arrived, following the dictates of ordinary courtesy, the latest guest stood up and pressed everyone around to join him in partaking of it.

'The one before you is a thoroughly inadequate host,' he announced, bowing graciously in the four direction; 'a worse combination of courses than those that he has chosen could not well be hit upon, and, as is quite befitting, the most inferior portion of each dish has been specially reserved for him. How great, therefore, will be your amiable condescension if you will but leave your own attractively arranged tables and endure the unappetising deficiences of his.'

'On the contrary,' came from every side, 'your nimble-minded wit makes you so desirable a guest that we must really implore your company here with us instead. As for the assorting of the dishes and the quality of the food, we can assure your high excellence that you are pleasurably mistaken in thinking that yours are worse than ours. Do, therefore – ' The remainder of the graceful compliment was lost in the agreeable rattle of chopsticks as all resumed their interrupted occupation precisely as before.

Now although Wong Tsoi had evolved no definite plan, he had come to the 'Abode of Harmony' in the full expectation of finding the unsightly produce merchant also there. Towards the outcome of that incident he had not neglected to burn a liberal supply of joss-stick, so that when his entirely expressionless gaze noted the gross outline of the objectionable Teen King seated at no great space away, he recognised that so far as the Doubtful Forces were concerned he was not ill-equipped for an encounter.

Teen King, for his part, fancied that the dignified inclination sent in his direction was perceptibly warmer than the other three. Wong Tsoi recognised as the loudest voice raised in complimentary greeting that of Teen King. The omens pointed to the mutual recriminations in the matter of a few kin of debatable birds' nests being forgotten, but so far neither was committed beyond one side of his face.

When Teen King rose to go it was not inevitable that he should pass Wong Tsoi's table, but with absent-minded detachment he took that course. Seeing this, the mandarin's preoccupied foot thoughtlessly moved a vacant seat so that it barred the way.

'Ten thousand sincere regrets that your honourable progress should be impeded in this manner,' exclaimed Wong Tsoi, drawing the chair aside with his own obliging hand. 'Have you appeased your virtuous stomach?'

'Rather is it my own incommodious bulk that disturbs your well-intentioned chair,' replied Teen King deferentially. 'Are they gratifying your enlightened palate?'

'Since an unlooked-for felicity has delayed you at this spot will you not occupy the seat so auspiciously provided?' suggested the other. 'After your laborious passage of this badly arranged room doubtless a moment's rest – ' and he pushed his snuff-bottle of priceless jade across the table for Teen King's use.

'Excellence,' began Teen King, after he had helped himself liberally from the snout of the recumbent pig that formed the bottle, 'with the exception of ordinary business transactions the one before you has led an integritous life. Why then should the path of his endeavour be edged with sharp afflictions?'

'It is truly said that a rogue may sit under a scaffolding all day, but if a righteous man ventures to pass beneath a ladder something offensive is sure to fall upon his meritorious head,' remarked Wong Tsoi with ready sympathy. 'Unload your over-weighted mind, Teen King.'

'Your warm compassion melts the crust of my under-bred reluctance,' confessed the merchant. 'Furthermore, I desire to lean somewhat upon your official counsel.'

'Speak freely,' replied Wong Tsoi, with but one thought, 'for in matters affecting the relationship of the inner circle – '

'That is a crow of quite another colour,' interrupted Teen King, his face not entirely gladdened by the plain allusion. 'Upon questions of that sort it is seldom necessary for a really humane and affectionate head to raise the shutter of his domestic interior.'

'Yet,' urged the exalted, 'the one before you, as high official of the district, stands in the position of a benevolent father towards every family within his province.'

'Assuredly,' agreed Teen King, 'but the truly considerate son hides a great deal of what might be unnecessarily distress-ing from a venerated parent's eyes. In the direction to which you are obviously leading, excellence, be satisfied that by patience and the use of a stick no thicker than that which is legally permissible the most opinionated of our lesser ones can ultimately be persuaded to bask in the light of reason.'

'This concerns Tsoo and the one called Fragrant Petal,' reflected Wong Tsoi in the pause that followed, 'and it clearly indicates that I was right in my conjecture. But with what other adversity is the misshapen thing before me harassed?' Aloud, however, he said:

'With your usual crystalline logic, Teen King, you compress an entire social system to within the narrow limits of an acorn-shell. Yet you spoke – '

'It is of it that I would speak further,' replied the merchant, lowering his naturally repulsive voice and arranging his ill-balanced form so that they should not be overlooked. 'Pass your esteemed judgment upon this obligation, highness.'

Wong Tsoi took the folded parchment that was offered him and submitted it to the test of a close scrutiny, even to the length of using an enlarging-glass to supplement his eyes.

'There is no ambiguity at any point of this, Teen King,' he said, courteously veiling his regret that it was not some tiding of disaster. 'Herein you authorise your secondary to recompense ten taels of silver and a like amount of store to the one presenting this, he having already rendered its equivalent to you.'

'Do you find no questionable line about the thumb-sign?' almost implored the merchant.

'I am as familiar with the signet of your pliant thumb as with the details of your prepossessing face,' freely replied Wong Tsoi. 'Should I fail to recognise you when we encounter in the Ways, or would I greet another by your ever-welcome name? Thus and thus. In every thread and indent is this your accepted impress.'

'Yet,' protested Teen King, so overwrought because he dare not shout aloud his frenzy or kick any of the lavish arrangements of the room that his always unbecoming neck increased to several times its wonted thickness, 'yet, high puissance, it is *not* the impression of my own authentic thumb nor had I ever seen the thrice-accursed draft until the mentally weak-kneed Chin discharged the obligation. What an infamy is here residing within Hoo-yang!'

At this disclosure Wong Tsoi achieved a sympathetic noise among his teeth, but he bent his face above the writing so that Teen King should not misread the signs of his compassion.

'This is an unheard-of thing to come about,' he remarked impartially. 'Hitherto it has been assumed that by a benevolent dispensation for the safeguarding of commercial intercourse no two thumbs would be created of identical design. It now becomes evident that something essential has been overlooked. Is there any more of this, as it were, questionable paper upon the market, merchant?'

'It is that qualmous thought that is eroding the walls of my tranquillity,' confessed the effete Teen King. 'Three misprocured drafts have I so far honoured and I tremble at the possibility of what may yet appear.'

'But,' objected the mandarin, 'if you are the victim of a

well-laid plot why should you not proclaim the falsity, repudiate the impression of this alien thumb, and warn the merchants of our city to be alert?'

'Therein you speak as an official and not as a man of commerce,' replied Teen King with feeling. 'Were I to do as you advise I might as well throw open the doors of all my marts for the four winds to blow in and out. My thumb-sign is the evidence of an inviolable word. To proclaim openly that it is henceforth more than doubtful would be to put the profitable house of Teen into the "formerly existed" class.'

'What then do you contemplate? To submit to this iniquity for ever?'

'That is the purpose of my confidence in you,' replied Teen King. 'As the ruler of the city you will assuredly put forth your straightforward hand and the sacrilegious dog will cease to prosper.'

Wong Tsoi thought for a few moments under the pretext of having inhaled a superfluity of snuff. Then his face resumed its usual expression of inscrutable profundity and he turned towards Teen King with a gesture of open-minded assent.

'Agreeably so,' he replied pleasantly. 'Deliver the abandoned leper into my keeping and your unblemishable name will be free from the shadow of this taint for ever.'

'Therein lies the key of this one's hardship,' exclaimed Teen King with some annoyance, for he began to describe Wong Tsoi to himself as a person of very stunted outlook. 'Could I but discover and take the offender myself, one of my refining vats would very quickly adjust the difference between us. As it is I rely on your authority to transact justice.'

'The one before you is a high official,' returned Wong Tsoi with appreciable coldness. 'Were he a dog doubtless he could follow a trail from this paper in his hand to the lair of the aggressor. Or were he a demon in some barbarian fable he might, perchance, regard a little dust beneath an enlarging-glass and then stretching out his hand into the void withdraw it with the miscreant attached.'

'Nevertheless,' persisted the merchant stubbornly, 'it behoves you for your own well-being not to suffer the rice to grow around your tardy ankles in the matter.'

'Teen King undoubtedly has something in his sleeve or he would not press me to this limit,' pondered Wong Tsoi. 'Perhaps it would be as well to tempt the distressing mountebank into disclosing himself more fully. An apt saying should serve here.' Accordingly he added: 'Anything to do with your graceful personality admittedly has weight, Teen King, but in questions of authority mere bulk is not everything. It might be prudent to take to heart the adage, "A toad has to pass a very severe examination before he can become a dragon".'

At this allusion Teen King changed colour several times and for a moment it seemed inevitable that the chair in which he sat must fail incapably under the weight of his displeasure. Seeing this, the one concerned rose abruptly to his feet.

'It is also written, "A pointed tongue, however keen a sword, makes an insufficient shield", and you, O contemptible Wong Tsoi, will soon be putting the analogy to a desperate trial,' he replied with vigour. 'Learn now how that incorruptible official Kao-tsz, of the Board of Censors, has been deputed to visit Hoo-yang before the next full moon. As he is somewhat heavily in this person's debt the nature of his report, should you maintain your headstrong front, need not tax your imagination. It is one thing to be technically degraded seven times, mandarin; it is quite another to be actually shortened at both ends, even once.'

With this illiberal forecast the outrageous Teen King shook hands with himself in a disagreeable manner and withdrew his contaminating presence.

'A person of true refinement would have expressed much of that very differently, but nothing will ever make up for the lack of a classical education,' reflected Wong Tsoi when he was again alone. 'However,' he added self-capably, 'though it will obviously become necessary to do something to counteract his malicious influence, there is no reason why the incident should be allowed to mar an otherwise well-arranged repast. This business clearly concerns Ho Hung, and he will doubtless be at home throughout the night.'

Ho Hung now steps into the narration, and in order to explain the unfolding of events it is as well to describe his outline. He was of middle stature and not ill-cast, but with the essentials of an appearance spoiled somewhat by his face. His ears were loose and ragged, his teeth as large as those of a moderate horse, but of several different colours, while his nose resembled a toucan's beak. One of his eyes was elsewhere; the other had a deceptive bend which enabled Ho Hung frequently to observe persons closely without their appreciation of the fact. At this period he was the admitted head and chief of all the thieves and assassins in Hoo-yang, but formerly he had conducted lotteries.

When Wong Tsoi, late that same night, knocked in a special way upon a certain door in the least-reputed quarter of the city, it was opened by Ho Hung himself. When he recognised the one who stood outside, the natural repugnance of his features changed to a look of welcome not unmixed with an arising lack of gravity.

'You do well to greet me cordially, Ho Hung,' remarked the official as he glanced cautiously about before he entered, 'for if I should be recognised in this doubtful situation it would certainly cost me my button.'

'As to that, mandarin,' replied Ho Hung with simple familiarity, 'should you ever be put to it, there are half a dozen openings I could tell you of, in which dignity combines with ease, and in any capacity you would very soon excel us all. But will you not honour this one's bankrupt home by entering, and there – if you can put up with its long-standing deficiency – partake of tea?'

' "For wine the top of the bottle; for tea the bottom of the pot",' quoted Wong Tsoi pleasantly as he stepped within. 'May worthiness never forsake your roof-tree, valiant Hung.'

'May winning numbers come to you in dreams,' responded Ho Hung heartily, standing aside in hospitable respect.

As they sat together and drank, Ho Hung broached the subject that had shaken his dignity on the mandarin's arrival.

'Some word of the inept misadventure that involved your conscientious secretary last night has already reached my threadbare ears,' he remarked discreetly, affecting to turn aside to catch a passing winged insect as he spoke. 'Doubtless it is upon that quest that you are here at all?'

'Up to a certain point the deduction is exact,' replied Wong

Tsoi, sprinkling a little snuff into Ho Hung's tea to mark his appreciation of that one's tact. 'But, as the saying is, "Although the T'ang road is long it does not lead everywhere." What is this that is being told of one whose thumb simulates the natural signature of Teen King, the produce merchant?'

At this inquiry Ho Hung became so excessively disturbed in gravity that he could only with difficulty retain his seat, while his endeavour to imply the reason of his mirth by rapidly opening and closing his missing eye began to have a disquieting effect upon Wong Tsoi's imagination.

'Thang-I the rogue's name is and he has but lately come among us from the Waste Lands to the south,' replied Ho Hung when he could speak with ease. 'The witling has no ready parts beyond this facile thumb, he being of the mulish sort. But Tong, the fabricator of salt-due seals, who chanced upon his gift, has put the business through. Tong it is who does all Teen King's resealing when he mixes – your nobility will understand – so that he was well familiar with that aggressive merchant's thumb-sign.'

'This is likely enough,' replied Wong Tsoi, 'but wherein lurks the essence of the jest?'

'It is not to be expected that a high official will have so gross an appetite for gravity removal as a mere sleeve-snatcher,' pleaded Ho Hung. 'The obese Teen King has ever been wont to press down an acrimonious thumb upon the feeble in Hooyang so that now the way that it has been turned against him has passed into a variety of questionable sayings. Indeed, it is become the matter of a most objectionable song that is being taken up by the river boatmen to the rhythm of their task.'

'Even the humblest of the muses is to be encouraged,' tolerantly observed Wong Tsoi. 'Should a superfluous copy of that ballad come your way – '

'It shall reach your discriminating hand without delay,' promised the other, marking a sign upon his tablets.

'There still remains the question of justice,' continued the high official. 'For the harmonious relation of our several interests it is vital that the overstepping of certain limits should not be unredressed.'

'That is admitted,' agreed Ho Hung, with a dutiful obeis-

ance. 'Your hand is that of a benevolent corrector, eminence,
and this one will not, for his part, fail.'

'In assaulting, as you have so correctly been informed, the
person of the one who takes down my spoken word, two unmentionable outcasts have been guilty of an attack – by deputy
– on me, thereby – obliquely – against the state, and thus – by
analogy – have finally as it were submitted the venerated person of the Sublime Emperor himself to the extreme indignity
of being projected into the tempestuous waters of an unclean
stream. For this iniquity two malefactors must suffer the fullest
penalty in order to appease the justly outraged feeling of a
loyal people.'

'Authority must be maintained,' replied the congenial Ho,
'or whereon do we stand? The very foundation of the Joined-
together Band of Superfluity Adjusters and Excrescence
Removers of Hoo-yang, with this one at its head, is
menaced.'

'We have always so far been able to arrange these necessary
formalities in mutual concord,' remarked Wong Tsoi. So
amiable at these recollections became the condescension of this
truly broad-minded being that after wiping the traces of tea
from off his lips he did not disdain to press the same cloth upon
Ho Hung. 'Nor,' he continued, 'is there any reason why we
should not now. As regards this slow-witted Thang-I: has the
lowly clown friends of any standing?'

'He is a stranger among us here, and therefore not of our
fraternity,' was the reply. 'Had his case not been thus and
thus he would have been driven forth ere this. Disclose your
mind, exalted.'

'To earmark Thang-I for this needful expiation would effect
a double turn. Have I your acquiescent word?'

'The dog has served an end but the jest has all but run its
course,' considered Ho Hung. 'There is none to raise a voice
against what you propose – save, perhaps, Tong, and he is of
slight account.'

'Tong – would he so do? Then nothing could be better
regulated. Two culprits are required: that being the case why
should not Tong be coupled with Thang-I and so still every
murmur?'

'Eminence,' interposed Ho Hung, 'even a goat and an ox must keep in step if they would plough together, and, as you have said, in matters of this sort we stand on a common footing. Let Thang-I fall to your deciding voice; for this one's share Teh-tang will serve.'

Wong Tsoi accorded a motion of dignified assent, for he had no concern in Tong, the seal counterfeiter, either one way or the other.

'But Teh-tang?' he asked with polite interest. 'Is not one of that name the prop of your right hand?'

'He was, he is, but he will not henceforth be. Of late Teh-tang's eyes have been fixed on a point somewhat above his head. It is as well that he should be removed before his aspiring footsteps seek to follow.'

'That is a detail that concerns your own internal state, nor would this one seek to probe into the routine of your well-conducted band,' declared the liberal-minded official.

Then as he turned to go he gave the courteous farewell: 'May your deserving path be smooth, even to the graveside.'

'May your warmth and cold always be correctly balanced,' replied Ho Hung, with no less feeling.

It was at a later date that the keeper of the door of Teen King's summer-house was roused from a profound meditation by an insistent knocking at the grille. The night being dark and stormy the menial did not hasten to comply, but a still more urgent summons brought him to his feet.

'Should corrosion reward your acrimonious knuckles, this one will gladly attend your funeral rites,' was the burden of his welcome.

'Is this a time for mere verbal pleasantries?' demanded the one who stood there in the harrying rain. 'Behold, the master whom you serve, stricken with an unlooked-for hurt, turns back home from your gate.'

'What is this that you say?' demanded the keeper sourly. 'If there is a tale to be told take hold at the beginning, friend, and not like the knife of some crafty juggler – haphazard as it comes.'

'My tongue and your ear stand on a different footing,' replied the other in a superior tone, 'I being employed about the counting-house and you a mere bolt-slider. Your offensively honourable name is Wang, door-keeper?'

'That indeed is the mediocre style of my distinguished line.'

'Let it suffice then, Wang, that the merchant has received various scars by the instability of one of his bearers on this misconstrued earth-road. He would have remained here through the night but for this affliction. As it is, he requires the delivery now of the one you guard. Here is the discharge of your answerableness for her.'

The dog-like Wang took the paper and held it to the light; then he compared the signature pressed on it with another that he had.

'This is well enough as far as the matter goes, but his memory is here at fault,' was the reply. 'Only a while ago he sent an urgent message, saying, "Accept no thumb-sign that is not made by me before your very eyes, for Dark Forces are about. This is my iron word." Yet now you say he waits?'

'This is beyond my office,' declared the stranger frankly, 'and you had better make fast your bolts and then come to the gate. It may well be that this is a snare on Teen King's part to try your firmness in his service.'

'If that is the case he will find me grounded like a limpet,' was Wang's crafty boast. 'I make no pretence to any range of subtlety, but what is nailed into this head sticks there.'

'Bring your lantern,' said the messenger. 'Things hereabout are none too bright.'

When they reached the outer gate two chairs were to be seen by the custodian's swinging candle. From the larger one a surfeit of groans and imprecations flowed, indicating, however crudely expressed, both pain and mental anguish. By the side of this a sombre-hearted carrier was still binding up his wounds.

'Commander,' pleaded the supine Wang, thrusting his head through the curtains of the chair, 'there has come to me one who bears a certain message, this requiring – '

The grossly outlined person dimly seen within did not cease to roll from side to side and to press a soothing cloth against his disfigured face. When he spoke it was with difficulty by reason of a swollen lip.

'Why then does not compliance hasten, thou contumacious keeper of my door?' he demanded with rancour. 'Is it not enough that I am to be broken bodily within sight of the lucky symbols hung above my gate, but that my authority should also be denied? Where is she whom I require of you?'

'Yet, master,' entreated the abject Wang, 'it may well be that this is but a snare to prove the tenacity of my allegiance. Was not your charge explicit: "Accept no sign that is not pressed before your very eyes"? How then – '

'Enough,' was the reply, and the one who spoke stretched out a requiring hand; 'it is not ineptly claimed. After all, you have a sort of stultish justice to protect you, loyal Wang. Now submit the paper for the full requirement.'

With this demand the keeper of the door at once complied, exultant that his stubbornness had been upheld before the others. The one whose authority he owned turned away for a moment as he searched about his sleeve for his pigment box. Then he pressed the paper and gave it back to Wang, who saw against the former signature another, identical in every line and still moist from the attesting thumb.

'Nothing now remains but to execute your will,' he freely admitted; 'my own part in the matter being amply hedged. Say on, chieftain.'

'In that I cannot stay, with my deep cuts unseen to, Fragrant Petal must accompany me back, the affair having taken a prosperous turn,' replied the other. 'Bring her out now, not staying for adornment, for my condition does not brook delay, but at the same time hastily put together all that she may have so that her face is not clouded among women.'

'It shall be done, O rewarder of great zeal,' exclaimed Wang, preparing to comply. 'How does this blossom among peach trees journey?'

'There is a chair at hand' – indicating the second that stood ready. 'My underling, who rode thus far, must make his way as may be.'

'Everything shall fall into its place like a well-oiled mill at work,' chanted the subservient Wang. 'I hasten to merit your extremely liberal bounty, princelet.'

'And this one,' murmured the underling, he who had first

summoned the custodian to the grille, as he prepared to follow, 'will meet the Embodiment of Beauty on the way and break to her ear the signification of the issue.'

'Unless,' came a guarded voice from behind the curtains, 'unless your father should have been an elderly baboon and your mother a standing reproach among she-asses, you will, on the contrary, withhold your egregious face until we are well clear of this stronghold of oppression.'

'Your strategy has been consummate throughout, great excellence,' replied the other, 'and this one bends an acquiescent knee to whatever you direct.' So that he faded into the imperceptible, nor was there anything to reassure the grief of Fragrant Petal when she was presently led forth.

'A thousand felicities, fountain of all largesse!' invoked the thirsty-handed Wang, as he stood at the opening of the first chair expectantly. 'May the vigour of a leopard sustain your high endeavour.'

'Ten thousand echoes to your gracefully phrased parting!' was courteously wafted back from between the curtains, as the bearers raised their burden. 'The moment is not propitious, but when next we meet do not fail to recall to me that the extent of my indebtedness cannot honourably be put to less than a full-weight piece of silver.'

*

Nothing could have been more in keeping than the greetings of Wong Tsoi and the merchant Teen King when they again encountered beneath the burnished roof of the 'Abode of Harmony.' If the latter person had suffered a reverse in an unexpected quarter he had the memorable satisfaction of having bent the mandarin to do his will in the matter of the unconscionable outlaw who had reproduced his thumb; if Wong Tsoi could not fail to recognise that in this affair the fullness of his countenance had suffered partial eclipse before the eyes of the superficial, he had the tangible offset that he had thereby been able to free his future of the Keu Chun obligation, and even yet he cherished an image that the one whose gravity would be the last to be removed might not prove to be Teen King.

Without waiting for any gracious intimation that his unin-viting presence would be suffered, the mentally ill-nurtured huckster on this occasion thrust himself into the forefront of Wong Tsoi's notice by sinking incapably into a chair at that one's table. To cover his grotesque behaviour the deficient-minded pedlar at once plunged into the subject of their late contention with the absence of refinement that stamped his uncouth footsteps whenever he appeared.

'It nourishes my heart to think that vice no longer triumphs about our city,' he remarked with annoying freedom. 'The two bodies now displayed in the Hoo-yang Public Relaxation Space prove that you have at length bowed your stubborn neck to the justice of this one's claim.'

'It is recorded of the enlightened Emperor Yu that on one occasion he rose from his bath and bound up his hair thrice uncomplainingly to listen to the doubtless unreasonable de-mands of quite negligible persons,' duly replied Wong Tsoi. 'Why then should not I, who am in every way so inferior to the imperishable Yu, inconvenience myself to that slight ex-tent to satisfy one in whom the parallelism is brought to an apt conclusion?'

At this well-guarded admission the preposterous Teen King bowed several times, his wholly illiterate mind leading him to assume that he was being favourably compared to the great First Ruler.

'In one detail an element of ambiguity prevails,' resumed the aggressive merchant, unable even at that moment to sub-due his natural canker. 'Admittedly the real offender in this case has suffered, for the thumb of one of the two bandits corresponds to the most rigid test against my own. Yet that extremity bears every sign of having been cut away and sub-sequently restored. Why – '

'It is, as you, merchant, must surely be aware, an essential of our pure code of justice that the offending member of any convicted felon should be summarily struck off,' replied Wong Tsoi dispassionately. 'Later, to satisfy the ignoble curiosity of the vile – those who are notoriously drawn to gloat upon the accessories of low-class crimes – the parts were crudely united.'

'Be that as it may,' persisted Teen King stubbornly, as he

began to regard the mandarin's well-rounded form with an awakening interest; 'someone has in the meanwhile counterfeited this person's exact figure – '

'Forbear!' exclaimed Wong Tsoi, raising his face-cloth as though to shut out the vision of iniquity. 'Such an atrocity is not possible among our chaste and graceful nation.'

'Yet nevertheless the fact exists,' continued the obtusewitted condiment-blender, 'and it is this one's intention now that you, mandarin, shall obtain a swift redress. Not only was that which has been stated done, but under the cloak of this deception the sanctity of an inner chamber has been usurped, a trusty henchman baffled, an unopened bud torn from the protecting branch – '

'Doubtless,' interposed Wong Tsoi firmly, 'but as you would be the first to advance, merchant, in matters affecting purely domestic culture it is hardly necessary for a really well-set and vigorous tree to disturb the soil that should conceal its roots.'

'Public action need not inevitably ensue,' maintained Teen King feebly, as he recognised the snare that he had contrived for his own misshapen feet. 'You, as high official of the district, stand in the position of a salutary despot who can administer justice in discreet obscurity.'

'Assuredly,' agreed Wong Tsoi, 'but the truly humane ruler turns a lethargic eye towards a great deal that might be actually pernicious in a cherished people's conduct. Should you be so ill-advised as to press your grievance further it would be as well first to recall the special application of the proverb, "It is better to lose nine changes of raiment than to win a lawsuit".'

'Yet what remains?' pleaded the ineffectual merchant. 'Shall these poverty-stricken hands be idly folded while an unending vista of spurious Teen Kings draws away my substance?'

'Suffer no apprehension on that score,' replied Wong Tsoi with meaning. 'Not again shall your notorious mould be counterparted in Hoo-yang.'

'Can that be definitely assured?' asked Teen King cautiously.

'Subject to the usual clause against demoniac intervention, it can,' replied the mandarin. 'For the rest, remember, "Even dragons know better than to appear too often".'

'If this is actually the case the prospect might have been

worse,' admitted Teen King. 'Indeed,' he added, with an unworthy impulse to ingratiate himself in the other's regard without incurring the customary outlay, 'had it been allowable a substantial token of esteem would have been forthcoming to mark appreciation of your prolific efforts.'

'What is this barrier that stands in the way of so laudable a craving, amiable Teen King?' inquired Wong Tsoi in a very agreeable voice.

'Surely it is not unknown to your pure excellence that in order to discourage venality an official of your degree is strictly forbidden to receive any gift whatever, save only – not to exclude mere courtesy – an offering of fruit. But as an earnest of this one's thwarted yearning a basket of the choicest Hooyang hedge-berries shall reach your hand to-morrow.'

'Nothing could be more delicately flavoured than the compliment,' murmured the engaging voice. 'Yet had not a wise provision set a check upon your open-handed spirit, what form would the tribute, to which an explicit reference has just been made, have taken?'

'In that case,' replied Teen King, seeing no reason why he should restrict himself in a matter that could involve him in no outlay, 'there would have been no limit to this one's profusion. Throwing open the door of his needy hovel he would have bidden you enter and accept what pleased you most, saying, "Put forth your hand on the right and on the left, and whatsoever it closes on is yours".'

'It is no more than what would have been expected of your untarnishable father's nimble-minded son,' replied Wong Tsoi, with a suitable display of appropriate emotion. 'And now let your generous heart expand in gladness, Teen King. You would appear to have misread – though only slightly – a single character in the official prohibition. Not "save fruit" but "save in the *shape* of fruit" is the carefully thought-out exception.'

'Yet wherein does the variation lie?' asked the merchant, in a deeply agitated voice.

'Embellishing your high-born serving-board there stands a lordly silver-dish, its cover in the likeness of a cluster of rich fruit, its base befittingly adorned with nuts,' replied Wong Tsoi pleasantly. 'Nothing could be more applicable or in severer keeping with the pronouncement of authority.'

At this disclosure Teen King rose up from his chair and then illogically sank down again until he was no longer capable of the exertion. His unbecoming mouth opened and closed repeatedly but it was not until Wong Tsoi had charitably begun to fan him that he disclosed his power of speech.

'What was spoken in the light of a graceful compliment is too delicate to be translated into the grosser terms of commercial equivalent,' he stammered effetely. 'The dish in question weighs not less than ten score standard taels, and its value in fine silver must be put at twice that indication. Why then should this almost bankrupt outcast tamely surrender it?'

'Nothing but the untrammelled purity of your upright nature could suggest so great a sacrifice,' replied Wong Tsoi.

'If that were all,' replied the other frankly, 'I could sleep to-night in peace. But the extreme moderation of your manner prepares me for the worst. What remains behind, Wong Tsoi?'

'Alas, merchant,' admitted the compassionate official, 'I had hoped to shield this latest menace from you. Know then how it is whispered in the Ways that the irredeemable Thang-I spent the last hours of his solitude thumb-signing countless sheets of unwritten parchment, which the dissolute hope to use from time to time as the occasions offer.'

'If,' considered Teen King, after a lengthy pause, 'if one from my house should in due course appear about your door bearing a weighty gift and crave your acceptance of it, what would be the nature of his reception?"

'That one so charitably employed should return empty-handed would put a barbarian out of the Outerlands to shame,' replied Wong Tsoi. 'The least that this person could do would be to send out into the Ways and beseech his many criminal friends, as a personal kindness to himself, to bring in all the offensive Thang-I's fabrications.'

'Could a favourable response be relied on?' asked Teen King.

'It has already been successfully accomplished, and the package now merely awaits your accommodating slave's arrival.'

'Would the third gong-stroke of the afternoon suit your distinguished leisure?' inquired Teen King, in very solicitous accents.

'Nothing could be more in harmony,' was the genial reply.

'Thus and thus,' remarked the merchant, rising. 'The hour approaches when this one displays his shutters. Walk slowly.'

'May your profitable commerce spread like a banyan tree and take root on every side,' pronounced Wong Tsoi courteously.'

'May swift promotion overtake your righteous footsteps and lead you to a more worthy sphere of usefulness,' replied Teen King, in a voice equally devoid of added meaning.

CHAPTER IV

At the Extremity of his Resource the Continent Kai Lung encounters one who leads the Unaffected Life

AT a later period Kai Lung emerged safely from the waste marshes of Yang-tze and set his face hopefully towards the mountain range beyond, confident that somewhere about those barren heights he would overtake Ming-shu and (aided by the ever-protecting spirits of his approving ancestors) settle a final and exacting balance with that detested upstart.

But in the meanwhile an arid and unproductive tract of country lay between him and the valleys of Ki-che, and the cake of dried paste that had nourished him so far had shrunk to a state of no-existence. For a lengthy day he had sustained a precarious life on a scanty cup of disconcerting water extracted from a laborious dug-hole, when, at evening, he espied one who wandered to and fro with a burden on his shoulders.

'This, doubtless,' considered Kai Lung, 'is the forerunner of others, who may, by an expedient, be assembled as a crowd, and surely to that, on one pretext or another, an applicable story should not prove fruitless.'

He looked anxiously for the gathering signs of habitation that would indicate a village street (for a feeling of inadequacy in all his attributes was beginning to assail him), but finding none and fearing to miss the settlement on the one foot or to increase his weary march upon the other he turned aside.

meaning to greet the loiterer whom he had already noted. When he had approached sufficiently near to observe the detail he saw that what the stranger carried was a coffin.

'Alas,' exclaimed Kai Lung, 'is this then so insalubrious a region that when a man goes about his daily task he takes with him the equipment for his obsequies? What scope is there for the story-teller's art in a spot so far removed from gravity dispersal or the leisured amenities of life?' Yet, there being none else to question and no abode in sight, he continued on towards him. When the other perceived Kai Lung's approaching form he laid down the burden off his shoulders and advanced to meet him.

'Welcome to this unattractive wilderness,' he remarked hospitably. 'Your becoming name and the number of your blameless years would be an agreeable subject for conversation.'

'I am of the worthless house of Kai, my forbidding name being Lung,' was the reply. 'As regards my years – they have been few and quite devoid of interest, as this immature pigtail will readily disclose. Now as regards your own distinguished self?'

'Thang, am I, my father's name being presumably illustrious but unfortunately misplaced,' replied the other. 'My ill-spent age exceeds two-score by one. By ceaseless toil I wrest a feeble livelihood from this tenacious soil.'

'The occupation is a venerated one in our enlightened land, being only second, both as regards honour and inadequacy of reward, to the literary calling,' replied Kai Lung. 'And touching that same office – as between one necessitous person and another – is there within not too great a distance from this well-favoured spot a refined community who by some stratagem or other may be drawn together to listen to an epic from the masterpieces, with a reasonable outlook of the narrator being finally rewarded in one form or another?'

'A community!' exclaimed the stranger, enlarging both his eyes. 'Know, traveller, that the one before you and those beneath his crumbling roof live so remote that they do not see an outside face from one moon to another. Whence, therefore, could even a sprinkling of bystanders be obtained to listen to your pleasing voice?'

'If this is so,' observed Kai Lung dispassionately, 'the voice to which you so flatteringly refer will very soon cease for ever. Yet how comes it that you who are an alert and vigorous man have selected a region at once so desert and remote?'

'That,' replied the peasant, 'is to conform to the integral fitness of things. In his milk days the one before you listened with becoming deference to the conversation of persons of every rank of life and studied what they said. From what he heard, when they were speaking freely, it was at once plain that he himself was so beneath all others both as regards the virtues and attainments, that it was only seemly for him to withdraw and live apart. Accordingly, selecting a lesser one as unworthy as himself, he retired unpretentiously to this forgotten spot; for it is related of it that after the First Celestial Emperor had formed the earth he wiped his toil-stained hands upon his heaven-born thighs, and this is what fell from him. Being neither earth, heaven, nor the region Down Below it was ignored by the deities and protective Forces, so that here there are no winds, dews, spontaneous growth, nor variable seasons.'

'Are there then no evilly disposed Beings either?' inquired Kai Lung with interest.

'For some reason or other they abound,' admitted Thang. 'Thus, in spite of what a fostering care could do, our only he-child – one who seemed destined by his fearless and engaging nature to raise a squalid Line to something like an equality with others – came under the malign influence of a resentful Spectre that drew his breath away. ... It is his coffined form that I am carrying from place to place to find if possible a spot immune from harmful spirits.'

'May the Many-eyed One guide your footsteps!' voiced Kai Lung with a look of wide compassion. 'Your condition is a hapless one. For how, being thus bereft, will your weak and trembling shade, when you shall have yourself Passed Beyond, obtain either food or raiment?'

'That is very true, but is it not tolerantly written, "Even a mole can turn its eyes upwards"? Within my stricken hut two sadly deficient she-children still remain. If some lenient-minded youth can be persuaded to marry one of these he may, when in charitable vein, include my shivering ghost in the offerings he transmits. As I am well inured to privations here below, it is only reasonable to suppose that what is, after all, little more than an unsubstantial outline will be satisfied with even less.'

'It is aptly said, "The strongest tower is built of single bricks," and your steadfast attitude justifies the saying,' remarked Kai Lung. 'Did I possess anything beyond a general feeling of concavity I would pleasurably contribute to your store. As it is, I endow you with the confident prediction that your upright House will flourish. Farewell, esteemed.' With these words and a deferential bow, in which he contrived to indicate his sympathetic outlook towards the other's unenviable lot and a regret that the circumstances had not conspired towards their more enduring friendship, the weary story-teller turned to resume the hopeless struggle of his onward march. An unpretentious voice recalled him.

'Hitherto, a sense of insufficiency restrained me,' explained the lowly Thang; 'for judging from the fullness of your garb and the freedom of your manner I thought you to be a rich official, travelling at ease. If, however, as certainly your words may be taken to suggest, you are not so well equipped and can offer no reward for that which is really worthless, I am emboldened to beg your high-born acceptance of the inadequate resources of my makeshift home. The more you can consume the less will be this self-conscious person's shame at the insipidity of what he puts before you; the longer you can tolerate his worn-out roof the greater will be the confidence with which he can henceforth continue to dwell beneath it.'

'Yet your humane task?' urged Kai Lung, in spite of the despair of his position. 'Should so slight a thing as the extremity of a passing stranger interrupt your rites?'

'About the city gate are many beggars, but on the plains all men meet as brothers,' was Thang's reply. 'Furthermore,' he added prudently, 'were you to die about this spot the duty of providing you with a suitable bestowal would devolve on me and even then your annoyed and thirsty ghost might haunt my door.'

'But you spoke of destitution. If less than a sufficiency for your own stock exists, how should another – '

'Where four can stand at all five can just squeeze,' replied the accommodating Thang. 'Unless my repellent face displeases you beyond endurance the last word of ceremonious denial has been uttered.'

When they were come to the peasant's hut, Thang excused himself on a simple plea for passing in before his guest. From the approaching path Kai Lung soon overheard the reason.

'It had been our natural hope to spend the night in grief and lamentation, but chance has set another – even more faint and needy than ourselves – to share our scanty hearth. Sorrow must therefore be banished to a more appropriate time, and in the meanwhile nothing should escape to dim the lustre of his welcome in this stranger's eyes.'

A lesser voice replied, graceful yet docile.

'Where the ox clears a way the sheep can surely follow. ... There is a little cake which I had secretly prepared of fruit and sifted meal, put by against the joy-day of our two remaining dear ones. This will to some extent disguise the leanness of our ill-spread board, and towards it we can ourselves affect a cloyed repugnance.'

'We,' said a still smaller voice, 'will cheerfully forgo our separate share to relieve the stranger's need. ... Have I not spoken with your polished tongue, Chalcedony?'

'Your fragrant words, O Musk, are my own feeble thoughts well set to music,' was the equally melodious answer.

'Then are we all agreed' – it was now Thang again. 'Conduct the politely waiting stranger to a seat beneath our ragged thatch, ye two uncouth afflictions, while I go hence to gather such decaying herbs as our stubborn ground affords.'

Kai Lung had moved to a more distant part – so that he should not seem to betray too gross an interest in the details of what was being prepared for his enjoyment – when the two sympathetic she-children approached together. Being dressed alike and so moulded that they varied in no single detail, it was beyond an ordinary person's skill to discriminate between them. Their years were somewhat short of half a score, and with a most engaging confidence each took the story-teller freely by the hand and drew him forward.

'She who leads you by the right hand is Musk,' said the one

who was thus positioned, 'the other being Chalcedony. To me no special gift has ever come beyond a high discordant voice, but Chalcedony can accompany this harmoniously with music blown on reeds. What is your attractive name, wayfarer, and are you as old as your meritorious aspect would lead one to suppose?'

When he had replied to these courteous inquiries in suitable terms the one referred to added:

'Since it is inevitable that we should spend some hours together, how is it possible to know one from the other among you when both are perceptibly alike?'

'It is for that very reason that our sounds have been chosen so diversely,' was the capable reply. 'Being two alikes, born at a single birth, we have been named so that it is impossible to mistake one for the other, nor do either of our revereds ever now fall into so culpable an error. ... That one, remember, is Chalcedony, your base slave here being Musk.'

As Kai Lung reached the door Thang's lesser one came forth and with a look of gladness made him welcome. When he had been protestingly composed into the one chair that the meagre hut contained, Musk and Chalcedony again approached and standing one on either side before him sought to beguile his weariness by the artless means within their simple power, Musk lifting up her resolute voice in a set chant – 'The She-Child's Invocation' – and Chalcedony by no means lagging in the sounds that she extracted from an arrangement of pierced reeds. Nor did either desist until the rice appeared and was enticingly set out.

'It is less than would satisfy a family of midgets, and moderately self-respecting dogs would turn from it with loathing,' remarked Thang, bowing before his guest. 'It is quite possible, however, that your excessive politeness will compel you to make something of a meal. Approach therefore – '

'One hears of the lavishness of rich country nobles,' aptly replied Kai Lung, standing before the board. 'But this – '

Afterwards a small pipe, charged with dried herbs, was passed from hand to hand and tranquillity prevailed. When it was dark and a single paper lantern had been lit they sat upon the floor and the story-teller claimed that as a circle had been formed it was, by ancient privilege, incumbent on him to gratify their leisure.

'So that,' he added, 'the history of Tong So and the story of his ingenious rise to honours will linger pleasurably within your minds long after all thought of the large-mouthed Kai Lung shall have come to be forgotten.'

The discriminating Thang, however, understood that the other wished to make some small return for the compassion shown to him, in the only way he had. He therefore indicated to Musk and Chalcedony (who were on the point of blending their energies in the exposition of a well-laboured ballad entitled 'The More-desirable Locality') that they should restrain their acknowledged zeal, and admitted to Kai Lung that he was now favourably prepared for whatever might ensue.

THE STORY OF TONG SO, THE AVERTER OF CALAMITIES

I

How there fell to him the Leadership of the Fraternity of Thieves within I-kang

When Tcheng the Earless, the accepted head and authority of the company of thieves that dwelt about I-kang, suddenly Passed Above, all of that calling came together to appoint another who should take his place. Finally, by an equal choice, the matter lay between Tong So, because he was able and discreet above the rest, and Pe-hung, who though gross and boastful possessed the claim that he was of the House of Tcheng. Those who favoured the cause of Tong So dwelt on the need of skill and resource in the one who should direct their strategy, while the voices raised on behalf of Pe-hung extolled authority and a dutiful submission to the fixed order of events.

'Illustrious brothers,' exclaimed Tong So at length, for those who were to decide had by that time reached the pass of two wrestlers who are locked in an inextricable embrace where neither can prevail, 'it is well said among us, "Although the door is locked the shutter may be pliant." The honey of smooth speech and the salutary vinegar of abuse having likewise failed to convince, it may be judged that the time now is to explore another way.'

'Say on,' urged those around, for both sides were weary of the strife. 'May the more integritous cause prevail.'

'What a thousand eloquent words cannot achieve, a single timely action may accomplish,' continued Tong So. 'Let a facile test be set. In the innermost secrecy of the Temple of Autumnal Winds there reposes the Green Eye of Nong, surrounded by a never-sleeping guard. Whichever of the two shall bear it off let him be acclaimed our head.'

'It is well said,' agreed the gathering. 'He who performs that feat is worthy to be our leader. Furthermore, the value of the spoil will, when equally divided, add greatly to the dignity of all.'

Standing somewhat apart, the contumacious Pe-hung would have declined the test had that been possible, but to do so then would have involved a greater loss of face than even he could stomach, for in the past he had never failed to speak of his own skill approvingly. He accordingly sought to attain his unworthy end by a more devious line, and while seeming to agree he contrived a hidden snare.

'The trial is a suitable one,' he therefore said, 'and its accomplishment is well within my own indifferent powers. For that reason and also because the idea sprang from the enriched soil of his productive mind, the distinction of the first attempt lies clearly with Tong So. Thereafter I will speedily outshine whatever glory he may obtain.'

Pe-hung's words, however, were but as the sheath wherein one holds a keen-edged blade, for his inner thoughts ran thus: 'Tong So will make the attempt and be slain by those who guard the jewel. Obviously it is unsuitable for a dead person to be a leader, so that the choice will automatically revert to me. Or Tong So will fail in the attempt but escape alive. In that case his ineptitude clearly unfits him to be our chief and there will no longer be any opposition to this one's cause. If, however, by an unforeseen perversity Tong So should succeed it will manifestly be impossible for another, no matter how competent, to carry away what is no longer there and so the contest fails in its essential. To this end it is aptly written, "He who would feast with vampires must expect to provide the meat".'

In the darkness of a stormy night the door-keepers of the

Temple of Autumnal Winds were aroused by the clash of conflict beyond the outer gate. As the repeated cries for help indicated that violence of a very definite kind was in progress they did not deem it courteous to interfere until the sound of retiring footsteps and a restored tranquillity announced that the virtuous might prudently emerge.

Outside, they found Tong So bearing all the signs of a speedy departure Upwards. His robe was torn and earth-stained, his eyes devoid of light, while the ground around had been lavishly arranged with bloodshed. To the ordinary passer-by, finding him thus, only one question would present itself: had those who had gone before efficiently performed their sordid task, or was there, perchance, something of value still concealed about the unconscious body?

'Danger lurks here, unless we move our feet with caution,' observed the chief keeper of the door to the one who served his hand. 'Should the inopportune wayfarer Pass Beyond in this distressing manner his offended and vindictive ghost will continue to haunt the gatehouse, regardless of our feelings, and of the possible loss of custom to the temple itself which so forbidding a visitation may entail.'

'Alas, master,' exclaimed the other, 'as it is the gatehouse has become overcrowded somewhat since the less successful deities have been thrust into our keeping. Would it not be well to take this distinguished personage, the one by the head and the other by the feet, and unostentatiously convey him to the doorway of another before it is too late?'

'If it could be prudently effected such a safeguard would undoubtedly be wise; if, however, while in the act we encountered a company of his friends or the official watchers of the street, no excuse would serve us. Better endure the annoyance of another's ghost than incur the probability of yielding up our own.'

'Nevertheless there is the saying, "He who fails to become a giant need not remain content with being a dwarf," and a middle way may yet be found. Beneath the innermost sacrary of the temple there is an empty vault. Should this ever-welcome stranger honour us by Passing while reposing in its commodious depth his nobly born apparition will occasion no alarm, for by closing the upper and the lower doors we can confine its discreditable activities to that secluded region.'

To this proposal the chief door-keeper turned an assenting ear. Together they drew Tong So through the lower door and along a narrow passage, until they reached the cave hollowed beneath the walls. Here they left him, first securing his robe and whatever else of interest he possessed.

When Tong So had thus penetrated beyond the outer limits of the temple he allowed a sufficient interval to elapse and then raised himself out through the upper door, using for this purpose a cord that had been wound concealed among his hair.

In the sanctuary above a band chosen for their vigilance kept guard by day and night. It was dark except for the pale lustre round about the jewel, for it would have been held disrespectful to the brilliance of the Sacred Eye to deem it necessary to require an added light. This favoured Tong So's strategy, but as he crept forward his benumbed foot struck against a column.

'One moves among us,' exclaimed the readiest of the band. 'Let each man touch his brother's hand so that nothing may escape between us, and thus go forward.'

Tong So pressed back into the wall, compelling his body to merge itself into the interstices of the sculptured surface. He closed his eyes, ceased to breathe, and composed his mind into an alert tranquillity. A hand swept across his face as the line moved past, but the rigorous confinement of the cave had frozen his outer surface so that its touch in no way differed from that of the marble images on either side. The searchers passed on and presently they stood before the farther wall.

'Nothing can have escaped our discovering hands,' declared the leader. 'He who was here has certainly crept out. Disperse yourselves about the inner courts, if haply we may yet take him.'

When they were gone Tong So came forth from his place of refuge and quickly forced the Green Eye from its setting. The jewel secured, he took his stand behind the open door and in a simulated voice raised a disturbing cry.

'Ho, keepers of the Sacred Nong, to your stations all! That which we guard is assailed by treachery!'

Like a wave of the flood-driven Whang-Ho, back swept the

band into the darkness of the sanctuary. When all had passed inside and were surging about the statue of the despoiled god Tong So slipped out, drew close to the door, and made fast the bolt. From that point the way of his escape was easy.

Memorable in the annals of the heroic brotherhood of thieves within I-kang was the night when Tong So returned among them and displayed the great green jewel called the Sacred Eye of Nong. A feast was called for the next day, all cheerfully contributing from their store, and when they were assembled Tong So was installed upon a dais with flattering acclamation. Pe-hung alone maintained a secluded air, although his gluttonous instincts impelled him to push forward at the feast, to which, however, he had contributed less than a righteous share. 'The larger the shadow grows, the nearer is the sun to setting,' was his invariable reply to those who taunted him with Tong So's success, moreover adding, 'And the lizard that essayed to become a crocodile burst at the moment of attainment,' until presently they ceased to molest him.

When the repast was over the most elderly person among those present rose to express himself, at the same time pointing out the patriarchal length of his venerable pigtail in furtherance of his claim to lead their voices. As his remarks were chiefly concerned with the inscrutability of the gods, the uncertainty of the price and quality of rice spirit, the insatiable depravity of the official watchers of the streets, and the unapproachable perfection of his own immediate ancestors, he was thrust somewhat impatiently aside and room made for another.

'The time approaches when the more industrious and less garrulous members of our praiseworthy craft would seek the Ways,' he reasonably declared, 'nor is it necessary to procure a sack wherein to bear away a single coin. A searching test has been made and Tong So has conformed to its requirements. Is it agreed that he should be our leader?'

'Haply,' interposed the foremost among those who had hitherto opposed Tong So's cause, 'yet Pe-hung still remains.'

'Inevitably – so long as any food likewise remains,' capably replied the other. 'Does Pe-hung then raise a claim?'

'The inference is inexact,' retorted Pe-hung assertively, 'nor is it necessary for this person to crave that which devolves by

right. Out of a courteous regard for his youth and inexperience
Tong So was given the first essay, and by chance the jewel fell
into his large open hand. Manifestly it is contrary to our just
rule that this person should now be set aside because through
his benevolence the accomplishment of the test is no longer
within man's power.'

'It is but seemly,' declared Tong So, checking with a persuasive glance those who would have answered Pe-hung's craft
with ridicule. 'Yet were the possibility still present would you
now maintain your former boast that you likewise could bear
off the jewel?'

'Assuredly,' replied Pe-hung, his confidence enlarged by the
impossibility of submitting him to the test, 'and that by so
daring and ingenious a scheme that the lustre of the deed
would have brought undying honour to our fraternity within
I-kang.'

'Then let your unassuming heart rejoice at the prospect of
our well-sustained felicity!' exclaimed Tong So. 'Learn now, O
fortunate Pe-hung, that the Green Eye of Nong again adorns
his sacred face and awaits thy supple thumb!'

'It has been recovered?' cried those around. 'You have
suffered this ineptitude?'

'By no means,' replied Tong So, 'but foreseeing this entangle-
ment I caused it to be restored to its socket after displaying it
to you, so that no ground for dissension should exist among
our harmonious band.'

For a measurable space of time all power of speech was
denied even to the most fluent tongue. Then those who had
favoured Pe-hung burst forth:

'But the loss to each one of us which this expedient entails –
therein you have done evilly, Tong So. The value was that of a
camel-load of jade.'

'Loss!' exclaimed Tong So reprovingly, 'who speaks of loss
while Pe-hung still remains? Not only will he duly fulfil his
spoken word, but with the jewel he will bring back the lusty
matter for an offensive song, which Chi-ching shall set to music
for our winter fires.'

'A full-throated verse shall therein be retained for your pestilential virtues, O ill-disposed Tong So!' replied Pe-hung with

heavy-laden breath, as he made ready to depart. 'Lo, I go to efface the memory of your puny efforts.'

When he had gone and there remained only Tong So and those who were wholly favourable to his cause, that broad-minded person further disclosed the reason of his course.

'It is one thing to cast a noose about a tiger's neck,' he remarked, 'but it involves another attitude to conduct it to an awaiting cage. Had we retained the sacred relic the undying enmity of the priests of Nong would have sought us out. That, perchance, we might have evaded had it not been that those who traffic in such stones one and all refused to face the risk of its disposal. Another outlet could doubtless have been found were it not that our spoil consisted of a worthless counterfeit, the real gem having been abstracted by an earlier one in the distant past. Thus the path of Pe-hung's success is fringed by many doubts and harassments, against which it would have been well to warn him had he been a person of sympathetic outlook.'

In such a manner Tong So became the chosen leader of the company of thieves about I-kang. In this he had their unanimous voice, for Pe-hung was never seen again among their haunts. The better disposed towards him contended that he had fallen beneath the vengeance of the priests of Nong during a valiant attempt to repossess the jewel. Others, however, claimed that in a distant city there was one resembling him in the grossness of his outline who endeavoured to extort a meagre livelihood from the large-hearted by publicly beating his head and body with a brick. But this does not concern Tong So

II

Showing how slight a Matter went Hand in Hand with Tong So's Destiny

At a convenient spot outside I-kang, where it was well protected from the attacks of passing demons by an intersecting gorge, stood the ornamental residence of Fan-Chin, a retired ginseng merchant.

In spite of this, Fan Chin did not enjoy an immunity from every kind of evil, for, as the proverb says, 'However deep you dig a well it affords no refuge in the time of flood,' and the distant and solitary position of the house encouraged those who were desirous of sharing in Fan Chin's prosperity. No matter the fierceness of the hounds he procured or the vigilance of the watchers he employed, few moons ever passed without some industrious person penetrating beyond his outer walls. Indeed, the hounds frequently attached themselves to those thus introduced, for the training of all creatures of this kind lay in the hands of Tong So's associates, while the hired watchers were generally those of his company who had for the time found it desirable to seek a less violent manner of living owing to some injury received in the course of their ordinary occupation.

So convenient was it to despoil Fan Chin's possessions that Tong So himself charitably refrained in order to encourage deserving but inexperienced members of his band or to leave a facile certainty for the aged and infirm. It was by such considerate acts that the affection of his followers was nourished, so that in time Tong came to be regarded as the Father and the Elder Brother of all good thieves.

One night, towards the middle part of the darkness, Tong So was walking with the hunchback Chu when by chance they found themselves outside the walls of Fan Chin's garden.

Up to that point their discourse had been of a philosophical nature, concerned with the Essentials, the Ultimate Destinies, and the like, but discovering an iron implement within his sleeve Chu thereupon displayed it and began to speak to a more definite end.

'Ill fortune has of late attended all my efforts, while a misbegotten blow from a wooden staff, carried by an officious watcher of the street, has corroded my left thumb with acrimony. You also, Tong So, are but sparsely clad. Let us therefore accompany one another into the secluded part of this well-stocked mansion and there replenish our necessities.'

'The project is a worthy one and this person would gladly enter into it and perform an allotted part, were it not that for a specific reason he has hitherto refrained,' replied Tong So candidly. 'Nevertheless, without requiring any share of the expected profit, he will cheerfully remain here in an alert attitude and will at once fell to the ground any who should attempt to impede your intrepid progress.'

Upon this understanding Chu went forward and quickly forced his way into the remoter portions of the house. The watchers whom he encountered greeted him familiarly and courteously indicated in which direction the path of safety lay. Thus guided Chu had no difficulty in filling his sack with suitable merchandise, and was on the point of withdrawing when the avaricious Fan Chin, whom an unworthy suspicion had kept awake, suddenly appeared at an angle of the wall. He was heavily armed at every point of his attitude, while the hunchback's movements were involved with the burden under which he staggered. In this extremity it would have gone doubtfully with Chu had he not already resourcefully filled his mouth from a flask of Fan Chin's raisin wine against such an emergency. The stream of this he now vigorously propelled into the other person's menace-laden face, compelling him to drop the weapons in order to clear his eyes of liquid bitterness.

As Tong So and Chu again turned their steps towards I-kang they resumed their former discourse, nor did either refer to the details of the undertaking until they reached the parting of their ways. There the latter person raised a detaining gesture.

'Although you have not actually shared in the full flavour of the adventure, yet by remaining aggressively outside and by sustaining me with your virtuous encouragement you have undoubtedly played an effective part. Accompany me, therefore, to my criminally acquired hovel and there select from this much-distended sack whatever is deemed worthy of your tolerant acceptance.'

'The suggestion is a gracious one,' replied Tong So, 'and fittingly illustrates the high standard of benevolence which marks those of our band. Observe how the sordid-stomached Fan had been in possession of these goods for a score of years or more but never during that period had he once invited this necessitous person to share the most attenuated fraction of his store; yet no sooner do they pass into your hands than you freely bestow on me the fullness of my choice.'

'Your indulgent words cover me with honourable confusion,' stammered the gratified Chu. 'How should I divide an egg with you, who are my father and my elder brother too?'

Conversing in this mutually helpful manner they reached the

hunchback's home. Here they quickly made themselves secure and then proceeded to display the rewards of their industry. These included wares and utensils of many kinds, silks and fabrics from the walls and seats, suitable apparel as well as coverings for the head, the ears, and feet, food of the richer sorts, and here and there a silver-mounted carving.

'Beneath my decayed but hospitable roof all things are yours,' declared Chu, indicating by a gesture that he pushed the entire contents of the sack away from him.

'That which grows on the tree of enterprise should be eaten off the bough,' replied Tong So no less generously, and he was indicating by means of a like gesture that he renounced all claim to any part thereof when the vigour of his action laid bare an object which an inadvertent movement on Chu's part had hitherto successfully concealed beneath the sack.

' – Nevertheless,' continued Tong So as he took it up and regarded it with deepening interest, 'a solitary fruit may sometimes legitimately fall into the basket of another. Whence blows this fragrant peach?' and he held out the depicted image of a maiden of surpassing charm, traced with inspired skill upon a plate of ivory set in a golden frame.

'Doubtless it was hidden away among the folds of a piece of silk and thus escaped our scrutiny,' replied Chu freely. 'Humiliating as the admission is, this person will not deny that he had until now no inkling of this distinguished prize.'

'There will then be no sense of loss in its withdrawal,' observed Tong pleasantly. 'Out of the bountiful flood of your opulent profusion, O worthy Chu, this one object alone will I accept. From this resolve do not attempt to move me.'

For an appreciable moment it seemed doubtful whether the hunchback would tamely submit to this decision, so deep and wide was the stream of his devotion, but at the sight of Tong So's impassive face he bent an acquiescent neck.

'Truly is it written, "It is better to keep silence than yield wisdom",' was his discreet reply. 'I bow, chieftain.'

III

*His Meeting with Fan Chin and the Manner
of his many-sided Qualities*

On the following day Tong So again turned his footsteps in
the direction of Fan Chin's mansion, but this time he went
alone. At the outer gate he spoke little, but that to a pointed
edge, and the one who held the bolt admitted him, so that very
soon he stood face to face with Fan Chin himself.

'Greeting,' remarked Tong So affably. 'Have you eaten your
meritorious rice?'

'So much of it as an ill-nurtured outcast has generously left
behind him,' replied Fan Chin, indicating the despoiled confusion of the room. 'Nevertheless, you are cheerfully welcome
if you have anything to reveal.' He was a man of middle
height, dispassionate in manner and evenly balanced in his
speech. From time to time he caressed an eye with a cloth of
some soft fabric.

'Your moments are as pearls while my worthless hours are
only comparable with lumps of earth; therefore, I will trim
short my all-too-wordy tongue,' was the reply. 'In the deeper
solitude of the night this person chanced upon two who strove
over the division of their spoil. By a subtlety he possessed himself of that which they most esteemed. This he would
now justly return to the one who can prove his undisputed
right.'

'What you say is very surprising, especially as you yourself
have all the outward attributes of a hired assassin,' replied Fan
Chin, after a moment's thought. 'Can reliance be placed upon
your mere assertion?'

'There are four witnesses here to all that I declare; how then
can anything but the truth be spoken?'

'Four witnesses?' repeated Fan Chin, to whom this form of
testimony was evidently unknown. 'Disclose yourself.'

'The heavens above, the earth beneath, and the two who here
converse together,' explained Tong So.

'That is undeniable,' admitted Fan. 'On the whole I am inclined to credit what you say.'

'Furthermore,' continued Tong, 'here is the painted plate of

ivory held in a band of gold,' and he displayed the painting
that had been the mainspring of his actions. 'Is not this a
valued part of your possessions?'

'There can no longer be any reasonable scruple as to your
integrity,' exclaimed Fan Chin. 'You have restored that which
alone occasioned an emotion of regret.'

'Doubtless,' assented Tong So; 'yet there is an up and a
down to every hill, and having convinced you of my virtuous
sincerity it now devolves on you to satisfy me of yours.'

'The angle of your misgivings remains somewhat obtuse to
my deficient mind,' admitted Fan Chin. 'Fill in the outline of
your distrust.'

'On the back of the plate of ivory there are traced these words
in characters of gold, "Tsing Yun, of the righteous House of
Fan". Produce, therefore, the one thus described, so that the
similitude may stand revealed, and the essence of your claim is
indisputable.'

At this bold challenge the nature of Fan Chin's breathing
changed and he walked round the room several times before he
could frame his lips to a sufficiently discreet reply.

'The requirement is unusual,' he replied at length, 'though
the circumstances are admittedly out of the common. But in
any case that which you ask is unattainable. The one depicted
is the least of those of my inner chamber, and to add to the
burden of this person's harassment she now lies suspended in
the vapours of a malign distemper.'

'Then it is not unlikely that my intervention has been brought
about by the protecting powers, desirous of our mutual happiness,' declared Tong So with confidence. 'In the past I rendered
a certain service to a learned anchorite, who in return disclosed
to me many healing virtues of the hidden kind. What is the
nature of the stricken one's malady?'

'It takes the form of a dark stupor, whereby the natural
forces of the mind and body are repressed. To counteract this,
an expert healer from the Capital counselled a decoction prepared from tigers' bones.'

'The remedy is well enough, but there are subtler and more
potent drugs than tigers' bones,' said Tong with some impatience. 'Moreover, you who have been a ginseng merchant

doubtless know that every bin has two compartments. Were the bones submitted to a searching test?'

'A lavish price was paid and a thumb-signed assurance of integrity was given. What added precaution could have been taken?'

'Do any still remain?' demanded Tong.

Fan Chin summoned an attendant and issued a command. This one quickly returned with some broken fragments, which at a sign he placed before Tong So. The latter blew shrilly from between his teeth, and the next moment the largest and fiercest of Fan Chin's watch-dogs leapt among them in answer to the call and fawned upon Tong So.

'Oi-ya!' cried the one in question and threw towards it the weightiest of the pieces; without a moment's hesitation the hound caught it between expectant jaws and fled in the direction of its lair, closely followed by the bewailing Fan, striving to recover his possession.

'Restrain your ineffective zeal,' exclaimed Tong So. 'You are pursuing the wrong dog if you look for restitution.'

'Which dog is that?' asked Fan Chin, gazing round expectantly. 'I see no other than the hound escaping.'

'The one from whom these goat ribs were procured. Where does the usurious mongrel dwell?'

'He is She-Ng, the son of Ho, carrying on his necessary traffic beneath the Sign of the Magnanimous Pestle, and spoken of as both upright and exact.'

Tong So drew a figured ring from off his thumb and gave it to the awaiting slave.

'Hitherto,' he remarked in an unsympathetic voice, 'traffic with Ho She-Ng has doubtless been on a somewhat mutual basis, thou equivocal bondman. Enlighten that obscene refuse-chafferer as to what has taken place and displaying this very ordinary ring before his short-sighted eyes require of him a double measure in place of what he has fraudulently withheld. To this add that he who sends requires no thumb-signed bond, but should the fiercest hound not tremble and retreat before the bones he now provides, on the morrow the emblem of his sign will be changed from the Magnanimous Pestle to the Discon-nected Hand. To this obsequious message append the name of

Tong So and let your sandals be in shreds on your return.'

'I listen and obey, high chieftain,' replied the submissive slave.

When they were alone again Fan Chin turned towards his visitor and spoke with some reserve.

'Your name and your general line of conduct remind me of what I have heard concerning one who haunts the secluded Ways. Is it unreasonable to conjecture that you cast the same shadow as that So, of the line of Tong, who is the admitted leader to the thieves about I-kang?'

'To deny it would be superfluous,' replied Tong So. 'My revered father was of that craft before me and his venerated sire likewise in turn. How then could I, without being unfilial to a criminal degree, seem to disparage their hallowed memories by rejecting what was good enough for them?'

'That certainly is a point of view which cannot lightly be dismissed,' confessed Fan Chin, who was a staunch upholder of tradition. 'In the past this person himself had leanings towards the insidious cravings of a literary career, until he saw, as in a vision, seven generations of ginseng-providing ancestors beckoning him to follow. Recognising the brink on which he stood, the one who is now speaking immediately burned all that he had written, together with the varied utensils of the art, with the happy result that to-day he is able to command a congratulatory ode of any length whenever he feels the need of one, instead of merely having to compose them for the delectation of another.'

'It is well said that there are three of every man: that which he is, that which he only thinks he is, and that which he really had intended to become,' agreed Tong So. 'In the meanwhile, this person would seek, by tracing the origin of the adorable Tsing Yun's disorder to its hidden source and there controlling its malignity, to establish a claim on your approval.'

'It would be inept to spread a fabric of evasion between our mutually straightforward minds,' replied Fan Chin, as one who strives to be urbane and at the same time to disclose an unpalatable truth. 'Already you have appreciably risen in my esteem since the first moment of our meeting, but your inopportune profession stands as an ever-present barrier against an alliance of a really definite kind. In any other direction doubtless our congenial feet may continue side by side.'

'Yet,' pleaded Tong, 'by the exercise of a frugal industry I should soon be in a position to lay before you an adequate proposal. Hitherto I have regarded the pecuniary side of our venture with a perhaps undeserved contempt, but the business is one that is admittedly capable of a wide development under more vigorous methods, and if only inspired by a well-founded hope of the one whom I have named, very soon the puny records of the past will be obliterated – '

'Forbear!' exclaimed Fan Chin in an access of dismay. 'Already the insatiable rapacity of your never-tiring band is such that this care-worn person would gladly submit to a yearly tribute of a hundred taels of silver to be preserved from their assault. If these activities should be increased, a flood deeper than the Yang-tze will sweep over the awakening growth of our mutual esteem.'

'Yet if, on the other hand, you should be wholly freed from the exaction, would you then be impelled to regard this person in the light of a favoured suppliant for the lady Tsing Yun's lotus hand?'

'That is a longer stride than one of my age can take forward at a single step,' said Fan Chin guardedly. 'The tree of reciprocal goodwill would certainly be cherished by such an act, but the obstacle of the means whereby your rice is earned remains.'

'To change that, even were it possible in this strenuously competitive era, would risk alienating the protective spirits of my ancestors,' remarked Tong So. 'Unless,' he mused thoughtfully, 'unless, indeed, by some adroit syncretism the conflicting elements could be harmoniously reconciled so as to appeal to all.'

'My moss-grown ears – ' interposed Fan Chin politely.

'A passing invocation to the deities,' apologised Tong So. 'But touching a possible arrangement of our various interests. May the suggestion of five-score taels of silver be regarded as a concrete proposition?'

'The remark was more in the nature of a flower of conversation than a specific offer,' replied Fan Chin, somewhat annoyed that he had thus incautiously named so formidable an amount. 'Even allowing for the most ruthless energy of your painstaking crew, the full annual tale of their depredation would not approach that sum.'

'Yet there are incidental contingencies from which an assured immunity cannot be weighed in a money-changer's scale even against fine gold,' suggested Tong, meeting Fan Chin's drooping eye sympathetically. 'But among obliging friends a tael more or a tael less does not lead to strife. Assuming that fivescore could be laid before my trustworthy gang as a basis for discussion – '

'You have spoken of your knowledge of the hidden qualities of healing things,' remarked Fan Chin, turning abruptly from both the subject and the path that they had been treading; 'let us approach the one who stands in need of such an art and put your subtlety to a deciding test. Afterwards, perchance, a jar of almond wine may be unsealed and matters of a varied kind discussed.'

IV
In which he becomes both Virtuous and Esteemed

When it was passed from mouth to mouth among the thieves throughout I-kang that an assembly had been called of the full Brotherhood, to which all were summoned on pain of ejectment from the Order's protection and estate, it was understood that affairs of distinguished moment were involved. In the face of so emphatic a command none ventured to abstain, so that when Tong So entered he saw before him all who recognised his leadership, whatever their degree. His first act, after the ceremonious rite of greeting, was to require a written tablet of their names and attributes, and this being taken it was thereupon declared to form a full and authentic record of the Guild, with all other thieves outside.

'Let each one present now declare against his name the yearly sum of taels that his industry procures, judging it as he reasonably thinks fit, but with the full assurance that the sum once set down stands for good or ill unchangeable.'

'Imperishable chief,' ventured one, whose calling it was to steal tribute rice on its passage to the north (voicing the dilemma of many of his fellows), 'we be mostly men of stunted minds and alien to the subtleties that lurk in the casting of accounts. Could but an indication of the outcome of this affair be given it would greatly assist our stolid wits.'

'One with wit enough to draw out an axle-pin, while walking on his hands beside a cart, need not tremble at the task,' replied Tong So, amid a general melting of their gravity. 'Whether it be to reward you according to your proficiency or to tax you in the light of your success will presently appear.'

'Doubtless you, as our ever-cherished leader, will be the first one to attest?' suggested another hopefully.

'Not first but last, according to my unconquerable regard for your superior virtues,' politely declared Tong.

Thus baffled, as it were, each one considered well, and in the end declared himself according to his exact knowledge, lest haply he might fall upon the wrong extreme. When this was done Tong So stood up again.

'In the past we of this Brotherhood have laboured strenuously for an inadequate reward and have had, moreover, to endure the maledictory word of every rival. The powerful mandarin, holding towards each suppliant three expectant hands, the lesser official, pursuing the tribute-payer with three unrelenting feet, the merchant blending among that which is costly that which is similar but cheap, the stall-keeper propelling a secret jet of wind against the trembling balance of his scale, even the beggar in the Way, displaying that upon his body which is not really there – all these do not hesitate to extend towards us the venomed tongue of calumny. Who considers the perilous nature of our enterprise, its hidden dangers, its sudden alarms, its frequent disappointments wherein much that appears solid and of good repute by the feeble rays of the great sky-lantern proves to be hollow or of fictitious lustre when submitted to a corrosive test by the one to whom we offer it? Does any man ask us as we enter to remove our sandals and recline at ease, any maiden greet us with tea and a song of welcome? Plainly we are no longer wanted in I-kang. Thus positioned we will toil no more. It is better to live in luxurious idleness than to labour for a meagre wage and salt our rice with broadcast words of scorn.'

'Assuredly,' interposed one of some authority, as Tong So paused to take up a cup 'Your lips drop rubies, chieftain, but when picked up they transmute to points of fire. For if we toil not at our craft whence come the means to live in any state?'

'You are plainly behind your era, worthy Li, and your deliberative type of mind is fast becoming obsolete,' replied Tong So. 'Henceforth, instead of being compelled to take what we desire by stealth or force, men will freely press it into our awaiting hands, and greet us with regard and courtesy. The distinction hangs upon a subtle word: instead of working we will covenant to abstain and thus by our unanimity protect from loss those who hitherto we have endeavoured to despoil.'

'The outlook is so attractive that it must inevitably conceal some hidden spring to take us unaware,' said one. 'Men will not consent thus to reward us to remain in idleness.'

'Bend then your ears,' replied Tong So, 'and listen to the scroll of those who are already pledged: Fan Chin, a retired ginseng merchant, in consideration of a hundred taels less five; Ling-hi, who keeps a den, for twenty-eight; Hieng, the dog-butcher, at two score and a half; Tang-tso, of late reputed to possess a million taels, who offers twice what any other pays; Fung-san, at the Sign of the Upright Tooth-remover – but why drive home a wooden skewer with an iron mace? Be assured that already to each man will fall more than he earned by toil and before a final count is made his portion will be double.'

'How then shall we contrive to pass our time?' inquired another rapturously. 'We who shall henceforth be as mandarins walking the earth!'

'Thus and thus,' replied Tong, as this became a general cry. 'In the morning you will doubtless remain undisturbed or smoke a fragrant pipe among your kind. After the middle rice, attired in seemly robes and moving leisurely beneath a shading umbrella, you will approach those on our scroll whose dues have run their course, be graciously received, and give an official seal (the only form of evidence we shall recognise) for that which you receive. To each one will be apportioned a certain limit of the city, and as you make this dignified and pleasurable round you will look from side to side and observe such houses as do not display our Company's protective sign. At each of these you will present yourself in turn, pointing out to the one whose ear you gain the period of his ease, warningly – but at the same time enlivening the argument by appropriate jests and instances. Of all the profits due to your persuasive threats an added share falls to your sleeve, beyond your general portion.'

'This is the Golden Age of the Han dynasty returned,' murmured one whose method was to enter into conversation with those whom he could entice by confidence. 'But assuredly we shall very soon awaken.'

'In the evening,' continued Tong alluringly, 'you will perhaps give yourself to homely mirth among those of your choice, to witnessing a play of a kind according to your mood, or, in season, to planting the earth around your flower-clad bower. Soon, in the fullness of your leisure and content, some may even become immersed in the art of attempting to ensnare fish upon a cord, to propelling a resilient core from point to point across a given space by means of weighted clubs, or in regulating the various necessary details of the city's management. And when, in the course of time, you Pass Beyond you will lie in well-appointed tombs and your Tablets will be kept. If any should dissent from the prospect thus held out let him now speak freely.'

'Your vision is that of an above-man, chieftain, and a monument of many heights will certainly be erected to your immortal name,' a voice at length declared. 'Yet this one pitfall still remains. Men of dissolute and improvident habit from other cities will from time to time pass through I-kang and by unscrupulously robbing those whom we are pledged to guard will bring us to disrepute.'

Tong So looked round on the company that wrought his will and raised his hand with a gesture of all-confidence.

'It is foreseen,' he replied in a level voice, 'and the hazard will be met. We know The Ways by day and night; we know each other and those who are not of our confederacy; and we know The Means. Those who come will not return, and that which is had away will be restored in full, to the vindication of our unbending name. Aught else?'

They made way for the next with laughter and applause: an aged man named Jin, who was only proficient in the simplest forms of crime.

'Gracious commander,' said the ancient diffidently, 'I who speak am beyond the years of pliant change, having been a robber of the commoner sort outside the memory of most. Now touching this new-garbled plan whereby we are to lift fish on a noose, or armed with a heavy club to go openly by light of day into the houses of those who display a certain sign – '

'Set your mind at rest, honest Jin,' declared Tong reassuringly. 'None shall dispossess you from your time-worn way.' He came down and took the venerable affectionately by the shoulder, adding in his ear, 'There will always be those who would obstinately withstand our proffered help, to whom persuasion – in its various forms – must be administered. Do not despair.'

Thus in the eleventh of the Heaven-sent Emperor Yung, Tong So became the first who undertook to ensure to those who bargained with him protection against loss. Being now rich and well esteemed, Fan Chin no longer maintained a barrier before his hopes, nor, it is to be assumed, did the spirits of his discriminating ancestors regard him as having transgressed their honourable traditions in any essential detail, for they continued to uphold him in his virtuous career. So zealously inclined and sought after did he soon become that on the occasion of his marriage with the enchanting Tsing Yun he caused to be erected a many-tiered place of commerce at the meeting of the four busiest streets within I-kang, and outside this he hung a sign of polished brass, embellished with these words:

TONG SO

AVERTER OF CALAMITIES

In time he added to the nature of his commerce protection from the peril of fire, of being drawn under the wheels of passing chariots, and the like. Yet in spite of his benevolent concern for the misfortunes of others he was not wholly devoid of enemies, and these did not hesitate to declare that while Tong So could – and admittedly did – restrain his outrageous band from despoiling those who bought exemption, he was no demon to grant immunity from fire and the contingencies of life. To this narrow-minded taunt the really impartial would reply that if *some* among those who sought Tong's aid *might* occasionally experience fire or fatal injury, *all* those who stubbornly refused to do so inevitably *did*.

CHAPTER V

The Meeting by the Way with the Warrior of Chi-U, and what emerged therefrom

At daybreak Kai Lung left the scanty hut of the hospitable Thang and that obliging person accompanied him to the boundary of his knowledge.

'Before you now,' he declared significantly, as they paused at the point of his return, 'there lies an unknown and therefore, presumably, a barbarous and immoral country, doubtless peopled by wild and unintellectual tribes. Few travellers have reached our clay-souled plain from the quagmires of Yang-tze, but out of these misty slopes that lead through interminable valleys to the very peaks of Teen no message has ever come. It would be well for you, Kai Lung, to consider again before you tempt the doubtful Forces lying in wait for you ahead. The demons here are bad enough, but those elsewhere may prove much worse.'

'That is a necessary evil to be faced,' was the frank admission. 'But I place very great reliance on the energetic influence of my ancestors Above. I do not despair of their invoking an even more potent band of worthy Powers to lend their aid, and my lucky ascendant has certainly so far triumphed.'

'The connection between your auspicious number and this one's misguided age is both conclusive and exact,' acknowledged Thang, to whom the story-teller had disclosed the obliging soothsayer's prediction. 'Still, it is as well not to push these auguries too far; there is generally a concealed spring in them that releases itself when least expected. May your virtuous Line prosper in the end, however. Keen eyes and quick-moving feet in the face of danger is the last wish of the abject Thang.'

'May all the felicities ultimately be yours,' was Kai Lung's no less staunch rejoinder. 'Were there no darkness we should never see the stars, but by the light of your compassion the planets cease to be. Much happiness, esteemed.'

At a distance they raised their hands again, Thang waving a short woollen cap that he wore about his ears and Kai Lung lifting his almost deficient scrip high upon his staff. Beyond, an intervening barrier of rock hid them from one another.

*

As Kai Lung approached the border town of Chi-U he could not fail to notice that a feeling of anticipation was in the air. Kites in the form of aggressive dragons floated above every point likely to incur assault, and other protective measures were not lacking, while the almost continuous discharge of propitiatory crackers could be heard even before the mud walls appeared in sight.

'All this,' argued Kai Lung, 'may not unreasonably concern Ming-shu and his invading host. Thus ambiguously positioned it would be well to enter into affable conversation with one of leisured habit before disclosing myself too fully.'

With this inoffensive object the story-teller looked for some wayfarer whom he might casually approach with an unstudied request about the gong-stroke of the day, or to whom he might haply predict a continuance of heat. But all those whom he observed were at a distance and moving with extreme rapidity in one direction or another – those from the east flying to the west as though in no other way could they preserve their lives, and those from the west pressing on to the east as if pursued by demons.

'It is well said, "Men fear the noise more than they dread the missile",' considered Kai Lung. 'Rumour is here at work.'

At length one who neither hastened nor glanced back approached, but so assured was the dignity of his bearing, and his attire so rich, that had the circumstances been less urgent than they were Kai Lung would not have ventured to address him. The stranger had something of a martial poise although he bore no weapon; instead, he carried in one hand a polished cane from which an eager bird, attached by a silken cord, sprang divertingly into the air from time to time and caught a fleeting seed cast in its direction; from about the other arm a substantial rope, with one end fashioned as a noose, depended. His nails were long and delicately sheathed, his skin like the outer surface of a well-grown peach, and as he moved his person diffused an attractive perfume even when several paces distant.

'Greeting, high eminence,' was Kai Lung's obsequious salutation. 'Has your rice settled?'

Without exactly replying in terms that would infer acceptance of this courtesy the other made an indifferent gesture of assent and then began to regard Kai Lung more closely.

'You have not the appearance of being a Chi-U man,' he remarked with some display of interest. 'Are you from the Waste Lands of the South?'

'For such and such a length of days I have journeyed on a northward track, seeking a certain end,' was the reply. 'Say on, magnificence.'

'I am in this difficulty: If I am to Pass Upwards and rejoin my celestial ancestors under the most propitious sign it is very necessary that I should find a suitable banyan tree, growing in a valley that affords protection against spirits drifting from the east and west,' explained the stranger; 'my lucky direction being north and south, and the banyan my adopted tree. Have you in your passage marked such a spot?'

'Yet how comes it,' ventured Kai Lung, 'that you, who appear to possess all that an ordinary person could desire, should wish to self-end your being so unpleasantly?' and he indicated the cord that the other carried.

'It is better to miss a few superfluous years here below than to go through all eternity in the form of a headless trunk,' replied the one who thus forecast his own misshapen future. 'Being over-captain of the Ever-Valiant Camp of Tiger-Eating Braves stationed about Chi-U this one is bidden to attack the impure Ming-shu's rebellious lair without delay and to send that corrupt leper's obscene head to the Capital as a badge of his submission. This being clearly impossible, my own head will be held forfeit and it is to avoid this distressing humiliation that it becomes necessary to act thus and thus.'

'Yet why, with so valorous a troop of death-deriders, headed by one whose mere appearance is calculated to strike despair into the hearts of the prudent and diffuse, should it be possible for the effete Ming-shu to defy your band?'

'That,' was the reply, 'arises from the complexity of our military system. Three hundred braves are the avowed total of this one's company, but in order to foster a becoming spirit of thrift the monthly inadequacy of taels is computed for half that number.'

Kai Lung experienced a moment of regret that so many of those whom he had hoped to join in an attack on Ming-shu's fastness should be, as it were, struck down at the very outset. The emotion passed.

'There is a saying in the Books, "Two willing men can cleave a passage through the rock while four pressed slaves are moistening their hands",' he remarked. 'Seven or eight score valiants would set Ming-shu at naught and so uphold your face.'

'Perchance,' agreed the other, 'but the path from the office of the Board of Warlike Deeds and Achievements, in the Capital, to the door of the military stronghold here in Chi-U, is both long and tortuous and whoever travels it must receive the protection of many important officials on the way. There is the immaculate President of the Board itself, who checks the silver out on leaving, and the incorruptible civil overling here, who counts it in on arriving, while between lurk the administrators of three districts, the chief mandarins of eight townships, and the headmen of seventeen villages. All these integritous persons are alert to see that the consignment has not suffered attrition in its passage through the previous zone, and each has a large and instinctively prehensile hand. Thus and thus – '

'Excellence,' besought Kai Lung, not without misgivings, 'how many warriors, each having some actual existence, are there in your never-failing band?'

'For all purposes save those of attack and defence there are fifteen score of the best and bravest, as their pay-sheets well attest,' was the confident response. 'In a strictly literal sense, however, there are no more than can be seen on a mist-en-shrouded day with a resolutely closed eye.'

'None, illustriousness? Not one with which to bring the unanswerable Ming-shu to justice?'

In the ensuing pause the over-captain threw a dexterous succession of choice seeds to the expectant bird and applauded its unfailing effort.

'Despite all that a sordid economy can accomplish, there remains only so much – after allowing barely enough to maintain the one essential officer in a state befitting his position – as will keep the three hundred uniforms and the flags and banners of the imperishable company in a seemly condition of repair,' replied the other. 'That, and something inevitable in the way of joy-making and esteem-promoting when the appointed red-knob journeys hither to survey the band.'

'Yet if the band is in a state of no-existence does not disgrace ensue from that same one's report?'

'Wherefore, if the necessary formalities have been becomingly observed and mutual politeness reigns? Fifteen-score hard-striving and necessitous persons are never lacking in Chi-U, who for the honourable distinction and a few assorted cash are willing through a passing hour or two to obey the simpler signals of command and to answer to a name.'

The sugared seed being no longer offered, the brilliant captive poised on the apex of the upraised rod and folded its tranquil wings. The stilling point of yellow took Kai Lung's eye with a deeper meaning. '"A golden bud set on a leafless stem",' leapt his immediate thought. 'There is more than the outer husk herein.'

'In this affair of Ming-shu, however,' he prompted, speaking at a hazard and merely to detain the stranger, 'does not your meritorious service in the past call for official mildness?'

'That which is only painted should not be washed too often,' replied the over-captain with broad-minded resignation. 'Therefore, if you can aid this person's search to what he now requires do not refrain, and the obliged shade of Hai Shin will speak a good word for you in season.'

'Truly, importance,' agreed Kai Lung, 'yet this matter is not one that can be settled as between the drinking of a cup of tea and the filling of another. In your illustrious proximity this one now recognises the fulfilment of an inspired portent. Have you, on your side, no indication of his menial presence?'

'There certainly was a remark made by a priestly mendicant, to whom I threw a doubtful coin at the Camel Gate,' replied Hai Shin. 'This was to the effect that, "Even a paper leopard can put a hornless sheep to flight", but the analogy is admittedly abstruse.'

'High prominence!' exclaimed Kai Lung joyfully. 'Surely nothing could be more pellucid in its crystal depth. As a leopard is the symbol of indomitable valour what could so explicitly proclaim your own consternating image? And inasmuch as this one is a minstrel and a reciter of written tales the reference to paper is exact. How apter could the invincible alliance of the two persons standing here be classically portrayed? The paper leopard: device and intrepidity.'

'The simile might strike the undiscerning as coming somewhat from a distance,' conceded Hai Shin, not altogether unimpressed. 'But who is to be sought in the allusion to a hornless sheep?'

'Who, high commander? Who but the promiscuous Mingshu, for what could be more truly said to counterfeit the goat than to forgo an assured life for the uncertain fruit of insurrection? – but a goat whose horns are predestined to be very closely shorn by your all-conquering sword.'

'The prospect is not wholly devoid of glamour,' the over-captain agreed, 'but how are we, the one being an unspecified retailer of delusive fables and the other a fugitive devoid of followers, to overthrow Ming-shu – camped in a mountain stronghold and surrounded by armed men?'

'Is it not written, "Every hedge has a rotten stake somewhere"? and Ming-shu's defence will prove no exception to the rule. What cannot be pushed in by force may yet be drawn out by guile. This involves a stratagem.'

'If you have any definite plan it might be worth considering,' admitted the other, 'but the prospect of a speedy and not inglorious end – especially at an hour when the very cracks of hell are voiding their vapour upwards to consume us – compares favourably with a long-drawn-out and speculative existence,' and he continued to fan himself at leisure. 'Disclose your artifice more fully.'

'That is best explained by a recital of the story of Lin Ho

and the Treasure of Fang-tso,' replied Kai Lung resourcefully. 'If, therefore, you will but inconvenience your refined and well-trained ears to the extent of admitting such harsh and ill-chosen phrases as I have at my illiterate command I will endeavour to impart the necessary moral as painlessly as possible.'

With this auspicious foreboding Kai Lung arranged his mat so that it might offer an agreeable shade to both, and then without permitting the more leisurely minded Hai Shin any real opportunity for dissent he at once raised up his voice.

THE STORY OF LIN HO AND THE TREASURE OF FANG-TSO

In the days before the usurper Wung-che arose to destroy the land (may the daughters of his outcast Line slant their eyes in vain along the byways of our desecrated city!) a conscientious lacquerer, Li Chu by name, plied his inoffensive craft in the township of Ki-ting. He had an only son, Lin Ho, whom it was his care to instruct on all occasions in the pursuit of excellence.

'Yet how comes it, revered,' inquired Lin Ho, when he was of an age to discriminate these things, 'that I who am the outcome of your virtuous life should go in homely cloth and oft-times gnaw the unappetising husk while the sons of other lacquerers wear silk array and speak familiarly of meat?'

'It is even as it is,' replied Li Chu, applying a pigment of a special brilliance to the work beneath his hand. 'Doubtless if this person hung out a flagrant sign, hired one to chant his praises in the market-place, and used a base alloy to simulate pure gold, you also might wear rich attire and eat your fill.'

'Why then, since others of your guild do this to their advancement, should you not act thus as well?'

'It is not the Way,' answered Li Chu simply. 'Have you already forgotten the words of the upright official Thang to those who inquired of him an easy road to wealth: "All roads are easy if you do not disdain the mud"?'

'Nay,' assented his son, 'I had not forgotten. But to what does this Way you speak of ultimately lead?'

'To this end: that among future races, even in far distant lands, men searching for that which is precious will take up

perchance this very casket and examining it will say "Here is
the thumb-mark and the sign of Li Chu, the obscure craftsman
of Ki-ting in the ancient days – lo, we require no further
guarantee".'

Thus inspired, it will occasion no surprise that Li Chu himself soon after Passed Beyond, stricken by a low distemper
against which the natural forces of his ill-nourished frame
could not contend. Lin Ho, still many years short of manhood,
was left destitute and would doubtless have likewise perished
had not the fear of barbed whispers impelled his wealthy uncle
Leung to succour him.

When Leung took Lin Ho into his household he did so
reluctantly, partly forecasting his meagre wife's displeasure but
no less by reason of his own prevailing greed. Although full
brother to Li Chu they resembled each other only to this degree: that where the one succeeded the other failed, and likewise in converse, so that he who amassed five cart-loads of
taels as the fruit of a sordid usury was at once forgotten, while
he who was buried in a hired coffin is extolled by a thousand
lips to-day when they declare: 'Behold, the colours are as
bright as those of the unapproachable Li Chu.'

The smaller ones of Leung's house were not slow to bend
towards this unworthy attitude, for, as the Verse proclaims,
'When the dragon breathes out fire, the dragonets begin to
blow forth smoke,' and very soon Lin Ho found that extended
hands were not to welcome him and that the feet turned in his
direction so far from accompanying him in a friendship propelled him forward with undisguised hostility. The most degrading and obscure of the household tasks were thrust upon
him, so that ere long his state in no way differed from that of
a purchased slave. Nevertheless, Lin Ho remained sincere and
obsequious and whatever he was bidden to do he did in a
superior manner.

'Even if it is but the scouring of a cracked utensil my aim
shall be to scour it so that anyone taking it up will say, "This
is the work of Lin Ho and none other",' he was wont to remark, with well-sustained humility. This, indeed, actually occurred on several occasions, but it did not enlarge Lin Ho in
the eyes of those around.

When the years of Leung's hospitality had reached about a single hand-count that person was the victim of a severe and ill-arranged misfortune. An obsolete and heavily burdened junk – the outcome of his enterprise – in making a hazardous passage along an uncharted course was not wrecked, and in spite of the distinguished efforts of the one in command – an adherent to Leung's cause – the undisciplined crew succeeded in bringing the superfluous vessel to its inopportune anchorage. Leung was obliged to take up his share of the merchandise (which he had already disposed of at an advantageous loss) and to extricate himself as best he could. The blow was an unbecoming one.

'Henceforth,' remarked the pioneer of commerce to the discreet beneath his roof, 'henceforth the rigid line of economy must be strenuously maintained until this person's credit is sufficiently robust again. Restrain the generous impulse to outvie all others in the cost and dimensions of everything procurable. Cultivate originality of taste in the direction of the inexpensively severe. Forbear to provide your table with lotus shoots when it is difficult to walk without treading on rice worms but when there are no lotus shoots within ten thousand li, and with rice worms when lotus shoots abound around your door but when rice worms have to be brought in tanks from distant provinces at vast expense. In the matter of fans and general attire, that which was entrancing when the moon was crescent need not inevitably be regarded as unendurably grotesque by the time it is at the full –'

'Haply,' interposed the leader of those chiefly concerned; 'but he who is clumsy with his feet will be weak in his reasoning also. Turn your eyes inwards, O thou financially concave Leung, and, as the adage counsels, eat what you have roasted. Henceforth, in place of the exclusive brands you habitually affect, learn to inhale the frugal "Tame Chrysanthemum", of which two brass cash procure five. For peach wine of the choicest sorts substitute Ah-kong's Stimulating Orange-Joy at seven taels the gross. Avoid the robe marts of the Western Quarter and about your lavishly proportioned form wrap the already prepared garments – '

'Desist,' exclaimed Leung ungracefully; 'you cannot mend

things with a broken needle and your words are quite destitute of point. These are but trifles, and in any case they constitute this person's commercial frontage. Meet his wishes in a thoroughly large-hearted manner and he, for his part, will give up something really substantial.'

'In what direction will the promised economy tend?' inquired the speaker of the band, in a spirit of well-grounded mistrust.

'For upwards of four years Lin Ho has consumed our rice and beyond a little manual labour of the unskilled type he has done nothing in return. Admittedly the one who is speaking has carried family affection too far and he must now deny himself in this respect. Lin Ho shall go.'

'That loss were an undivided gain,' agreed the other. 'But will not the ever-ready voice of censure assail our trembling prestige if we thrust him forth?'

'Refrain from instructing your venerated ancestress in the art of extracting nutrition from a coco-nut,' replied Leung concisely. 'One whose ships are incapable of foundering on the perfidious Che-hai coast is scarcely likely to lose his bearings in so simple a matter as the marooning of Lin Ho.'

It will thus be seen that already this mentally bankrupt speculator was deceiving himself by an illogical grasp of the ordained sequences. Can we deny the aptness of the saying, 'He who has failed three times sets up as an instructor?'

Early the following day Leung took Lin Ho aside and proceeded to unfold his ignoble plan. He was (to set forth his misleading words, though the discriminating, who will by this time have taken his repulsive measure, should need no warning cough) on the eve of initiating a costly venture and would enlist the special protection of certain powerful spirits. To this end it was necessary to sacrifice and observe the ceremonies at a notorious shrine on an indicated mountain. For this service Leung had chosen Lin Ho, and having provided him with all things necessary he bade him set out at once.

With no suspicion of treachery the painstaking Lin Ho proceeded on his way, determined to conduct the enterprise in such a manner as would redound to the credit of his name. It was noon when he reached the foot of the mountain, the spot being a wild one and austere. Before ascending to the shrine Lin Ho sat down upon a rock to partake of food and gather strength for the lengthy rite. He opened his wallet and found therein an adequacy of mien paste, a flask of water, and an onion. There was also a little spice to sprinkle on the food and a few score melon seeds.

'If he whom I serve is not so light as day, neither is he quite so black as night,' observed Lin Ho, for the nature of the fare surpassed what he had expected.

'To speak one's thoughts aloud, even in a desert, betrays a pure and dispassionate mind,' exclaimed an appreciative voice from behind a crag. 'I need have no hesitation in affecting the society of such a person.'

With this auspicious presage the one who spoke came into view and stood before Lin Ho. He was above the common height and wore a martial air, to which his fiercely bristling whiskers gave a sombre increase. His robe was faded by the long exposure of a rigorous life; where the colours could be seen they were both harmonious and rich. Whatever arms he bore he had laid aside in deference to the reputation of those heights whose shadows lay upon them, but he retained his iron sandals and a metal covering for the head. His manner had in it both something of the menace of the mountain brigand and the subtlety of the wayside mendicant, so that Lin Ho was not wholly reassured. Nevertheless he waved his hand in greeting and indicated a smooth rock at no great distance from the one he sat on.

'You are two thousand times welcome,' he declared hospitably. 'If you are about to refresh yourself before you perform your rites there is no occasion why we should not eat together.'

'It would be churlish to refuse an invitation so delicately advanced,' replied the stranger. 'Foreseeing the necessity of this halt the one before you carried with him baked and steamed meats of various kinds, condiments of the rarer flavours, rice and sweet herbs, fruit, wine, and a sufficiency of snuff. All of these – '

'Beside your rich abundance my own scanty fare is a shrivelled weed beneath a towering palm,' confessed Lin Ho in deep humility. 'Nevertheless, if you will but condescend to share – '

'All of these were swept away at a perfidious and ill-conditioned ford a short li distant to the north,' continued the other. 'Of what does your welcome and appetising store consist, O brother?'

'Very little, and that quite unattractively prepared,' replied Lin Ho, his face by no means gladdened at the direction in which the episode was tending. 'Accept this cake of paste and a cup of water to refresh your weary throat when it is finished. More I cannot allot, for I have an exacting service to perform and shall need all the sustaining vigour that food bestows.'

'What is offered in friendship should not be weighed upon a balance,' assented the stranger pleasantly, but at the same time so arranging himself that he could closely overlook all Lin Ho's movements. 'With what is your own meritorious meal supplied, in addition to this wholesome though undoubtedly prosaic foundation, comrade?'

'The staple of it is a large but unsightly onion,' replied Lin Ho, as he began to peel it. 'Had there been two I might have prevailed on you to overcome your high-born repugnance to such crude fare.'

'An onion!' exclaimed the one beside him, stretching out his hand to take it, so incredulous were his eyes of their service. 'An onion at this momentous hour! Would you affront the deities on whom you call by carrying so impolite a taint into their sacred presence?'

'That is very far from being my purpose,' replied Lin Ho, colouring at the unbecoming imputation. 'Nor shall so gross a misdeed ever be set to my account.'

'Yet do you not hold that the breath of your petition will rise before the faces of the gods you supplicate?'

'Such is the essence of the rite,' Lin Ho admitted. 'How else should they hear and concede my prayer?'

'Then how can your breath ascend on high without conveying in its wake the pestilential reek of onion if you permit yourself this rash indulgence? It is well for you that we encountered, friend!'

'That certainly presents the matter in a disconcerting light and one that I had never up to now been warned of,' said Lin

Ho in a very downcast spirit. 'Must the better part of my sustenance then be wasted?'

'By no means,' replied his companion, beginning to eat; 'it shall not be lost. My own business with the Venerable Ones is the mere formality of rendering thanks for an enterprise achieved and at the moment I have nothing to solicit. It therefore matters very little whether they maintain a sympathetic front or turn their backs on me disdainfully. In this matter of the onion, neighbour, be content: Lam-kwong will requite you to the full at some appropriate time.'

'That may be,' agreed Lin Ho, 'but "To-day is a blistered foot; to-morrow but an itching hand". It is no easy thing to prostrate oneself continuously on a stomach sustained by mien paste alone.'

'You have suffered no great loss,' said Lam-kwong in a voice that began to lose its truculent assurance. 'Already I am experiencing certain grievous inward qualms. Whence comes this dubious root that you have so noticeably pressed upon me?'

' "Wan Tae, falling into the river while catching fish, accuses them of his misfortune",' quoted Lin Ho, stung by the injustice of the taunt. 'Touching the thing that you have eaten I know no more than this; that it is from the hand of one who is not prone to bounty.'

'Is this enmity so great that he would conspire to your destruction if it could be prudently achieved?' inquired Lam-kwong faintly.

'He is capable of any crime, from reviling the Classics to diverting water courses,' freely declared Lin Ho. 'If you desire to speak openly to Leung do not let the fact that he is closely related to the one before you impede the zealous fountain of your doubtless fluent tongue. Without question he laid a dark spell upon the onion for it to contort your limbs so unnaturally.'

'It is a spell that writes Lam-kwong's untimely end,' exclaimed the one who thus alluded to his own Up-passing. 'The device is an ancient one, the pungent juices of the herb cloaking the natural flavour of the poison until it is too late. Between you you have outdone me who have outdone all others – may the two of you grill at a never-slackening fire throughout eternity! Him, neither my resentful hand can reach nor my avenging ghost discover, but you at least shall suffer for your inept share in this one's humiliation. Take Lam-kwong's last message!' A weighty stone, propelled with all that one's expiring vigour, accompanied this short-sighted curse, and chancing to inflict itself upon Lin Ho at a vulnerable point of his outline, the well-meaning and really inoffensive person groaned twice and sank to the ground devoid of life.

Lin Ho being dead his spirit at once sped to the Upper World and passed the barriers successfully. An inferior Being received and questioned him and setting a certain mark against his name led him into the assembly of those who sat in judgment.

'Lin Ho,' said the presiding chief in some embarrassment, 'the circumstances of your abrupt arrival here are rather out of the formal order of things and the necessary records are not as yet available. For this irregularity Lam-kwong shall answer sharply. As for you, in view of your frugal and abstemious life and taking into consideration the mission on which you are now engaged, it has been decided to send you back again to earth. Regard the Virtues, sacrifice freely, and provide an adequate posterity.'

Lin Ho then had the sensation of being violently projected downwards. When he recovered sufficiently from the exertion to be able to observe coherently he found that he was floating in spirit above the spot on earth where he had lately been. Beneath him lay two lifeless bodies – those of Lam-kwong and of himself. For the first time he was inspired by an emotion of contempt towards his own placid and unassuming features.

'It is one thing to lead a frugal and abstemious life,' Lin Ho reflected; 'it is another to partake of meat whenever the desire arises. Hitherto this person has accepted servitude and followed the integritous path because with so narrow-minded a face as that any other line of conduct was not practicable. Had he possessed fiercely bristling whiskers and a capricious eye he would not have meekly accepted the outer husk of things nor would the maidens of Ki-ting have greeted him with derisive cries, that he should not respond to them when they encountered about dusk in the waste spaces of the city.'

For a few short beats of time the spirit of Lin Ho considered further. Then he looked this way and that and saw that there was none to observe him there, nor had any attending Being accompanied him to Earth. He took a sudden resolution and before a movement could be made to intercept him he slipped into the body of Lam-kwong and animated it.

When Lin Ho, wearing the body of Lam-kwong, rose up, he was conscious of possessing an entirely new arrangement of the senses. The thought of Leung no longer filled him with sub-mission and he laughed sonorously at a recollection of the labours he had lately been engaged in, though hitherto he had regarded all forms of gravity-removal as unworthy of his strenuous purpose. The sound of his iron shoes grinding the rocks he walked on raised his spirits and he opened and closed his great hands to feel their horny strength. From time to time he leapt into the air to test his powers and he shouted a de-fiance to any unseen demons who might happen to be lurking in the caves around.

So careless had Lin Ho grown that he had walked and leapt at least a li before he recalled his new position. To return to the house of Leung was now useless, for however passively dis-posed that one had formerly been towards a kinsman of his Line it would be vain for a stranger of formidable hirsute guise and martial mien to appear and claim his bounty. In search of a deciding omen Lin Ho turned to the inner sleeves of the one whom he now was and he did not turn in vain. Among a varied profusion that he left for future use he found a written mes-sage. It bore the name of Kuei and conveyed an affectionate greeting from one who dwelt beneath the sign of Righteousness Long Established, in the Street of the South Wind, within the city of Tsing-te. Towards Tsing-te Lin Ho now turned his ad-venturing feet.

It was not until three days later that Lin Ho reached the gate of Tsing-te called the Lepers' Gate and entered by it. He had not hastened, for the encounters of the way were not dis-tasteful to his newly acquired temper. Those whom he greeted with a single upraised finger and an unbending neck acknow-ledged him obsequiously in turn, and when he spoke of the appetising air food was at once forthcoming. Some made a claim to know him and talked familiarly of things, but though Lin Ho would have welcomed whatever led him to a fuller understanding of himself he could not pursue the arising conversation to any lucid end. From one it would appear as though he controlled a Hall of Melody; from another that he dealt extensively in yellow fat. A third spoke as if the public lotteries lay beneath his guiding thumb, and yet a fourth cautiously disclosed a secret sign which Lin Ho had some difficulty in ignoring.

'The wealth of analogy possessed by our inimitable tongue admittedly lends itself to a classical purity of style, but it certainly tends towards a baffling ambiguity in the commonplace needs of life,' reflected the one involved, and with a gesture of qualified agreement he passed on.

Once in the city he had come to, Lin Ho recognised that his course would be no less devious there. He forbore to ask the way lest it should be of any who might know him, so that it was the time of between-light before he chanced upon the street he needed. It was a deserted part and sombre and the house that showed the symbol of a golden bar disclosed no window to the passer-by. Lin Ho struck the well-protected door, and as no answer came at once he beat upon it with an iron shoe.

'What errant lord stands there to wake the Seven Echoes with his unbecoming clamour?' growled a contentious voice within, and there came the creak of a shutter being more firmly wedged.

'One who is not wont to be questioned either before or after,' replied Lin Ho, stamping with his massive heel upon the door-sill. 'Let that suffice.'

An iron plate slid open and an eye appeared. Then the defences of the door were drawn.

'Why was the usual sign withheld, chiefling?' protested the one within. 'Had I not identified that richly mellowed voice you might have stamped in vain.'

'It was but to try thy wariness, reliant Ying,' answered Lin Ho with a confidence engendered by success. 'I am newly returned from a lengthy journey and thought to test the watch you keep here.'

'Your mood was ever light and whimsical,' retorted the keeper of the door tolerantly, as Lin Ho entered. '"Ying" indeed! For three-score years plain Wong has served, but "Ying" is well enough.'

'Do any await me now?' ventured Lin Ho, putting his lightness from him with an indulgent nod.

'She of the inner chamber broods expectantly,' replied the docile Wong, bending a meaning look. 'Furthermore, she laid a charge on me to bid you hasten to her presence.'

'Then lead me there,' Lin Ho commanded. 'Her engaging interest fills me with a pleasurable confusion.'

'Lead, forsooth! Surely by this time you must know the way,' began the one who sought thus to excuse himself, but:

'I would have it so,' replied Lin Ho, touching his efficacious whiskers significantly, and Wong obeyed.

From the nature of her written greeting Lin Ho did not doubt the depth and weight of Kuei's devotion, and he was reconciled to the necessity of reciprocating it to the full when he should have discovered in what direction the requirement lay. In a chamber hung with bright silks of eight appropriate blends she was seated on a dais covered with a leopard skin when he entered, and the colours and arrangement of her robes exceeded anything that he had yet encountered. At the same time he could not fail to recognise that her years somewhat overlapped those of the one whose obligations he had assumed, and as regards his natural self the comparison was even more remote.

'Ten thousand jewelled greetings!' she exclaimed with a dignified absence of restraint that convinced Lin Ho of their mutual affection. 'Have you indeed returned?'

'Admittedly,' and to impart a fuller flavour to the assurance he added, 'What could detain this person's hurrying footsteps from your virtuous and attractive side?'

The one addressed rewarded him with a well-considered glance of approval from her expressive eyes and then indicated by a refined gesture that he should seat himself where they could converse without exertion.

'Tell me then of the various adventures of your quest,' she commanded graciously, 'for these bankrupt ears droop to learn your tidings.'

'There is neither length nor width to the limits of that story,' replied Lin Ho cautiously. 'In which particular direction does your gratifying curiosity extend?'

'That needs no trumpet to proclaim it,' was the ready answer. 'Have you accomplished this one's freedom?'

'He who would deny it is malformed from birth, nor is his father's line unsullied,' exclaimed Lin Ho, deeming his strategy to lie in a judicious evasion until he could satisfy himself more fully; and he would have raised a menacing hand to touch his responsive cheek, had he not doubted whether the gesture would be correct in Kuei's presence.

'Your sublime assurance is a never-failing support to the weak-kneed scruples of my own embarrassment,' confessed the lady Kuei gracefully. 'There is, however, a time to speak in the flowery terms of poetical allusion and a time to be distressingly explicit. Descending to the latter plane for one concise moment, O my dragon-hearted, state definitely whether you have or have not at last succeeded in slaying this long-enduring one's offensive and superfluous lord, and in attaching to yourself his personal belongings?'

Alas, it has been truly said, 'He who flies on an eagle's back must sooner or later drop off', and Lin Ho was experiencing the justice of the verse. But when it seemed as though he could no longer maintain an equivocal poise an inspired recollection of Lam-kwong's boast – that he had achieved his enterprise – came back and decided him to accept the hazard.

'With these unworthy hands have your unmentionable sufferings been ended,' he accordingly declared, 'and here' – at this point he poured out before her feet the varied contents of Lam-kwong's inner sleeve – 'here is the evidence that I do not lean on words.'

'Truly your little finger is more achieving than the whole of Fang-tso's two-faced body,' exclaimed the one beside him exultantly. 'Here are his keys and signet and his personal authority as well! Who can any longer doubt that the band will acclaim you its chief and ruler in Fang-tso's stead – and this person has ever gone with the band!'

'It is more than enough to hear such gratuitously expressed words,' said Lin Ho courteously; whereupon Kuei sang to him a melody expressing her deep emotions.

The next morning, after they had refreshed themselves with food brought in on silver plates by richly attired slaves and had smoked from a single pipe, Kuei took up the ring of keys that Lin Ho had brought and indicating by a suitable movement of her swan-like hand that two bearers should attend with lights, she called that one to accompany her.

'Come,' she remarked pleasantly, 'it is fitting that you, who are shortly to be the chieftain of the place, should now learn the extent of the treasure that its vaults contain.'

'It is an agreeable mark of confidence on your part,' replied Lin Ho with polished unconcern, but he followed her down the ladder closely, for there was his own strategy to consider and he had a far from tranquil stomach about the one called Fang-tso, whom, in an outside manner, he had heard spoken of as comparable with gods in strength and with demons in resentment.

'Doubtless in these remote beneath-parts there will be a store of gold and silver and precious stones which will smooth this person's path very appreciably should it become necessary for him to withdraw in unobtrusive haste,' thought Lin Ho as he descended full of hope and resolution.

The first cave, from its earthen floor up to its arching roof, was filled with rags. There were shreds of every colour, variety, and usage, from the wrappings which the afflicted cast off in obscure byways to the unused scraps such as the charitable bestow on persistent mendicants about their door.

'Nothing is too insignificant to have some use; nothing too ample to be beyond our power of assimilation,' remarked the broad-minded Kuei with far-seeing pride as she contemplated the mass, but Lin Ho was not disposed to linger.

The next cave was filled in a like manner with bones, and it was no less spacious than the first. Again the one who led him spoke encouragingly of the profits of this obscure traffic, but here also Lin Ho pressed forward dumbly, so involved were his feelings.

Jars, cruses, and receptacles in their several grades were the staple of the third enclosure; fragments of torn and rejected paper of the fourth. In immediate succession there were vaults of broken and abandoned umbrellas, of wornout and cast-off sandals, of unserviceable fans and fabricated flowers.

'This is the very dust-bin and the ash-heap of the city's void-ance,' reflected Lin Ho, as he passed a cave pressed to the full with driftwood, bungs, and half-burned joss-sticks. 'What scope is there for one of my distinguished personality in this har-bourage of refuse?' Twice or thrice he would have turned had not Kuei urged him on, and presently the nature of the com-merce changed more in keeping with Lin Ho's mood, for here were cloaks and coverings for the head and face, the better sort of garments, and such things as could be worn with fitness. Weapons of all kinds there were and armour both for men and horses, ceremonial flags and wands of office, tablets and even chairs.

'Yet how comes it,' he remarked, 'that these things are com-paratively few and sparse, while of the cruder stock an inter-minable line of caves extends?'

'The answer to that requires no lantern to discover, seeing that the brigands of our band scarce number now a dozen, and they old and infirm in service, while of the mendicants a stal-wart and increasing tribe responds daily to the roll,' explained Kuèi readily. 'But, speaking as one in authority to another, there is no great matter for regret in that. The rewards of men-dicancy, if severally minute, are sure and the market is a never-failing one. The fruits of brigandage are uncertain and difficult to garner, indeed several of the band are scarcely worth their rice and had it not been for the local distinction that the gang confers, even the vainglorious Fang-tso would ere this have dispersed them to their homes. But in the end he was always wont to say, "What we scatter on the brigands we gather up by the mendicants," and thus and thus it remains.'

'Her thoughts are for ever set on gain and truckage and her mind is ordinary in the extreme,' reflected Lin Ho. 'This one can have no lasting permanence for me.'

'And now,' continued she whom he thus inwardly denounced, 'I have freely shown you all. Will you not, in return, disclose to me the one thing that is lacking?'

'When you open your golden lips nothing is wanting to complete the circle of felicity,' politely replied Lin Ho, his ex-perience not being sufficient to enable him to detect the peril underlying Kuei's speech and judiciously to avert the impending sequence. 'What pearl is missing from the rope of your desire?'

'Somewhere about these caves is hidden Fang-tso's private store of gold and jewels. That secret you would have extorted from him before you suffered him to Pass Beyond. Let us together now draw them forth and put them to a more appropriate use.'

This request threw Lin Ho into a very complicated meditation. It disclosed that such a store did undoubtedly exist, but it led no farther on a beneficial line. In the vastness of those caves to dig at a hazard would be as profitable as a scoop for a grain of salt in a cask of water. And a moment might arise when Lin Ho would not be given the leisure to dig at all. Despite much that had cast a favourable shadow the Destinies were not really well arranged so far.

'Can it be that one on whom this person has lavished so much disinterested affection maintains an ambiguous pose towards her only expressed wish!' exclaimed the lady Kuei reproachfully as Lin Ho remained aloof, and despite the restriction of the spot she prepared to indulge in a very extensive display of many-sided agitation.

'Defer your refined exhibition of virtuous annoyance to a more convenient gong-stroke,' cautioned Lin Ho. 'One in no way concerned approaches,' and as he spoke the sympathetic Wong discovered them.

'Well chanced upon, O chieftain,' exclaimed Wong, with obtuse self-satisfaction. 'The company of beggars are about to take their stations in the Ways. Would you exchange the usual greeting with them in the courtyard?'

'Let them disperse with an entire absence of ceremonial rite,' replied Lin Ho, in a tone of no-encouragement. 'Dismiss them at their ease.'

'Things were very different in the upright days before the coming of the Competitions,' muttered Wong supinely. 'What next, perchance? Indeed,' he added at the recollection, 'there is a case in point. One stands about the outer door, protesting to all who pass, that he, in spite of every outward sign, is no other than the bountiful Lam-kwong.'

'What is this one like?' demanded Lin Ho sharply. 'Seeing that you have listened to his feeble pretensions.'

'Nay, but I did no more than question him, by warrant of my office,' replied Wong stubbornly. ' "If you indeed are our noble chief Lam-kwong" (I said, be it understood), "there is a ready test," and I held out my hand, palm uppermost, towards him, "For" (I continued, this being the snare), "that compassionate and high-stepping leader suffers no single day to go without a piece of silver passing to my sleeve – and so far today the custom has escaped him." To this the uncongenial dog made no adequate response and thereby stood exposed. "Begone, witless," I cried, justly annoyed, and I beat him about the head and shoulders with my staff. Then, as he put up no defence, I added, "Wert thou his very likeness and the wearer of his embossed ring, still, after this, thou couldst not be Lam-kwong." ' '

'There is more herein than hangs upon a wooden nail, as the saying is,' pondered Lin Ho. 'Describe him whom you beat,' he commanded aloud. 'Haply he is some obscure member of my clan who bears a portion of the name.'

'He is small and undersized and his expression vile,' declared the ready Wong. 'His eyes are badly placed and have a complex bend, his forehead insincere, and the sound of his breathing unpleasant to the good-class ear. His dress is meagre and ill-fitting, his – '

'Enough,' interrupted the one who recognised himself, although he was little disposed to hear from another what he had spontaneously avowed; 'I would sift the essence of this mixture to the dregs. Remove the impostor to a cell apart and there I will confront him.'

'It is as good as done, commander,' replied Wong with easy assurance; and he went.

When Lin Ho and Lam-kwong, each in the semblance of the other, encountered, the moment was a concentrated one. The former person had required that all should withdraw to a distance from the cell so that there was none to overhear their words. Lam-kwong was the first actually to speak.

'It is useless to curl your whiskers and blow out your cheeks in this one's direction,' he remarked, and he spat familiarly and sat upon the ground.

'Yet how comes it,' demanded Lin Ho, 'that you, who could not oppose the feeble-minded Wong, should remain unmoved by a display at which the boldest tremble?'

'It is in the nature of things,' replied Lam-kwong. 'It must already be known to you that with so ineffectual a face as this, and all that it implies, subservience and a meek demeanour are forgone. Only one aspect fails to impress me and that is the one you wear, for it having been my own so long I cannot but know the hollowness behind. The contentious Wong may indeed be effete, but I am less familiar with his weakness.'

'What you say is very reasonable,' admitted Lin Ho, 'for from my own angle of observation I have already experienced something of the kind. Since there is nothing to be gained by acrimony let us disclose our minds,' and he related to the other what – up to a certain point – had taken place.

'It is difficult to see that you are much to blame,' admitted Lam-kwong courteously, 'and in any case the involvement sprang from this one's short-sighted gluttony. Had he not coveted the onion that you would have eaten everything might still be going on satisfactorily. Were it not for the thought of you and the now unobtainable Kuei – ' and he fell to pulling out much of his carefully arranged pigtail by the roots.

'Beware of jealousy,' advised Lin Ho. 'Remember it is written, "Not everyone who comes down your street enters by your door." Rather, occupy your mind by disclosing in turn how the High Ones arraigned you before them.'

'That is easily explained,' replied Lam-kwong, 'and they doubtless acted for the best. I must have Passed Upwards at a slightly later period than your own distinguished flight, for as I went up I encountered your high-born Shade descending. After having very properly been kept waiting for a lengthy interval this one was at last called in for sentence. "Lam-kwong," pronounced an authoritative voice, "you have over-ridden the Edict and set the Principles at naught. Your instincts are largely criminal and your tastes obscene. By this last act of violence you have seriously inconvenienced those who keep the Books, for it was not intended that Lin Ho should close his record yet. To reward him for the wrong that has been accomplished he has been returned to an ordinary state of life and given the opportunity to inhabit your body; to punish you in the most offensive way that can be thought of you also will be sent back to earth and in place of your own attractive and courageous frame you will be condemned to take up his. In this manner your defiant and salacious nature will be quelled, whether you like it or not." "Omnipotence," I craved, "before the word goes forth hear an inserted plea : let the judgment be extinction, the sulphur pit, or being transformed into the likeness of one of the lower insects, but not – " "Enough; it is too late," interposed the voice. "The sentence has been written and the ink is dry." I then found myself lying among the rocks and suffering excruciating pain from the wound that I had inflicted upon you.'

'That is no doubt your angle of regarding what took place, but there is certainly another, more acute,' said Lin Ho coldly. 'However, being in that barren place alone and with nothing in your sleeve, by what means did you extricate yourself?'

'Through the night I lay there and nourished my hurt on the dew that fell. Towards the dawn came one seeking, and presently from his rancour and the familiar knowledge of his greeting I recognised in him that ill-conditioned Leung of whom you spoke, come to see that his vengeance was complete. "Much gladness!" exclaimed the misshapen outcast when he discovered me. "Have you eaten your rice?" "What little of it there was," this one replied. "Is it your humane purpose to supplement it with a further portion?" "Will another onion serve?" he inquired smoothly, thus to test the limits of what I knew, and to this, seeing no profit in concealment, I replied, "Assuredly. Being under the direct protection of the gods its venom will pass from me." At that, recognising the frustration of his crafty plan, he disclosed himself without reserve. "If you lie beneath the bosom of the gods, let them suckle you," he scoffed. "See to it that you cross my path no more," and he drove me on with blows. Feeling incapable of raising a defence this person fled as best he could and thenceforward, begging diffidently from door to door, he made his laborious way.'

'Yet what can you hope to achieve by coming here?' demanded the one who had usurped him. 'Nothing awaits you but a place among the band of mendicants.'

'A beggar in these Ways!' exclaimed Lam-kwong, changing colour. 'Not even Lin Ho's face would countenance that. This one, before whom all others quailed, save Fang-tso only!'

'Doubtless,' was the reply, 'but no one fears the bull when he has lost his horns. As regards the one whom you have named I would speak further, for I have cherished an uneasy feeling from the outset that Fang-tso was somewhat beyond our common measure. What passed between you at the last encounter?'

'We two being on a journey alone and in a desert place, I overcame him by a stratagem, and having securely bound his hands and feet I sold him into slavery among a passing tribe of barbarian Khins.'

'That was short-sighted to the last degree,' declared Lin Ho. 'Why, he being in your power, did you not then destroy him?'

Lam-kwong hesitated and would have turned the subject aside by a timely stress of coughing, but Lin Ho took him by the ears so that he could not avert his face and thus compelled the truth.

'I would have done so for several reasons,' admitted Lam-kwong, seeing evasion useless, 'but necessity ordained it otherwise. Fang-tso possessed a certain secret – not of any outside moment but essential to my plans – and this he would not disclose. In the end I bargained with him on a mutually inviolate oath, covenanting his life in exchange for what he told me.'

'This concerns the hidden wealth,' thought Lin Ho instantly, 'but Lam-kwong has now so little left in life that he will inevitably submit to death rather than disclose the spot. Adroitness alone will serve.'

'The private affairs of Fang-tso and of yourself do not engage my mind,' he accordingly remarked, with well-sustained no-interest – for he had also acquired Lam-kwong's duplicity as well as that one's valour – 'but I would gladly learn what form the wealth took that he must undoubtedly have gathered.'

'He has heard nothing so far of Fang-tso's buried hoard,' considered Lam-kwong, more easily deceived than he was wont to be. 'If I can but secure even a short time alone in the beneath-parts all may yet be well.' Aloud he said:

'He spoke more than once in the past of conveying it for

safety to the stronghold of Hsin Foo, a well-walled city in the tranquil south, of which his brother, Hoang, is the governor. If there is no evidence of luxury about, this has assuredly been done.'

'Assuredly,' agreed Lin Ho; 'for all that this place holds would appear to be the wind-sweepings of the city byways.'

'Naturally to a being of your superior tastes such commerce would seem gross,' ventured Lam-kwong. 'Very soon, however, the one before you must turn his reluctant feet upon an outward path, nor has he any trade whereby to earn his rice. If out of the large-stomached forbearance that you must feel for his in every way second-hand condition you would suffer him to carry off in his pack a few poor remnants of unserviceable traffic, he would secure the nucleus of a sordid livelihood, the store would not appreciably be lessened, and your imperishable name would be written in letters of pure gold above the Temple of Munificence.'

'What was begun in friendship should not be wound up in malice,' assented Lin Ho, taking out the keys that he had retained. 'So much as you can bear away upon your shoulder shall be yours.'

'I must contrive to divert Lin Ho from accompanying me,' argued Lam-kwong; 'but to suggest it too abruptly were to raise suspicion,' so he remained silent.

'It is necessary to allow Lam-kwong to work in secret, so that he shall find the treasure,' reasoned Lin Ho; 'though to leave him for no good cause might defeat its end,' and he also held his peace.

Together therefore they reached the opening to the vaults and Lin Ho having unlocked the strong door they would have entered, but at that moment the supple Wong appeared.

'Fearless chieftain,' exclaimed that officious person, 'Tse, of the intrepid mountain band, has ridden in on an urgent rein and seeks your pressing ear.'

'It distresses me beyond measure to leave you so inhospitably at the very outset of your laborious undertaking,' declared Lin Ho; 'but – '

'It grieves me inexpressibly to be deprived of your entertaining society just when I was looking forward to enjoying that

felicity for a further period,' retorted Lam-kwong; 'however – '
And with a mutually appropriate gesture of regret they parted,
the latter person descending to his task and Lin Ho unobtrusively locking the door upon him.

The one described as Tse stood at the outer gate and caressed
his weary horse. He was of repulsive outline, having one eye
only and an ill-cast face, but he seemed upright and he accorded the sign of deference as Lin Ho approached.

'High commander,' was his greeting, 'when they would have
buried alive this person's mother, in that she was an admitted
witch, and your benevolence intervened and spared her, the
one who speaks took an oath to discharge the obligation and
bound himself thereby.'

'Proceed,' encouraged Lin Ho, 'the occasion may fulfil your
pledge.'

'We have a saying, "A word whispered in the ear can carry
a thousand li", and it would doubtless surprise you to know
what details of the private doings of you upper ones reach us.
Howbeit, that is neither caught on a hook nor shot by an arrow,
as the motto goes, but herein lies the gist of it : As this one
kept his station by the Gridiron Pass at daybreak, there came a
wayfarer who pushed on his failing horse, and every time it
stumbled he raised a curse of vengeance against one whom he
did not name outright. Hearing this and seeing him, although
no name was spoken, your menial hid among the rocks and
when that other one had gone he came past him by a secret
way and has conveyed the warning.'

'Wisdom has guided your feet so far,' acquiesced Lin Ho,
well knowing by the indications that the one anathematised
was that Lam-kwong whose form he himself wore. 'Did the
horseman bear no sign by which he might be known?'

'He showed such marks as disclosed that he was escaping out
of bondage,' replied the other. 'But to the robbers of our tribe
his upraised whip-armed hand was a not-forgotten symbol.'

'Fang-tso returned!' uttered Lin Ho beneath his breath, and
Tse bent his head in token, well content that he had done what
he had and that no incriminating name had passed his lips.

'This embodies something of a paradox for it both compli-
cates and simplifies the matter,' remarked Lin Ho, after he had

U.M.—5

stood a while in thought. 'You spoke of encountering him at dawn and avoiding his passage by a hidden track. Thus and thus at what hour may we expect to greet him with our loyal devotion?'

'According to the various influences his ever-welcome feet should reach this gate at a gong-stroke before noon,' replied the brigand.

'You have done well throughout and have all but repaid your oath. One thing alone remains. Achieve that and not only what you set out to effect will have been accomplished but five ingots of the purest will reward your zeal.'

'Though one eye is useless, both ears are copiously alert,' responded Tse. 'Say on, most opportune.'

'In the first place it is necessary that your accomplished and bewitching mother should be here, for my business lies with her.'

'That is easily done,' was Tse's reply, and from a hidden fold of his ample garment he produced a lean grey rat and sat it upon his hand. 'Since the incident referred to, she has generally accompanied me in one shape or another, to be out of harm's way.'

'Filial piety carried to such a length deserves to be set to music,' declared Lin Ho. 'Nothing could be more propitious. Perhaps in the circumstances, as we are unobserved, she would graciously revert to a condition in which mutual conversation will be on a more normal level.'

'That also presents no obstacle.' Tse shook off the docile creature down on to the ground, sprinkled a little salt upon it as he pronounced a magic word, and instead of a rat an aged and unsightly hag appeared before them.

'I have heard all that has been said, high excellence,' remarked the ancient. 'So that it only remains for you to disclose your need.'

'To one of your venerable charm it should not be a weighty matter,' suggested Lin Ho. 'For a certain reason it is necessary that I should leave my ordinary body for a trifling moment and float in the Middle Air at will. Can you ensure me this?'

'If that is all you require,' declared the witch, 'it will involve no eclipse to contrive it. You have seen that this one is in the habit of changing herself into the similitude of various creatures of the lower part as the necessity arises, and for this one way is as well as another. Drink but a single drop of the liquid of this phial and presently a languor will assail you. Under this influence your unfettered spirit will float away at its own volition, free to enter any untenanted shape that it encounters or to return to its own body as it may desire.'

'You have earned a full requital,' admitted Lin Ho, counting the silver to the one who stood by expectant. 'Yet what period spans the pause between the drinking of the potion and the lethargy descending?'

'It can be rated as the time in which an agile man might walk a li,' was the reply. 'May a coronal of shining lights illuminate your hazardous path, esteemed.'

'May the immortal principles of equipoise be maintained within your venerable body,' rejoined Lin Ho, no less agreeably, and they parted.

Had this position been a less ambiguous one Lin Ho would certainly have called upon the shadows of his immediate ancestors to rally to his aid in their strength at this crisis of his fate. In view of the two-sided nature of his being, however, he deemed this to be inexpedient, so that, instead, he devoted the time that he could spare to perfecting his arrangements. It then wanting about two gong-strokes to the hour of noon, he unlocked the strong door of the caves and found Lam-kwong below.

'A few jars of one kind and another, an assortment of rusty iron, and a sundry profusion of rags wherewith to pack the whole,' remarked the one in question, indicating the bale that he had bound with leather. 'A scanty cash or two in the market-place at most, but the limit for these degenerate shoulders.'

'The rewards of industry were ever ill-allotted,' sympathised Lin Ho. 'When you have refreshed yourself at my poverty-stricken board perchance you will be able to sustain more.'

'Alas,' replied Lam-kwong evasively, 'the honour of sitting at the same table with your distinguished self would be so excessive that I should certainly sink under its weight alone. A crust as I go on my uphill way – '

'Should it become known that I allowed so illustrious a guest to depart fasting, the stones of Tsing-te would leap into indignant hands when next I passed,' Lin Ho insisted firmly; and because he was unable to withstand, Lam-kwong yielded.

When they were come to a suitable room, set at a distance from the rest, Lin Ho called for a repast of a generous sort and he also indicated wine. At this Lam-kwong raised a protesting hand.

'For,' he said, 'we have no certainty of what shall thence arise. Should you in consequence become too self-centred to accompany me the acrimonious Wong may resist my going with this bale of stuff and delay me at the gate.'

'That is a point to be considered,' admitted Lin Ho; 'but because leprosy exists there is no reason why one should not enjoy the shelter of a tree. Let Wong attend.'

'I hear and obey, magnificence,' said the voice of the one indicated, as he appeared from around the open door. 'Understanding that a feast was being prepared – '

'In due course a portion shall be assigned,' interposed Lin Ho. 'Meanwhile, feast your ears upon my words. This inoffensive youth will shortly be proceeding on his journey hence. See to it that nothing untoward occurs about our gate. Let neither hand nor foot be stretched in his direction or I who speak will prune their overgrowth. Furthermore, all that he takes is his by special grace and free of any mulct or usage.'

'A line of bowmen shall be drawn up to do him honour,' replied the outrageous Wong, unsettled by the thought of the approaching meat; 'and muted trumpets sound an appropriate march.'

'Take heed lest their office is to play one who shall be nameless towards a hole made in the ground,' remarked Lin Ho with sombre freedom. 'An added duty, keeper of the latch: when our guest shall have departed your charge is that none approaches or disturbs me here on any pretext, for I have deep matters to consider. Now let all withdraw so that we may eat negligently.'

Lam-kwong being eager to get away and Lin Ho no less anxious not to delay the parting their etiquette was neither ceremonious nor involved. The former person, indeed, did not scruple to convey the choicer morsels of each dish to his inner sleeve, and Lin Ho, though he must have observed the movement, forbore to challenge him. Presently, turning aside, he filled two cups with a special wine.

'Let us, as the custom is, pledge our mutual enterprises,' and he pressed one of the cups upon Lam-kwong.

'There is no reason why we should not do so,' replied the other. 'Nor would I stand churlishly aloof were it not that I observed your surreptitious hand to linger somewhat about the cup that you have passed to me.'

'That is a very one-sided view to take,' exclaimed Lin Ho in some annoyance. 'If I wished to effect your end there hangs a trusty sword upon the wall and none to question how or why I use it; though where your unsophisticated death would profit me, the Great Serpent alone knows.'

'Be that as it may,' argued Lam-kwong, ' "It is too late to learn to swim as the vessel sinks".'

'However,' continued Lin Ho resourcefully, 'in order to convince you of your error I will drink the wine myself,' and recovering the cup he did so.

'In that case there can be no harm in accepting yours,' declared Lam-kwong, who was feeling thirsty, and taking Lin Ho's cup he drained it.

'This only goes to show how our natures have become blended, neither maintaining a full share of any quality,' remarked Lin Ho. 'Thus, although I possess your strength I wholly lack your deftness. The skill with which you bound Fang-tso – '

'That is a very simple matter,' contended Lam-kwong, who plainly had not entirely lost his former self-assurance among the milder nature of Lin Ho; 'nor, despite your theory, has this hand grown less proficient.'

'Such a boast is easily maintained across a peaceful table, and the method even traced in spilled wine on the board, but here are ropes and one who will submit his body to the trial. Bind this person so that his strength cannot surmount the bondage and he will forfeit a resolute-minded mule to bear your load, so that you yourself may walk in comfort.'

'There is nothing to be lost in this encounter,' reflected Lam-kwong, 'since – like the fig-tree at Ka-pi's boundary – the fruit is wholly on one side. It would be gratifying to humiliate the egregious Lin Ho, and the mule that he holds out is certainly worth having.' He therefore took up the challenge with alacrity, and, Lin Ho submitting, he bound him hand and foot.

'Now, braggart,' he announced, 'the test is in the balance. Do what Fang-tso failed to achieve and you will deserve a peacock feather in your hat.'

Lin Ho strained at the knots but failed to move them. He rolled his great form from side to side and threw his body into sudden jerks, but nothing would avail. Lam-kwong could not withhold derision.

'Already I seem to hear the hoof-beats of the mule upon the outward earth-road,' was his taunt. 'But give one heave more, princely warrior, and the coils may fly asunder.'

'I must not be pressed for time,' panted Lin Ho, 'for that was not provided. Admittedly the bonds are capably arranged, but, more than that, a strange and sudden lethargy assails me.'

'There is certainly a deficient look about your eyes and your face has gone a very inferior colour,' declared Lam-kwong. 'Perhaps some inward cord at least has yielded. Would it not be prudent to summon an attendant?'

'Should you do so and I am found thus bound and helpless, your priceless body would be piecemeal-sliced before a word is spoken.'

'It is well to bear that in mind,' Lam-kwong confessed. 'However, I can release you,' and he made a movement of advance.

'In that case,' came from Lin Ho very faintly, 'the mule necessarily fades from the engagement.'

'The path of compassion,' remarked Lam-kwong, 'seems beset with sharp-edged borders.' Even as he spoke the magic began to involve him also and he abruptly lay down on the floor. 'This is highly distressing,' he contrived to say. 'The languor of which you spoke is now sapping my forces. What is this spell that has descended suddenly upon us both?'

Lin Ho made no reply. He was already in the Middle Air, watching his opportunity, and before the limit predicted by the witch had passed the spirit of Lam-kwong had likewise left his body.

*

When Lin Ho contrived, through the other person's incapable suspicion, that he should drink the potion first, he recognised that this would give him a sufficient pause of time in which to outwit Lam-kwong. But in this he judged that ill-developed outlaw by a larger helmet than he could ever fill. No sooner did the spirit of Lam-kwong see its own discarded body lying there than it uttered a shriek of triumph and projecting itself through space occupied the empty tenement without a thought beyond the present. At the same moment the spirit of Lin Ho came down and resumed its rightful cover.

'Hai!' exclaimed Lam-kwong, displaying his teeth with all his former arrogance. 'At last the day of vengeance dawns, and your downfall is achieved, O most treacherous Lin Ho!'

'Doubtless,' replied Lin Ho deferentially, as he tore a shred from the bundle by his side and then approached Lam-kwong. 'How is it your enlightened purpose to set about it, omnipotence?'

'When I have enjoyed your terrors to repletion I shall raise my voice and the guard, finding me thus bound and helpless, your offensive body will be piecemeal-sliced before a word is spoken.'

'Perchance,' agreed Lin Ho, and with every indication of humility he pressed the pad of cloth into Lam-kwong's slow-witted mouth. 'Do not distress your already overtaxed throat unnecessarily, chieftain. Presently one will enter and release you. Though,' he added thoughtfully, 'who that one will be and the manner of the release which he effects it would be hazardous to forecast.'

There being nothing now of a helpful nature to detain him, Lin Ho took up the bundle on his shoulder and turned to go, but in response to the message of Lam-kwong's outspoken eye he paused to add a farewell.

'Prosperity, mightiest,' was his unpretentious message. 'Here at last our ways diverge. You remain stretched out in luxury, with a stalwart band of trusty followers responsive to your call. This one sets forth on an unknown path, with nothing between him and penury but the traffic of these simple wares which your forethought has provided. May you live a hundred years and beget a thousand sons!'

Lam-kwong would certainly have said something equally appropriate in reply but he was unable to release the words that filled his throat and the occasion faded.

At the gate the covetous Wong eyed Lin Ho's load aslant,

but the warning laid on him had been too explicit to be disregarded, and with a cheerful saying the well-intentioned guest passed out and on his way.

At a crossing of the road he paused to listen. In the direction of the house of Righteousness Long Established silence hung like the untroubled surface of a tranquil dream, but from the opposite direction there was a sound that caused Lin Ho to press back into a secluded angle of the wall. Presently one came in sight riding upon a careworn horse which he beat with a naked sword. He was of the height and width of two ordinary persons, his teeth jutting forward, and his face like the rising sun when the day portends a storm. As he passed Lin Ho he cleared his throat of a curse against one whom he would very soon encounter. It was Fang-tso returning.

CHAPTER VI

The Ambiguous Face upon the one found in a Wood and the Effete Ming-shu's Dilemma

As Kai Lung told the story of the treasure of Fang-tso the overpowering heat and stupor slowly faded from the day, and when he had made an end of Lin Ho's trials Hai Shin looked up with a much more alertly sustained air than he had before disclosed.

'Certainly the ingenuity of the diffident Lin Ho enabled him to triumph where less crafty means would have left him in subjection,' he remarked. 'Yet, this being a relation of the strategy by which you hope to outwit Ming-shu, explain to my deficient mind how the devices that were appropriate here can be shaped to that contumacious rebel's downfall.'

'Omniscience,' replied Kai Lung frankly, 'it would be bootless to interpose a verbal screen between my very threadbare wit and the piercing rays of your all-revealing vision. The strategy involved in the story of Lin Ho was not that by which Ming-shu may be circumvented but the more pressing detail of how to retain you alive to effect our common purpose.'

'Have you then,' demanded Hai Shin, in a not wholly sympathetic voice, 'no plan whereby to reduce Ming-shu, and is the plea on which you held this one from his pious errand merely an empty boast?'

'Exalted,' was Kai Lung's just reply, 'let your agile mind become an upright balance and weigh this person's claim. The story of Lin Ho was told to a specific end. Up to the moment when he began it, the notoriously incompetent Kai Lung had not so much as heard of that obscure one's being, and each of his successive involvements with its appropriate extrication was contrived from word to word. If, therefore, the one before you can so easily direct the fortunes of a person in whom he has no real concern, is it to be thought that he will fail to involve in destruction the opprobrious Ming-shu against whom he has a very deep-set grievance?'

'There is certainly something to be said for that,' admitted the over-captain, in a more conciliatory manner. 'How then will you set about beginning?'

'That will doubtless be revealed to me at the proper moment by the powerful spirits that are interesting themselves on my behalf,' replied Kai Lung, assured that he had gained his point. 'Even a weed requires congenial soil if it is to fructify, and the one discoursing with you is noticeably short of moisture.'

'In any case it is now too late in the day for me to think about self-ending, my lucky hour being past,' assented Hai Shin; 'so we may as well return to Chi-U together.'

'Your favour will protect me as a mantle, and on the strength of our being seen together I shall doubtless be able to arrange for shelter through the night and an occasional bowl of rice without an actual payment in advance,' was the story-teller's hopeful forecast. 'To-morrow, at an early gong-stroke of the day, I will present myself before your charitable door with a scheme devised to meet the situation.'

'When he specified "together", this custom-regarding person did not presume to imply the honour of going hand in hand,' remarked the other, with an unworthy note of coldness in his tone. 'Here, however, is a piece of money that will support you no less capably,' and at the same time he indicated that Kai Lung should follow at a more respectful distance. 'Let your leisurely footsteps keep time with a well-digesting mind, Kai Lung.'

'Would that your ever-protecting shadow might cover a whole province,' was the response, as Kai Lung shouldered his penurious burden.

*

It was characteristic of Ming-shu's low-minded taste that he had chosen as his stronghold a mountain pass that was inaccessible to force. Although the sides of this retreat were high and precipitous the gorge in which the repulsive outlaw had pitched his camp was too wide for rocks or offensive messages to be hurled upon him from above, while the only portals that the fastness offered – one to the north and the other to the south – were so narrow that two defenders standing there abreast could resist an army.

'This calls for a more than special effort on the part of my sympathetic ancestors if they are not to see their menaced Line dwindle incapably away,' ran the burden of Kai Lung's thoughts when he grasped the position as it then existed, though to Hai Shin, who fanned himself leisurely near at hand, he maintained an unbending face. 'Even if no official band exists, pre-eminence,' he remarked to the one who stood beside him, 'there are doubtless many resolute-minded persons in Chi-U who would not scruple to lend their aid on the side of loyalty and justice once they were assured that it could be prudently achieved?'

'Suffer no derangement of your confidence on that account,' replied the over-captain definitely. 'In this matter of the extermination of Ming-shu's discordant horde we stand on a common footing and each will play an effective part. If you will but involve these chicken-stomached rebels in headlong flight I will lead out a sufficiency of trusty henchmen to desecrate their shrines, pillage their abandoned tents, and stab fatally between the shoulders any who tarry too long about the scene of their undoing.'

'A concrete plan is in the process of being revealed to me by inner sources, but I must have a substantial force behind, even though their tactics are a purely spectacular function,' bargained Kai Lung. 'That much is assured?'

'Short of taking part in actual warfare, blood-thirst in its most intensive guise may be safely looked for,' was the agreeable reply. 'There are not a few among the habitually disinclined of Chi-U who have grown respected and obese in this form of belligerency, they being, indeed, the mainstay of this person and his forerunners in office on those occasions alluded to, when from time to time it has been desirable to anoint the eyes of those higher in authority. Say on, O fount of ingenuity.'

'It is no longer possible to doubt that inspiration decides my path,' exclaimed Kai Lung as his mind sought backwards. 'In Ming-shu and the treacherous Shan Tien, opposed as they are by the empty arraignment of authority, it would be inept not to recognise the two hyenas and an effete tiger so presciently foreshadowed by the soothsayer of Ching; while the hollow sovereignty of a devastated province may be fitly likened to a sick cow's bones. This is the very quintessence of prognostication and all uncertainty must fade and hesitation vanish.'

'So long as you are foreordained to sweep the despicable rabble from our path none will gainsay that inspiration gilds your palate,' assented Hai Shin freely. 'Indicate where we can the fittest lie concealed while you clear out this nest of pirates.'

'Thus and thus shall you act,' began Kai Lung; and he then proceeded to unfold his plan. 'Anything that is still elusive in the way of detail will certainly be communicated by the attendant spirits of my ancestors as the occasion rises.'

'It shall be as you ordain; for, "Tranquillity will roof a house but discord can wear away the foundations of a city",' was Hai Shin's notable admission. 'Lo, minstrel, I go to instruct the apter of the hirelings in the simple parts they have to play.'

*

When, on the morning of the day that next ensued, certain of the rebels were searching the ground that lay between Chi-U and their own ill-conditioned lair, to see if perchance an ambush lurked there (or haply a misdirected duck had opportunely strayed in that direction) the upraised voice of one in torment drew them to a grove of cedars. There nailed by the ears to a tree of suitable girth and standing was he who claimed their pity. He had the appearance of being a stranger from one of the outer-lands near beyond, for his skin was darker than the wont, his hair unplaited but trimmed in a fantastic spread, and his speech mild though laboured. For covering he wore crude cloth of an unusual pattern and his manner was sincere and profuse.

'Here is a fitting target for our barbs,' cried some of the more illiterate of the band, and they would have shot their arrows forth but one who wore a mark of stentority upon his sleeve spoke out.

'It is not thus that refined warfare should be waged among polite and civilised communities,' he cried, 'nor could such an action be logically upheld. Inasmuch as the one before us has been harassed by the foe it is only reasonable to sustain him. If on inquiry we are dissatisfied with what ensues he will still be available for the more gravity-removing spectacle of wading blindfold among pits of boiling water, or being pegged down naked on a stirred-up ant-hill. In the meanwhile, to have taken him alive increases our repute for zeal.'

Accordingly they drew out the spikes that held the stranger to the tree and led him back in triumph to the camp, where presently Ming-shu impeached him in his tent.

'Every detail of your two-faced past and discreditable present is recorded on our unfailing systematic tablets,' asserted the pock-browed outcast, displaying his aggressive teeth in his usual manner, 'so that no defence is lawful,' and he continued to throw about the various weapons that were hung around him so as to confuse the other. 'Now confess your various crimes unflinchingly.'

'Magnificence,' replied the supine captive, 'your lowly thrall – '

'Slave!' interposed the insatiable Ming-shu.

'Your excrescence,' amended he who stood there, docilely. 'Mang-hi my ill-sounding name is and I am of the outer-land of Kham.'

'When I have consumed Chi-U, it is my fixed purpose to reduce Kham to an evil-smelling cinder,' vaunted Ming-shu.

'It is as good as done – at the mere opening of your lordly fiery mouth,' was the confident admission. 'Howbeit, hearing in Kham that the Banners of the Knife had been raised in this our Over-State we held a muster and the lot fell upon me that I should secretly encroach and extricate the truth.'

'Ha!' exclaimed Ming-shu. 'Then are you now an admitted spy. Yet herein lies the obvious falsity of what you say, for if they of Chi-U had caught you thus, not your ears, but your narrow-minded life would have been forfeit.'

'Such was their warm-hearted purpose, highest, and without doubt it would so have been done, but as they led my too unworthy steps towards the roasting-vat, an eagle, a mole, and a tortoise crossed our path. At this manifestation the augurs dare not proceed until the Books had been opened and the Omens searched, whereupon it appeared that the cause of those who destroyed me would be fated from that moment to be ruined.'

'If this is as you say, how comes it then that the elders of Chi-U did not set you free, but rather ensured that you should pass as a captive into our requiting hands?' demanded Ming-shu in slow-witted uncertainty.

'Omnipotence,' replied Mang-hi, not without an element of reprehension in the voice, 'wherefore? Why, but in the hope that you would fall into the snare and yourself incur the doom?'

At the disclosure of this pitfall much of the assurance faded from Ming-shu's dog-like features and he caught several flies to gain time before he spoke again, but when he did so it is doubtful if his heart was single.

'A person of your stunted outlook need not be expected to know the Classics,' he remarked, 'but it is no less truly written, "One cannot live for ever by ignoring the price of coffins", and your case, Mang-hi, is clearly analogous. Sooner or later in the day that powerful thinker, the Mandarin Shan Tien, will wake from his virtuous slumber and then your fate will be decided. Meanwhile' – here the insufferable rebel beat upon an iron gong to summon an attendant – 'you are, except for the formality of being tried, provisionally sentenced to one of the more distressing forms of ending. You, Li-loe, take charge of the condemned, and your head shall answer for his keeping.'

'That, chieftain,' grumbled the mulish Li-loe as he led the captive forth, 'is the only part of me that can ever answer for the others.'

CHAPTER VII

*The Concave-witted Li-loe's insatiable Craving
serves a Meritorious End and Two (who shall be
nameless) are led towards a Snare*

WHEN they were come to a convenient distance from Ming-shu's tent, Li-loe indicated to Mang-hi that they should sit down upon the ground and converse more at their leisure.

'For,' he explained, 'it seldom occurs that nothing may be gained by the interchange of mutual ideas. Thus, for instance, it lies with me, as the one who holds the rope about your neck, to lead you along comparatively smooth paths, for the short time that you are destined to be here among us, or to bring you up sharply against the rock-strewn traverses of my disfavour, and this almost entirely depends upon how you treat me from the outset.'

'Yet if I am to be confined meanwhile, awaiting this high lord's pleasure, how shall the merit of ways or rock-strewn barriers affect our intercourse?' inquired Mang-hi simply.

'It is very evident that you are certainly a barbarian from an outer-land,' replied Li-loe, with an air of superior culture. 'The reference to the prudence of arranging for my priceless friend-ship was in the nature of a primitive analogy that would have been very well understood by a person having the least experi-ence of refinement. As it is, the only path you seem likely to discover is that leading by very short stages to the public execu-tion ground.'

'But surely it ought not to be beyond our united effort to discover a path leading to a discreet seclusion where for a suit-able consideration a jar of wine might shortly be obtained to quench our common thirst.'

'It is scarcely credible,' exclaimed Li-loe, pausing as he scrambled to his feet to regard Mang-hi with a look of wonder, 'that one who is so obtuse at grasping a well-meant suggestion should be so alert in going to the very essence of the matter, as it were unaided. ... What is the full extent of your negotiable worth, O brother?'

'Those who so charitably released me from the tree have already roughly computed that,' explained the prisoner, 'but we of the outer-lands are not prone to wear our taels about our sleeves,' and by a movement which the covetous Li-loe could not satisfactorily follow he produced a piece of money from a hidden spot among his garments. 'Lead on, thou lodestone of moisture.'

When the piece of money had been spent and Li-loe had consumed the greater part of what it purchased, that shameless bandit sought by dropping his voice to a sympathetic cadence to penetrate still farther into Mang-hi's bounty.

'Behold,' he urged, 'between now and the moment of your extinction a variety of things may happen for which you are unprepared, but wherein a trusty friend standing by your elbow and furnished with a few negligible coins to expend on your behalf would be worth his weight in jasper. Reflect well that you cannot carry money with you to the Above, no matter how ingeniously it is concealed about your person, and if you delay too long you will certainly incur the fate that overtook the procrastinating minstrel.'

'It is good to profit by the afflictions of another,' agreed Mang-hi. 'Who was he to whom you so dubiously refer, and what was the nature of his failing?'

'Kai Lung the dog's name was, and this person succoured him as though we had been brothers. Yet in the event he played a double part, for having found a cask of wine concealed among some rocks he shunned this one ever after, so that at the last he came to a friendless and a very thirsty end and his secret perished with him.'

To this recital Mang-hi made no response at first and his head was sunk in thought. Then he looked round with a slowly gathering sense of recognition.

'What you tell me is very unaccountable,' he remarked at length, 'for in some ambiguous way it is woven into the fabric of a dream that has accompanied me about the Middle Air for three nights past. This concerned a barrel of the rarest grape-juice spirit, as large around as three men's arms could span and very old and fragrant. Furthermore one whom I now recognise as you accompanied me.'

'Proceed, O eloquence, proceed,' encouraged the dissolute Li-loe. 'Even to talk about a dream like that is better than to exist in a state of ordinary repletion.'

'Together we searched for this keg of potent liquid, which, be it understood, was hidden from our knowledge ... until we at last came to a rocky valley which I now recognise as this.'

'This!' exclaimed Li-loe, leaping to his feet to regard the gorge with acquisitive eyes. 'And you dreamed the dream three times? Come, O sharer of everything I have, let us explore its length and breadth until you recognise the very rock that guards this treasure. Employ bamboo upon your sluggish mind, O would-be grateful friend; quicken as with a mental goad each fleeting image, and by means of an intellectual crowbar raise the barrier that separates the dimly grasped from the half forgotten.'

'None of these will, alas, avail – ' demurred Mang-hi.

'We will, if necessary, regard each point of the landscape from every variety of angle,' pleaded Li-loe. 'In a dream, remember, you would inevitably be observing what is below from above, whereas now you are regarding what is above from below. Adapt your supple neck to this requisite inversion, comrade. Are we to be duped in the matter of this cask of wine of ours – '

'It fades,' rejoined Mang-hi definitely, 'in that the keystone of the arch is missing.'

'Disclose yourself more fully.'

'When, in the progress of the dream, we reached this valley, we were met here by a being of the inner room whose face was like the petal of a perfumed flower. "Inasmuch as she before you is a mouse," she said with some significance, "she creeps through narrow ways and she alone can lead you to the threshold of what you seek." The vision faded then, but in a camp of warlike men it ensues that no such being – '

'Manlet!' exclaimed Li-loe, casting himself bodily upon Mang-hi's neck and embracing him moistly and repeatedly in the excess of his gladness, 'your lips are honey and the ripple of your voice is like the music made by pouring nectar from a narrow-throated bottle. Such a being as the one you designate *is* here in our midst and this cask of wine of mine is as good as on the spigot.'

'Here in this martial valley!' doubted Mang-hi. 'Who then is the one whose furtherance we need and how may we approach her?'

Before committing himself to speech Li-loe looked round several times and made a displeasing sound among his teeth to imply the need of caution.

'It is necessary to have a thin voice now to escape the risk of a thick ear in these questionable times,' was the modulated warning. 'She whom you describe fills an anomalous position among us, for though a prisoner here, by balancing Shan Tien's rashness against Ming-shu's caution and setting the infatuation of the one against the disinclination of the other, she not only contrives to sway more authority than the leader of five companies of archers but walks along a muddy road dryshod.'

'If she exercises so much rule among the high ones, how can we, being both men of the common sort, hope to engage her ear?'

'Leave that to me,' replied Li-loe vaingloriously. 'Although I have said nothing so far about it – for, after all, what is it to one who has occasionally held an umbrella above the heads of nobles? – when she was known as the Golden Mouse (whence the analogy of her saying to you) this Hwa-mei relied very greatly on my counsel in all affairs, and though she has deteriorated overmuch in the ensuing years she seldom fails, even now, to return my greeting when we encounter. ... I will contrive to cross her path when nobody else is by, but it may be another matter to persuade her to give ear to an Out-land man.'

'As to that,' replied Mang-hi, 'I have thought out something of a plan. I will gather for this purpose a red flower growing on a thorny stem (as she was wearing in the Middle Air) and this you shall give to her saying that the one of whom she has dreamed of late has made his way here to rejoin her. Thus she will be somewhat prepared for what may follow.'

'It may serve,' admitted the short-sighted Li-loe. 'The one thing needful is that you and she should have an opportunity to put your wits together to determine where this cask of mine is hidden.'

'Under the fostering eye of our benevolent authority that should not be beyond our united skill,' was Mang-hi's pronouncement.

*

As Hwa-mei, warned by the sign that Li-loe had been enticed into conveying to her, did not fail to recognise Kai Lung through his disguise it would be obtuse to maintain the figment of Mang-hi's existence any longer. Let it be understood, therefore, that when, later in the day, the summons came and the feeble Li-loe led his prisoner to the tent where Ming-shu and Shan Tien sat in judgment, a movement of the curtain disclosed to Kai Lung that one who was not unmindful of his welfare was there to play a part.

'Before you, High Excellency,' deposed the calumnious Ming-shu, 'is the ferocious brigand chief, Mang-hi, whom a mere handful of our intrepid guard, while peacefully engaged in gathering wild flowers outside the camp, surprised in the act of lurking in a wood, and made captive.'

'They would appear to have picked a very untamed blossom,' remarked the gifted Mandarin pleasantly. 'Why does his misfitting head still disfigure his unbecoming body?'

'Doubtless to afford your all-discerning brilliance the high-minded amusement of deriding the obscene thing,' replied Ming-shu, with his usual lack of refinement. 'To a less degree, it has been judged more profitable to hold the dissipated thug as hostage, rather than dispose of him offhand. Subject to that, he is at the will of your unquenchable sense of justice.'

'Let the perjured transgressor give his own fictitious account of himself, then,' commanded Shan Tien, closing his eyes judicially.

'Greatness,' replied Kai Lung with a submissive gesture, 'my unassuming name and the pacific nature of my journey have already been declared. What more remains?'

'Clearly something, or the contumacious rebel would not be so desirous to conceal it,' interposed a melodious whisper from behind the hangings.

'The difficulty obviously arises, criminal, that being a prisoner here before us it is essential that you should have committed something by which you become imprisonable or the whole of our well-thought-out judicatory system falls to pieces.' Here the inspired law-giver placed the ends of his fingers together in an attitude that never failed to convince even the most hardened of his rigorous impartiality. 'If your naturally retiring mind is not equal to the strain of disclosing what the offence may be it will automatically devolve upon this unworthy but incorruptible upholder of the peace to supply it.'

'Well-spring of authority,' prompted the hidden voice, 'in that the recalcitrant clown has no obvious business here, is not the inference that he is an unusually determined spy reasonable?'

'The imputation that you are an alien intruder seeking to acquire military information occurs to us,' continued the enlightened official tentatively, 'and the crime, punishable as it is with every form of correction from ridiculing your immediate ancestry to extirpating your entire posterity, would serve as well as any. But – '

'As the insensate buffoon has been moving about the district freely, does not the opportunity present itself of enticing him into revealing something of the intentions of our adversary, high intelligence?' came the low-voiced suggestion.

'But in order to incriminate you on this head, felon, it is necessary that something of a definite nature should be allegable against you. The details of our own impregnable position offer no scope for your admitted talent, but doubtless some interesting points in connection with the obvious weakness of the defences of Chi-U have come under your many-sided notice?'

'All-grasping,' was the meet reply, 'the one before you is a man of Kham and Chi-U is of our Over-State. Is it becoming that a vassal should disclose particular information to those in arms against his suzerain?'

'There is marrow in this bone, sublime, if you will but probe it,' was the sage monition. 'The backward oaf has knowledge that he will not readily disclose.'

'That remains to be tested,' muttered the credulous Shan Tien, while Ming-shu, ever insistent, cried aloud:

'Who is this scrofulous Mang-hi that he should speak before a provincial governor and one who is destined to lead the all-conquering Knife to victory of what is or is not seemly? Words fade at nightfall, but a branded sign of guilt upon the forehead endures while life remains. Let the irons be made ready.'

'Benevolence,' entreated the one thus threatened, holding out his hands suppliantly towards Shan Tien, 'is it your august will also that the unwitting should endure so oppressive a correction?'

'Maintain your autocratic upper lip, exalted, and you will yet wrest information of great value from the misgiving knave,' was the whispered counsel.

'The mortar must harden if the wall is to hold good,' replied Shan Tien inexorably. 'Look for no flaccidity in this direction, culprit,' and from outside there came the sound of dry wood being kindled.

In the ensuing pause the captive raised a fold of the garb he wore and drew it across his face, and for a space of time wherein a man might count a hundred, nothing could be heard but the sound of preparation taking place beyond and the offensive beat of Ming-shu's low-class breathing. Then the one arraigned before them bared his face.

'It is contrary to the rites and strict observance of our high rule that the son of a chief's son should submit to this misusage. In our remote upland we have an adage designed to meet most of the contingencies of an ordinary person's everyday experience, and among us it is said, "If when escaping from a dragon you should meet an advancing demon, turn back again".' He lowered his hands submissively and bent an appropriate neck. 'On this understanding, high puissance, ask what you will.'

Shan Tien and Ming-shu exchanged glances of ill-hedged satisfaction and the latter person cleared his self-willed throat.

'In what way is it possible for us to inflict a calamity upon those of Chi-U without incurring any danger to ourselves?' he asked.

Kai Lung thought for a moment, while the others watched him narrowly to see by the changing phases of his emotion whether his disclosure would be sincere.

'The weakness of Chi-U lies in the leanness of its stores, not in any effeteness of its walls or vacillation among its intrepid guard – '

'There is no official band,' interposed the stiff-necked Ming-shu

'Your knowledge is exact,' replied Kai Lung, 'but each man of the city is trained to bear a part, while at no far-off date a strong company of the Tiger-clad is promised in relief.'

'It would be well to make our presence felt before those weak-kneed miscreants impede our footsteps,' remarked Shan Tien with well-arranged anxiety.

'Thus and thus,' explained Kai Lung. 'To-morrow about noon a convoy designed to replenish Chi-U's need will slip through the western gorge. Without knowledge, the chance that you would be there to intercept them is remoter than the clashing of two stars. For this reason there will be no armed guard – for the cities of the route have none to spare. None will be there but the bearers of the loads and drivers, and this you will verify from a distance off before you swoop upon them. Baffled in the hope of this relief Chi-U will succumb and its gates will open to the summon of your lifted hand. Lo, I have spoken, and a noose is round my neck.'

'It is well – or it may be,' was Shan Tien's pronouncement. 'Yet of what does this train consist that it should be worth our while to seize it?'

Ming-shu could not forbear a gesture of despair at the ineptitude revealed by this disclosure, for even to his unbalanced mind it was plain that the essence of the strategy lay in the deprivation of their foe rather than in the replenishing of their own store. He was recalled from this funereal mood by the gross elation of Shan Tien, rejoicing at what Kai Lung unfolded.

'Nothing could be more auspicious, for it is by the lack of these very things that we most suffer: had Chi-U sent a messenger to ask what we would have it could scarcely have been bettered.' (From behind the screen a thread of silver laughter gladdened Shan Tien's fatuous heart.) 'This project carries.'

'How many of our company will the enterprise require?' demanded the more practical Ming-shu.

'Ten or fifteen score of your indomitable horde will baffle every chance of failure.'

'That is as the destinies ordain,' was Ming-shu's guarded

answer; 'for although we may protect the fruit we cannot see the roots. But' – here he bent on Kai Lung a sudden look of menace – 'they will go armed and alert for guile, and you, Mang-hi, will travel in their midst with a gag closing your mouth and your throat chafed by a rope.'

'Yet even then, esteemed, my unfettered mind will be free to dwell on the bright vision of your rising fortune,' replied Kai Lung discreetly.

*

'Ming-shu and Shan Tien were ever of a cast,' pondered the Golden Mouse, 'and, as with a crystal jar, whatever is poured in at the neck can be seen filling the body. Had one come to them, freely offering knowledge, they would have derided his pretension, but now that they have had the appearance of exacting it by force, demons could not dissuade them. Truly it is written, "It is easier to put an ox into an egg-cup than for a man full of conceit to receive wisdom".'

CHAPTER VIII

In which the Position of the Estimable Kai Lung is such that he must either go up or down

AT an arranged gong-stroke after daybreak, three hundred men – one-half of Ming-shu's ill-clad force – marched from the rebel stronghold with Kai Lung in their midst, a gag filling his mouth, his arms bound, and a degrading cord (the noisome Li-loe controlling it) hung about his neck. From the opening of a spacious tent Shan Tien and Ming-shu stood forth to see them pass.

'At the first sign of treachery pull the noose tight and drive a heavily projected knife well between the uncouth shoulders of the repellent outcast,' was Ming-shu's offensive order, and the supine Shan Tien concurred.

'Is it not due to the dignity of your button to be informed how the affair proceeds, mightiness?' enjoined an insidiously alluring voice from the shadow of the tent, and the obtuse Shan

Tien coughed several times and arranged his girdle clasp to indicate high-minded unconcern. 'Li-loe would prove a speedy runner in any case, so that his absence would entail no loss if there should be a fray. Would it not be in keeping with your special office that he should hasten back, either with or without the repulsive-featured hostage as the outcome may require, when the issue has been cast? This one, at any rate, will know no rest until the success of your strategic-minded foray gladdens her yearning ears.'

'It was balanced on my finger-tips to make some such command,' replied the egregious Shan Tien, and he beckoned to a lesser chief and spoke as had been said.

When the band had proceeded a short march to the west, Li-loe, under a pretext, dropped behind the rest and as soon as they were unobserved he removed the gag from the story-teller's mouth.

'It is well enough to talk to you about this wine of mine that we are on the point of recovering,' he said, 'but it would be even more attractive to hear your assurance in reply. Now as regards the exact size of the cask, whereof you spoke of three men's encircling arms? In this respect men vary, yet it would be manifestly unjust to take three of only meagre stature. Last night, on the feigning of a jest, I induced three sturdy fellows to join hands and the full measure ... '

In this strain the niggardly Li-loe filled himself with his own imagination until, about noon, the company reached the border of the rocky terraces that overlooked the plains. Here they lurked in hiding, not daring to emerge until the defenceless nature of the convoy was disclosed, and on this hung Kai Lung's fate. When, soon after the appointed time, a column of unarmed men was seen winding along the track that led towards Chi-U, the rebel host raised a loud cry of triumph and launched headlong forward in pursuit. At this display the assemblage of bearers cast down their loads in terror, and without staying to make any retort whatever fled back to the safety of the intricate passes they had come by. At the same time the horsemen cut loose their charges and urged them incessantly on towards the safety of Chi-U. The effect of the surprise was immediate and complete and Ming-shu's unbridled

horde at once began to take possession of the spoil, for many of
the bales had burst open in their fall and the contents lay scattered.

'There is no longer any doubt as to the success of the foray,'
declared the under-chief to whom Shan Tien had spoken.
'Ordinary warriors Li-loe and Kong are instructed to return
without delay and relate to the High One in Command the outcome of the venture. And should the name of the reticent Ip
Chan be favourably garnished in the telling,' added the one
who thus described himself, veiling his voice discreetly, 'it will
be mutually creative of profitable esteem.'

To this the sombre-mannered Kong made no reply beyond a
servile flourish of his open hand, but Li-loe (distrustful for his
share of what was taken) would have raised a dejected plea had
not Kai Lung contrived to pluck him by the sleeve and whisper
in his ear.

'It is better to have the chance of netting a turbot than to
have already caught a shrimp,' was his admonition. 'Now,
with the camp more or less denuded, is our chance to search
unseen.' And the ever-craving Li-loe assented.

With about half the distance still untravelled they came to a
cleft cut sharply through the rock, where each must pass alone.
It was towards this spot that Kai Lung had shaped his preparation when he had stood in the open space within Chi-U and
called for six intrepid men who should be the standard-bearers
of a righteous cause. 'If there be any who have suffered the
unforgettable offence at the unclean rebels' hands now is the
opportunity to exact a strict account,' he cried, and twelve had
answered to the call. 'Your names will be extolled in characters of gold,' had been his forecast as he made a choice, and
to the remnant, 'and yours no less than these, for to all a part
will in due course be given.' These chosen six now crouched
beyond the rock, and as Kong and Li-loe passed through their
arms were seized and they were held securely.

'The time for dissimulation has gone by,' pronounced Kai
Lung in his natural voice, 'and this business will shortly assume
another colour. Which rogue of the two has the more supple
tongue?'

The only reply Kong deigned was to spit in that direction.

but the pusillanimous Li-loe fell upon his knees and beat the unyielding earth beneath his two-faced forehead.

'All-conquering,' he exclaimed, to the steady clash of his abasement, 'there is no evasion to which I would not bend my pliant throat to retain my worthless life. Lay the weight of your authority upon my allegiant shoulders to practically any extent, for I am not yet fit to face the Records.'

'Not only will your life be spared, but enough wine will be allotted to float you in a state of bliss through three quarters of each moon – if you but play your part.'

'Omnipotence,' declared the other freely, 'on those terms I am with you in this world and the next.'

'Take heed lest you precede me very substantially in both,' was Kai Lung's stern menace. 'It is not befitting that the more abject is the one who must be spared, but yonder dog would maintain a stubborn end at any hazard. Howbeit, he has had the chance and made a becoming choice. ... Now take the un-compromising outlaw to a little space apart and there, with as slight an inconvenience to his distinguished self as possible, remove his attractive head.'

'May your perjured-hearted father grill in Hades to the end of all time and apes void upon the fallen Tablets of your race,' was Kong's farewell parting, and he was led away by those who held him.

'It is enough to recall the worthy Yen-tsu in a similar position – "Blessings will cause a strong town to flourish, but the curses of the vicious cannot destroy even a mud-built wall".' Thus Kai Lung reassured his fellows, and he added, 'Let each now move to his appointed task, and aptly.'

Leaving one of the band to guard Li-loe, the rest fell to their different parts and very soon a transformation had been wrought. One brought Kai Lung a special kind of lye in which he washed off his stain, while another combed and drew out his matted hair and trimmed it as a tail. In place of his out-land garb and barbarian trappings they robed him in everything that Kong had worn and in various ways changed him to that one's likeness. Without much hurt, an appearance of wounds was given to his face and body and blood was splashed both on him and on Li-loe, though it was not deemed necessary to indicate actual violence towards the latter beyond a spear-thrust through the rear part of his trousers. In the meanwhile Kong's severed head had been transformed no less completely, a stain deepening its tone, the hair spread out as Kai Lung's hair had been and the gag forced between his rebellious teeth; nor was the knife withheld to disguise wherein they differed. Thus prepared, the two resumed their journey, Li-loe, at a command, bearing the burden.

'Mightiness,' ventured that feeble person when they were alone again, 'so far a feeling of unworthiness has sealed these slow-witted lips. Yet have we not been as the two sons of one father, with all things shared in common? Now touching this ambiguous head I bear – '

'Peace, dullard,' replied Kai Lung with some dignity; 'for you are as you are and it is very necessary that I should now instruct you. Dwell well on this: that when we approach the camp my wounded face will be all but concealed within this bandage, and, for support, my clinging arm will be about your shoulder.'

'So long as I am by your side, esteemed, you need fear no stumble.'

'So long as you are, I shall not,' was the admission. 'But should you attempt to disengage yourself or to vary what you are to say, I may, perchance, and in slipping this small but extremely pointed knife that I shall hold beneath my cloak and against your middle ribs will inevitably be thrust forward. ... '

'Revered,' protested Li-loe very earnestly, 'I clearly begin to foresee that in whatever tale we are to tell our words will blend together as harmoniously as the two parts of a preconcerted ballad – though between the madness that has assailed you on the one hand and the madness that will certainly assail the blood-thirsty Ming-shu shortly on the other, I see very little likelihood of our song reaching a happy ending.'

'That is because you have a weak, deficient mind or you would have begun to deduce an ordered scheme emerging,' explained Kai Lung more kindly. 'What was in progress when we left the captured spoil, O witless?'

'That is easily expressed,' was the overcast reply. 'The sordid-hearted crowd were seizing what they could. The greater part of this by some mischance consisted of the dress and insignia of a strong company of the Imperial guard and the ragged barefoot crew were triumphantly refitting.'

'Thus,' agreed Kai Lung. 'And by a benevolent conjunction of the time and place they will return at nightfall waving the captured banners of authority and wearing the Tiger-garb. How regrettable will be the outcome if Ming-shu, having heard our tale of treachery and rout, should mistake them for the foe and fall upon them in the darkness unaware!'

'Stripling,' declared Li-loe with a gathering look of insight, 'what I hitherto took to be an empty shell would seem to enshrine a solid kernel. Yet this scheme of yours must proceed along the razor-edge of chance, so that a single false step will undo it.'

'The same path confronts those who oppose us also,' replied Kai Lung, 'and Ming-shu and Shan Tien are notoriously uncertain on their feet. For the emergencies that may arise, remember that it is better to have an ingenious mind than a belt adorned with weapons.'

'In the circumstances there is nothing unreasonable in disclosing that I too have long nourished a secret ill-bred grudge against the obtuse Ming-shu,' declared Li-loe profusely. 'We go therefore hand in hand.'

'Truly,' agreed Kai Lung. 'Yet it would be as well not to forget meanwhile that the unusually sharp-tempered knife to which this person has already reluctantly referred will still be grasped in the other.'

*

When Ming-shu and Shan Tien learned of the crafty snare in which one half of their followers had perished, and had seen the offensive head of the profane Mang-hi, it is questionable which of the two expressed himself with less regard for the pellucid style of the Higher Classics. The former person indeed had become so involved in a complicated analogy based on Mang-hi's remoter ancestors, that Li-loe, urged on by something that he felt rather than saw, did not deem it unwise to interrupt him.

'Thereafter, High Excellences,' he continued, 'lurking together in a cave we overheard their truculent war lords conferring. "Let us," proclaimed the highest in command, "seek out this misbegotten nest of lepers, led by a weak-kneed upstart, and put them to the sword. The feeble-witted earth-worm thus described" (so ran his veracious words, nobilities) "can no longer have anything beyond a cringing remnant answering to his call. Added to this, we will so contrive that dusk shall mask our coming and the surprise will be complete." To this they all agreed, rejoicing, and seeing that the assembly had begun we crept away unseen.'

'Wisdom guided your feet,' murmured the recreant Shan Tien, after he and his Chief of Military Arrangements had engaged each other in a somewhat lengthy silence. 'To retire unobtrusively is often the most unspeakably galling form of contempt with which it is possible to treat a despised antagonist. ... The Way is still open to the north, and clad as two wandering pilgrims – '

'Mandarin,' interposed Ming-shu, in a not entirely grateful voice, 'when the path is slippery it is safer to go two paces forward than one pace back. In the words of the not wholly felicitous apophthegm, we who stand here banded together are wedged in between the Head Evil Spirit and the illimitable Whang Hai. ... Not even a sightless mendicant would take either of us for anything but a steady eater.'

'High Presences,' came a meek but very attractive voice from somewhere unseen, 'is it permissible for so small and abject a person as myself to whisper in your weighty ears?'

'Speak,' was the grudging assent. 'Even a gnat may disclose a hidden point somewhere.'

'What is this sudden misgiving that has for the moment eroded your usually large-hearted stomachs?' exclaimed Hwamei reliantly. 'The valiant Ming-shu was undoubtedly correct when he spoke of the danger of going back and the ever-prescient Shan Tien was no less inspired when he shrank from the repugnant thought of pressing forward.'

'Thus and thus,' rose from Ming-shu's acrimonious throat. 'That leaves us where we are.'

The Golden Mouse struck her symmetrically formed hands together with a refined gesture of well-expressed relief.

'Ming-shu has gone to the very nucleus of the matter and

plucked the ill-set words from my all-too-loquacious mouth,' she exclaimed. 'As he so epigrammatically insists, this is the spot on which to meet the uninventive foeman and overreach him.'

'Haply,' conceded Shan Tien, with a hasty assumption of one of his most telling magisterial bearings, 'but the versatile Arranger of Martial Exploits did not carry the analogy to the extent of revealing how the suggested snare is to be effected.'

'Truly,' agreed Hwa-mei; 'your mind is like a crowded storehouse and unheard-of wisdom drops from your ripe lips in masses. ... As the Inscrutable was on the point of saying, the obvious way to baffle the frozen-witted interloper is to turn the looked-for surprise on his part into an even greater astonishment on ours.'

'Doubtless,' was Ming-shu's sombre comment; 'and having thus exposed the far-seeing Mandarin's inner thoughts, would it be too excessive a labour to penetrate a little deeper into the rich mine of strategy and disclose a specific detail?'

'The deduction is inexorable,' replied Hwa-mei, with a delicately balanced look of gratitude at both together. 'When the loathsome marauders seek to creep up at the dusk of evening they will find nothing interposed between them and success. The paths will be unwatched and the sentry of the gate engaged in the insidious charms of fan-tan elsewhere. Half, perchance, of the offensive crowd will have passed in and be assembled when our one heavily loaded but never so far discharged weapon of assault will be exploded in their direction. At the same preconcerted moment a chosen band concealed in the heights outside will loosen an avalanche of rock down upon the throng lurking beyond the gate. When the confusion is at its zenith our intrepid host will launch itself against the unsightly rabble and the distressing affair will be all but over. Was not that, Highest, the trend of your enlightened meaning?'

'Crudely expressed, you have indeed struck the skewer on its business end,' admitted Shan Tien, rising. 'Where is this person's most terror-inspiring suit of armour laid?'

Ming-shu made no remark, but he left the tent with a settled look and presently his two-edged voice could be heard emitting orders.

Kai Lung was meanwhile seated on a high place apart, with

his arm still cherishing Li-loe's support. Hwa-mei went from point to point, speaking hopefully to the various defenders of the camp and inspiring them to put up a stubborn resistance to the end. Thus the afternoon was worn away and the time of Middle light arrived.

*

The battle of Running Mandarin Valley (as, for some reason, those who were there have designated it) has been so often described in terms of literary perfection that it would be almost profane for this attenuated brush to attempt its details. It is generally admitted that the mutual surprise of all concerned might have been less effective had not certain of Kai Lung's most intrepid followers imperceptibly joined the returning throng under cover of the withdrawing light and at the first shock of attack raised the enlightening cry, 'Treachery is here at work and the camp has, in our absence, been carried by assault. Let us retake it at any hazard!' From that stage onward every man on both sides fought with the tenacity of vampires, so that when Hai Shin, somewhat later, ventured to lead in a hastily collected bodyguard by the neglected northern gate, with the avowed intention of 'obliterating as with a sponge the embers of rebellion', he found none to bar his passage. So evenly matched had been the two divisions of the force – the opening assault on the part of the defenders being exactly balanced by the superiority of the weapons with which the others had been refurnished – that from the outset a common extinction was the only logical and possible solution. So harmoniously was this accomplished that in practice every ordinary warrior slew every other ordinary warrior, every stripe-man every other stripe-man, every under-chief every other under-chief, and thus and thus up to the two overlings of the two contesting sides whose bodies were found locked together in a tiger-like embrace. Ming-shu and Shan Tien alone survived (owing to both remaining), together with Kai Lung, Li-loe and the Golden Mouse – these latter not being officially 'in the vigour' as the melodious phrase of military usage has it. It is owing to this unshrinking demonstration of the Essential Principles of Poise and Equipoise, leading up by an inexorable chain of uncontroversial subordinates to the only rational and

conceivable termination, that this otherwise commonplace encounter is so often given as a subject for antithetical treatment
in the triennial competitions.

When the last person had been killed on either side Kai Lung
made his way to Ming-shu's tent, confident of coming face to
face with that opaque-eyed usurper and of wringing from him
an admission of his ill-spent life before he Passed him Upwards.
For this purpose the story-teller, who still wore the habiliments
of Kong, had removed the covering from his face, and he had
rearranged his hair as Mang-hi's had wont to be and resumed
some of that warrior's trappings, so that he might the more
readily convince Ming-shu of his knowledge of those matters.
In this the destinies intermingled to an unexpected close, for no
sooner had the conscience-haunted rebel discovered the one
who sought him, standing in the admittedly deceptive light of
the great sky lantern outside the open door, than he threw up
his abandoned hands effetely and sank down to the floor.

'Behold,' he exclaimed in an uncertain voice, 'when an
event of this sort happens it is no longer profitable to deny that
the one subsiding here has spent a thoroughly abandoned life
and practised every sort of infamy. Kai Lung has been pursued
relentlessly in the past and is now doubtless Beyond; Kong
has been struck down in this one's service, maintaining a dis-
loyal cause, and he has obviously Gone Up, while Mang-hi's
picturesque head is at this moment somewhere about the tent.
That these three industriously disposed persons should spare
their priceless time to appear in a composite Shape before me
pithily indicates that I have nothing more to hope for.' Ming-
shu accordingly loosened the hold by which he maintained his
Constituent Elements together and his liberated Shadow at
once set off towards the Upper Air.

The agreeable-minded Mandarin Shan Tien was never exactly
seen again by any actual person. On this account it has sometimes been claimed that he must have thrust himself into the
most fiercely contested quarter of the battle and there been cut
to pieces. Others, however, contended that rather than suffer
the indignity of so important an official being touched by the
profane hands of those inferior to his button, the High Powers
had invited him to Pass Above without going through the

ordinary formalities of defunction. At a later period an unworthy rumour was wafted about the province that an impressive personage, who was liable in any emergency to assume
a richly magisterial manner, was in the habit of making a desul-
tory livelihood in a distant city by picking up articles of apparent value before the eyes of wealthy strangers. But this can
only be regarded as being in the nature of a craftily barbed
shaft from the invidious lips of malice.

· CHAPTER IX

Wherein the Footsteps of the Two who have induced these Printed Leaves assume a Homeward Bend

NOTHING could exceed the honourable distinction with which
Kai Lung was greeted by all classes of those dwelling about
Chi-U after the destruction of the rebel host. The lean and ex-
pectatious were never weary of professing their readiness to
consume an unspecified abundance of rice spirit to the accompaniment of a hope that the story-teller's sinews would be
thereby strengthened, and no matter how urgent might be the
business on which he was engaged, rich merchants did not disdain to stop him repeatedly as he went about the Ways to enjoy
the gladness of shaking hands with themselves before him.
Some of the actually charitable expressed a willingness, in view
of the obviously threadbare state of the one with whom they
conversed, to supply him with the needs of life at an appreciably lower rate than was usually imposed on strangers, and on
Kai Lung displaying the empty folds of his deficient sleeve a
special edict of the Chi-U Confraternity of Impost Adjusters
was issued, permitting him to pass round his collecting bowl at
any time without being liable to any humiliating regulations.
   But among the marks of approval showered upon Kai Lung
that devised by Hai Shin was perhaps the most delicately arranged of all. In some obscure way unknown to the artless
over-captain himself, the valour displayed by Hai Shin, so
soon after the taking of the camp that it imperceptibly merged
into the forefront of the battle, had reached the ears of his

higher-lords in office, and to mark appreciation of the economical way in which he had conducted the affair throughout he had been raised to the position of under-overling, with authority to command six hundred warriors and permission to carry a green silk umbrella when on duty. Not to be outclassed disinterested persons in Chi-U had suggested to others that to entice the unsuspecting Hai Shin into an assembly and there to weight his sleeve with a bag of silver would be a suitable return for their deliverance.

'So that,' explained Hai Shin, on the morning of the day in question, 'after this person has recovered from his bereft-of-words surprise, and has suffered the one seated upon a chair to compel acceptance of the tribute, there will ensue a more or less unpleasant gap before dispersing, to be filled up as inoffensively as can be. If, therefore, you could be induced to lift up your always harmonious voice it would relieve the admitted tension, and at the same time, without any actual outlay to yourself, you would be privileged to witness the interesting ceremony from one of the foremost benches. Nor should it be ignored that early rice, enhanced by a reasonable allowance of health-giving raisin wine, will be provided.'

'It suffices,' replied Kai Lung gracefully; 'and since a virtuous outcome could never have been reached without the miraculous protection of the watchful spirits of my ancestors, the mediocre story chosen for this seasonable occasion will be that which concerns Kin Weng.'

THE STORY OF KIN WENG AND THE MIRACULOUS TUSK

In the golden days of the enlightened dynasty of Ming a company of artificers who have remained illustrious throughout all later time dwelt about the Porcelain Tower in the city of Tai-chow. Their crafts were many and diverse, there being workers in gold and silver, in jade and precious stones, in wood, in lacquer and the various lustres, even in brass, leather, horn and material of the cruder sorts on which the resource of their inspired art conferred an enhancing grace, but most highly esteemed among them all were those who carved ivory with patient skill and cunning lore and of this favoured band Chan Chun was the admitted head.

For many years Chan Chun had dwelt beneath the gilt sign of The Conscientious Elephant, gathering in honours with his right hand and the more substantial profits with his left, until nothing that an ordinary person could desire lay outside his grasp; but whether this unvarying prosperity was due to the directing efforts of good Beings, or whether Chan Chun was in reality the sport and laughing-stock of malignant Forces, who, after the too-frequent manner of their kind, were merely luring him on through a fancied security to an end which should be both sudden and inept, cannot yet be suitably revealed. Nevertheless, it is aptly written, 'The reputation through a thousand years may depend on the conduct of a single moment', and Chan Chun was no magician to avoid the Destinies.

As befitted his position, Chan Chun had an underling whose part it was to do the more menial service of his task. This youth, who bore the unassuming name of Kin and the added one of Weng, had thus long been accustomed to shape the blocks of ivory in their rougher state, to impart an attractive polish to the finished work, and to apply appropriate pigments in cases where the exact representation might otherwise have been in doubt. He also removed the evidence of toil and re-stored the work-room to a seemly state of order at the earliest beam of light on each succeeding day, sharpened the tools that had been in use and reassembled them on an appointed plan, bargained with tribes of beggars (when they were too numerous to be expelled by force) as to the price of an agreed immunity, intervened with reasonable excuses of Chan Chun's absence, infirmity or, if necessary, death, before those who presented themselves inopportunely, and the like. Yet in spite of the ad-mittedly low-conditioned nature of his duties Kin was of a sincere mind and a virtuous heart. Next to his own immediate ancestors he venerated the majestic carvers of the past, while to Chan Chun he gave an unstinted admiration, hoping that one day he might follow unostentatiously and at a sufficiently respectful distance in his master's well-established footsteps. Every moment that could be snatched from the rigorous exercise of his unremunerative task he spent towards the attainment of this end, either in a contemplation of The Symmetrical or by making himself more proficient in the practice of the art, using for this purpose Chan Chun's discarded tools and such scraps of ivory as he himself might legitimately throw away and then pick up again. Thus the seasons passed, but Chan Chun saw in Kin only the one who served his hand.

To the south of Tai-chow lay a dense and pathless forest wherein might be found every kind of wild growth which the soil of that province could sustain. Recognising in the harmonious contrasts afforded by this profusion all the essentials to a style of classical purity, Kin was in the habit of resorting to these glades in order to imbibe the spirit of their influence. Too often the few hours which the parsimonious usage of the exacting Chan Chun allowed were only sufficient for a meagre contemplation of the outer fringe, but sometimes, on a sufficiently convincing plea or during that one's absence, he was able to secure a longer respite.

It was on one of these occasions, when he had penetrated more deeply into the funereal recesses of the wood, that Kin (guided admittedly by the protecting shadows of his grateful ancestors) reached a grassy place, sufficient in extent to tax the skill of an expert bowman to shoot across. In the opening thus provided stood an ancient pagoda, its pinnacle merged among the branches of a spreading cypress tree, within whose shade a maiden of engaging personality sat in an attitude of graceful unconcern as she arranged her abundant tresses.

'Plainly there are things which I am yet ignorant of, in spite of a lifelong contemplation of The Symmetrical,' remarked the youth aloud. 'Here are three objects as widely differing in their forms as a maiden, a venerable pagoda and an overhanging cypress tree, yet each fully conforms to the most rigid standard of a classical perfection nor is any one less harmonious than another. In view of the frequently expressed apophthegm that all Art is a matter of selection, to find these three, among which it is impossible to distinguish any one as pre-eminent, within so narrow a limit as a woodland glade introduces an element of doubt.'

'Such words would seem to indicate a student of the Higher Excellences,' remarked a sympathetic voice, and turning, Kin perceived, close at hand, one who had all the appearance of an elderly philosopher. 'Doubtless you are a person of some literary attainment, qualifying for the Competitions?'

'Far from that being the case, my occupation is wholly menial in its ignoble outlook, nor does the future stretch beyond to-morrow's toil,' replied Kin freely. 'If, therefore, your agreeable condescension sprang from a mistaken cause do not hesitate to continue our discourse in your ordinary voice.'

'On the contrary,' replied the other affably, 'I would willingly learn somewhat more of your condition. As you unsuspectingly approached this spot, I cast the outline of your destiny according to the various signs you bear. Although I possess certain supernatural powers I am not really proficient in this branch of geomancy and my only thought was to obtain a trifling practice, but to my surprise I found that in some unaccountable way the lines of our future destinies converge.'

'Even a snail can fly through space if it attaches itself to a dragon's tail,' replied the unpretentious Kin, and thus encouraged he willingly laid bare the mediocre details of his threadbare life. When he had finished the stranger continued to regard him narrowly.

'A noticeable career of one kind or another certainly awaits you, although my meretricious skill is unfortunately not profound enough to indicate its nature,' he remarked benignantly. 'Rest satisfied, however, that henceforth I shall certainly be exerting my unnatural powers in your direction.'

'If the destiny is already assured, might it not more prudently be left wholly to the more experienced Forces?' suggested Kin cautiously. 'You have spoken of your efforts in terms which indicate that the outcome of their use may prove somewhat disconcerting to the one on whose behalf they are invoked.'

'Do not nourish any misgiving on that account,' replied the philosopher with a reassuring smile. 'Certain things lie beyond my admitted power it is true, but I could, without inconvenience, change you into an edible toad or cause a thick growth of fur to cover you from head to food by the exercise of a single magic word. If you doubt this – '

'By no means!' exclaimed Kin hastily. 'Your authoritative word puts me entirely at my ease. Yet as the acrimonious Chan

Chun will by this time have discovered an empty stool I will, without further attention of your precious moments, walk backwards from your lordly presence.'

'You have been honourably welcome to my feeble entertainment, which henceforth you can associate with the obscure name of Cheung,' courteously replied the one who thus described himself. 'In the meanwhile, frequent indications of my protecting hand will disclose themselves from time to time to preserve intact the silken thread of your remembrance.'

'If the suggestion should not be deemed too concise, a favourable occasion will present itself when the one upon whose bounty I depend stands at the gate to welcome my return.'

'The occasion is befitting,' replied Cheung graciously, 'and a timely intervention shall arise. Furthermore, in order to guide you through the forest by an unknown path – one more suited to your present haste – Fa Ming, the sole remaining blossom of my attenuated tree, shall, in a suitable guise, precede you on your way.'

With these auspicious words the venerable personage raised his necromantic staff and waved it towards the maiden who was still engrossed in the arrangement of her glossy hair before a shield of burnished copper. Immediately she disappeared and in her place there stood a sleek white bird intent on preening its resplendent plumage. When Cheung again made a magic sign, however, no further manifestation took place, the shapely creature remaining immersed in a gratified contemplation of its own attractions. A faint line of annoyance corroded the austere smoothness of the philosopher's brow.

'It is one thing to turn ordinary persons into the semblance of apparitions of a different part, but it is quite another to induce them to preserve the unities in their new habit,' he remarked, with engaging frankness, towards Kin's ear. Indeed, the graceful being continued to regard itself approvingly from one angle after another, despite the formidable magic projected against it by the persistent waving of Cheung's all-powerful staff, nor was it until, in an access of engendered bitterness, the painstaking wizard cast the wand violently in its direction, that the one whom he had referred to as both the Hand and the Foot of his declining years began to bend her acquiescence towards his wishes. Thenceforward, however, her amiable compliance did not falter and she hovered continuously before the grateful Kin, guiding him along a secret track so that presently he came clear of the forest at a point much nearer to Tai-chow than the most skilful woodfarer might have found possible.

It was not long before Kin encountered what might reasonably be accepted as a token of Cheung's sustaining care. In the few hours that spanned his absence from its walls a great caravan of merchants had reached the city from the Outer Lands and filling the narrow Ways with laden beasts and hurrying slaves were even then vying with each other to extol the richness of their wares and to announce at what resort their commerce should be sought. Some, more zealous than their fellows, did not halt to shake out their sandals and partake of tea, but pressed forward without pause to offer the enticement of an early choice to those whose custom they esteemed. Thus it befell that at the gate before The Conscientious Elephant a laden camel stood while a sombre attendant, who restrained its impatience by means of a cord passed through its nose, from time to time spoke of his master in terms of unfavourable comparison with the Keeper of the Pit.

'Prosperity attend your gracious footsteps,' remarked Kin in polite greeting (and also because he wished to learn their purpose there) as he raised the latch. 'The Street called Fragrant is honoured by your restful shadow.'

'It would not be, had not a misbegotten planet of the unluckier sort been in the ascendant at the moment of this person's ill-timed birth,' replied the attendant darkly. 'Is it not enough to have toiled across a self-opinionated desert, leading this perverse and retaliatory daughter of two she-devils by an utterly deficient cord, without being compelled to wait interminable gong-strokes in a parched and plague-infected byway of Tai-chow while the rest-house of the Garden of Musical Virtues spreads its moist allurement but a short span farther to the east?'

'Your well-expressed offence causes the strings of my compassion to vibrate in harmony,' replied Kin with genial sympathy. 'Who is he who has thus misused your forbearance and what is the nature of his errand here?'

'Pun Kwan is his repulsive name – may the stomach of a Mongolian crow prove to be his tomb! From the Outer Land of Zam are we come with a varied commerce of the finer sort, so that, forestalling the less grasping of our band, he now seeks to make a traffic of six horns of ivory to the one within.'

'My ineffectual voice shall be raised on your behalf,' said Kin, as he passed on. 'Do not despair: the fiercest thunderstorm is composed of single drops.' With this amiable pledge, however, he merely sought to end the conversation in a manner congenial to the other's feelings, for his own hopes did not extend beyond entering unperceived. In this (aided, doubtless, by the exercise of Cheung's secret magic) he was successful; the upraised voices of two, each striving to outlast the other, revealed that the hazard of the bargain was still in progress in a farther room, and Kin reached his bench unchallenged. Then, as if a controlling influence had been lifted when this effect was gained, Pun Kwan and Chan Chun began slowly to approach, the former person endeavouring to create the illusion that he was hastening away, without in reality increasing his distance from the other, while the latter one was concerned in an attempt to present an attitude of unbending no-concern, while actuated by a fixed determination not to allow Pun Kwan to pass beyond recall. Thus they reached Kin's presence, where they paused, the sight of the outer door filling them both with apprehension.

'It were better to have remained through eternity in the remote desert of E-ta, leaving these six majestic tusks to form an imperishable monument above our bones, rather than suffer the corroding shame of agreeing to accept the obscene inadequacy of taels which you hold out,' declared Pun Kwan with passionate sincerity. 'Soften the rebellious wax within your ears, O obstinate Chan Chun! and listen to the insistent cries of those who call me hence with offers of a sack of rubies for six such matchless towers of ivory.'

'If,' replied Chan Chun, with equal stubbornness, 'I should indeed, in a moment of acute derangement, assent to your rapacious demand of a mountain of pure silver for each of these decaying fangs, the humiliated ghosts of an unbroken line of carving ancestors would descend to earth to paralyse their degenerate son's ignoble hand. Furthermore, the time for bargaining has passed, thou mercenary Pun Kwan! for pressing forward in the Ways behold a company of righteous merchants, each proffering a more attractive choice for less than half the price.'

Before Pun Kwan could make a suitable reply there came from beyond the walls the sound of one who raised his voice at dusk. It was the evening chant of the cameleer, who, after the manner of his tribe, had begun to recite his innermost thoughts, in order to purify his mind before he slept. After listening to the various analogies in which his name was blended, Pun Kwan's expression gradually took upon itself a less austere cast.

'It is not unaptly written, "When the shield is bent the sword is also blunted", and neither person can reproach the other with a lack of resolution,' he remarked pacifically. 'Added to this, we are but men of natural instincts and must shortly seek repose.'

'Say on,' replied Chan Chun, as the other waited for his acquiescence. 'Provided that a mutual tolerance is involved this one will not oppose you with a brazen throat.'

'Let the price be thus and thus, so that my unattractive face shall suffer no compression, while your enlarged munificence will be extolled. Then to the balance of my offer will I yet add another tusk, freely and devoid of charge. By this, each shall seemed to have profited at the other's expense though neither is the loser.'

'Perchance,' assented Chan Chun doubtfully. 'But touching that same added tusk – '

'Admittedly the six cannot be matched, did one comb the forests of the land of Zam and pass all matter through a potter's sieve. Seen side by side with these any other tusk deceives the eye and takes upon itself an unmerited imperfection. Is it not truly said that what is gold by night – '

'That which needs so much warming up may as well be eaten cold,' observed Chan Chun in a flat-edged voice. 'Behold the scales and an amplitude of silver bar. Let the promised tusk appear.'

Thus challenged Pun Kwan withdrew and presently returned with an object which he bore and set before Chan Chun. For an elaborate moment the ivory carver was too astonished even to become outwardly amused (a poise it had been his previous intention to assume), for the tusk was of an ill-shapen kind never before seen by him or any other of the craft. It was of stunted form, gnarly and unattractive to the eye and riven by some mishap while yet in growth, so that it branched to half its length.

'What infirmity contorts your worthy sight and deflects your natural vision from its normal line, O scrupulous Pun Kwan?' said Chan Chun indulgently. 'This is not a tusk of ivory at all but doubtless the horn of some unseemly buffalo, or of one of the fabled monsters of the barbarian Outer World. This should go to those who fashion drinking cups from commonplace bone, who dwell about the Leafy Path, beyond the Water Gate.'

'Peace, brother,' said Pun Kwan reprovingly. 'To revile my wares is in the legitimate way of fruitful bargaining, but to treat them as a jest assails the inner fibre of one's self-esteem. Is there not justice in the adage, "Eat in the dark the bargain that you purchased in the dusk"? The tusk is as it is.'

Alas, it is truly said, 'If two agree not to strive about the price, before the parcel is made up they will fall out upon the colour of the string,' and assuredly Pun Kwan and Chan Chun would very soon have been involved as keenly as before had it not been for an unexpected happening. Ever concerned about the smallest details of his art, Kin had drawn near to mark the progress of the conflict and to lend a stalwart voice to his master's cause if Chan Chun's own throat should fail him. Judge then the measure of his wonder when in the seventh tusk he at once recognised the essential outline of the fair white bird as it hung poised above the path before him! Misshapen as the ivory seemed for the general purpose of the carver's art it was as though it had been roughly cast for this one service, and Kin could no longer doubt the versatile grasp of Cheung's fostering hand.

'A word in your far-seeing ear, instructor,' he said, drawing Chan Chun aside. 'If the six are worthy of your inspired use do not maintain an upper lip rigid beyond release. This person has long sought to acquire a block sufficiently ill-formed to conceal his presumptuous lack of skill. This now offers and in return for a tusk of admittedly uncouth proportions he will bind himself to serve your commanding voice for four hand-counts of further moons and ask no settled wage.'

'It suffices,' replied Chan Chun readily, seeing a clear advantage to himself. 'Yet,' he continued, with a breath of slow-witted doubt, 'wherein, at so formidable an obligation, can this profit you whose reputation does not reach any higher than the knee of a sitting duck?'

'The loftiest mountain rises gradually at first,' replied Kin evasively. Then, on the excuse that the auspices of Chan Chun's purchase required the propitiatory discharge of a string of crackers, he withdrew, to venerate his ancestors anew.

As the days went on it grew increasingly plain to Kin that he was indeed under the care of very potent Forces, while the likelihood of Cheung's benevolent interference from time to time could not be ignored. Despite the unworthy nature of the scanty tools he used and the meagre insufficiency of light remaining when Chan Chun's inexorable commands had been obeyed, the formless block of ivory gradually took upon itself the shining presentment of a living bird. When any doubt assailed Kin's mind as to the correct portrayal of a detail, an unseen power would respectfully but firmly direct his hand, and on one occasion when, with somewhat narrow-minded obstinacy, he had sought to assert himself by making an inaccurate stroke too suddenly to be restrained, the detached fragment was imperceptibly restored while he slept.

It was at this period of its history that Tai-chow reached the cloudy eminence which marked the pinnacle of attainment among the illustrious arts. The provincial governor, an official of such exalted rank that it entitled him to wear a hat with a yellow feather even when asleep, returned after a long absence to gladden the city with his presence. To indicate the general satisfaction and at the same time allow the prevailing excess of joy to evaporate in a natural and, if it might be, painless manner, mutual feasts were given at which those most proficient in the sonorous use of words were encouraged to express themselves at various lengths upon whatever subject most concerned their minds. When by these humane means the city had been reduced to a normal state of lethargy, the Mandarin Tseng Hung (the one referred to) testified his enduring interest in the welfare of the company of craftsmen by a proclamation and a printed sheet displayed on every wall.

'He is a peacock among partridges, the one who rules our laws, and will doubtless become the founder of a promiscuous line of kings,' exclaimed Chan Chun vaingloriously, on his return from the market-place where he had listened to the reading of the edict. 'Has any rumour of the honour now fore-shadowed to the tree of Chan already reached my usually deficient home?'

'None save a resolute collector of the bygone water dues has crossed your polished step,' replied the chief one of his inner room. 'Is then your fame proclaimed again, thrice fortunate Chan Chun?'

'Not in so many explicit words,' admitted the unbecoming Chun, 'but the intention cannot be obscured. Thus is the matter set forth at ample length: On a certain agreed day any crafts-man who dwells about Tai-chow, or even within the shadow of its outer wall, be he worker in the finer or the cruder sorts of merchandise, may send the most engaging product of his hand to the Palace of the Lustres, to be there beheld of all. Chief among these will come the enlightened Mandarin Tseng Hung himself, wearing his fullest robe of ceremonial state. After glancing perfunctorily at the less attractive objects ranged about the Hall he will stop with an expression of gratified ad-miration before the one bearing the sign of Chan Chun and the seal of the Reverential Company of Carvers in the Hard. Then to an accompaniment of laudatory trumpets he will an-nounce this to be worthy of the chief reward – and doubtless soon after that retire, leaving the disposal of inferior honours to integritous but needy Young Brethren of his suite.'

'Haply,' remarked a shrewd maiden who was present, one who did not venerate Chan Chun, 'yet the Wisdom has de-clared: "It is easier to amass a fortune in a dream than to secure ten cash by the light of day". By what inducement do you hope to sway the strict Tseng Hung, thou Conscientious Elephant?'

'The necessity does not arise,' coldly replied Chan Chun.

'The craft of carving ivory being the most esteemed of all, and this superlative person the acclaimed leader of that band, it inevitably results that whatever he puts forth must be judged to transcend the rest. To decide otherwise would be to challenge the Essential Principles of stability and order.'

In an obscure corner of the room Kin bent his energies upon a menial task.

'You have spoken without limit of those who may compete, esteemed,' he said diffidently. 'Is it then permitted even to the unassuming and ill-clad to incur this presumption?'

'Save only malefactors, slaves, barbers, official guardians of the streets and play-actors – who by an all-wise justice are debarred from holding any form of honour – even the outcast leper in the Way may urge his claim.' Chan Chun restrained his voice to an unusual mildness, in order thereby to reprove the maiden who had challenged his pretension. 'If,' he continued benevolently, 'it is your not unworthy purpose to strive for some slight distinction within the bounds set apart for the youthful and inept, any discarded trifle from my own misguided hand is freely at your call.'

'The compass points the way but one's own laborious feet must make the journey,' replied Kin tactfully. Then to deflect the edge of his evasion and to recall Chan Chun's mind to a brighter image he adroitly added: 'What is the nature of the chief reward, so that we may prepare a worthy place, revered?'

'That,' replied Chan Chun, 'is as the one who achieves it may himself decide. The large-hearted Mandarin binds himself by his father's sacred pigtail that on this unique occasion whatsoever shall be asked will be freely given.'

'That may aptly be related to the Ever-Victorious!' exclaimed the contumacious maiden with the conciseness of contempt. 'Think you, O credulous bone-chipper, that if the one thus singled out should demand the life, the wealth, or even the favoured wife of the Mandarin himself – '

'To do anything so outrageous would clearly proclaim a subverter of authority, and thereby a traitor to the state. A traitor is essentially a malefactor, and as all criminals are definitely excluded from competing it automatically follows that the triumph of this particular one is necessarily null and void and another – more prudent – must be chosen in his stead. Thus justice moves ever in a virtuous cycle and the eternal properties are fittingly upheld. For myself,' added the not undiscriminating Chan Chun reflectively, 'I shall gladden the face of this remunerative patron by the suggestion of a striking but more or less honorary distinction.'

'To surmount above our sign the likeness of an official umbrella would cast a gratifying shadow of authority upon The Conscientious Elephant,' remarked the keeper of his hearth.

'Accompanied by the legend: "Under the magnanimous thumb of the auspicious Tseng Hung",' amplified Chan Chun. 'The hint is by no means concave.'

*

As the day of the great event drew near the air above Tai-chow grew dark with the multitude of rumours that went up on every side. While many of these were of a gratuitous and inoffensive nature, it cannot be denied that others were deliberately cast abroad by thrifty persons whose business it was to make a profit from the fluctuating hopes and fears of those who staked upon the chances of competing craftsmen. Few were so lacking in respect towards the Omens as not to venture a string of cash in favour of the one who appeared before them in a lucky dream. Even the blind, the deaf and the dumb, and the mentally deficient, lying about the city gates, forecast portents at their leisure in the dust and esteemed from the passer-by a predictive word whispered behind a screening hand more than they did the bestowal of a coin in silence.

In the meanwhile Chan Chun and Kin laboured at their respective tasks secretly and alone – Kin because the only leisure he obtained was in his own penurious room, the former person owing to his cold and suspicious nature. The task upon which he engaged was one wherein ingenuity combined with art to a very high degree. Selecting his purest and most massive block of ivory he skilfully fashioned it into a measured counterpart of the great Palace of the Lustres as it stood. Then, to continue the similitude, within this outer shell he carved the core into a smaller likeness of the same, perfect in every detail, and thus and thus down to the seventeenth image – a pigmy Palace no larger than the capacity of a cherry stone but equipped to the slenderest point. Yet despite the complex nature of the task none of the sixteen smaller Palaces could be removed away from its encircling walls, all the cutting being achieved by Chan Chun through succeeding openings as he worked inwards. When this truly elaborate piece should be placed within the walls of the Palace itself the analogy would be complete and the craftsman did not doubt that a universal shout of accord would greet his triumph.

On the eve of the day of trial Chan Chun crept out secretly at dusk and distrusting all hired assistance carried his work by unfrequented ways to the Palace of the Lustres and there deposited it. As he reached his own door again he encountered Kin, who would have avoided him, but Chan Chun was feeling very pleasantly arranged within himself at the thought of his success and would not be disclaimed.

'Within the four walls of the arts all men are brothers,' he speciously declared. 'Remove the cloth that covers your achievement, worthy Kin, and permit my failing eyes to be rewarded by a blaze of glory.'

'Even a sightless bat would recognise its grotesque imperfections,' deferentially replied Kin, and he disclosed what he had done.

For a measured beat of time Chan Chun continued to observe the ivory bird with outstretched wings that Kin had fashioned, and although the expression of his face slowly changed from one extreme to another he was incapable of speech, until the youth, deeming the matter sufficiently displayed, passed along and into the outer way. Then the master sought a solitary chamber and having barred the door he sank upon a couch as he exclaimed:

'Assuredly it breathes! I have carved with a chisel, but Kin Weng has endowed with life itself.'

That same night at the middle hour of the darkness the keeper of the door of the Palace of the Lustres was roused from his sleep by a discreet but well-sustained knocking on the outer wall. For some time he did not attach any importance to the incident, but presently the unmistakable sound of a piece of silver being tested against another caused him to regard the

matter as one which he should in duty probe. On the threshold
he found Chan Chun, who greeted him with marked consideration.

'You alone stand between me and humiliation on the morrow,' said the craftsman with engaging freedom. 'When the
painstaking Mandarin who is to judge our efforts selects as the
worthiest that which I have brought, how will his inspired
decision be announced?'

'Should your hopes be fruitful, a full-throated herald of the
court will cry aloud your name, the sign beneath which you
dwell, and the nature of your handicraft. On hearing these a
chosen band outside will repeat the details to the far corners
of the earth, to symbolise the far-extending limit of your fame,
their voices being assisted when necessary by a company of
lusty horners ... and thereupon this necessitous person will seek
out one with whom he has wagered on the strength of your
renown and claim from him an indicated stake. May your
valiant cause succeed!'

'Doubtless it may in its essence, yet none of these things you
speak of will ensue – particularly the last,' replied Chan Chun.
'By an incredible perversity the written tablet of my name and
the like required details has been omitted so that when the
choice is reached no announcement can be made. The van-
quished, not slow to use this sordid weapon put within their
reach, will claim the forfeit of my chance, urging that by this
oversight I have not fulfilled the declared terms nor can those
who hold the balance resist the formal challenge. Not to further
this act of iniquity permit me to pass inside, gracious Pang, so
that I may complete what is now lacking.'

'This is a somewhat knotty tangle, chieftain,' said the keeper
of the door uncertainly, 'and one not over-clear as to which
end leads to wisdom. Thus it was laid upon me as a solemn
charge, that at the sounding of the eighth gong all further
traffic in this matter ceased – that which is within remaining so
and all beyond excluded from the Hall. Should it come to the
ears of high ones that in this I have failed incapably – '

'It is foreseen,' interposed Chan Chun; 'nor is your com-
plicity involved. As I awaited you a piece of silver slipped down
from my grasp and rolled some way apart. Should you seek

this your eyes will be upon the ground and nothing else will come within their sight, while being at a little distance from the open door you will have no knowledge that anyone goes in or out. Thus, with well-chosen words you can safely take the most convincing oath, nor will your phantom's future state be thereby held to bondage.'

'That which has an inlet has an outlet also,' assented Pang, now fully reassured, 'and your mind is stored with profitable wisdom. Yet,' he added thoughtfully, 'it is no less truly said, "As the glove smells, so the hand". Is the piece of silver which is the basis of this person's attitude lawful in weight and of the stipulated purity?'

'If anything, it exceeds in both respects,' affirmed Chan Chun. 'Preserve a virtuous front in all contingencies and none can implicate you.'

It has already been discreetly indicated that in a moment of emergency Chan Chun's character might undergo a downward bend. So far he had been able to withstand all the ordinary allurements placed about his path by evil Forces, none of these being on a sufficiently large scale to make the hazard profitable. But in Kin's great achievement he plainly recognised the extinction of his own pre-eminence among the craftsmen of Tai-chow, for none could miss its matchless qualities nor fail to accord to it an excellence above his own. To this contemplation was added the acuter barb that the one who should supplant him thus publicly was the disregarded underling who served his bench. In this extremity Chan Chun sent forth a message of despair to any passing demon who would succour him and even yet assure his triumph. To his weak and superficial mind the solution at once afforded by one seemed both adequate and just, and he accordingly proceeded to that end. Having gained admission to the unguarded Hall by the stratagem set forth, he treacherously removed the tablet of Kin's name from off its owner's work and placed it on his own, and in like manner transferred his own name and description to the creation of his servant's hand, well knowing that Kin had none to support his claim and that if dissent arose the word of an obscure hireling would not emerge above Chan Chun's outstanding voice. Then after again exhorting Pang to maintain an unswerving denial in the face of any question he returned to his own abode, quite satisfied that in a very difficult matter he had acted up to the requirements.

On the following day Chan Chun would have denied to Kin any respite from his task, the better to effect his crafty scheme, but as soon as it was light a herald passed along the Ways announcing in the Mandarin's name that to mark so special an occasion no one should engage in any work that day, but should instead receive a double wage, and so great was the respect now paid to Tseng Hung's slightest wish that among all those who laboured in or about Tai-chow there was not one who did not instantly comply.

At the appointed hour every person in the city and the boundaries round who was capable of movement was clustered about the Palace of the Lustres, Chan Chun and Kin among them. The former of the two had purchased a position upon an erected structure draped with red, which enabled him to maintain an attitude of ease and arrogance towards those who stood below, while Kin had been content to arrange himself among the feet of the foremost line. When the Mandarin Tseng Hung appeared, surrounded by his guard, so loud and continuous was the thunder of his welcome that several flashes of lightning are credibly asserted to have followed, owing to an excess of zeal on the part of the conscientious but inexperienced Being who had charge of it. Yet it is to be doubted if Kin heard a sound or saw any of the moving crowd, for at a single glance he plainly recognised in Tseng Hung the agreeable philosopher who had assured him of protection when they encountered in the wood.

In order to avoid the possible profanity of the Mandarin being actually touched by a person of no distinction the Hall of the competition had not been opened since the preceding night nor were any allowed to pass within when Tseng Hung entered it, save only his chosen band. To those among the throng outside who were competing craftsmen the moments were as leisurely as the shadow of a branchless pine tree moving across a level sward.

At length one in authority came forth and at the sight of him, expecting this to be the herald who should proclaim the victor, speech and movement died away, so that the only sounds heard throughout the vast multitude were the indignant cries of those who enjoined silence on each other.

'Let two approach and with downcast eyes prepare to be received into the very presence of the august Tseng Hung himself,' announced the messenger, in an all-powerful voice. 'These be Chan Chun, who carves ivory beneath the sign of a golden elephant, and Kin, the attendant of his hand. Hear and obey.'

'Your wholly abject hastens to comply,' cried Chan Chun, almost casting himself bodily from the height of the barrier in a passion of servility, and still more in a praiseworthy determination to be there before the inopportune Kin should gain the Mandarin's ear. Kin, however, was no less speedy, although the obstruction of his passage was equally involved, so that as a result they reached Tseng Hung and prostrated themselves, each with his face pressed submissively into the dust, side by side.

'Rise, unassuming ones,' said the Mandarin, with a consideration almost unparalleled in an official of his illustrious button. 'Your attitude, though complimentary in itself and eminently suited to a merely formal greeting, is frankly embarrassing to all in the light of well-extended conversation.'

'Your gracious words sink through the back of my threadbare head and reach even this ill-nurtured brain, so clear-cut is the penetration of their brilliance,' replied Chan Chun, scarcely daring to obey so indulgent a command.

'Doubtless,' assented the Mandarin, with high-born tact, 'but owing to the necessary inversion of our respective postures yours unfortunately do not possess a reciprocal capacity. Furthermore,' he continued, in a voice from which the sympathetic modulation began imperceptibly to fade, 'in order to avoid a very regrettable strain upon your neck, it will be necessary for you to use your eyes adroitly. Raise yourself to a position in keeping with your wide repute, upright Chan, and state deliberately wherein lies the path of associating your ornate name with a merely shapeless block.'

The matter having thus become too intricately arranged to be parried by evasive flattery Chan Chun raised so much of himself as was permissible and looked towards the indicated point, but at the benumbing sight he dropped back into his original abandonment, partly because his two-faced joints betrayed his flaccid limbs, but also to gain a precious moment in which to rearrange his mind. What he had seen was the foundation of Kin's work indeed, still bearing the tablet of his own name and sign, as he had unostentatiously contrived, but the bird itself was no longer there. So lifelike had been Kin's inspired touch that the sound of one of its own kind calling from outside had enticed the creature into flight.

'In order to give your inventive mind an unfettered range we will pass for the moment from the question of punishing contumely to that of rewarding merit,' continued the justice-loving Tséng Hung impartially. 'This ingenious but by no means heroic device of concentric palaces, bearing the name and symbol of Kin Weng, the underling of the momentarily indisposed Chan Chun, must be selected to receive our highest commendation. Let the herald therefore proclaim – '

'Imperishable!' exclaimed Chan Chun, unable any longer to retain between his teeth the bitterness of seeing his achievement surrendered to another, 'before the decisive word is spoken hear the ungilded truth of my misshaped lips. In the darkness of the night, having discovered an essential detail to be lacking from my task, I sought to remedy this. Deluded by the misguiding beams of the great sky-lantern my inept hand must have stumbled in the direction of its quest and thus the tablet that I would have placed about my work found a resting-place upon the immature effort of this inoffensive youth.'

'His in like manner – ' inquired the painstaking Mandarin.

'Possibly unseen Influences have therein been at work,' Chan Chun ventured to suggest. 'Or, perchance, one of those concerned about the Hall, seeing a deficiency removed a tablet from the space where two appeared, and thus and thus – '

'What fits the right foot does not necessarily fit the left,' remarked the judicial-minded administrator, keeping a firm grasp upon the intricacies of the case. 'Is there present anyone who can bear witness to your case, Chan Chun?'

'Pang, who guards the outer door of the Palace, will uphold what I have said,' replied Chan Chun, endeavouring to convey

by a veiled glance toward the one in question a knowledge of
the changed necessity pursuing him. 'He it was who, measur-
ing the extremity of my need with a forbearing rod, admitted
me by night.'

'High excellence,' declared the inauspicious Pang, thrusting
himself forward from among those who were stationed round,
'may my lot through all futurity be a rigid arm and an itching
sore if my discovering eye beheld the sight or if this forbidding
hand was raised to suffer any man to pass,' and the slow-witted
person who had spoken closed one eye in the direction of Chan
Chun in order to reassure him that he would, despite all enticement to the contrary, tenaciously follow his instruction.

'We have heard it said, "One may ride upon a tiger's back
but it is fatal to dismount", and you, Chan Chun, are experiencing the wisdom of the verse,' declared Tseng Hung. 'Pang
having bent within your hand it behoves your expectant eyes
to seek another prop. Is there, by chance, none who has seen
you busied at your task?'

'Alas, omnipotence, I wrought in secret lest another should
forestall my plan.'

'Can you then implicate Kin Weng with this emblem of
contempt and save your own repute by calling to your aid those
who have marked it beneath his fashioning hand?'

'I also strove unnoticed at my toil, benevolence, nor has any
ever deigned to tarry as he passed my despised bench by,' interposed Kin, not thinking it necessary to declare himself more
fully until it became apparent on which side justice lay.

' "He whose sandals are in holes is seldom asked to ride",'
quoted Chan Chun, plainly recognising that disgrace would attract few towards his need. 'Having reached the end of my
evasion, mightiness, I bend an acquiescent neck.'

'Great Head,' cried a captain of the guard which stood outside, entering with an absence of all seemly form, 'there is an
omen in the sky to justify my uncouth haste. A strange white
bird has three times circled round the tower above and now
remains suspended in an unnatural poise, high in the Middle
Air.'

'All this is according to a definite line of augury and moves
towards an end,' remarked the Mandarin, leaving his cere-

monial chair and indicating that those concerned should follow him. 'If this celestial creature can be brought to earth and is found to fit a place upon the sculptured block, Chan Chun's contention need not be gainsaid, while distinction of a very special kind will appertain to Kin. Let the most skilful with his bow stand forth.'

'Wang, of the Crouching Leopard Band, display the opening attitude!' commanded an under-captain of the guard.

'A weighty bar of silver for thy needy sleeve if the first shaft shall reach its destined mark,' promised Chan Chun in a beseeching voice.

'Begin to prepare to affix a trusty arrow to thy bow in accordance with the prescribed requirements of the distance to be attained,' continued the one who led the movements. 'Extending a propitious hand in the direction of the upper – '

'All-powerful chief!' exclaimed Kin suddenly, casting himself before the Mandarin's feet. 'Suffer the inoffensive bird to live in safety and the penalty that Chan Chun has merited I will myself incur.'

'Rise, estimable Kin,' replied Tseng Hung, raising a jewelled hand with a gesture indicating that if his position had been slightly less exalted he might even have extended it; 'your orthodox way of behaving in this emergency, together with the low-class efforts of the usurpatory Chan Chun, make any display of judicial alertness on this one's part superfluous. Your humane wish is granted.'

'In any case,' remarked the morose Wang, as one who forbodes oppression, 'the discriminating bird has by this time passed out of the range of a merely human skill. Yet as a certain sum was specified – '

'Revert to your original attitude of unalertness!' interposed the under-captain definitely.

'There is still another page to be unrolled if the Destinies are to be fulfilled as the Omens would direct,' declared Tseng Hung expectantly. 'Turn your capable eyes towards the west, Kin Weng, and search the path that gives access to our weed-grown park.'

'None approaches from your well-kept grounds, esteemed,' replied Kin, after a penetrating scrutiny.

Tseng Hung leaned upon his staff and his lips moved, but so discreetly that none save Kin (who saw in this an added likeness to the one called Cheung) detected the enchantment.

'A vision of the inner chamber lifts your latch and makes as though an unseen power directs her steps this way,' reported Kin.

'Is she known to your remembrance?' asked the other, with a warning glance.

'He who dreams by night may also dream by day, but who shall recall the colours of a rainbow that is past?' was the guarded answer.

Tseng Hung signified his approval of this speech and moved his staff again.

'Should any further auspice seem worthy of remark do not hesitate to free your mind,' he said protectingly.

'She holds a white bird in her arms, which nestles there; but to presume a mutual bond from that would not be opportune,' replied Kin with ingrained diffidence.

'Do not hesitate: remember that it is better to be the forefront of a rabbit than the hind-quarters of an ox; and should the portents be maintained your pre-eminence is well assured. But the moment for the final test is now at hand. Come.' With this condescending familiarity of speech the unworldly Mandarin led Kin aside and brought him back into the Hall where they had lately been. Here, without actually concealing themselves, they stooped behind an upright beam of sufficient size and thus screened they watched the maiden enter. Straight to the spot where Kin's work had stood she bent her feet, then stopped and there from her releasing hands the bird flew lightly down and taking up again its exact place upon the sculptured block passed at once into its former state of lifelike poise.

'Fa Ming, daughter of my all-but-extinct Line, what aim has brought you to this spot?' mildly inquired Tseng Hung, discovering himself to her.

'That is a matter which lies beyond my feeble lore, revered,' was the suitable reply. 'As I sat in my leafy bower, sewing pearls upon a golden ground, a white bird entered by an open lattice and flew into my heart, filling its empty void. Then with a message that I may not speak it drew me on and on until about this place, its purpose being fulfilled, it passed into another state, leaving me tranquil.'

'This is the end to which I have striven through many gloomy years and it was with this in view that I finally applied myself, with varying results, to the questionable arts,' remarked the gratified father, beckoning Kin Weng forward and addressing himself chiefly to that one's ear. 'At an early age the last enduring offspring of my decrepit trunk came under the perfidious influence of the spirit of an uprooted banyan tree, who, to revenge itself for an imaginary slight in the choosing of her name, deprived her of the gentle and confiding habit which up to that time she had invariably displayed and in its stead imposed its own unbalanced and vainglorious nature. To neutralise this powerful influence was by no means so simple as an ordinary person might at first imagine, as it necessitated gaining a profound knowledge into the customs and circumstances of every kind of Being, Force, Spirit, Demon, Vampire, Shadow, Ghost and other supernatural creatures inhabiting earth, air, water, fire and wood. The possible intervention of dragons, phœnixes, tortoises, and unicorns, both ill- and well-disposed, had also to be delicately balanced, and the contending influences of tides, planets, winds, inundations, eclipses and dynastic changes accurately divined. In addition to these no single omen, portent, augury, prediction, conjecture, foreboding, dream or imprecation could safely be ignored. In the end, the movements of practically every living person in Tai-chow and its surroundings were more or less drawn into the scheme, so involved had the counter-charm become, while the discovery that only one short measure of time during the next ten thousand years was really auspicious for the test necessitated an immediate effort.'

'Your labours have been both wide and profound, esteemed,' remarked Kin deferentially. 'Yet,' he added, with an admiring glance in the direction of Fa Ming, 'were they multiplied by ten their troubles are repaid a hundred-fold.'

'It will be gratifying if all concerned, Chan Chun specifically, prove as outspoken in their loyalty,' replied Tseng Hung.

'Omniscience,' reported a privileged slave, entering hurriedly, 'the populace has begun to assail the keepers of the routes with missiles of the riper sort, and the official few, fearing a popular rising, await your gracious word to announce that the promised entertainment is not yet commenced or has already reached its determined end.'

'Let all be freely admitted whatever their degree and bid the several troupes of music-players to engage at once in harmony to the full extent of their capacity,' commanded the Mandarin resourcefully. 'We ourselves will display our interest in the animated scene from the seclusion of this conveniently arranged cupola.'

Yet despite the attraction of his urbane presence Kin Weng and Fa Ming neglected to accompany him, and when the Hall became thronged with persons of the usual kind it was noticed by the more observant that the two referred to stood side by side apart, and that, although without having anything in the nature of spoken language to exchange, they did not appear to realise a deficiency.

*

When Kai Lung had related the story of Kin Weng there was no longer any reason for his presence, nor, with sincere courtesy, did the hospitable band around make an actual effort to detain him. For a moment he had the low-minded impulse to pass round his penurious bowl, but seeing that those about had become inextricably absorbed in conversing with each other he judged that the movement would be deemed inept.

Outside the door Hwa-mei was waiting, an inconspicuous bundle at her feet and a trimmed lantern placed beside it.

'The oppressive closeness of the day has gone and presently the great sky light will rise to guide our footsteps,' she remarked agreeably, after they had exchanged words of an appropriate nature. 'Is there any reason why we should not at length return to the scene of our disturbed felicity?'

'It had been somewhat to my purpose that the trivial Li-loe might journey by our side, he having in a measure contributed to our cause,' was the rejoinder. 'But the witling was ever of a stunted warp and now he steadily declines to forsake the valley. He is even now there, digging – doubtless for the cask of wine, of which he cannot recognise the no-existence.'

'Doubtless,' assented Hwa-mei abstractedly, and they set

forth together, she still maintaining a grasp upon the slight
burden she had brought while he sustained the lantern. The
lights of Chi-U grew fewer, less, and vanished, and soon even
the melodious clamour of hollow wooden drums, resonant
stones, bells, gongs and cymbals that marked Hai Shin's exultant homeward progress sank to a faint tremor on the unruffled
air ... then, when sought for again, had faded.

'Though it was but a small cottage it was seemly,' remarked
Kai Lung, with the first trace of sadness. 'Alas, this time,
cherished, there is nothing but a ruin.'

'He who can command four hands shall never lack a shelter,'
replied Hwa-mei, undaunted; 'and that which is built on mutual
affection has a very sure foundation. Furthermore, if the roof
is low it will be the nearer to our thoughts. Is it not, O story-
teller, written, "When the wine is rich we overlook the gilding
in the cup"?'

'Yet the peach tree at the gate has been destroyed, the sown
field wasted, and the scanty store put by against the day of
drought has melted.'

'As to that,' said Hwa-mei, with a certain gaiety in her
manner, 'an adequacy of, as it may be expressed, seed, has by
the forethought of the Sustaining Ones been provided for the
renewal of our harvest.' Thus speaking she untied the knots
that bound the cords, and then disclosed her burden. It consisted chiefly of a nest of pearls but there were also eleven other
varieties of precious stones and a reasonable amount of both
gold and silver. 'Ming-shu and Shan Tien would each seem
to have provided for the morrow and since neither of them will
have occasion to pass that way again it would have been inopportune not to search beneath the ground whereon their
tents had stood.'

'As you must clearly have been led by the guiding spirits of
your – no less than my own – ever-to-be-reverenced ancestors,
it would, perhaps, be impious not to accept their gift in the
way it was intended, and to make use of the various possessions
here, in a good sense, gradually,' declared Kai Lung, after he
had tested a chance selection of the gems and metals. 'Inexorable is the saying, "However much the river winds it finds the
sea at last".'

PART II

THE GREAT SKY LANTERN

*

CHAPTER X

How Kai Lung sought to discourage one who did not gain his Approbation

To Kai Lung, reclining at ease within the lengthening shadow of his own mulberry tree, there came the sound of contest, as of one strong in his assurance and the melodious laughter of another who derided what he claimed. Recognising therein the voices of Chi Lin, the son of a rich neighbour, and Precious Jade, the matchless blossom of his own matured years, the discriminating relater of imagined tales slowly closed the scroll upon which he had been absorbed and imperceptibly composed himself into an attitude of wary unconcern – not with the ignoble purpose of listening to their words but so that he might haply correct any inelegance of style in such stray phrases as should reach his ear.

'Thus and thus, perchance, it has been in the past,' came the boast of the vainglorious youth, 'but this person will yet pluck a whisker from the tree of Fame, and even hang the silver buckle of his shoe upon the crescent of the great sky light itself.'

'Thus and thus indeed?' mocked the answering voice, and a laugh, musical as a stream of pearls falling into a crystal lake, stirred the perfumed air. 'Beware of arousing the envy of the sleeping shades of Yaou and Shun, O thrice-valiant one!'

At the mention of these unapproachable heroes of the past Chi Lin plainly realised the unseemly loudness of his challenge, for he moved yet closer to the maiden's side and began to express himself very ardently into her well-placed ear. Kai Lung, therefore, had no alternative but to leave the shelter of his arbour and to display himself openly before them.

'Noble youth,' he remarked with becoming mildness, 'consider, if but for a breathing-space of time, the harmonious balance of the unisons. Trees put forth leaves, flowers, and fruit, each in due season; men – those who attain the honourable appendages of virtuous old age – wear whiskers or moustaches and the like. The analogy was ill-contrived.'

'Venerated master,' replied the self-confident one whom he had thus arraigned, 'in the unsophisticated days of your distinguished minstrelsy it was doubtless well enough to speak of things as they really were. In our own more exacting times, however, in order to entice the approbation of the throng it is necessary to cultivate a studied obliquity of style. To pluck the natural verdure of a tree foreshadows no romance, but what imagination is not stirred by the bold conception of a doubtless retaliatory arboreal whisker being torn from its parent stock?'

'Alas,' admitted Kai Lung sadly, 'it is well written, "The shell must crumble when the young emerge", and this obsolete person's literary manner is both thin and very fragile.'

'Yet,' protested Precious Jade, rearranging his pigtail affectionately, 'it has been freely said that no arising emergency has ever found you unprovided with an appropriate theme.'

'Who stoops to gather fallen leaves when the full fruit bends to meet his hand?' replied the one concerned. 'Since your curiosity clearly tends that way, however, doubtless this opportune and intellectually replete young man will relate by what means the great sky lantern came to have that crescent point towards which the latter part of his painstaking ambition is directed.'

'The requirement finds me unprepared,' stammered Chi Lin, by no means grasping how the exigency had arisen. 'It is one thing to speak in terms of classical allusion, as of a "peach"; it is quite another to have to declare who grafted the stem that bore the analogous fruit and where he performed his Rites. The words were but in the nature of an imagined feat.'

Kai Lung shook his head as one not wholly satisfied.

'Before setting out for a distant and barbarian land it is prudent to learn all that is available of the difficulties to be encountered by the way,' he stubbornly contested. 'Turn accordingly, your highly connected footsteps in the direction of my very incommodious summer-house, O Chi Lin, and then, after this deformed and altogether unattractive she-thing of my decaying Line has brought fruit and wine wherewith to sustain you through the ordeal, I will endeavour to remove your lamentable want of historical polish as agreeably as possible.'

Chi Lin would have refrained, it having been his intention to pass the time pleasurably in Precious Jade's society without any reference to Kai Lung himself, but this no longer seemed feasible and he began to recognise that he had conducted the enterprise in a manner unworthy of his all-embracing reputation. Nor did the engaging maiden return with the promised viands, her place being taken by a one-eyed hag of forbidding outline, but the self-opinioned story-teller behaved with all the narrow-minded obstinacy of his unsympathetic tribe, for ignoring his reluctant guest's well-displayed air of no-enthusiasm he seated himself upon the floor and proceeded leisurely to unfold the story of the alluring Chou.

THE STORY OF THE PHILOSOPHER KUO TSUN
AND OF HIS DAUGHTER, PEERLESS CHOU

In the reign of the patriarchal Chun-kuh a venerable philosopher occupied a position of some distinction outside a small village in what is now the Province of Shan Si. This versatile person, Kuo Tsun by name, had an only she-child, Chou, in whose welfare he was sincerely concerned. In view of what happens even within the limits of this badly told and ill-constructed story, it is hardly necessary to describe Chou's outward semblance, beyond stating generally that for some time afterwards it was not unusual to meet quite elderly ascetics whose necks had become permanently bent from an inability to remove their eyes from her perfection after they had passed.

At that remote cycle of time matters had not become organised on stable and harmonious bases. A thick mist still obscured the land (for the canals were not yet dug), and under the cover of its malignant shade Forces of various kinds, both Good and Bad, were accustomed to frequent the earth and to reveal their conflicting energies more openly than they are prone to do to-day. Dragons of all the eleven sorts might be encountered anywhere. Winged snakes and phœnixes disturbed the air. Unicorns and celestial tortoises wrought the omens of their presence, and from numerous watercourses the voices of singing serpents – whose song is like the clashing of melodious rocks – tempted the passer-by. The more ordinary manifestations of spectres, ghouls, vampires, demons, voices, presages and homeless shadows excited no comment. For lengthy periods, sometimes exceeding years, the rain never ceased to fall, the lightning to be displayed, and the thunder to announce the labour of the High Ones, as the Immortal Principle strove to adjust the Eternal Equipoise. Owing to the absence of fixed barriers between the Upper and the Lower Airs many of the deities strayed down upon the earth and formed connections of the more intimate kind with ordinary beings. From this cause it came about that not a few people found themselves to possess qualities for which it was difficult to account, and it was widely admitted that sooner or later anything might be expected to come to pass.

Besides being a discriminating sage, Kuo Tsun was also a powerful magician, and it was, indeed, chiefly due to his attainments in the latter capacity that he was able to procure the means of sustenance. While not failing to profit by the circumstance, the contrast was one that did not gladden his understanding.

'It cannot cease to be an element of bitterness in this one's stomach,' he was wont to remark, 'that while he has no difficulty, as a mediocre wizard, in converting the baser metals into gold, as a far-sighted philosopher the full extent of his laborious system has been to reduce Everything to Nothing.'

Chou, also, was not entirely devoid of unnatural gifts. She could, she had learned by chance, transform herself into the appearance of certain of the lower creatures, and in moments of concentrated emotion, when words became inadequate, she had the power of breathing out fire. But with a seemly regard for the proprieties she gradually relinquished both these practices, although a few sparks occasionally betrayed the sincerity of her feelings even in later years. Her own she-children enjoyed the same corrosive attribute to a less visible degree, while her he-children walked in the integritous footsteps of their ac-

complished grand-sire. One became a high official, the second a
fearless warrior, and yet a third a person of commercial eminence. All possessed the serviceable capacity of transmutation,
but the process was rather more protracted and involved than
it had been with the inspired founder of their Line, and it was
not infrequently discovered that what looked like gold in its
creator's hands had in some obscure way assumed another and
inferior guise after it had been successfully disposed of.

In the interval of his meditations Kuo Tsun did not disdain
to take Chou indulgently by the hand and to point out to her
the properties of things and the inferences that his well-trained
mind evolved.

'We perceive,' he thus explained, 'that by a beneficent scheme
of spells and counter-charms when the light goes darkness
gradually appears, and when darkness has run its appointed
span the light is ready again to take its place. What, however,
would occur if by some celestial oversight this had not been
foreseen, and both light and dark had been withdrawn together? The logical mind bends almost double beneath the
weight of so dire a catastrophe, but it is inevitable that in place
of creatures of the day and creatures of the night the Empire
would have become the haunting-place of a race of pale and
uncertain ghosts.'

'You are all-knowing,' replied Chou with ingratiating can-
dour, though it did not escape the philosopher's notice that she
was gazing in several other directions as she spoke. 'Your eyes
see round the corners of the earth, and wisdom distends your
waistband.'

'Say on,' remarked Kuo Tsun dispassionately. 'Yet should
this appreciation forecast another robe of netted gold, or a
greater sufficiency of honeyed figs, let it be cheerfully understood among us that this afflicted person's eyes are practically
opaque and his outline concave.'

'Your large-handed bounty satisfies in every way,' declared
Chou openly. 'The reference to your admitted powers was
concrete and sincere. Something in the nature of an emergency
confronts the one before you and she would lean heavily upon
your sympathetic lore.'

'In that case,' said the magician, 'it might be well to have all the support available,' and he would have proceeded to trace the Symbols on the ground with his bamboo wand had not Chou's lotus hand restrained him.

'It is by raising your eyes, rather than bending them upon the earth, that enlightenment will come,' she urged. 'Behold, before us stretch the disputatious waters of the Ch'hang Ho.'

'Truly so,' agreed Kuo Tsun; 'yet by pronouncing a single word of magic, I can, should you desire to cross, cause a solid shaft of malachite to span the torrent.'

'The difficulty is not so easily bridged as that,' replied Chou, directing an evenly balanced glance of some significance. 'What detail on the west bank of the river most attracts your never-failing gaze?'

'Upon a convenient crag there rises the strong tower of Ah-mong, the robber chief,' announced Kuo Tsun. 'At the moment it is rendered doubly conspicuous by the fact that the revolting outlaw himself stands upon the highest pinnacle and waves a two-edged sword in this direction.'

'Such is his daily threat,' declared Chou with a refined shudder of well-arranged despair, 'it being his avowed intention to destroy all people by that means unless this one will consent to grace his inner chamber.'

Although Kuo Tsun could not repress an element of surprise that the matter had progressed to so definite a complication without a hint even of its inception warning him, he did not suffer the emergency to impair the broadminded tolerance of his vision.

'Thus positioned,' he judicially remarked, 'it might become more prudent to recall the far-reaching length of Ah-mong's sword rather than the distressing shortness of his finger-nails, and to dwell on the well-lined depth of his treasure-store to the exclusion of his obvious shallowness of mind.'

'Perchance,' asserted Chou; 'yet now direct your all-discerning glance to the east bank of the river and indicate what feature of the landscape most forcibly asserts itself.'

'The meagre hut of the insolvent scholar Yan is in itself a noticeable landmark,' was the reply. 'As the versatile student of the Classics is even now – by a process quite outside this inefficient person's antiquated wizardry – projecting a display of lightning flashes from a revolving wheel, the spot assumes an added prominence.'

'The perfection of that device is the assiduous Yan's continual aim,' expounded Chou. 'This effected, it is his lamentable design to require the diffident one now conversing with you to share his penurious cell, and should this be withheld to consume the world with fire.'

At this further disclosure of the well-spread range of Chou's allurement Kuo Tsun did not deem it inept to clear his throat of acrimony.

'Doubtless it is as it was designed from the beginning of time,' he took occasion to remark, 'for had the deities intended that men should control the movements of their lesser ones, instead of two eyes in front they would have endowed us with sixteen, arranged all round.'

'Doubtless,' assented Chou with commendable docility, 'but pending the arrival of that Golden Age by what agile display of deep-witted philosophy is it your humane purpose to avert these several ills?'

'The province of philosophy,' replied the one who thus described his office, 'is not so much to prevent calamities befalling as to demonstrate that they are blessings when they have taken place. The only detail that need concern us here is to determine whether it is more unpleasant to be burned to death or to perish by the sword.'

'That is less than my conception of the issue,' declared Chou with an indomitable air. 'Is then mankind to become extinguished and the earth remain a void by reason of this one's inopportune perfection? Rather than suffer that extremity she will resolutely set out to conform to the requirements of both positions.'

'Restrain your admitted reluctance to jeopardise the race for at least a few beats of time,' counselled Kuo Tsun, withdrawing his mind from a deep inward contemplation. 'There is an apt saying, "What appear to be the horns of a bull by night stand revealed as the ears of a mule at daybreak", and something in the nature of a verbal artifice occurs to me. Exactly what form this should take eludes the second-rate functioning of my misshapen brain at the moment, but light will doubtless be vouchsafed. ... Had the ill-dispositioned chieftain of an unsightly band of low-caste footpads possessed even the rudiments of a literary style an eliminating test in the guise of an essay in antitheses might have been arranged between them.'

'With so unexacting a trial the contingency of both succeeding should not be overlooked,' interposed Chou decisively.

'Leave that to one who in his youth composed an ode containing seven thousand conflicting parallels, so deftly interwoven that even at the end the meaning had to be sought in what was unexpressed,' replied Kuo Tsun with inoffensive confidence. 'Putting the same glove on the other hand, if the effete seeker after knowledge known to us as Yan had any acquaintance with the martial arts a well-contested combat would seem to be the obvious solution.'

'Yet with so formidable an encounter the possibility of both succumbing must not be ignored,' urged Chou with humane solicitude; but Kuo Tsun did not applaud her bias.

'It is easier to get honey from the gullet of a she-bear than sincerity from between the lips of an upright woman,' he declared with some annoyance. 'If it is neither your will that both should fail nor yet that both should triumph, indicate plainly which of the two permeates your eye with the light of gladness.'

'That,' replied Chou modestly, 'is as it will of itself appear hereafter; for if it is no part of the philosopher to avert misfortune, neither is it within the province of a maiden to hasten it.'

As she made this unpretentious reference to the one who should in the fullness of time possess her, the radiant being took from her sleeve a disc of polished brass to reassure herself that her pearl-like face would be worthy of the high occasion, and she also touched her lips with a pigment of a special tincture and enhanced the slanting attraction of her accomplished eyes. But when she would have fixed at a more becoming angle the jewelled comb of scented wood that restrained the abundance of her floating hair it slipped from her graceful hand and was lost in the darkness of a crevice.

'Alas,' she exclaimed, in an access of magnanimous despair, 'that is by no means the first which has escaped my unworthy grasp among these ill-constructed rocks. Would that I might have a comb fashioned of the substance of the great sky lantern hanging there, for then its shining lustre would always reveal its presence.'

'Even that shall be accorded if in return you will but share this degraded outcast's sordid lot,' cried a harsh and forbidding voice from near at hand, and at the same moment the double-faced Ah-mong disclosed himself from behind a convenient boulder. At the first distant glimpse of Chou he had crept up unheard to gloat his repulsive eyes on her complicated beauty as his obscene habit was. 'Entitle me to the low-minded felici-tations of my questionable friends and all the resources of a nimble-fingered band of many-footed mercenaries shall be pressed into your cause.'

At this proposal an appropriate saying, in which a bull-frog sought to pursue an eagle, rose to Chou's lips, but before she had made the unflattering reference Kuo Tsun contrived a sign enjoining caution.

'All this shapes itself to some appointed goal,' he whispered sagely. 'The actual end of Ah-mong will certainly be painful and obscure, but in the meanwhile it is as well to play an am-biguous role.'

'Disclose your mind,' continued the obtuse chief robber (the philosopher having, by witchcraft, propelled his speech towards Chou's ear alone); 'for the time has arrived when it is neces-sary to be explicit. On the one hand is raised this person's protective arm; on the other his avenging sword. Partake of either freely.'

'Your amiable condescension retards for the moment the flow of my never really quick-witted offspring's gratitude,' in-terposed Kuo Tsun tactfully. 'I will therefore lift my discordant voice on her behalf. Your princely dignity requires that your lightest word should be unbending as a wedge of iron and in this matter my verbal feet are hastening to meet your more than half-way spoken gesture. Procure the slice of heavenly luminary to which allusion has been made and the ceremonial interchange of binding rites will no longer be delayed.'

'The task is so purely a formality that among broad-minded friends the suggestion of delay would imply a distorting reflection,' remarked Ah-mong, hoping to outwit Kuo Tsun among the higher obscurities. 'Let mutual pledge be made on this auspicious spot.'

'Friendship,' replied the philosopher no less ably, 'has been aptly likened to two hands of equal size dipping into one bowl at the selfsame moment. How well-balanced must be the shadow cast by so harmonious a group!'

'May two insatiable demons dip their rapacious claws into your misbegotten vitals!' exclaimed Ah-mong, throwing off all restraint as he recognised his impotence; and with all-advised precipitancy he seized the alluring form of Chou in his unseemly arms, intending to possess her. In this, however, his feet moved beyond his mental balance, for as his offensive touch closed tenaciously upon her, Chou merged her volition inwards and with maidenly reserve changed herself into the form and condition of a hedge-pig. With a full-throated roar of concentrated anguish Ah-mong leapt back at any hazard, and escaping thus she found safety in a deep fissure of the earth. Not to be wholly deterred in his profane endeavour Ah-mong then turned upon Kuo Tsun and advanced waving his voracious sword and uttering cries of menace, but as soon as he was assured of Chou's security the far-seeing sage passed upwards in the form of a thin wraith of smoke. Brought up against a stubborn wall Ah-mong threw a little earth into the air and tried several of the simpler forms of magic, but so illiterate was his breeding that in no single instance could he pronounce the essential word aright and the extent of his achievement was to call down a cloud of stinging scorpions through which he struggled back to his tower morosely, arraigning the deities and cherishing his scars.

On the day following that of this encounter Chou walked alone along the east bank of the river. Owing, doubtless, to the involved nature of her meditation she was within sight of Yan's obscure abode before she realised the circumstance; nor did she at once turn back, partly because so abrupt a movement might have seemed discourteous if he had observed it but also because she knew that at that hour Kuo Tsun would be safely asleep within his inner chamber. As she advanced, slowly yet with graceful ease, the following inoffensive words, sung by

one to the accompaniment of vibrating strings, indicated the
nature of her welcome:

'Seated on the east bank of the Ch'hang river,
'I turned my lute into accord with its dark and sombre waters;
'But presently the sun appearing every ripple sparkled like a
    flashing jewel,
'And my glad fingers swept the cords in unison.
'So when this heaven-sent one approaches all sad and funereal
    thoughts are banished,
'And my transported heart emits a song of gladness.'

'The time for such palatable expressions of opinion is, alas,
withheld,' remarked Chou, as Yan stood hopefully before her.
'The calamitous Ah-mong has brought things to a sharply
pointed edge among our several destinies and the future is
obscure.'

'So long as our mutual affection thrives no time can be otherwise than bright,' replied the scholar.

'From a poetical angle that cannot be gainsaid,' admitted
Chou. 'None the less truly is it written, "Even flowers turn their
faces from the sun that sets", and my revered father is, after
all, semi-human.'

'Are then the feet of the profound Kuo Tsun's regard still
reversed in my direction?'

'Detestable as the admission is, your imperishable Treatise
on the Constituents of Voidness is his daily execration,' acknow-
ledged Chou. 'From this cause a line of dissimulation has necessarily arisen and the one whom we are now discussing regards
you merely as a studious anchoret, instead of a rival philosopher of dangerously advanced views.'

'How then – ' began Yan, but Chou interposed her efficient
voice.

'The situation has slipped somewhat from its appointed
base,' she explained, 'and the commonplace strategy by which
I sought to entice his esteem in your direction has taken a
devious bend.' In a few well-arranged words the versatile
maiden disclosed the unrolling of events, adding, 'Foiled in his
besotted might the intolerant Ah-mong now kowtows to the

requirement of a no-less grasping strategy. He has sent a written message of contrition to the all-wise of my noble Line admitting that his punishment was just, but holding him to the promise by which he may yet acquire me.'

At the mention of his low-conditioned rival's name Yan could not restrain a gesture of dignified contempt.

'Admittedly Ah-mong's mouth is large,' he declared, 'but the seat of his intellect, if indeed it has not completely shrivelled up, must be stunted in the extreme and of less than average quality. Furthermore, so corrupt is his daily life that, even on the most lenient scale, it can have very little longer now to run, while the greater likelihood is that a large adverse balance will have to be expiated by his weak-kneed descendants and all those connected with his effete stock.'

'In what way is this – this doubtless just punishment incurred and how will it affect the lesser persons of his household?' demanded Chou, with a manifest solicitude that Yan was too high-minded to impugn.

'Besides his ordinary crimes,' he replied, 'Ah-mong is known to do things of which a strict account is kept. These are punished by shortening his span of life here on earth before he goes to the Upper Air, where he will atone for the more serious offences. Thus he has been seen to point repeatedly at rainbows, to tread on grain destined for food, to annoy working bees, and to cook his rice, when pressed for time, over unclean sticks. In the extremity of danger he hisses noisily between his teeth and he has an offensive habit of spitting up at shooting stars. Taking one thing with another, his end may come at any moment.'

'Yet if in the meanwhile he conforms to the imposed condition and procures the comb of silver light, how regrettable would be this one's plight!' exclaimed Chou, restraining with some difficulty an impulse to breathe out her sentiments more forcibly.

'Set your mind at rest on that score,' replied Yan with ready confidence. 'An obvious solution presents itself to one of philosophical detachment. This obscure person will himself bear off the stipulated spoil, anticipate the sluggish-hearted Mong, and then, despite the shadow of his inimitable theme, hold your honourable unnamed to the performance of his iron word.'

'That would certainly smooth out the situation appreciably,' agreed Chou with more composure. 'But how shall you,' – thus corroding doubts again assailed her – 'being small and badly nurtured, as well as unskilled in the proficiency of arms, succeed where the redoubtable Ah-mong falters?'

'It is a mistake to judge the contents from the size and fabric of the vessel,' declared the one who made reply; 'nor is the assurance of the branded label always above corruption.'

'Your whisper,' admitted Chou with inoffensive tact, 'is more far-reaching than the vindictive outlaw's loudest summons. Yet has it not been written, "Beggars point the way to fortune"?'

'Not less aptly does the saying run, "No stream is mighty at its source",' Yan made rejoinder. 'Let mere misgivings fade. One who has brought down to you a diadem of stars to set upon your brow' – in this expressive way he indicated the string of poems extolling Chou's perfection that hung about his stinted cell – 'is scarcely prone to tremble at the thought of ravishing the moon to deck your floating hair.'

'It is enough to have reached this apex,' confessed Chou as she listened to Yan's discriminating tribute; 'for my unworthy name will shine by the pure light of your renown for ever. I am a queen upon a golden throne and the people of the earth will bow down before my glory.'

At an early gong-stroke of the following day, after performing his simple Rites, Yan took up his staff and set forth on a journey. Distantly related to him by an obscure tie, there lived in a cave among the higher Quang-ling mountains an elderly astronomer, Cheng his name and his house the reputable one of Chang, who had chosen that barren and austere retreat out of a painstaking resolve to miss no portent in the starry sphere. To consult this profound recluse was now Yan's object, for who could advise him better than one who had spent the full-ness of his life in watching the movements of the Inner and the Outer Upper Paths and the ever-shifting flux of the Beyond? As he passed Ah-mong's stronghold that truculent leper him-self appeared upon his rugged tower and began to whet his great two-handed sword meaningly upon a marble hone, purposely throwing the drip in Yan's direction. To this insult the scholar replied with a suitably barbed apophthegm, but beyond this they ignored each other's presence.

Chang Cheng received his kinsman gladly and set out a choicer sufficiency of food and wine than was his own abstemious custom. For some time their conversation was restricted to a well-kept-up exchange of compliments but gradually the visitor introduced the subject of his ambition. When he fully understood what was required of him Cheng's face altered somewhat but he betrayed no resentment.

'In temporal matters involving force or strategy it is this one's habit to be guided almost wholly by the wisdom of misshapen Mow, the dwarf who waits upon his person,' he remarked. 'Retire now to your inner recess of the cave and when the pigmy alluded to returns from gathering herbs some scheme advancing your felicity may be propounded. In the meanwhile – prosperity, and an absence of dragon-dreams from about your couch, attend you!'

'May the planets weave the lucky sign above your virtuous head!' replied Yan with equal aptness as he lay down upon the floor. Weary as he was with the long exertion of the day, thoughts of Chou and of the great enterprise upon which his feet had entered kept him for many gong-strokes from floating off into the Middle Air, but as long as he remained awake whenever he raised his head he could hear the distant murmur of thoughtful voices as Chang Cheng and the gnomish Mow discussed the means of his advancement.

The next morning Yan would have questioned Chang Cheng as to the outcome of the discourse but the astronomer parried the inquiry with a ready saying.

' "He who can predict winning numbers has no need to let off crackers",' he made reply. 'What we shall offer for your enlargement will be displayed at the proper moment.'

'If it is not inopportune I should like to exchange greetings with one whose cunning stands so high in your esteem,' said Yan. 'Will the dwarf Mow presently appear?'

'He has set out upon a distant journey,' replied the other evasively. 'Now that the light is here let us go forth.'

He led the way across the mountains, avoiding the path by

which Yan had come and soon they were in a hidden valley, between two projecting crags.

'These two rocks have been called Jin and Neu for a certain reason,' remarked the astronomer, stopping midway through the ravine and searching the stunted growth around his feet. 'Formerly a learned sorcerer lived about this spot, but he was changed into a rivulet by an even stronger power whom he had rashly challenged.'

'Doubtless in a modified way he can still disclose his wisdom?' suggested Yan.

'For a time he did so and the spot had some renown, but during an excessive drought the wellspring of his being dried up and nothing now remains of him. He left a pair of magic iron sandals, however, with the message that whoever could wear them would get his heart's desire.'

'Was the accommodating prediction verified?' inquired Yan with heightened interest.

'It has never yet been put to the corroding test. Of those who tried to profit by the charm many were unable to don the gear at all and of those who could none were successful in moving from the spot. Therein the requirement failed.'

'If it is not taking up too much of your meritorious time, I would gladly make the essay,' declared the student. 'Priceless as your help will be it is as well to remember the saying, "Do not carry all your meat held on one skewer".'

'It is for that very reason that I have brought you to this forgotten place,' replied Chang Cheng. 'Here are the sandals lying among the brake; it only remains for you to justify your boldness.'

Yan knelt beside the iron shoes and with some exertion adapted his feet to their proportions. The astronomer meanwhile lent his aid, and at a certain point he bent down and pressed the fastenings of the sandals in a special manner. This done he stood aside.

'The omens of success are not wanting,' exclaimed Yan, standing upright but remaining on the spot. 'Yet so far my self-willed limbs betray my exalted spirit.'

'That is not to be wondered at, seeing that the iron rings, now inextricably fixed about your feet, are chained to the rocks Jin and Neu, one on either side,' replied Chang Cheng, speaking in an altered voice. 'The time has now arrived when sincerity may prevail and subterfuge be banished. This design to bind the planets to your purpose, O short-sighted Yan, is a menace to the orderly precision of the Paths and it cannot be endured. Desist you shall, either by force or by entering into a bond pledging your repose, and the repose of the one whom you most covet, throughout futurity.'

'That oath will never be exacted, thou detestable Chang Cheng!' cried Yan, straining at his chains. 'Is this then the hospitality of the house of Chang, that was a kennel in the courtyard of my forebears' palace? Or do malignant change-lings haunt the Quang-ling heights?'

'It is better to destroy a shrub than to mutilate a tree,' stubbornly maintained Chang Cheng, but he kept his face averted from that time onwards. 'However, as it is truly said, "If there is meat at one end of a boar there are sharp tusks at the other", and so long as you reject the pacific course there still remains the coercive.' With these insatiable words the perfidious astronomer took from beneath his cloak a cake of paste and a jar of water and placed them on an adjacent rock. 'From time to time further sustenance will be provided and when you are ready to bring your weak-eyed period of restraint to an accommodating close a pacific sign will not find me hard-stomached. May the All-knowing lead your feet to wisdom.'

'May the Destinies guide you even on the edge of a yawning chasm,' responded Yan with absent-minded courtesy, though on recalling what had passed he added, 'and also over.'

In such a manner the inoffensive student Yan came to be abandoned in a narrow pass among the desolate Quang-ling mountains, with the noon-tide sun sapping the inner source of his nutrition. Resolved never to relinquish the hope of procuring that which alone would enable him to claim Chou's fulfilment, the likelihood of remaining chained to two massive rocks to the end of all time did not seem to be a far-distant one. Presently, his thirst having become intolerable, he began to drag his reluctant fetters towards the place on which his food was spread, when for the first time the deep-laid malice of the offensive plot revealed itself. Thrust how he would, the rock was a full half-score of paces still beyond his reach.

In setting forth the exploits of Yan towards the attainment
of peerless Chou, later historians have relied on a variety of excuses, some even describing the exact Forces that lent him their
aid. Yet this should be deemed superfluous, for putting aside
the protecting spirits of his devoted ancestors (who would
naturally assist in a matter affecting the continuance of their
Line), the outcome was one of logical conclusion. Yan's determination to avail himself of the challenge ruling Chou's disposal was unbending and sincere; to do so it was necessary that
he should remain in a condition of ordinary existence; and in
order to sustain life food and drink were essential to his being.
... Towards sunset Yan stretched out his hand and drank and
ate, for by the tenacity of his purpose he had plucked up Jin
and Neu from their rooted fastness and drawn them at his need.

The next morning he awoke encouraged and sustained. A renewed adequacy of food and water had been placed there in
the night but at a yet greater distance from him than the other.
By the time that the heat of the day was at its full Yan had
reached this also, nor was the exertion so strenuous as before.

For a period of which no exact record has come down, Yan
continued chained within the valley of the rocks and during the
whole of that time of inauspicious trial the false-hearted Cheng
did not disclose his two-headed face. Yet no day passed without
bringing its sufficiency of food, but each time with the labour
of obtaining it increased, until Yan had to traverse the entire
space of the ravine. This he could at length achieve with con-
temptuous ease.

When there was no greater test of endurance to which Yan
could be there submitted, Chang Cheng one day appeared suddenly before him. Already Yan had striven to escape out of the
valley, to confront that most perfidious kinsman eye to eye, but
the ill-arranged protrusion of his prison walls had thrown back
his stubborn efforts. Now with the thwarter of his ambitions
and the holder of the key of his release almost within his grasp
a more concentrated range of the emotions lent a goad to his
already superhuman power and with a benumbing cry of
triumph Yan gathered together his strength and launched himself in Chang Cheng's direction. But in this he was, as the

proverb has it, dining off fish for which he had yet to dig the
bait, for with a vigour astonishing in one of his patriarchal cast
the astronomer easily outdistanced him and by his knowledge
of the passes gained the upper peaks. Howbeit, Yan had thus
reached a higher point along the outward path than he had
ever before come to, and the noise of his progress, as he
dragged Jin and Neu crashing from side to side and destroying
in his wake, spread the rumour far and wide across the Province
that the Hoang Ho had again burst through its banks in flood.

After that, Chang Cheng frequently appeared at this or that
spot of the valley and Yan never failed to extend himself in
furious pursuit. Each time he attained a higher level on the
barren slopes enclosing him but the last peak ever defied his
power. Observing this, the astronomer one day cast back an
unbecoming word. Under the lash of this contumely Yan put
forth a special effort and surmounted the final barrier. Outside
he found Chang Cheng waiting for him with no diminution of
his former friendship.

'The moment has arrived when it is possible to throw aside
the mask for ever,' remarked the astronomer benignly. 'The
course of your preparation, Yan, has been intensive and compact, for in no other way was it possible for you to gain the
necessary aptitude within a given time.'

'Revered!' exclaimed the student, recalling the many occasions on which the venerable must have suffered extremely in
his dignity at the hands of the pursuit. 'Can it be – '

' "Our troubles are shallow; our felicities deep-set",' replied
the other, tactfully reversing the adage for Yan's assurance,
'and in contemplating your spreading band of sons I shall have
my full reward. When I have removed your shackles be guarded
in what you do, for the least upward movement will certainly
carry you out of sight into the above.'

'Has not the hour arrived when I may put my presumptuous
boldness to the test?' inquired Yan.

'It will do so at a certain instant of the night, for then only,
out of the millenaries of time, all the conjunctions will be propitious. Should you fail then through instability of mind or
tenuity of will, demons could not preserve you.'

'Should I fall short in so unflattering a manner,' replied

Yan capably, 'I would not preserve myself, for all hope of possessing Chou would thereby have faded. Yet out of your complicated familiarity with the heavens would it not be possible to indicate some, as it were, sharp-pointed ends for guidance?'

'There are no abbreviated ways across in the infinitive,' replied the profound, pointing. 'There wheels the shifting target of your adventurous flight and should you miss your mark your fall into the Lower Void will be definite and headlong. Now wrap your inner fibre round my words, for when you wing your upward track through space the rush of wind and the shrieks of adverse Forces will be so marrow-freezing that all thoughts which are not being resolutely held will be blown out of your mind.'

'Proceed, esteemed,' encouraged Yan. 'My ears stand widely open.'

'When you take your skyward leap from off this plateau my staff will guide your initial course. If your heart is sincere and your endurance fixed, the momentum will carry you into the Seventh Zonal Path whence your drift will be ever upwards. Speak to none whom you encounter there.'

'Yet should I be questioned by one who seems to have authority?'

'In that case your reply will be, "I bear the sword of Fung", as you press on.'

'The reference to a sword being doubtless an allusive one,' suggested Yan, with a diffident glance at his short-coming side.

Chang Cheng moved his shoulders somewhat, though the gesture was too slight to convey actual impatience, and he raised a beckoning hand.

'At a convenient break in the instruction it was this ill-balanced one's purpose to disclose the point,' he remarked concisely. 'However, for strictly literary exigencies yours is doubtless the better moment. Let the dwarf Mow appear.'

'I obey, high excellence,' was the response. 'Here is the sword, indomitable Yan.'

Yan took the weapon that the gnome had brought and balanced it upon his hand before he slung it. Of imperishable metal it was three-and-thirty li in length and three across and had both an upper and an under edge for thrusting. The handle was of brass.

'I have somewhere seen the dual of this before,' thought Yan aloud. 'Yet few warriors have come my way.'

'It was formerly the sword of that Ah-mong who lived in a strong tower above the Ch'hang river, being both the secret of his power and the reason of his confidence that he should achieve the test,' explained Chang Cheng.

'That accounts for much that was hitherto obscure,' admitted Yan, and he would have inquired further but the astronomer's poise did not entice discussion.

'The instant presses on when you must make the cast,' declared the latter person, closely watching the movements of the Paths through the medium of a hollow tube. 'The Ram's Horn has now risen and lying off its sharper end there winks a yellow star. Mark that star well.'

'I have so observed it,' declared the student.

'That is the Eye of Hwang, the Evening Star, and on it your right foot must come to rest. For the grounding of your left you must take Pih, the Morning Star, for that conjunction alone will form the precise equilibrium on which success will hang. Now gird yourself well and free your mind of all retarding passions.'

'I call upon the revered shades of my imperishable ancestors to rally to my cause,' exclaimed Yan boldly. 'Let none refrain.'

Chang Cheng indicated that the moment had arrived and held his staff at the directing angle. Mow, who knew the secret of the clasp, cast off the shackles. Then Yan, gathering together the limits of his power, struck the ground a few essaying beats and fearlessly cleft upwards. Freed of the clog of Jin and Neu there was no boundary to his aspiration and he sang a defiant song as he spied the converging lines of spirits string out to meet his coming. When he looked back the earth was a small pale star between his ankles.

The details of Yan's passage through the Middle Space would fill seven unassuming books, written in the most laborious style, but wherein would Chou reside? Only one spoke of her – Ning, who with a flaming faggot at his tail, as the Supreme had ordered, was threading his tormented path among the Outer

Limits. Ning had the memory still of when he dropped to earth to become enamoured of the slave girl Hia, and as he shot past Yan he threw back a word of greeting and would have liked to have Chou's allurement described in each particular. Let it suffice that 'Between He and Ho', as the proverb goes, Yan gained his celestial foothold and bending forward cut with the sword of Fung what he deemed a sufficiency out of the round-ness of the moon. As he withdrew a shutter was thrown open and a creature of that part looked forth.

'What next!' exclaimed the Being rancorously when he saw what Yan had taken. 'Truly does this transcend the outside confine! Is it not enough that for a wholly illusory crime this hard-striving demon is condemned to live upon an already inadequate sphere and burnish its unappetising face for the guidance of a purblind race of misbegotten earthlings?'

'There will be so much the less for you to keep polished, then,' replied Yan competently. 'Farewell, moon-calf. I bear the sword of Fung.'

'May it corrode the substance of the hand that holds it!' retorted the other with an extreme absence of the respectful awe which Yan had relied upon the charm producing. 'Hear a last word, thou beetle-thing: that once in each period of measured time I will so turn this lantern which I serve that all may see the havoc you have wrought, and suffering the loss of light thereby will execrate your name for ever.'

Yan would have framed an equally contumacious parting had the time at his disposal been sufficient, but remembering Chang Cheng's warning and his design being now accom-plished, he turned and set a downward course back again to earth.

His purpose would have been to embrace the astronomer affectionately, but owing to some deflection which lay outside his sphere of control, he found himself transported to the re-gion of his own penurious dwelling. As he neared it he saw Kuo Tsun, who led Chou by the hand, approaching.

'To confess a former error is but a way of saying that exact-ness now prevails beneath one's housetop,' remarked the philo-sopher auspiciously. 'Owing to the misreading of an obscure symbol this deficient person had hastily assumed that matter originally began as Everything and would ultimately resolve itself into Nothing. He now perceives, on a closer perusal of your inspired thesis, that its first principle was Voidity and that the determinate consummation will be a state of Allness. In addition to being a profound thinker you have competently performed an exacting test.' Here Kuo Tsun pushed Chou slightly forward. 'Take, therefore, the agreed but wholly inadequate reward.'

'Yet, munificence,' urged Yan diffidently, 'this meagre hut – '

'All that has been suitably provided for by the justice-loving System under which we live,' replied Kuo Tsun. 'During your absence the decayed Ah-mong has Passed Beyond and as he was a person of notoriously corrupt views I invoked my own authority as District Censor to dispossess his band and to transfer your Ancestral Tablets to his tower.'

'It is well said, "The Destinies arrange, but under our benevolent government all must help themselves",' commented Yan, after he had suitably referred to Kuo Tsun's undoubted service. 'Yet what was the nature of Ah-mong's Out-passing?'

'An element of vagueness shrouds the incident,' confessed Kuo Tsun. 'It is whispered that a mysterious Being appeared among the gang and proving his authority by the precision of his knowledge enticed Ah-mong with the promise of a certain way to gain his end. This consisted of a stupendous javelin, having bamboo cords attached, with which it was proposed to transfix the great sky light and draw it down to earth. In the end the contrivance proved so unwieldy that the cloven-footed outlaw fell upon its point from off his lofty tower, when there was none but the Being near. Thus and thus – '

'This concerns Mow, the subtle dwarf,' thought Yan, but he said nothing then, being desirous of keeping the full recital until he could compose it as a song, to give Chou gladness at some winter fire. He had, indeed, arranged an opening antithesis when Kuo Tsun's voice recalled him.

'By a complexity of circumstances, rare in this belated person's experience of the Province, very little appears to be wanting to create a scene of ideal felicity,' the venerable sage was remarking. 'The Ch'hang river, for probably the first time in history, is neither in flood nor completely evaporated; an almost poetical verdure has suddenly appeared where no vegetation was ever known before; several of the rarer kinds of feathered creatures have raised their harmonious voices, and now and then it is quite possible to see the great grandfather of the sky above the mists. If only a company of musicians could be inspired – '

Even as he spoke a band of village dwellers of the younger sort began to pass that way. The maidens carried ropes of flowers which they had gathered at some toil, but many of the most powerful of the other kind had iron gongs and hollow metal tubes, sonorous ducks and fish of wood or stone, and a variety of implements capable of producing sound, with which they beguiled the time. Chou's many-sided interest in the welfare of all had raised her in their esteem and Yan's unassuming virtuous life was a byword far and wide. When the leaders of the band grasped how the position stood they covered the two with whose involvements this threadbare narrative has largely been concerned with sprays and garlands and set out with them upon a joyful path, the minstrels, urged to a more tenacious vigour, leading the way. Thus, at the conclusion of their exacting trial, Yan and peerless Chou were brought in some triumph to the strong tower of the turbulent Ah-mong that was henceforth to be their home.

For several æons after these commonplace events the comb was a venerated relic among the descendants of Yan and Chou, but during the insurrections of a later age it passed into undiscriminating hands, and being then much worn and broken it was thrown aside as useless. It fell in the Province of Kan Su and became the Yue-kwang range. It is for this reason that the upper peaks and passes of those sacred heights are always clothed with brightness, while at certain periods of the year the lustre they reflect equals the splendour of the great sky light itself.

PART III

THE BRINGER OF GOOD NEWS

*

CHAPTER XI

Whereby the Angle at which Events present themselves may be varied

IT was still the habit of Kai Lung to walk daily in his garden and to meditate among the shady walks of the orchard grove beyond; but in this exertion he was prone to rely increasingly on the support of a well-tried staff and even with this assistance Hwa-mei was disinclined to encourage him to go unless Valiant Strength, Worthy Phœnix or some other supple branch of his now spreading tree was at hand to sustain his elbow.

'Revered,' exclaimed Hoo Tee, who thus attended on the occasion with which this pointless relation is concerned; 'behold, there approach along the stone path nine persons of distinction and with them one of official rank. Would it not be fitted that I, on whom their high-minded conversation would certainly be lost, should serve a useful end by bringing forth an assortment of choice food to refresh their weary throats?'

'Restrain your admitted zeal in that direction,' replied Kai Lung, 'until they have declared themselves. Should they come with expectation in their step, whatever you could offer might fall short of their desire; should they have no such purpose it would equally prove too much. Your pigtail has still some length to grow, Hoo Tee.'

When the nine wayfarers drew near they disclosed themselves as three philosophers of the district round, three young men of literary tastes, and three who without any particular qualification or degree were in the habit of attaching themselves to

whatever seemed to offer a prospect of reward. In their midst
was the stranger who displayed a badge.

'Greeting, venerable Kai Lung,' remarked the leader of the
band. 'May your meritorious Line increase like the sprouting
of a vigorous ear of corn in the season of Much Rain.'

'May all your virtuous tribe be no less favoured,' replied
Kai Lung, with a desire to be courteous but not yet convinced
of the necessity for any special effort. ' Are your constituents
well balanced?'

As they slowly passed along the conveniently arranged ways
of Kai Lung's flower-strewn garden, with a due regard to the
ceremonial precedence accorded to their age, the nature of the
occasion was presently made clear.

'He whom we have guided was in the out-paths seeking the
house that bears your worthy sign,' explained the chief of the
philosophers. 'Plainly the occasion would seem to merit our
felicitations.'

'My superfluous task,' enlarged the one thus pointed out, 'is
to be a Bringer of Good News, and in this pursuit I take my
daily stand before the Official List board of our provincial city.
There your pleasant-sounding name is honourably displayed,
Kai Lung, and in accordance with the immemorial right of our
exclusive guild I have hastened hither to be the first to reach
your grateful ear.'

At this agreeable announcement the nine neighbours of Kai
Lung shook hands with themselves effusively and several
admitted that it was what they had long foreseen, but the story-
teller himself did not at once step into the full lustre of the
moment.

'What,' he inquired, with a rather narrow-minded precision,
'is the nature of the title and are the initiatory expenses set
forth in detail?'

'The latter part of the subject would appear to have been
overlooked,' replied the other, after glancing at his tablets.
'The distinction carries with it the privilege of unrolling your
mat and relating one of your inimitable tales before any member of the Imperial House who strays within three-and-thirty li
of your Domestic Altar – providing that you are able to reach
his exalted presence and that he is not at the time engaged on

serious public business. It also entitles the holder to style himself "Literary Instructor to the Shades of Female Ancestors"
in all official pleas.'

'It is doubtful if so exceptional an honour was ever bestowed
before,' passed from lip to lip among them, though one of the
less worthy added beneath his voice, 'It is more profitable to
step upon an orange-skin before a cloyed official than to offer
pearls of wisdom to a company of sages.'

The venerable story-teller, however, continued to shake his
head with supine misgivings, nor did the added prospect of
having to compose a deferential ode in answer tend to restore
his spirits.

'Tou-fou and Li-tai-pe were not distinguished in their life-
times, nor was a crown of leaves ever offered to Han Yu,' he
demurred. 'Why then should I, who only stumble in their well-
made footsteps, be thus acclaimed? The ungainly name of
"Kai" is easily mistaken and "Lungs" greet one on every side:
the brush of some underling has, perchance, blundered to this
arisement. ... Yet, which of my negligible productions was
singled out for mention?'

'Munificence,' replied the expectant messenger, 'the quality
to which you owe your distinctive popularity would not appear
to have been specifically of a literary trend – '

'The frustration of Ming-shu's detestable rebellion might
certainly have been deemed a notorious public service by a too-
indulgent eye,' continued Kai Lung more cheerfully. 'The delay
of some two-score years in extending recognition is not unusual
in a State Department connected with – '

'Truth adorns each word,' interposed the Bringer of Good
News, not in any way desirious of becoming involved in a speculative discourse, 'but your flattering reputation does not stand
on that foot either. Rest assured, benignity, that it is wiser not
to test a coin found by the roadside, but to spend it.'

'Speak frankly,' urged the insidious voice that had already
murmured, 'we being all friends here, one among another,'
and he looked pleasurably forward to hearing something of an
offensive nature.

'A wet robe is more becoming than a borrowed umbrella,'
was Kai Lung's tolerant pronouncement as he signified

assent that the stranger should proceed. 'Withhold nothing.'

'However dubious the soil the rice conveys no taint,' aptly replied the other. 'But since you persist – the unexpressed part of the occasion is as follows. A rumour has of late sprung up, esteemed, that you have been miraculously endowed with the unusual gift of being able to walk on the side of a house, or in any other upright place, with the superior agility over our own race possessed by all winged insects. "If," the analogy has thence continued, "the one in question (of whom we have never previously heard), is so remarkably conformed, it necessarily follows that his inspired productions must possess a very unusual blend." Within a moon, benevolence, you have thus become what among those who put forth the printed leaves is termed a "leading cash enticer". Seeing this, it behoved authority to move. "For," flowed the rhythm of their thoughts, "inasmuch as flowers turn their faces to the sun and all men, when untrammelled, seek the highest, he who can claim the greatest number of adherents in any walk of life is necessarily the worthiest of his kind, and for our own repute we must profess acquaintance with his works and do him honour." '

'Alas,' exclaimed Kai Lung, when he understood that he was thus indebted to a fallacious comparison with an illiterate insect, 'how shall I meet the shades of Toù-fou and Han Yu hereafter? In our highly favoured land of unparalleled refinement is it essential to a just appreciation of his literary style that an unassuming relater of imagined tales must stand upon one foot for a record span of time, or be secretly conveyed to an unknown spot by a providential dragon, or consort with apes upon a trackless desert, or by some other barbarian wile appeal to the trite and superficial?'

'Who shall ordain in what form the deities bestow their gifts or question the wording of the inscription upon the outer wrapper?' asked the philosopher Wan Fo – he who in earlier life had provided for a virtuous old age by arranging competitions. 'The husk which, in the case of the salubrious nut, protects the desired food is, when we turn to the equally nutritious date, itself similarly surrounded – clearly with the humane intention both of warning mankind against hasty generalities and of exercising the teeth diversely. That which – as may be demonstrated with a coin – is round when looked at from above, is flat when seen edgewise – '

'Besides, O instructor,' interposed one of the studious youths (less, perchance, with the desire of assuaging Kai Lung's umbrage than of deflecting the profuse Wan Fo), 'have you ever yet attempted to progress upon an upright wall in the manner indicated?'

'This one has never bent his commonplace feet to so grotesque an essay,' replied Kai Lung, with an appreciable distance in his manner.

'Then for all that an ordinary person can declare you may be gifted to that extent, and as you are certainly now too patriarchal to put the contention to a test it will never be possible to gainsay the achievement. How then,' concluded the disciple, 'can you logically reject a distinction which in addition to being founded on an admitted merit may even in its circuitous process be exact?'

To this plea the others joined their voices, especially the Bringer of Good News, who foresaw no certain gain if the one whom he had come to apprise maintained a stubborn outline. Therefore, as they slowly trod the walks and admired the ingenious vistas – being prompted thereto by a whisper in his ear that he might thus induce Kai Lung to forget resentment – he approached the story-teller more directly.

'Beguiler of men's leisure,' he remarked astutely, 'it is asserted out among the more trodden Ways that in your time you have framed stratagems, led armies and fought battles. How is it possible for one who has thus controlled events to have passed his later life in a state of unbroken ease, plying his simple calling?'

Before replying, Kai Lung led his guests among the remoter outskirts of his orchard where on a few neglected trees a shrivelled aftergrowth of fruit still lingered. These he laboriously sought out and pressed on each in turn, with hospitable insistence.

'Had we been earlier here the fare might have been more full-flavoured,' was his mild extenuation. 'But who shall blame the tree that has already of its nature yielded crops when autumn finds it wanting?' Then turning to the Bringer of Good

News he added, 'Since you put it in that way, it will be necessary for me to explain matters by relating for you, to the best
of my decayed proficiency, the Story of Ching-kwei.

THE STORY OF CHING-KWEI AND THE DESTINIES

I

*The Manner of his Setting Forth, his Encounter by the Way,
and the Nature of his Reception at Wang Tae's Hostile Door*

Not idly is the warning given, 'Destiny writes with an iron
spear upon a marble stele; how then shall a merely human
hand presume to guide her pen?'

This concerns Ching-kwei of the dwindling Line of Ying,
Wang Tae the dauntless warrior, and the philosopher Ah-Yew;
no less also Shen Che, known later as the Poising Butterfly
from the graceful lightness of her movements, and her sister
Mei, to whom no other name was ever given. It involves likewise the aged grandmother of Ching-kwei, the sorcerer who
dwelt beneath the rugged tower of Ya, Shang king of the upstart power of Tsun, certain friends, associates and relatives of
those chiefly engaged, warriors and captains of the various
armies raised, usurpers and upholders of the dynasty, sages and
historians, merchants and artificers, holy men, outlaws and
peasants, and a great variety of persons of the ordinary sort
for whom no particular description here is necessary.

Ching-kwei was of the age of manhood when he first beheld
Shen Che. Thereafter he marked the day with a special sign
(binding a knotted cord about his wrist), so that on it he might
initiate any great enterprise on which his mind was fixed. It
was the thirteenth of the Month of Peach Blossom and on that
day he united with Wang Tae in the Compact of the Cedar
Grove, led the assault on the walled city of Hing-foo, and, last
of all, turned home again.

'Truly art thou thy father's very son!' exclaimed his grandmother one day, at a period before any of these things had
come to pass. 'Are we to starve by slow degrees? Here are but
nineteen goats where yesterday a score responded to my call.
Pursue the misshapen recreant with all speed before another
shall have killed and eaten it. Take with you rice sufficient for
a lengthy search, and if in the course of your wanderings you

should fall in with a reputable magician sitting by the wayside, do not neglect to traffic a portion of it with him for a written charm against this person's pestilential cramps.'

'Venerable one,' replied Ching-kwei dutifully, 'your spoken word is my unwritten law. Yet how, encountering a recluse of this description, may it be assumed with confidence that he is all you would desire and not an unscrupulous impostor?'

'Commiserate with him upon the malignity of his own afflictions. If he enlarges on the subject pass him by.'

'Your words enshrine the essential germ of wisdom,' agreed Ching-kwei. 'Although,' he added sombrely, 'to one whose forefathers bore banners in the van of many famous wars, the pursuit of an erratic four-legged creature across a precipitous land is an enterprise neither dignified nor heroic.'

'Those who cover themselves with martial glory frequently go in need of any other garment,' replied the ancient capably. 'Be content that by peaceful industry you have goats to pursue.'

Being of a docile and obedient nature – and also because no adequate retort occurred to him – Ching-kwei respectfully withdrew and at once made his simple preparations for the search. In this he was assisted by the praiseworthy honesty of that region, for so humiliating was it felt to be that the animals of one family should ingratiate themselves into the herds and flocks of an unsuspecting neighbour and enjoy his confidence that to render this contingency as remote as possible it had become the time-honoured custom for each household to stain all its removable possessions with a distinctive dye. Thus Ching-kwei's inquiries tended to a definite end.

'Has there by any chance a base-born interloper lately appeared among your lordly herd of distinguished-looking goats?' he might have vainly asked at every farmstead.

'Is the one whom you address a hungry dog that the odour of one goat differs from that of another across his path?' would have been the discouraging reply. 'Or have you counted the hairs of that which you claim to have lost, so that you shall describe it. Behold, within my flock are goats of every shape and kind, and by a meritorious fruitfulness their numbers increase from day to day. Begone then with this quail-and-dragon story of a wandering goat, the counterpart of one of mine, and seek a less wary victim.'

Truly; but what words of evasive contumely could be directed against one who should draw near remarking:

'Greeting, opportune possessor of this majestic flock of vermilion goats which so decoratively sets off the fertile hill-side.'

'Greeting,' courtesy would demand in answer. 'Yet the creatures are themselves evil in every bone and the pasturage is meagre and full of bitterness.'

'On the contrary, only one blemish mars the harmonious unity of the engaging scene. Have I your genial permission to disclose it?'

'Say on – if you must,' would be the morose reply, the one addressed seeing no other course before him. 'But a virtuous life speaks louder than a brazen trumpet.'

'Your gracious encouragement moistens my laborious tongue. Among such perfection even these afflicted eyes at once recognise yonder ungainly outcast, whose ineradicable coat of blue is very thinly disguised beneath a recent dressing of red earth. Permit me, therefore, to attach this commonplace thong to its rebellious horns and to free your nobly descended herd of its distasteful presence.'

In this mutually inoffensive way Ching-kwei had already on several occasions recovered defiant members of his flock, and had himself not infrequently suffered a similar loss at the hands of equally determined neighbours. But this time an unstinted measure of no-success marked all his efforts and his persistent endeavour to implicate one after another of those whom he distrusted led to nothing but a spot ever increasingly distant from his own domestic hearth.

It was towards evening on the second day of his quest that Ching-kwei encountered a brighter omen. He had then reached a barren and forbidding waste and was contemplating turning back from so cheerless a prospect when he noticed a little wizened mendicant seated upon a rock a few paces further on. As even the rock had not been there the previous moment Ching-kwei at once doubted the ordinariness of the occasion and this emotion was added to when he perceived that the Being's teeth were composed each of a separate jewel of unusual size and brilliance, and that he had four eyes and held four books in either hand. A golden centipede was coiled about his feet and from his escaping breath there was formed a river of clear water. Ching-kwei's first impulse was to render obeisance of the lowliest kind, but as he would have done so it was put into his mind that the one before him, by invoking the threadbare garment of an aged beggar, wished to assume a part. He therefore approached the venerable one in an upright position but saluted him obsequiously.

'Ching-kwei,' remarked the vision in some embarrassment, 'the fact that you see me half as I really am, and half in the appearance I have assumed, plainly shows that you yourself are not entirely normal. This foreshadows a life of chequered fortune, nor would it seem to be wholly settled yet to what end your destiny will tend. All this, however, is for your inner ear alone, for it would certainly involve me in humiliating censure if it became known in the Upper World that I had, in a moment of indiscretion, exceeded my imposed task. This is simply, in the guise of an aged native of these parts, to influence you from turning your dejected feet on a homeward bend by observing in your hearing, "Many hoof-marks point inwards at Wang Tae's gate but few lead out again", adding, "To the deaf ox a meaning word is as efficacious as a detailed statement".

'Your timely warning falls on a nutritious soil,' replied Ching-kwei gratefully, but without any especial reverence for one who was so inadvertent. 'On your return you can safely claim that your message has not failed.'

The venerable made a gesture of familiar understanding.

'Anything that I have said beyond, regard strictly as between one semi-supernatural Being and another,' he remarked diffidently. 'At some future period in The After doubtless an opportunity of doing no less for your accommodating Shadow will occur.'

Having thus discharged his mission the one in question sought to vanish, but being still confused by the mischance of their meeting, he failed to pronounce the charm efficiently, so that while he and the rock disappeared entirely, the robes of the patriarchal mendicant remained in a seated attitude upon a void.

'Clearly it would seem that you do not necessarily act like a deity merely by being one,' thought Ching-kwei as he resumed his forward path. The intimation that he was himself of remote kinship with the Immortals did not gild his imagination, for he had often recognised that he was in some undetermined way superior to those around him, although the circumstance did not appear to have any direct pecuniary advantage.

He had soon other things to engage his mind upon, for as he advanced he heard from the scanty peasants of that inhospitable tract that Wang Tae's dwelling was near at hand. It was spoken of as being strongly staked about, but when Ching-kwei would have learned something of the nature and attitude of the one whom he was seeking, those he questioned ceased to speak and replied only by signs of such profound significance as to be wholly unintelligible.

'It is truly said, "A fly on the window may be taken for an eagle in the sky", and Wang Tae is doubtless no more formidable than any other man upon two feet,' reasoned Ching-kwei aloud, as he approached a stronghold of the kind described to him, and he would have continued in the strain when a defiant voice caused him to turn. One whom he had not observed in his eagerness to press on had stepped forward and now stood barring the path of his retreat.

'Perchance,' retorted this inopportune stranger, 'but Wang Tae does not go upon two feet, and as he therein differs from the generality of men so are the depth and lustre of his power not to be measured by a wooden rule,' and the one who spoke indicated with a gesture of contempt the staff that Ching-kwei carried. 'If our agreeable conversation is to continue in the same harmonious vein let your persuasive tongue acquire a more businesslike point,' and he struck the handle of a sword he wore.

'It is certainly my intention to speak a few pacific words at Wang Tae's door, touching the movements of an erring goat I seek,' replied Ching-kwei mildly. 'Should his reception of what I have to say not be entirely thus and thus, however, it will then be time to shape my tongue to a more incisive edge.'

'Your well-chosen language fills me with the most joyous anticipation,' said Wang Tae, moistening his hands with gross elaboration. 'Here is the gate of my neglected hovel. When you have seen all you want of the outside world, pass within.'

It is in this not entirely sympathetic manner that Wang Tae now comes into the narrative and it is chiefly owing to that voracious person's large military appetite that the onward history of Ching-kwei moves to the measured clash of arms. At the time of this encounter Wang Tae was of a middle age and very lusty in his strength. His hair was long and matted, his eyes open and sincere, and the expression of his face both bold and menacing. So bushy were his eyebrows as to give rise to the saying that phœnixes might build there, and with the closing of his hands he could crush a rock. In height he would have been above the ordinary had not both his feet been lacking; for having at an earlier period displeased the ruling lord of Tsun that prince had caused them to be sawn off, to correct, he said, Wang Tae's rising ambition.

'Henceforth,' declared the conscientious ruler, when this act of justice was accomplished, 'it can no longer be hinted that your aspiring footprints point towards a throne, Wang Tae.'

'Benevolence,' replied Wang Tae unmoved, 'by cutting back the branches of a tree you do but increase the vigour of its fruit, and I will yet leave the impress of my thumb upon the age.'

Carrying with him the echo of this vainglorious boast Wang Tae retired to a desert place apart and there built himself a strong retreat, guarding it with a trench and a palisade of teak. He lived by establishing a system of taxation for the benefit of travellers of the richer kind who passed that way and gradually he found around him a company of necessitous persons who were of his own way of thinking. From time to time secret messengers went to and fro throughout the province and as the land continued to grow more troubled, men's thoughts began to turn towards Wang Tae as to a lofty banyan tree when the rain threatens to fall.

II

The influence of the wise Philosopher Ah-Yew and the
inspired Assurance of his parting Forecast

When Wang Tae with a ceremonious welcome threw wide
the gate of his outer yard, Ching-kwei did not hesitate, nor did
the sound of the bolt being wedged against his escape cause
him to stop. He found himself overlooking a considerable enclosure wherein every sort of beast displayed every variety of
colour; a goat stained with his own distinctive shade of blue
sported among its kind.

'In the matter of the colour of my herd I am content to preserve the harmonious blend of nature,' remarked Wang Tae,
reaching his side again and speaking with polished insincerity.
'What is good enough to arch the heavens is good enough to
adorn my pastures.'

'It is well said,' agreed Ching-kwei. 'Furthermore, by the
same analogy both manifestations would appear to be of spontaneous origin.'

'The honey of your continual approbation is too rich for my
weak mental appetite,' said Wang Tae, by no means pleased at
the insidious courtesy of Ching-kwei's replies. 'Is there haply
nothing here to displease your fastidious eye?'

'On the contrary, there is that which amply rewards my inefficient sight, for at no great distance this person perceives the
object of his foot-weary search. Permit him, therefore, to lead
the truant home in triumph and your virtuous name shall ever
remain a synonym for uprightness.'

'Put forth your self-reliant hand and take it then,' replied
Wang Tae, leaping down into the yard to draw his impatient
sword. 'There is but one slender bar between.'

'No obstacle is both too high to get over and too low to get
under,' retorted Ching-kwei no less resolutely, and he suddenly
thrust his staff forward in a way that Wang Tae was not prepared for.

In considering the various facets of the not altogether dignified encounter that ensued it is necessary to hold an impartial
balance. Admittedly Wang Tae was by repute one of the most
skilful sword-users of his day, while Ching-kwei was then
wholly deficient in the simplest passes of that weapon. The

latter person, however, was wont to rely in every emergency on the dexterous manipulation of his herdsman's pole, while Wang Tae in all his numerous encounters had never yet gained experience of so contemptible an arm. The inevitable outcome was that neither could subdue the other, for while the length of Ching-kwei's weapon kept Wang Tae at a humiliating distance, the thickness of the outlaw's leather armour saved him from the full impact of the blows propelled against him. Yet it is not to be denied that Ching-kwei by concentrating his efforts upon a spot somewhat lower than his adversary's waistband, found a means to corrode the tempered surface of Wang Tae's self-confidence and the loud cries of defiance which that person had at first raised in the hope of sapping the other's valour began imperceptibly to assume a more personal tone. It was at this point, while they thus strove, that one of benign aspect and patriarchal cast drew near and held up a restraining hand before them.

'It has been wisely said, "If he is a stranger do not give offence; if he is a friend do not accept it",' remarked the auspicious person judicially. 'How then does strife arise between you?'

At this interruption both lowered their weapons, Wang Tae because he was not desirous of adding to the pain he already felt, while Ching-kwei had not sought the encounter.

'I have no wish to conceal my part in the arisement,' replied the latter person unassumingly. 'I am of the forgotten Line of Ying and the separate names conferred on me are Ching and Kwei. Touching the cause of this, I did but claim my due.'

'That is the essence of all dissension,' remarked the philosopher, but he averted his face at the mention of the stranger's name lest the conflict of his thoughts should mirror there. Then he took Wang Tae aside.

'Say what you will,' declared the outlaw, forecasting the reproach awaiting him, 'but suffer me at the same time to continue rubbing the seat of my affliction.'

'If Ching-kwei's blows remind you of the teeth of vampires, my words will associate themselves in your mind with the tails of dragons,' continued the sage, who may now be disclosed as Ah-Yew, the crafty counsellor. 'You have done ill, Wang Tae, and by the anger of a moment imperilled what the patience of a year may not restore.'

'Continue in the same entrancing strain, excellence,' interrupted Wang Tae bitterly. 'Already this person's bodily pangs begin to fade.'

'When the time is ripe for action, who is there that is most essential to our common hope?' continued the wise adviser with measured sternness. 'Not you, Wang Tae of the lion heart, nor I, venerable Yew of the serpent tongue, nor yet any of the ten thousand nameless ones who, responding to our call, will sweep on like driven leaves in autumn and with as little compunction be crushed down into the earth. But with us we must have, at every hazard, one of the banished Line of Ying to give a semblance to our unstable cause and to proclaim a mission accepted of the gods. Such a one, inspired by his destinies and suitable in every attribute, came to your gate to-day with a supplication in his hand, and you, with contumely, have flung him back again. Could demons do more to bring about your fall, Wang Tae, than you have done yourself? Let me hence, that I may cleanse my throat of the memory of this ineptitude!'

'Press your correcting heel on my submissive neck, instructor,' murmured Wang Tae penitently, 'for my all-too-ready sword admittedly outruns your more effective tongue. But in this matter surely it is not yet too late to walk backwards in our footsteps. Ching-kwei, despite his royal line, is but an inexperienced villager and a few words of well-directed flattery – '

'Mayhap,' replied the prescient one, 'but even the guileless turtle does not put his head out twice. However, proceed to unfold your verbal strategy.'

On this understanding they returned to where Ching-kwei was endeavouring to entice the goat into a noose, and at that moment, by a device, he succeeded in doing so. To Wang Tae this seemed a fitting opportunity.

'Nimbly cast!' he cried effusively. 'Never has this one seen it better done.'

Ching-kwei wound the loose excess of rope about his arm and still grasping the staff he turned to go.

'Your experience is both far-flung and all-embracing,' he

made reply; 'nor would the confines of your landmark seem to be any barrier to your exploiting loop. Henceforth our goats must learn to become more nimble.'

'You have come on a bleak and irksome march,' continued Wang Tae, ignoring the venom of the thrust. 'At least honour my deficient hut by venturing to recline at ease and to partake of tea. To do less is to brand this person far and near as a bankrupt outcast.'

'I have already tasted of the hospitality of Wang Tae's stock-yard; that of his house will certainly be still more overwhelming. As it is, I have so far preserved my life. I go.'

In this extremity Ah-Yew came dispassionately forward and stood between the two.

'May the Three-fold Happiness be yours, Ching-kwei,' he said benevolently, 'but for a single pause of time listen to my voice, for I am old and very fragile and doubtless we shall never meet again.'

'The venerable length of your blameless pigtail compels my profound respect,' replied Ching-kwei deferentially. 'Proceed.'

'There is a ready saying of these parts, "The northern men ride horses, but the southern men sail boats", thereby indicating the various paths assigned to us by nature. Similarly, Wang Tae is rude and strenuous from the shock of continual warfare, while you, Ching-kwei, living in a sequestered valley, have a bland and pacific guise. Yet when you go into the street of potters, there to bargain for a jar, how do you proceed to make a choice?'

'Selecting one that seemed to meet my need, I would strike it sharply, thus to detect its secret flaws,' was the reply. 'Should it fail beneath the test I would pass it by.'

'Therein lies Wang Tae's policy and the enigma of your welcome,' declared the subtle Yew. 'From afar, Ching-kwei, you have been marked out for great honour of a very special kind and to that end were your steps attracted to this place. Should you prove diligent and apt there is no ambition to which you may not rise. But first it was necessary to submit your valour, enterprise and temper to the test of sudden action; had you in this disclosed some hidden flaw the call would have passed you by.'

'What you say is certainly plausible,' admitted Ching-kwei, 'but the industrious bee is not attracted by the brightest flower,' and remembering his grandmother's rebuke he added, 'Those who cover themselves with martial glory frequently go in need of any other garment.'

This reply was far from meeting Ah-Yew's expectation, for he had hoped that so definite a prospect would not fail to entice one of a simple mind and the refusal found him unprepared. Seeing this, Wang Tae interposed his voice.

'Those who cover themselves with martial glory do not stand in need of any other garment,' was his arrogant retort. 'It is both food and raiment and an elder brother too, so that he who wears it feels neither heat nor cold, neither does he sleep alone by night.'

Whatever might have been the outcome under other auspices this speech finally decided Ching-kwei's course. 'Wang Tae is admittedly my superior with the sword,' ran the current of his inner thoughts, 'and when she who has authority over me put forth that argument I was unable to disclose its weakness. Herein Wang Tae has also proved his mastery and it is not agreeable to a person of even remotely divine origin to be both physically and mentally inferior to the one whose rice he eats.' From this resolve nothing occurred to move him, so that, now leading the recovered goat upon a cord, he presently set out again along a homeward course. The last words between them were those spoken by the aged Yew as the closing of the gate marked their diverging ways.

'Ching-kwei,' he observed on parting, 'it is well always to remember that men are not conquered by their enemies but by the decree of fate. This enables the wise to bear an unruffled front in all extremities. Sooner or later ambition will lead your footsteps here again to seek Wang Tae's assistance, but who shall compel the flower to fruit out of its season by plucking off the petals?' To this, Ching-kwei would have waved an appropriate farewell had not the goat leaped forward and thus foiled his purpose. When he looked back again, later, the patriarch had withdrawn.

III

*His Visit to the Soothsayer who dwelt beneath the Tower
of Ya, and the coming of the Two Maidens whereby the
Destinies become involved*

It was not until Ching-kwei had reached an intermediate
village on the following day that a chance allusion to a holy
man recalled the second detail of his journey. The gifted hermit referred to lived beneath a ruined tower on the wildness of
a certain hill, at a convenient distance from the village. He was
spoken of as being reliable and not exacting in his demands.
To keep his mind from dwelling on merely worldly details he
unceasingly counted from one up to four when not engaged
upon matters of divination and the like, and in this scrupulous
manner he had succeeded in regaining a state of natural purity.
At one time a rival soothsayer, encouraged by the repute of
Ng-tung's sanctity and by the stream of pilgrims attracted to
his shrine, sought to establish himself upon another hill, but
presently it was discovered that this later one, in order to endure the monotony of his life, found it necessary to count up to
ten, and the craving for variety in his mind thus being revealed
he became discredited in consequence.

Bearing a gift of rice, Ching-kwei accordingly turned aside
and sought out Ng-tung. The way led through an avenue of
flowering trees where the sunlight came in shafts, it then being
past the middle hour. As he proceeded, a distant sound of
melody came down the aisle, and on its near approach Ching-
kwei stood aside to watch. Soon two maidens came in sight,
one dancing as she sang, the other more restrained but equally
attractive. There being a sward about that place they loitered
there, the one displaying a variety of very graceful attitudes to
the rhythm of her words while the other moved apart and
sought for certain chosen flowers which she broke off between
her shining teeth and held there. This one wore a cloak of
plaited straw dyed an engaging shade, and having once seen
her face Ching-kwei watched her unceasingly, scarcely sparing
a glance to regard the other.

'She is certainly a high official's daughter,' was his thought.
'Were it otherwise I might offer her a gift of rice, but it is extremely unlikely that she eats anything beyond the scent of

flowers and possibly an occasional fruit of the more sumptuous kind.' While he was debating with himself how he should inoffensively attract her notice an incautious sound betrayed him and seeing one of another kind so near at hand the maidens fled, the cloak-wearer dropping the flowers she had gathered in her becoming haste, but the other still continuing to sing and to dance along her path.

'Plainly my fitness for. the society of goats and outlaws is self-evident,' thought Ching-kwei in an access of despair. Nevertheless he recovered what the one had dropped and secured them in an inner sleeve, remarking:

'To-day I have only occasioned her this loss; doubtless in future years I shall find an opportunity to restore them.'

It was but a short li farther on to Ng-tung's retreat and the anchorite welcomed Ching-kwei affably when he understood what was required of him and had received the rice. The nature of the task occasioned him no concern, as with unfailing accuracy he at once detected, by a few well-chosen diagrams, the personality of the malign influence at work.

'Should any of the indicated substances be difficult to procure do not let that disturb the confidence of your venerable progenitor,' he remarked considerately, as he inscribed certain words and symbols on a shred of parchment. 'If she will inconvenience herself to the extent of swallowing the written directions in the suitable form of a pill the result will be equally beneficent.'

'Your mere words carry conviction,' replied Ching-kwei. 'No wonder your harmonious name is sown broadcast through this land.'

'Agreeably so,' admitted Ng-tung diffidently. 'Yet there is necessarily a period between seed-time and harvest. Thus to-day, until your noteworthy shadow obscured my prosaic meditations, I had only been called upon to forecast the destinies of two adventuring maidens at the recompense of an inadequately made pair of unfitting sandals,' and the versatile recluse displayed his brightly adorned feet disparagingly.

'Did they whom you mention proceed from your hospitable door towards the west, and was the more symmetrical of the two covered by a plaited cloak of straw dyed an attractive shade? If so, I would willingly devote two or three brass cash to learn towards what end your divinations led.'

'It is never my aim to frustrate a natural thirst for knowledge,' agreed Ng-tung, passing across his wooden bowl. 'The one cloaked as you specifically describe, Shen Che by name, is foreordained to become a queen and in the end to jeopardise the throne. In the case of the other, her sister Mei, nothing particular is indicated.'

'This is sufficiently surprising, although her mien admittedly suggests a royal destiny,' said Ching-kwei, endeavouring to subdue his strong emotion. 'Perhaps, though, their distinguished father is some high noble of the court?'

'By no means,' replied Ng-tung. 'He is an indifferent maker of the least reliable variety of threadbare sandals, his name being Kang and his dwelling-place about the cattle pools, beyond the marsh expanse. So humble is his craft that in times of rigour he is glad to make straw coverings for the feet of swine.'

'While you are in the mood perhaps you would be so obliging as to become inspired as to this one's ultimate future also,' suggested the other. 'There must surely be occasions in after life when such knowledge could be of practical value even to an ordinary person.'

'Undoubtedly,' replied Ng-tung. 'Thus, if one's prescribed end is to be drowned at sea it is possible to ensure a favourable extent of life by never venturing away from land until the natural end approaches.'

'Yet in such a case,' reflected Ching-kwei, 'would it not be possible to remain here on earth for ever by not venturing away from land at all?'

'It is never well to carry such matters beyond a reasonable length,' explained the soothsayer with an experienced smile. 'Without actually eating their words the destinies generally contrive some hidden outlet, by which, if unduly pressed, they are able to give an unexpected meaning to a stated fact. However, in your straightforward case, at an added expenditure of eight brass cash, I will prognosticate to the outside limit of my power.'

To this Ching-kwei assented and Ng-tung at once engaged himself upon the task, skilfully contriving a fabric of deduction upon the stable foundation of the inquirer's nativity and the outstanding features of his life. Yet from time to time he seemed to have occasion to begin anew and even when he had sufficiently tested the precision of his chart he had resource to the manipulation of the sacred sticks. Finally he prepared a little tea and poured its leaves upon the ground.

'There is no getting away from the fact,' he at length admitted. 'Long-armed as the coincidence will doubtless seem to later and less romantic generations, all the tests confirm that the drama of your life also will reach its zenith within the shadow of a royal palace. The indicated outcome of your destiny, Ching-kwei is this: that at the call of some great passion you will end a sovereign's life and by the same act terminate a dynasty.'

This intimation threw Ching-kwei into a profound abstraction. If the beautiful Shen Che, who in so short a time had grown inseparable from his thoughts, was destined to become a queen, while his own fate was to destroy the existence of a king, it was difficult not to attribute some link of connection between their lives, and in any case a not unnatural desire to trace the progress of the involvement to a slightly later period arose within his mind. To this inquiry Ng-tung turned a not wholly warm-hearted face.

'It is one thing to forecast destinies,' he said, 'that being an integral part of this person's occupation. But it is quite another branch of the art to explain how these things arise and what occurs thereafter. Furthermore, Ching-kwei, in the matter of the eight brass cash agreed upon, it has not escaped my inauspicious eye that an unworthy deficiency still lurks within this unpretentious bowl.'

'The oversight might have been more tactfully referred to in the circumstances,' declared Ching-kwei with dignity, as he made up the full amount. 'Between one who is the mouthpiece of the destinies and another who is foreordained to overthrow a dynasty should two brass cash this way or that lead to discord?'

'The amount may not in itself be formidable but an essence is involved,' maintained the seer. 'Even the gods must live.'

'It is equally true that no dust rises from an unstirred soil,' replied Ching-kwei. 'Clear your mind of acrimonious currents, O Ng-tung, and integrity will no longer be obscured.'

Upon this slight derangement of the harmonies the visit ended, and although they exchanged appropriate quotations from the poets at their parting, Ching-kwei did not ever again contrive to pass that way nor did Ng-tung allude to a hope that he would do so.

In the days that followed Ching-kwei found a new distaste towards his former occupations and he who in the past had been content to lead a company of goats from one place to another, to open watercourses and to secure the harvest as the seasons came, now took little pleasure save in listening to the recital of tales of bygone valour from the lips of passing minstrels or in strengthening himself by contests with the most expert whom he could meet. Under the plea of an advantageous bargain to be pursued he made an early journey to seek the house of Kang, near the cattle pools beyond the marsh expanse, but he found it deserted. The sandal-maker, replied an argol-gatherer about the pools, had fled to avoid being seized to satisfy a debt and his household was now scattered. Shen Che and Mei were spoken of as going north to crave a refuge at the hands of one who professed a kinship with their Line, but the seasons were lean and bitter and who should say? Fine argols, in particular, were hard to come by. ... Ching-kwei returned in a headlong mood and for a while he would contend with any but hold intercourse with none. Later, he sought out his grandmother and reproached her.

'Where is the sword of finely tempered make that our devastating ancestors were wont to bear? In former times it had its place above the Tablets of our race, but now that honourable space is empty.'

'It now has its place above the board on which the goats' food is chopped, out in the farther shed,' replied the one addressed. 'Thus for the first time in the history of our race it serves a useful purpose. Should you need it elsewhere, see to its safe return.'

'Its only becoming use is to add further lustre to our diminished name,' declared Ching-kwei with feeling. Then remembering Wang Tae's retort and being desirous that his grandmother should recognise the falsity of her argument, he added, 'Those who cover themselves with martial glory do not stand in need of any other garment.'

'It is well that you should have reminded me of the gem-like truth in time,' replied the other. 'I was on the point of contriving for your use another pair of lower garments to hide the open deficiencies of those you wear. Henceforth, cover the outstanding portions of your lower limbs with martial glory and I will save my cloth.'

'Probably Wang Tae could have matched this saying with another still more pungent,' thought Ching-kwei, 'but I have yet something to learn from him in most respects,' and having no seemly retort in view he silently withdrew.

Nevertheless he took down his father's sword and as the days went by he began to bend his powers to its use. At first, among the peace-loving dwellers of that untroubled part, he could find none able to instruct him or even willing to stand up against assault, but eventually he discovered an aged gatherer of water-weed, Hoo by name, who in more prosperous times had been a pirate. Inspired by the promise of an occasional horn of rice spirit this accommodating person strove to recall the know-ledge of his youth and in the end he did indeed impart to Ching-kwei the outline of most of the positions both of defence and of attack. Let it however be confessed that owing to his instructor's style having been formed at the capricious angle of a junk's unstable deck, where he was either being cast bodily upon his adversary or receiving that one's full weight upon himself, Ching-kwei's swordmanship to the last conformed to the rigid canons of no existing school but disclosed surprises and benumbing subterfuges against which a classical perfec-tion could accomplish little. To this day the saying lives, 'Like Ching-kwei's swordplay – up, down, and sideways all in one,' to testify to the baffling versatility of his thrust.

When Ching-kwei had learned all that the well-intentioned Hoo was competent to teach him, and could parry each of that hard-striving person's fiercest blows and beat down his defence, he cast about again for a means whereby to extend his know-ledge further. In this extremity he was visited one night by the shadow of a remote and warlike ancestor and a means dis-

closed to him under the figment of a dream. Profiting by this
timely intervention, on the following day Ching-kwei made a
shield of toughened hide and took it to the forest. There he
bound it in an appropriate position on the sweeping branch of
a giant cypress tree. To the relentless force and gyrating onslaught of this indomitable foe Ching-kwei now fearlessly
opposed himself. Whenever a storm of exceptional violence
shook the earth he hastened to take up the challenge, nor was
the blackness of the wildest night any bar to his insatiable zeal.
Often he was hurled reeling a full score paces back, frequently
struck, stunned and bleeding, to the ground. More than once,
being missed, the one who sought him found him lying there in-
sensible; but he carried at his heart the flowers dropped from
the lips of the maiden in the glade and after every overthrow
he returned again with an unconquered look of cheerful acquiescence. It is even claimed by poets and history-makers of a
later time that in these dark encounters Beings, and those concerned with the outcome of the age, gathered about the spot
and strove to various ends – some entering into the fibre of the
tree and endowing it with special qualities while others protected its antagonist through all and sustained his arm. In
this painstaking way Ching-kwei rose to a great mastery with
the sword.

IV

*The offensive Behaviour of Shang, usurpatory King of
Tsun, and the various Influences under which
Ching-kwei resolved to menace him*

In the seventh year of his reign the usurper Shang exceeded
all restraint and by offering sacrifice in a forbidden place he
alienated the goodwill of his own protecting gods. What was
even more important at that moment, by this act of defiance he
roused the just suspicion of the neighbouring power of Chung,
and the potent ruler of that State withdrew the shelter of his
indulgent face. From that inauspicious day Shang's strength
might be likened to a river on the summit of a hill.

Nearly twelve moons had come and gone since the recovery
of the wandering goat. Ching-kwei was drawing water from a
pool when he looked up and saw a solitary wayfarer who

leaned upon his staff as though the burden of the heat and dust was too great for him to carry. Remembering the many occasions when he himself had experienced a similar distress the sympathetic one hastened forward with his jar and offered it, remarking:

'It is too trivial an act to merit even thanks, to pass on to one that which heaven freely sends for the use of all. Drink to repletion, therefore, and what you do not need pour out upon your weary feet so as to strengthen you in each extremity.'

'May the All-providing reward you with a hundred sons and a thousand grandsons, to sustain your age,' exclaimed the grateful stranger as he thirstily complied. Then he returned the vessel to Ching-kwei's hands, but as he moved away his rod touched it, seemingly by chance, so that it gave out a ringing note. This incident, and the exchange of looks accompanying it, at once recalled to Ching-kwei his encounter with the broadminded Yew, and suspecting something deeper he would have questioned the wayfarer, but before he could frame the substance of his speech it was too late.

'Had there been a spoken sign I would willingly have met that upright man again,' thought Ching-kwei, and he was stooping to refill the jar when a gleam within its depths arrested him. He turned it over and there fell out a golden fruit growing on a silver stem. He could no longer doubt the message of the sage's beckoning hand.

As Ching-kwei returned he met his grandmother at some little distance from the door, for the passage with the stranger had delayed him beyond what he was wont and she had grown to misgive his absence. Seeing him, she would have turned back, but he called to her to stay, and when they were come together he delivered the jar of water into her hands.

'My sword is by my side,' he said; 'the only wear that I possess upon my back. In the first wood I can cut a staff; in the last village earn a bowl of rice. Henceforth, I must follow the pursuit of my destiny.'

'If you will but tread this path far enough, it will bring you to what you seek at last,' was her reply.

'Were we on the great earth-road, a few li farther to the

north, that might well be,' assented Ching-kwei; 'but you forget that this unfrequented track leads only to our door. Furthermore, there is a certain peerless maiden now wholly necessary to my very life, whom I must find.'

'In that case you had better stay at home; for if you are equally necessary to hers, be well assured that she will infallibly find you.'

'Customs have perhaps changed since the days of your own venerable youth, esteemed,' replied Ching-kwei tactfully. 'Nor is the one whom I indicate to be computed by our earthen measure, inasmuch as she exists on the smell of flowers, wears a robe formed of floating light, and is fated to became a queen – whose king it is my destiny to slay. Her imposing father, being a merchant of the princely sort, has gone hence on business of the state and I would follow. Nothing delays my journey now but your ceremonial blessing.'

'May the concentrated blight of eighteen generations of concave-witted ancestors ride on your back!' exclaimed the one invoked. 'Is she who cherished you in your infancy to perish in her own old age like a toothless dog whose master's house is closed? Where is this person's future recompense for twenty years of disinterested care and self-denial if contending camps are now to swallow you?'

'What you have done is assuredly recorded in a golden book,' declared Ching-kwei with flattering conviction; 'and for this the High Ones will one day reward you.'

'Doubtless,' replied the other adequately, 'but not in the exact way that I should myself select. However, as was truly said when this person left her father's palace, "pity leads to love; love leads to madness". If it is to be, it will be, but first return with me for a purpose that I will inform you of.'

On this persuasion Ching-kwei accompanied her and being now free of her dissuasion stayed to partake of food. When this was finished she led him to an inner room and there unlocked a box that had lain concealed beneath the floor. From this she took a complete suit of the finer sort, together with a cloak richly trimmed with costly fur, a shield of polished steel inlaid with gold, and a lavishly embossed scabbard fitting to his sword. When these were arranged about his person she drew five bars of silver from a secret place and leading him to the door put them into his hand.

'Go, son of my own son, and fittingly uphold the imperishable glory of our noble race!' was her parting word, and behind him Ching-kwei heard the hurried thrusting of the bolt.

That night Ching-kwei slept in a ruined temple and at a little after noon on the following day he stood once more before the strong stockade of Wang Tae's fortress. He measured the width and depth of the ditch with an appraising eye and judged the stoutness of the palisade, deeming each one sufficient for its purpose. Then he examined the resources of the massive door and the tower protecting it and could find no weakness there. Afterwards he beat upon the metal of the outer gate with a heavy stone and continued until a watchman appeared at the grille.

'Greeting to the valiant Wang Tae,' he called across the space. 'Bear word to him that there stands one without who would disclose towards his private ear a weakness in the chain of his defence.'

'He sleeps upon that side; begone, O clown,' scoffed the keeper of the gate, seeing no profit to his own sleeve from the encounter (for Ching-kwei now carried what he had received wrapped in a skin and stood there as a meagre goat-herd), and he turned away.

'Perchance a familiar sign may awaken him,' came back Ching-kwei's retort, and with it his trustworthy staff winged past the menial's head, carrying with it the lattice from the door. 'Give him that message, brother.'

With gratifying promptitude the door swung open, an ample beam was thrust over the gulf and Wang Tae passed across. When that large-stomached person recognised Ching-kwei most of the fury with which he had set out upon the enterprise melted from his expression and finally he shook hands with himself cordially.

'Ching-kwei,' was his open-hearted welcome, 'whether you are now come to claim tithe of the ill-assorted offsprings of that prince of profligacy you sought, or whether you are come to hazard for a throne, my roof is equally above you.'

'These things must take their proper turn,' was the discreet reply. 'But first of all, Wang Tae, I would disclose to you a serious error in the scheme of your protection.'

'Some word of this affair has already reached my backward ears,' said the warrior. 'Bring me to the point at which the danger lies.'

'Willingly,' replied Ching-kwei, and taking from the pack his sword he unsheathed it. 'So long as there is a mightier one outside your walls than there is within, your security is menaced.'

'That is a matter which is very easily put right,' said Wang Tae, suffering his gravity to become very grossly removed at the well-planned jest. 'Join the felicity of our commonplace circle and the inference will manifestly be reversed.'

'Before I can do that it is necessary to see what sort of entertainment your hand provides,' declared Ching-kwei, fastening on his shield. 'When last we met you were somewhat lavish of receiving and sparse to give – perchance being a stranger then I kept you too much at a distance. Now we can mingle freely.'

'It is impossible to misunderstand the challenge of your two-edged meaning any longer,' said Wang Tae, taking up an appropriate poise and unsheathing also. 'Your genial invitation warms me like the glow of very old wine. If only you are able to speak at all when I have done, nothing will be wanting to complete my happiness.'

The nature of Wang Tae's appearance has already been described so that it is only necessary to declare wherein he differed from it. His armour was more massive than before, being embossed on every plate with studs of shining brass, and in place of one sword of awe-inspiring size he now wore two. But his great height obscured all else, for having lately found his shortened limbs to thwart his reaching stroke he had contrived wooden pegs to replace the missing feet and these his domineering nature led him continually to lengthen until he towered above a world of dwarfs. When he spoke his voice resembled a multitude of corncrakes, calling at variance.

'Should you have any preference for retaining a right or a left ear, speak before it is too late,' said Wang Tae as they engaged. 'But do not plead for more than one.'

'Take both freely,' replied Ching-kwei, offering them in turn, 'for so far nothing favourable to Wang Tae has come near either. First, however, let me correct your ill-balanced outlook,' and by a movement which the other person could never clearly understand he cut off at a single blow the lower part of one of Wang Tae's props.

It has already been admitted that Wang Tae was an expert swordsman and in an ordinary sense he was able to maintain his supremacy in a variety of attitudes, but the necessity of bending his mind to carry on the conflict with one side so materially lower than the other soon began to disturb the high level of his skill. Seeing this, Ching-kwei assumed a sympathetic voice.

'What ails the great Wang Tae that his blade no longer slices where his hand directs?' he said. 'Take out your other sword, chieftain, and see if haply you can accomplish something more with two. Or beg a moment's rest whereby to find your scanty breath. Or call one from your inner room to wipe the drip out of your smarting eyes. Or suck the juice up from a bitter fruit to ease your gasping throat. Or – '

'May the nine bronze tripods of Yu fall upon your pest-infected tongue!' exclaimed Wang Tae with concentrated feeling, and he made an incautious stroke that laid his defences bare.

'Plainly I took too much before and I must restore the balance,' remarked Ching-kwei and with a blow similar to the former one he cut through the other of Wang Tae's supports. 'Now that you are somewhat come down in the world, eminence, we can associate more on a level.'

At this fresh indignity Wang Tae cast away his sword and bent his neck in shame. Finding that it was not Ching-kwei's intention to triumph over him he recognised the justice of that one's victory and after embracing him affectionately he led him into the stronghold of his walls with every mark of ceremonious deference.

V

Wang Tae's just Tribute to the Prescience of Ah-Yew, and the Conference of the Cedar Grove, wherein Ching-kwei learned how Shen Che was scheming towards a Throne.

That night there was a feast given in Ching-kwei's honour and at it he was the recipient of many flattering compliments, although it was not considered prudent by the more discreet to refer to the recent encounter within Wang Tae's hearing. When they were all come together Ching-kwei looked round.

'There are assembled here a hundred swords capable of putting me upon a throne,' he remarked, 'but I have yet to hear one voice able to keep me there. Where is the far-seeing Ah-Yew, whose counsel is a better safeguard than a towered wall of seven heights?'

At this there was a sudden and profound silence, each man looking towards another who should speak. At last Wang Tae was forced to make reply.

'He had finished his ordinary work among us here and he has now Passed Above,' he said.

'When did this take place?' inquired Ching-kwei sadly.

'Yesterday, at such and such an hour,' they told him.

'If that is indeed the case how can we gather here to feast together?' he demanded. 'It would be more seemly to be eating dust rather than drinking wine. I, at any rate, will have no part in it,' and he began to rise.

'It is easier to judge than to administer justice,' replied Wang Tae, 'and in this matter your exactitude is much at fault, Ching-kwei. Learn now how this has come about. Foreseeing your return and being desirous that no untimely omen should arise to mar its complete success, the one whom we all venerate laid a most strict injunction on our band that not even his own Up-passing should be allowed to interfere with the rites of hospitality whenever you arrived. Thus in feasting we are really exalting his decree above mere custom and by rejoicing we mourn an irreparable loss.'

'This admittedly puts another face on the affair,' confessed Ching-kwei, permitting his cup to be refilled. 'Yet it is aptly said, "When the tree has gone, only then do we appreciate its shade", and before long the fierce rays of a retaliatory sun will certainly attempt to reach us.'

By most of those assembled this speech was well received, but there was one present who in the past had been rebuked by Yew for the ordinariness of his character, and seeing now an opportunity to barb an insidious dart he looked ingratiatingly towards their chief and spoke.

'So long as we have in Wang Tae a well-lined silk umbrella, the fiercest sun will shoot its beams in vain, nor is the reference to a defensive wall wholly to be praised. Ah-Yew was well enough in his proper sphere but the present need requires a warrior's voice and this one has yet to learn that he who has been so servilely extolled had ever drawn a sword.'

Almost before he had finished speaking a score were on their feet to express their indebtedness to Yew, but Wang Tae himself waved them all aside.

'When we who are here shall all have passed away and our swords have corroded into rust, our names will then be utterly forgotten,' he declared in a loud and compelling voice. 'But to the end of time men will come together in moments of great stress and being perplexed will say: "In such a case thus and thus enjoined the clear-sighted Yew, the wily counsellor of the ancient days in the State of Tsun, and his advice was good." In that lies immortality.'

This testimony so pleased Ching-kwei that he rose up from his place, and taking Wang Tae by the elbow he exclaimed:

'It is one thing to reach behind your sword, Wang Tae, but I can never hope to get level with your supple tongue. Yet I would rather have said that about Ah-Yew than have found a ballast-load of topaz.'

'If you have felt it what need of further speech, and why then should there be a rivalry between us?' replied Wang Tae, and from that time they were close in friendship.

When the repast was over Ching-kwei and Wang Tae walked together in the cool fragrance of a cedar grove, beneath the full radiance of the great white daughter of the sky, and the warrior freely then disclosed his plans.

'As yet,' he said, 'it would be unwise for us to aim at the throne-direct, for by doing so we should alienate the weak and doubtful without attracting to our incipient cause those who have wealth or authority to lose. Nor have we a walled city on our side in which to raise our banner and to give protection to a sufficient host. For this reason it will not be prudent to declare you publicly just now, but before those whom we trust your sovereignty shall be maintained.'

'I regard you as the living symbol of the profound Ah-Yew,' replied Ching-kwei. 'For that reason I am wholly in your guiding hand.'

'I am not without hope that he will occasionally find time among his important duties elsewhere to return to counsel us. In the meanwhile he left an explicit chart of how to act in every arising circumstance. For the next year our course is one of wariness, sowing ferment like a flung mesh across the land and enrolling the dissentious to our cause, but moving ever with our faces to the ground. At the end of that period of repression we must, by a single well-planned blow, seize and contain an influential town.'

'Where the Shay river bends far to the north and then bends south again, there lies the great walled city of Hing-foo, which once this person beheld,' remarked Ching-kwei.

'Hing-foo is the target to which our arrow wings its devious flight. Thrust like the menace of a hostile elbow out into the plains, Hing-foo holds all the land south of the Shay and at the same time threatens irruption to the north. Already there are many worthy officials of the town who acknowledge our sign and give the countersign, and when the time arrives the more intelligent of the defenders – after a few examples have been made – should have no difficulty in recognising on which side virtue lies.'

'What follows next?'

'Turning over on his perfumed couch, the usurping Shang will languidly exclaim, "Two armies to the south and stamp these contumacious beetles down into their native mire", Yung and Wen-yi will rally to the call and begin to enrol their forces to that end. Wen-yi is incompetent and old, Yung vigorous and a commander by no means to be despised.'

'If that is the case,' suggested Ching-kwei, 'would it not be prudent, at the essential moment, to ignore the menace of Wen-yi's advance, but, concentrating all our resources upon Yung, to offer him a sufficient price to turn the scale of his allegiance?'

'The arrangement has already reached completion and the amount is fixed,' replied Wang Tae. 'Yung will be delayed outside the Capital and suffer Wen-yi to proceed alone. This chance to achieve the greater glory to his single arm, and so discredit Yung, Wen-yi will greedily accept, and regarding prudence less than speed he will urge on his weary force beyond a judicious limit. At a convenient obstruction in his path our troops will bar the way and checking his advance without permitting him to hazard a decision, will crush him between that agile wall and Yung's arriving hosts. ... It is almost inevitable that Wen-yi will also discover the justice of our cause when he realises his position, but it is difficult to see in what capacity we could make use of one so senile and inept.'

'Yet Tsun must have other leaders besides these and other armies ready to be led, nor can Shang dare to remain acquiescent in the face of a defeat.'

'There are other leaders without stint and doubtless other armies can be raised, but to keep them from falling down again their sustenance must be assured and here another force among the intersecting lines of destiny appears to play a tortuous part. ... In the seclusion of your native valley has the rumour penetrated yet of the wonder of Shen Che – why do you pause?'

'I heard something that held me,' apologised Ching-kwei. 'Pray continue.'

'A shout doubtless from the banquet-hall; some still linger there. In any case a reliant watch is kept.'

'It was nothing but a distant echo. You spoke of one – '

'Shen Che, to whom the fashion of the day has given the name of Poising Butterfly, from the winged balance of her grace. Her life recalls a passage from the missing epics of T'ai Chang, traced on bamboo slips and strung on cords of silk. A year ago she cooked her father's rice in a meagre hut set in a barren place – if haply there was any rice to cook, he being but an indifferent worker in some cruder staple. The household scattered by misfortune, Shen Che, together with her sister Mei, went forth into a larger sphere and being seen dancing by an affluent merchant she cast her spell so that he lavished the surplus of his gold upon her capriciousness. From the feet of the merchant Shen Che stepped into the yamen of a powerful mandarin, from the knees of the mandarin into the inner chamber of a high official, and from the shoulders of the functionary into the palace of the king. Now the whisper grows that Shang's royal wife will shortly fall into an obscure decline, and being thus removed that Shen Che will take her place.'

'She will then become a queen!' murmured Ching-kwei.

'She will become a queen but in the end her influence will jeopardise the throne,' replied Wang Tae. 'In her, all the attributes grow to a large excess, her matchless beauty being rivalled only by the resistless witching of her charm, and the sum of both equalled by the splendour of her wanton prodigality. Shang is besotted with desire and beneath her scattering hand the hoarded wealth of Tsun is already gnawed by dogs. To chase a dark look from her face a loyal counsellor will be disgraced to-day; to win a passing smile ten thousand foot-sore men pressed to a futile task to-morrow. When that time of which we speak arrives there will be nothing left to support another army on. Men may be procured by force, but the bare earth cannot be compelled to fructify by blows.'

VI

The Standard of the 'Restoring Ying' being raised, Ching-kwei is hailed as Rightful Lord of Tsun. The Capital is Besieged and an unworthy Dissension thereat engendered

The history of Ching-kwei and the nature of his deeper thoughts, his outspoken words, the omens cast about his path and the genealogy of each of those who rallied to his cause – these might perchance be fittingly set forth in nine-and-forty meritorious books, but though the finest paper and the smoothest ink were used, who should remain to read? Rather, in these later times of groundless stress, men would reach for their street attire, the one exclaiming as he went, 'What *befell* this long-throated goat-herd, story-teller?' and, 'Impart a movement to thy tardy brush,' another.

Let it suffice, therefore, that for the space of moons Wang Tae had spoken of, the confederacy persisted in its righteous task, linking the members of its scattered force into a living bond, and sapping the power of Shang's detested rule by various means. Then when the fruit was ripe the gatherers appeared, for in a single night they fell upon Hing-foo from every side and carried all its gates. Ching-kwei, seeing in the significance of the day a portent of success, led the assault and acquired much renown. All the more worthy of the citizens at once recognised in him the fulfilling of an ancient prophecy and the city keys were laid before his feet.

'Not that their necessity exists in the case of one who wears a master-key about his waist,' declared the spokesman of the band, 'but Hing-foo has been taken and restored three score and eighteen times in the history of its walls and the polite formality has ever been observed.'

After the lukewarm and contentious had been humanely dealt with the remainder of the populace settled down to existence as before, the unchanging motto of their city being: 'Above Hing-foo are the heavens, on three sides of it the Shay, and on the fourth a ruler.'

At a later period Ching-kwei was publicly enthroned in the Temple of the King and greeted with the royal salutation of, 'Ten thousand years!' The execrated name of Shang was removed from every seal and record amid an outburst of tumultuous joy, it being proclaimed that all documents and obligations in which it had appeared should henceforth be held as void. Having by these acts definitely cut off the path of their retreat every person in the city was set to the task of repairing the shattered walls and mounting a sufficient guard.

Events in the meanwhile followed on Yew's prescient course. Yung and Wen-yi converged as specified and the former person brought a pacific face into Hing-foo, and with him the stores and furnishing of all his force together with the staunchest of his men. On this foundation Wang Tae and Ching-kwei began to build the wedge that should drive the usurper ignominiously from his throne, for until he lost that last vestige of authority Ching-kwei might hold the handle of the sceptre but Shang still grasped the head. Across the intervening land trustworthy spies were ever on the watch in suitable disguise, and no day passed without a message of encouragement being brought. Sunk into a deeper lethargy the effete Shang scarcely deigned to turn upon his marble couch to listen to each succeeding recital of disaster; by his side Shen Che rose to more unbridled heights of recklessness until in despair at the inadequacy of her own desires she caused slaves to shoot priceless jewels from hollow tubes against the stars; while at the palace gates men and women fought for the sweepings from the kennels, and in the Ways the changing prices of a he-child and of a she-child went from mouth to mouth. It was at this pass that Ching-kwei and Wang Tae launched their force against the Capital.

At the northern water-gate of Hing-foo flat boats were drawn across by bamboo ropes, and in this way the army of the 'Restoring Ying' moved out. As the different companies with their appointed chiefs passed across the river a notched record of their strength was kept so that Wang Tae should have an exact knowledge of the various kinds of warriors under his control. Of iron-caps, armed with spears, there were as many thousands as could be counted upon the fingers of one hand; of bowmen, each with three-score crimson arrows in a sheath, the same; almost as many slingers with their gear; five chosen groups of fierce-voiced leapers clad in striped and spotted cloth to represent blood-thirsty creatures of the wild, and a suitable proportion of stalwart men equipped with horns and gongs. In addition, there were bannermen who waved insulting messages of scorn; firework throwers, of the kinds both loud and offensive to the smell; several stuffed animals propelled on wheels, and a full camp of diagram-men, whose secret craft it was to spread confusion by their mysterious artifice. Every warrior possessed a wooden bowl, a fan and an umbrella, and many had also brought iron swords and leather shields. Stores and utensils of the necessary sort followed the army on two thousand wheelbarrows in the charge of the elderly and weak. Many of the chief leaders rode small horses of a hardy build, and in front of all went a cloud of war-chariots filled with picked fighters of established valour. The omens had been duly sought and nothing was wanting to assure success.

When this great army – which despite its vast extent moved with such precision that no part of it at any time completely lost sight of all the other – arrived before the Capital, the craven defenders at once retired behind its gates, nor could the most offensive taunts or gestures of the keenest provocation induce them to emerge. On the other hand, with weak-kneed lack of originality they stood upon the well-protected walls and by remarks of an objectionable personal nature endeavoured to lure passing members of the 'Restoring Ying' to come within their reach, but all Wang Tae's troops were too highly disciplined to fall into the snare. Finding the defences stronger than it was prudent to assail, and despairing of the garrison ever having the refinement to come out and face a decision on equal terms, Wang Tae disposed his forces round about the city and proclaimed a siege.

Had the matter simply been left to its proper and foreshadowed course, the speedy subjection of the enemy could never have been in doubt. But it is truly said, 'Even black may become unclean', and the immediate conduct of the corrupt Wen-yi imparts a double edge of penetration to the adage. This squalid-souled person has already been fittingly referred to, so that it is unnecessary to do more than record the actual happenings. Not being deemed worthy of the honour of pursuit, after his troops were scattered in dismay, it was assumed that he would be driven to the necessity of sustaining life by begging from door to door – an occupation logically suited to his low standard of attainment. It must be inferred that Wen-yi had always played an insidious part, for instead of acquiescing to a defeat that was final and complete, he treacherously began to get together his ignoble followers again and even to induce other credulous and slow-witted outcasts to rally to his offensive cause. Working with the most unbecoming secrecy and assembling in distant and misleading spots, he brought on his illiterate and deluded rabble by a series of one-sided marches until he was able suddenly to insert his contaminating presence between the army of the 'Restoring Ying' and their essential city of Hing-foo.

Owing to this degraded act of perfidy, after several months of conscientious effort on everybody's part the position may be thus outlined: the defenders of the Capital were capable of resisting any onslaught but were powerless to emerge and free themselves from the encircling foe; the army of the 'Restoring Ying' was safe within its camp but was not adequate to the task of entering the Capital or of reversing a position on which all its system had been based and turning round to engage the despised Wen-yi; the garrison of Hing-foo was sufficiently protected by the river from the menace of Wen-yi's invasion but was itself too weak to march out and assist Wang Tae, and, finally, the decayed Wen-yi, having now exposed his feeble effort, was unable to move in any direction whatever.

But however badly arranged this unmentionable person's despicable strategy had been towards a martial end, it had an outcome which that superficial one had never even thought of, and very few more days had passed before Wang Tae called an assembly of the inner chiefs together at the council tent.

'When Yu, the pike, lay upon the river floor waiting for a bird to fall into the stream, and Yen, the kestrel, sat up in a tree waiting for a fish to leap on to the bank, both went supperless to bed,' he began. 'Hing-foo, from which we draw our daily sustenance, is now a thousand li beyond our reaching hand, and the case is thus and thus. Let any speak his mind.'

'Your words are ruled with accuracy,' agreed Ching-kwei, 'but let there be no fear on that account. It is decreed that I shall most certainly destroy the usurping Shang and by the same act end the sway of his ignoble line.'

'The fear to which reference has been made, imperishable,' interposed a discordant voice, 'is not so much whether you will kill the vindictive Shang but whether in the meanwhile hunger will not kill us. What store of food is there yet remaining, chief?'

'Some three-score sacks of rice – sufficient beneath a frugal eye for three days more.'

'Here again destiny sets whatever qualms one has at rest, for the third day hence is the thirteenth of the month of Peach Blossom, and that is your imperishable's lucky day,' declared Ching-kwei with confidence.

'Yet between now and the digging of our graves, what miracle will come to pass, omnipotence, unless we lay our elbow to the pole forthwith?' inquired another murmurer.

'What exact form our deliverance shall take will in due time appear, being doubtless revealed in the shape of a nocturnal vision,' replied Ching-kwei. 'To pray for rain and then give water to the drooping vine is to deride the faces of the willing gods.'

'The celestial air you breathe, supremest, is too refined for the gross nourishment of those whom I command,' declared a third. 'An empty bowl will come within their scope, but not the sustaining approbation of the unseen powers.'

'Peace – enough!' exclaimed Wang Tae, being in a double mind himself but fearing an open rift. 'Words make a deeper scar than silence can always heal. Let all consider well our present state until we meet again at a like hour to-morrow. Then when each one has contributed the weight of his deliberate word unto the common cause, we will blend the accumulated wisdom into the weapon best suited to our need. In the interval let mutual harmony prevail, for, remember: "Fire spreads of its own accord, but every jar of water must be carried".'

VII

The Nature of the Stratagem discovered to Ching-kwei and the Measure of its Success. His Meeting with One whom he had thought to be Queen of Tsun and the Rearrangement of the Destinies that then ensued. His return and the Greetings passed

That night Ching-kwei fasted and made sacrifice to the full extent of all he had, and having thereby purified his mind into harmony with the protecting influences around he composed himself into a tranquil state to await their guidance. At dawn he sought out Wang Tae before that quick-moving person left his tent.

'In the past, Wang Tae,' he said, when they had greeted formally, 'we have reposed an unshaken trust in one another and in the clash of battle my defending sword has struck out from underneath your weary arm, and your protecting shield has been held before my bleeding face.'

'It is true,' replied Wang Tae with dignified emotion, 'and the confidence that I still maintain in you is that of two men who walk along a narrow plank together at some great and rocky height. With me, at least, speak the first words as they rise upon your lips.'

'You are the front and authority of all our force, while in me resides the Immortal Principle. What, therefore, we two cannot do, shall the discording voices of a score attain?'

'I am with you in this also,' replied Wang Tae. 'Should you demand an attack upon the Capital, I will myself drive the first wedge into its gate.'

'Our united mind could split a granite rock!' cried Ching-kwei joyfully. 'But a less hazardous way has been revealed to me, as I indeed proclaimed. Is the extremity of our strait known beyond the camp?'

'Spies from both sides pass in and out as usual on one plea or another, nor hitherto has it been well to conceal our obvious strength. Now, this weakness also has inevitably been carried to the councils of both Wen-yi and Shang.'

'Let there be no uncertainty upon that head. Instruct a judicious captain of your own to conduct the spies all round our bankrupt store. At the same time let every warrior in the camp begin to furbish up his arms, to sing of victory and to create a general stir. This, to the spies, the various chiefs shall briefly indicate, with, "Thus", and "Haply", or "I might, if yet I would – ", but nothing more.'

'It shall be done,' replied Wang Tae. 'Before another gong-stroke sounds, a tincture such as you desire shall colour their reports.'

'Once they have left the camp there must be no return. Appoint a double line of sentinels and instruct them to use even force if necessary.'

'That, at any rate, will convince the spies that something unusual is in progress.'

'All shapes around that end. To-night a letter must be sent towards Hing-foo. This is its purport:

'"Illustrious Wang Tae to the ever-alert martial governor of loyal Hing-foo, greeting.

'"Our need is great, our stock being now but two-score bags of mouldy rice. In the mists of to-morrow's dawn we attack the Capital, having learned of vast hoards of grain and richer food of every kind secretly stored within the palace there. If at the same time we can tempt out the ill-made Wen-yi assail his rear with all your force. He is very credulous and may enter the snare." '

'The scheme might be well enough,' remarked Wang Tae, 'but it is doubtful if our messenger can pass through Wen-yi's line and reach Hing-foo.'

'To make sure of that miscarriage send the worst we have – in fact two had better go on separate ways: even the obese Wen-yi can scarcely miss both. How next shall a similar implication be contrived to fall into Shang's unruly hand?'

'I began to smell the gravy of your pig,' exclaimed Wang Tae with deepening interest. 'There was a discontented eunuch of the palace guard who at first conspired with us and messages have passed, but now the rumour goes that one being dropped incautiously out of his sleeve he has been charged and strongly pressed to tell everything he knows.'

'His name will serve. In this case it will run:

' "To – " '

'Tsan, of the Third Green Banner displaying Righteous Truth,' contributed Wang Tae.

' " – From one whom he has knowledge of, greeting." '

went on Ching-kwei, continuing to write.

' "Our need is great, our stock being now but two-score bags of mouldy rice. In the mists of to-morrow's dawn we attack Wen-yi, having learned that his camp contains vast stores of grain. Hing-foo will sally and assail his rear so that we shall have no lack of men. A snare has been contrived to take the ill-made Shang and all his force, if he can but be tempted out at the sound of conflict. Urge him to this and you and your well-born descendants in perpetuity shall be entitled – " '

'Eminence!' interposed Wang Tae hastily, 'the one in question is – '

'True.'

' " – you and your illustrious ancestors in retrogression shall be entitled to an open green silk umbrella with yellow tassels on all state occasions. He is very credulous and may enter the snare.'

Seal it with your special sign, Wang Tae, and despatch it by a thoroughly unworthy hand.'

'Whom, further, I will omit to recompense. It shall reach Shang's council without fail. This scheme of yours, Ching-kwei, whatever the final shape, has a meatiness about its bones that stirs my appetite.'

'When the camp is free of all whom we distrust, about the hour of dusk, let two-score chariots be emptied of their gear and drawn in secret to a hidden dell. To each pair appoint a tent of trusty men, some carrying digging tools, the others bearing for each car a sack of rice. The rest will soon unfold itself before your eyes, Wang Tae, but of this be well assured: the grain that we throw upon the earth to-night will bear a speedy crop and that a hundred-fold.'

*

Is there a single one, aspiring to a polished style to-day, who has not heard or even used the phrase: 'Like Wang Tae's rice – a little on the top?' Yet he who has followed these common-place words so far and put up with their painful lack of finish need not be told that the whole scheme and strategy devolved upon Ching-kwei. Who should then erect a public arch, or compose a written book, or even found a dynasty, if in a few thousand years his labour is thus to be accorded to another? Certainly it was not so in the glorious days of Yaou and Shun.

But in order to bring this badly-told narration even to an unpretentious close it is necessary to uphold the sequence of events and to state what followed after. That is the present way, and, as the saying goes, 'If you would dine with dragons you must not stay to chew the meat.'

On the succeeding day, before the hour of dawn, both the hosts of Shang and Wen-yi became aware of something very violent taking place elsewhere. In the obscure distance a noise composed of every variety of martial strain, shout, roar, boom, blast, shriek, firework, rattle, imprecation, thud, musical instrument and explosion grew and died down as it came across the intervening space at intervals, while fires at different points began to show and a great cloak of pungent smoke darkened the rising sun and shut out all the further details of the inauspicious scene. It was plain to each that the other was being vigorously attacked, while a demonstration in the nature of a feint was carried out against himself, but having been warned by intercepted messages neither fell into the snare but lay behind his own defensive walls or lines and watched.

When the battle had been in progress for a sufficiently convincing time a combined shout of victory rent the air and soon everywhere signs of rejoicing could be seen and heard. Shang and Wen-yi strove to pierce the veil of uncertainty surrounding them, to learn if haply any remnant of their ally stood, but the distance and the glow of fire and the drifting smoke conspired to baffle the most discerning eye, and presently each had a more convincing sign of the other's overthrow than all that went before. Winding through Wang Tae's camp, on its way to some secure place of storage, came a long and noble train of chariots, each one full and well heaped up with shining rice. Four well-trained horses went to the ropes of every car, with two henchmen at either wheel and four to follow after, so weighty was the load, and as they moved at certain parts more at their ease the men laughed and frolicked and threw rice by the handful on each other in wanton joy to see so much. Forty such chariots there were in sight at once, and then after a pause a score more, and then another score, and a little later a second forty as before. Wen-yi first saw the offensive sight and knew the worst, and after him in turn the abject Shang and all his court, for Ching-kwei's rice-train wound in and out among the camp for half a day.

'They have penetrated to the very heart and treasure of the citadel and taken what they would. Without doubt the garrison is all put to the sword and the ineffectual Shang now cast in chains or slain,' exclaimed Wen-yi. 'Get me four bearers and an emblem of surrender so that I may hasten to eat dust and make what terms I can with this new line of kings.'

'The flat-stomached Wen-yi has failed again – as usual,' remarked the ill-starred Shang in an accent of refined despair, at about the same time and inspired by a like sequence of events; 'and without doubt he has been taken in the snare. As our last hope is thereby brought to voidance, the hostile camp restocked, and their road to Hing-foo clear again, nothing remains for this much-depreciated sovereign but to put on an appropriate robe of sackcloth and to suffer himself to be deposed without further ceremony by the morally deformed Wang Tae.'

'Chieftain,' reported a lesser captain to Wang Tae, as Wen-yi and Shang set out, 'two separate groups approach the camp, one from the north, the other from the south, with banners of submission. What is your iron word concerning them?'

'At the peril of incurring each one of the seventy-five recognised ways of inflicting pain, let them be kept apart,' replied Wang Tae.

Thus it came about, Shang's band by this time being brought into camp, that a message reached Ching-kwei, who had stayed within his tent alone, of one who sought his ear.

'Suffer the messenger to pass the guard,' pronounced Ching-kwei, for the word brought in had seemed to speak, though darkly, of the time which he knew must now approach, and they led one in whose face was masked by a visor of worked steel.

'Omnipotence,' pronounced a low but very golden voice, 'I have a name to speak that merits your private ear. Furthermore, I bear no weapon anywhere while you have a notorious sword beneath your ready hand.'

'If I disclose my ear to you,' replied Ching-kwei, motioning to the attendants so that they withdrew, 'it is no less fitting that you should reveal your face to me,' and he indicated the covering which the other wore.

'Your magnanimity is itself a better shield than any I could wear,' was the gracious reply, and what he asked for being done they stood there for a poise of time, facing each other.

'Shen Che!' whispered Ching-kwei, falling back a step in wonder. 'You who are now a queen!'

'I recognise in you the one who loitered in the glade, that day the holy anchorite warned me that we should meet. But wherefore do you call me by my sister's name, and why greet me a queen?'

'Your sister's name?' replied Ching-kwei, with a great and sudden happiness singing like a nest of radiant birds about his head. 'Are you not then that Shen Che who should become a queen?'

'I am Mei, of the lowly house of Kang, and to me no other name was ever given. For her of whom you speak I come to plead, that being my errand here. Of your illusion that I was other than I am – doubtless it grew from this: that we encountered only once and that but for a single passing glance. Let it not weigh against my cause, high excellence.'

'Not once but many hundred times, O dazzling one, have we two met, for every day that meeting is renewed within my heart; and though it was a single glance so deep the image cut that the stone of life itself must be destroyed to wear away a line.'

'Benevolence!' pleaded the maiden, who had not expected to be involved in so abrupt and emotional an arisement. 'The one for whom I crave your countenance –'

'The fault lay with that hoary soothsayer,' continued Ching-kwei, who was by no means concerned about Shen Che now that he had learned that this one was no longer she. 'I described you beyond the possibility of doubt and he then played me false.'

'Great majesty,' murmured the bright vision, advancing more than the single step that the other had gone back, and gazing into Ching-kwei's eyes beseechingly, 'by what feeble attributes did you chance to depict this in-no-way-striking one?'

'How else than by the glory of your matchless presence, by the pearly splendour of your lustrous being, which at every point outshines that of all other dwellers upon earth, by the constant wonder of your deigning to remain among mere mortal things at all – there could be no mistake. Further, as the venerable necromancer's polite attention seemed to begin to wander at this point, I added that you wore a high-born cloak, your sister having none.'

'In this then, not the hermit but the very fates themselves have conspired towards a surreptitious end,' exclaimed the one henceforth to be described as Mei. 'Know now, all-powerful chief, that until we left the pious Ng-tung's cell, it was the more-admired Shen Che who wore that distressing cloak of plaited straw, which presently, to dance for joy at what the seer foretold, she cast about my form.'

'Then you indeed are not a queen, nor married to a king?'

'I am married to none,' replied Mei, indicating by a refined gesture that a contingency had been reached when it would be more suitable if she replaced the concealing mask, but to this Ching-kwei did not accede. 'Nor am I likely now to encounter so forlorn an end, for the divination ran that my destiny lay with a guileless one who herded goats and led a tranquil life. Thus I stand secure, for such a man could not be found in camps or capitals.'

'Yet I have herded goats and led a tranquil life,' maintained Ching-kwei. 'So that in me the prophecy takes root.'

'But can never come to fruit, esteemed, for from that life you have cut yourself irrevocably away, while to it I must straight return, like a homing swallow to its ingrained thatch.'

'Would you not instead become a queen, fair Mei, and found with me an undying line of kings?'

'Against that I am sworn. One queen from the inglorious house of Kang exceeds the moral limit, and having marked that same one's upward flight I trim my own wings now into a lowlier atmosphere.'

'Why then, I also would not be a king,' declared Ching-kwei, approaching her. 'And yet,' he added gloomily, 'the iron line remains – to "end a sovereign's life and by the same act terminate a dynasty", was the unbending fate. How else than by setting up my own?'

'Ching-kwei,' exclaimed a stern voice from the door, as Wang Tae threw back the fold, 'what note of doubt is this? The day is ours, gained by your stratagem. Shang and Wen-yi have both made full submission and recognised your claim. The army of the 'Restoring Ying' only awaits the sight of you to raise an overwhelming shout of triumph and to carry you upon the impulse of its valour to any misty height. This is the very apex of your destiny, but though the point is here for you to grasp, the sides are smooth and steep. Fail to assert your

right at once and all may yet be lost. Miscarry now, and you
end your sovereign life and by that act now and for all time
terminate the dynasty of your imperishable Line.'

For such a space of time as wherein one might count a score
the three chiefly concerned stood in their different moods. Then
Ching-kwei answered back and his voice rolled like a ceremonial drum.

'There spoke the several voices that conjoin in me to piece
my destiny and to reconcile all things! *This* is the kingship
that I put an end to now and *ours* the dynasty which I thereby
terminate. Wang Tae, your words have been inspired and you
at last have cut the knot of all my difficulty.'

'Yet what remains?' demanded Wang Tae darkly. 'Can the
people be left to revert to savagery, and Tsun, deprived of
every royal hand, become a vassal state?'

'Still less so than before. To-morrow, in the Temple of the
King within the Capital, Ching-kwei will voluntarily abdicate,
and turning to his right will crown Wang Tae first of a martial
line. That is what Tsun requires to-day – strong and vigorous
rule of natural force, not one whose kingdom is a dream and
his chosen throne a chimney-seat.'

'This is what generally happens sooner or later when a
capable general and a weak-minded sovereign are concerned,'
declared Wang Tae, not wholly reconciled, 'but in our exceptional case I certainly did not expect it yet.' Then as he turned
to leave the tent, Ching-kwei unsheathed his sword and raising
it before his face he very gladly cried: 'Ten thousand years!'

'Yet what remains?' repeated Mei, as they again stood there
alone. 'You have lost all, nobility, and for – for a vagarious
thought renounced a jewelled crown.'

'Not all,' replied Ching-kwei; 'I still have what I value
most,' and from an inner sleeve he took some faded flowers.
'These I have kept unharmed through the dust of weary
marches and the shock of furious battle, hoping perchance that
if I bore them worthily, when we should meet you of your own
free will might requite me for everything with one.'

'One is a very little to expect, high prince,' said Mei, turning
away her face as she received the flowers, 'though certainly
more might seem to be too much. Therefore the two I offer

you are now but one, and the one that you receive has hitherto been two,' and in a tumult Ching-kwei perceived that in the hand held out to him were two stems tightly bound together by the crimson thread of mutual betrothment. 'What more,' she continued with a still averted face, 'what more can one to whom all initiative is rigidly denied say – or even do – Ching-kwei?'

*

As Ching-kwei, leading Mei by the hand and at the same time controlling a wandering goat of his own flock that he had recovered by the way, neared his door, his grandmother came out to gather wood and seeing them awaited their approach.

'What is the latest apophthegm from the front just now, Ching-kwei?' she asked. 'And how does this new gear of martial glory fit about your limbs?'

'Those who cover themselves with martial glory appreciate a homespun robe at last,' was his reply; yet even as he spoke the thought went up: 'Wang Tae would certainly have produced something more keen-edged than that.'

'At all events, the maiden whom you sought has found you, it appears,' remarked the ancient, nodding sagely. 'Perhaps it was as well that you should have returned – another goat has cast off his allegiance and gone hence upon us.'

*

When Kai Lung, having thus successfully disposed of Ching-kwei, looked up, he discovered that he was there alone, not even one of the three whom he daily instructed in his art having lingered.

'It is doubtful if circles were quite so destitute of true refinement in the golden days of Tou-fou and Li-tai-pe,' he murmured; 'though the comparison is admittedly vainglorious. What call is that?'

It was the voice of Hwa-mei, seeking him in the darkness of the garden, and as Kai Lung went at once towards her they very soon encountered.

'There were nine of our neighbours here with me but now, to whom I owe some reparation,' he explained. 'In the nature of analogy I pressed sour fruit upon them so that now I would offer them both food and wine. Are they, perchance, awaiting me within?'

'There are none within, neither have there been any with thee here in the garden, save only Hoo Tee, who has already tasted bamboo for leaving thee alone musing by the arbour. Hast thou slept again, O dragon-hearted one, and dreamed a dream of ancient valour?'

'I may have mused somewhat,' confessed Kai Lung, 'as I sat there by the arbour. But I can hardly, as you say, have slept for a Bringer of Good News has sought me with a message.'

'Truly so,' replied Hwa-mei, with a ripple in her voice both of laughter and affection. 'Your evening rice awaits you.'